THE
MOTH THE
FLAME

WHEN RIVALS PLAY SERIES

B.B. REID

DEDICATION

For little brothers who adore their big sisters and
for sisters who never take it for granted.

ALSO BY B.B. REID

Broken Love Series
Fear Me
Fear You
Fear Us
Breaking Love
Fearless

Stolen Duet
The Bandit
The Knight

When Rivals Play Series
The Peer and the Puppet
The Moth and the Flame

NOTE

The Moth and the Flame is a continuation of the events that occurred in the previous novel. It is strongly advised that you read *The Peer and the Puppet* prior to reading this book. Content suitable for ages 18+.

PART ONE

BEST FRIENDS

PROLOGUE

The Flame

A STORM RIPPED THROUGH THE CITY THAT NIGHT.
The rain and hail sent dwellers scurrying for heat and shelter, and the ones who didn't have a home—like me—were left defenseless against the elements. I remember the wind and snow that followed most vividly, and it wasn't because of its harsh swiftness or icy chill.

It was because the wintry tempest had blown an even more unforgiving storm right into my path.

"It's colder than a witch's tits," Leo grumbled. He was a foster care runaway like me and a year younger at fourteen. In just a couple of years, he'd be beating girls off with a stick. His thick, blond hair, striking green eyes, and bubble gum pink lips made him an instant dream boy. It didn't help that he was kind, intelligent, and shy. I rarely opened doors around him, and he'd even absurdly offered me his jacket, willing to brace the biting cold in just his sweatshirt.

"Nah," Miles argued with a violent shiver. He was another runaway, and at sixteen, he was older than Leo and me. Where Leo was light, sweet, and easy, Miles was dark, broody, and complicated. Leo asked permission while Miles demanded. "It's colder than a pile of penguin shit."

"You're both wrong." I clutched my thin jacket and ignored the ache in my bones. The only thing useful about it right now was the pockets, and being a pickpocket, I *never* used them.

Instead, I entrusted everything I cared about to the camel-colored rucksack my mom wore when she used to hike and backpack across Europe. Other than the Polaroid camera my parents gifted me the Christmas before they took off, it was the only thing I never left behind whenever I took off, too. "It's colder than the hair on a polar bear's ass."

We huddled around the fire we had fought to make inside a trash can with only the fire escape hanging over a barbershop as our awning. We didn't have long before a cruiser ran us off, but I tamped down my rising dread for the hellish night I had ahead of me.

Both of their lips turned upward, and I knew they would have been laughing if it didn't require more energy than we had.

My stomach chose that moment to growl—a reminder of the other reason I had trouble keeping my strength up—and it was loud enough to be heard over the howling wind.

"Jesus, when was the last time you ate?" Miles grilled.

"I'm on a diet."

Miles ignored my sarcasm and pulled a shaking hand from his jacket pocket, revealing a half-eaten McChicken.

"So that's where you were earlier," I mused while ignoring his offering. "Begging for change." I turned my nose up, and his lips flattened into a line.

"It's better than risking my freedom picking pockets."

I met his dark gaze and almost laughed at the frustrated gleam. "We were never free, Miles."

"Take the sandwich, Louchana."

"No, thanks. I'm saving my appetite for steak and lobster. Those Wall Street jerk-offs really love to flash their cash around."

"Look around you, Lou! The entire city will be snowed in by morning. There will be no one to rob."

When he tried to force the sandwich into my hand, I snarled and said, "I'm not eating the fucking sandwich, so you can stop pretending you don't need it more than I do."

We both knew his run was almost up. He ran home as often as he ran away from it. Miles had type one diabetes and was on his last injection. Without insulin…

"I'll be fine."

"You'll be as dead as a doorknob."

I didn't miss the guilty look he exchanged with Leo or the way their bodies slowly straightened from their hunched positions.

"Please eat the sandwich," Miles urged, changing tactics.

I was immediately on edge. My gaze narrowed. "You're going back, aren't you?" At his reluctant tight-lipped nod, my attention swung to Leo. "You too?"

Leo weakly shrugged and shuffled his feet in the thin layer of snow that blew into the barbershop walkway. Leo was in the system like me, but Miles had a home that he shared with parents who didn't just decide one day that they didn't want to be parents anymore. And he didn't fucking appreciate it. Almost every other month, Miles ran away from home to show his parents he wasn't some fragile thing that needed to be coddled and protected. Leo, while possessing many virtues, didn't excel at thinking on his own, so whenever Miles called it quits and ran back home to mommy and daddy, he'd suddenly have this great epiphany that foster care wasn't so bad after all. The truth was he'd never survive on the streets without Miles's grit and temper, and Leo knew it.

"Why bother sticking around?"

"We were hoping to convince you to go back to the Hendersons," Leo meekly stuttered.

A second later, a harsh gust of wind slammed into me, and my body locked up tight in a feeble attempt to ward off the chill. At that moment, I considered the warm safety of my foster home before discarding the thought. It had been a week since I pretended to leave for school and never came back. By now, they would have reported me missing and asked my social worker to find me another placement. No, the Hendersons were no longer an option.

"I'm fine here, boys. Run along." I flicked frozen fingers toward the snow-dusted street.

Instead of looking relieved, Miles's scowl only deepened. "Come on, Lou. Don't be stupid."

"Don't call me Lou. Only my friends get to call me Lou."

"According to you, you don't have any friends and never will."

"Precisely."

Miles shook his head with a scowl while Leo whistled and said, "You're a cold piece of work, Louchana Valentine."

"Much better," I praised with my eyes firmly fixed on the dying fire. It was no match for the cold, wet wind.

They didn't stick around much longer after that although Miles took his time walking away. I made sure to keep my expression blank as I watched him glance over his shoulder before rounding the corner.

The breath I'd been holding shuddered out of me in relief and clouded the air. And even though I was alone in the middle of a storm, I was grateful. I knew Miles wanted more from me than friendship or someone to watch his back on the streets. I even suspected that the times he ran away from home weren't always because of his parents. Every single time, he sought me out, and it wasn't because he couldn't take care of himself.

The wind howled.

My body shook violently.

And then that howl began to sound strangely like a roar.

I didn't have the faintest clue why my heart skipped a beat, and my breath drew short as my stomach tightened. The part of my brain responsible for rational thinking told me it must have been a car approaching and not some monster searching for its next meal, but when a black muscle car with gleaming chrome jerked to a stop across from the barbershop, I was suddenly less sure.

There wasn't much that shocked or scared me anymore, but the figure that emerged unhurriedly, unlike his driving, did both without doing anything at all. Then again, I was so mesmerized by what my eyes were unveiling that perhaps my mind had chosen to record the moment in slow motion. I only wished I dared to capture it with my camera because one day, in the not-so-distant future, I'd call on this memory. I hoped for the sake of lonely, future me lying in the dark with her hand in her panties and a pleasured sigh on her lips that the picture my mind painted would be in vivid detail.

Because his fierce scowl did nothing to shroud his beauty.

And like the danger radiating from him, it was unbridled.

He was cloaked in a distressed brown leather jacket, matching worn gloves, and brown boots. The wind ruffled his dark brown hair as he carefully took in his surroundings, and I was glad he'd chosen not to wear a hat because hair that shiny, thick, and perfect was meant to be admired no matter the weather.

It wasn't so bizarre that I was attracted to someone who looked this damn appetizing, but I did find the voice in my head wondering if he were here for me and the answering clench of my gut unsettling. I could swear I heard the chime of a clock striking a new hour, telling me it was time. Or maybe it was more like the clang of a bell beckoning me. My feet even took a couple of steps toward him before I caught myself. It didn't help, though, because I felt my entire being reaching out for him. It was a magnetic feeling that only grew stronger as he slammed his car door shut and crossed the street with a purpose.

His eyes found mine, and I could have sworn his step faltered. Maybe he was just surprised to find someone else crazy enough to brave the storm. It took me a while to realize I hadn't moved, either. I was completely frozen. Not even a shiver shook my body despite the steadily falling temperature. Perhaps I believed remaining perfectly still would keep him from spotting me, but like a true predator, he had already locked onto his prey. His gaze never strayed as he stepped onto the sidewalk and his booted feet drew him closer.

"You got business here?" he said once he stood in front of me. His gray, maybe blue—I couldn't decide—gaze was colder than the wind and snow blowing around us as he passively assessed me.

"What's it to you?" Despite my instant infatuation, I couldn't keep my true colors from showing even if I tried.

He continued as if I hadn't spoken. "If it isn't worth your life, I suggest you disappear, kid."

"Kid?" I yelped as he moved around me. "Well, isn't that the pot calling the kettle black. I can still see your mom's nipple print on your upper lip!" I was thankful his back was to me so he couldn't see me wince. I didn't mean to be so crude or even angry, but I had the feeling that as of two minutes ago, I no longer had control of my emotions. I felt connected to him on a level I could never hope to reach and, therefore sever, and I didn't like it one fucking bit.

The hand reaching for the barbershop door fell by his side and balled into a fist. If it didn't already feel like the North Pole, the icy chill radiating from him certainly would've done the job. I knew I'd said something terribly wrong before he even spoke.

"Let me revise," he said in a deeper, deadlier tone. "If you want this wasted existence of yours to continue beyond the next three seconds, leave. *Now.*"

He didn't wait to see if I obeyed. Ripping open the door, he stomped inside and let the door reading Bear Cuts slam behind him.

I frowned at the realization that I could have stowed away inside all of this time. The lights were out, so I assumed, like everyone else, that the owner had gone home before it became too dangerous.

My stomach churned as I left my dying fire behind, but it wasn't for the loss of its meager warmth. I couldn't stop replaying the encounter or the words *wasted existence* in my mind. Never mind that he'd threatened me.

Apparently, I mused as my lip curled, *I cared more about what he thinks of me.*

Curiosity to know more about him kept me from going far. Across the street, in fact, where I huddled under a street lamp. Ten minutes later, when the chill in my bones became too painful to ignore, the door opened, and he emerged with something bright orange clutched in his fist.

And when he stepped off the sidewalk and headed straight for me, I was suddenly cold for a different reason entirely.

It was too late to run. He'd already seen me and could probably catch me even if I did, so I stood rooted to the spot under the dim yellow glow of the lamp like a red flag for a raging bull.

The only things that kept me from screaming were the stoic expression he wore and the fact that no one would hear me and probably wouldn't intervene even if they did. Besides, I wasn't a damn damsel, and if he forced me to try to kick his ass, then so be it.

What happened next I couldn't explain, but it would haunt my dreams for a long, *long* time. He stood in front of me, closer than he'd been before, and I took the time to study the odd hue of his eyes. It shouldn't have fascinated me so much.

The arm carrying what I realized was a coat—a super fugly one—extended, but before he could utter a word, my attention was stolen by a silver Acura rounding the corner on two wheels—snow and ice be damned. The passenger window rolled down, and a gloved hand pointed a semi-automatic with perfect aim.

I didn't stop to consider the fact that he'd threatened my own life before saving his. I screamed, "Watch out!" before dragging him behind a green Expedition sitting on oversized tires as bullets rained down on the spot he'd just been standing. I landed on top of him, still clutching his leather jacket for dear life. Our eyes connected the moment the shooting stopped. Rage began to effervesce, drowning the initial shock and turning the irises surrounding his pupils a startling blue. I was distantly aware of tires squealing and a roaring engine, but I couldn't be sure. I was only mindful of how close our bodies were and the hungry hum begging me to get closer. I got my wish seconds later when he grabbed me and rolled us underneath the SUV just as bullets sprayed the car, setting off the alarm and ripping a scream from my throat. With my eyes shut tightly and my face buried in his chest, I gripped his jacket as if my life depended on it. Evidently, it did.

I could hear the shooters' tires squealing as they raced away. I didn't dare exhale until long after the sound of the racing engine faded. My breaths came fast and hard, matching in tempo with the heavy rise and fall of the dude's chest.

For a while, the only other sound was the car alarm blaring above us, but once I caught my breath, I couldn't keep silent.

"That was—"

"God fucking dammit!" he roared.

"Not what I was going to say."

He gave me a withering look before swiftly rolling from beneath the SUV and out onto the street. I was less eager to depart. What if they came back to finish the job?

"Come out," he ordered a little impatiently. "They're not coming back, and we need to leave."

"No, I'm good. Thanks."

I heard him sigh before he dropped to the ground and peered under the car at me. "And when the cops come?"

Well, fuck. That got me moving.

Despite almost dying, I didn't care to be hauled back to my foster home or worse…a group home. And I sure as shit wasn't eager to be questioned by the cops. I'd rather have a rectal exam.

I inched toward him, and surprisingly, he held out his hand to assist me. When I was on my feet, I avoided his gaze and studied the car that now looked like molded Swiss cheese.

"That could have been you."

"And you," he pointed out.

I breathed in the cold night air, which then shuddered out

of me when I realized he was right. I doubt they cared if I was a casualty of whatever vendetta brought them here.

He rounded the front of the Expedition and bent to pick up the now shredded orange jacket.

Good.

I'm glad it was dead.

It was fucking *hideous*.

He sighed before wordlessly crossing the street and disappearing inside the shop. I was still deciding what to do and where to go when he emerged less than a minute later without the coat and then locked up the shop.

My heart skipped a beat when he hopped into his car without a "See you later" or "Sayonara." I knew it was going to hurt to watch him drive away, but I had no idea why. The car started with a roar as fierce as its owner, but instead of driving off down the street, he pulled up next to me. I didn't move an inch as he leaned over and rolled down the window.

"Let's go," he ordered.

"What?" Surely, he didn't think I was going anywhere with him? I was almost killed because I got too close, not to mention I'd only just met him, and he was clearly into some deep shit.

"Lets. Fucking. Go."

"No way."

"Did you hear me asking?"

I shivered, and it had nothing to do with the snow now falling steadily. "I'd rather die," I said with a snarl. "Wait, it seems I almost did!"

Before he could respond, the wind carried the sound of sirens closer. *Shit.* I quickly reached for the door handle, but he slammed his hand down on the lock just as I tugged on the door. Sure enough, it was locked.

"What are you doing?"

"Say please."

"Are you out of your fucking mind? Unlock the door!" I

tugged on the handle, willing to tear it off if I had to—although that would get me nowhere.

"Say 'Please, Wren. Rescue me, Wren. I need you, Wren.'"

So that was his name. Wren...

Silently, I tested his name with a wistful sigh. Aloud, I growled it. "Wren."

"Almost. I didn't hear *please*."

"Fuck you."

"Not what I'm offering," he casually retorted. His arrogance only infuriated me more.

"Fine." I let go of the handle and tapped my lip with my finger. "I wonder what I'll tell the cops when they get here. After all, I did witness *everything*."

His only response was to sit up straight, allowing me to see the gun that magically appeared in his lap. The warning was clear, and even though a chill worked its way down my spine, I somehow knew he'd never use it. At least, not on me.

"Please, Wren," I begged halfheartedly. He smiled when I punctuated my plea with an eye roll.

And just as the first patrol car turned onto the street a couple of blocks away, he popped the lock. I wasted no time diving inside. I barely got the door closed when the car shot forward, and we got out of dodge.

I nervously watched out the back window as two patrol cars parked next to the totaled Expedition, and four officers emerged with guns drawn. Only when we rounded the corner did I relax and sink into the leather bucket seats. I couldn't help admiring the interior. He'd kept everything classic and vintage and looking like he had just driven it off the lot days ago.

"What year is this car?"

"'66."

"Where'd you get it?"

"Why?" he sneered. "You thinking about getting one? Maybe turning it into a summer home?"

"Maybe I am," I snapped back. Wren snorted, which was clearly another dig at my homelessness. "Asshole," I hissed. He pretended not to hear. "Where are we going?"

Silence.

"Wren?"

He signaled before cruising down another street. I eyed the door handle and considered hopping out. As if reading my thoughts, he sped up.

I whipped my head around and glared until the seeping hole in his jacket caught my attention. "You're hit." Panic spread through my chest.

"Trust me, I'm aware."

I reached out a trembling hand before thinking better of it and letting it fall into my lap. "Shouldn't we go to the hospital?"

"I'll handle it," he said through clenched teeth.

"Better than an actual doctor?"

Once again, he didn't respond, and I was getting sick of it. "Fine," I said as my arms crossed, and I pouted. "Bleed out. Die. I don't care."

A crooked smile graced his lips. "It seems like you do."

I shrugged and crossed my arms. "You're my ride."

His deep-throated laugh sent the butterflies in my stomach scattering—fucking hormones. I never hated being fifteen more than I did right now. Not even when I realized I had no say in my own life for the next three years.

I whirled on him. "How old are you?"

Wren hesitated before mumbling, "Seventeen."

So I'd been right. He was young although I'd pegged him for at least twenty-one. He looked the part of seventeen, but I didn't need his story to know he'd grown up fast. Judging by the gun still in his lap and the near assassination, I'd say too fast.

"Which school do you go to?"

"Not in school."

I frowned. "Graduated?"

"Dropped out."

"Me too." I sighed. "Currently." Every time I was dragged to yet another foster home after days, sometimes weeks, on the streets, I was thrown back into whatever public hole would accept me.

"Why?" He voiced it in a way that instantly put me on the defensive.

"*Why did you?*"

Rather than answer, he shook his head as if disappointed.

I felt my teeth grind. How dare he judge me when he was no better?

I couldn't stand the silence, so I reached for the radio to play whatever cassette he might have, but his hand shot out and gripped mine before I could. It was like a thunderbolt had struck us both. The hairs on my skin rose as my body temperature sky-rocketed, and my next breath stalled. I knew he felt it too even though he recovered much quicker than I did and refocused on the road.

"Don't," he said, and it was almost a plea.

"Why not?"

"I like the silence."

"Yeah, well…I've had enough to last a lifetime." He didn't ask, and I didn't elaborate. Those days before my parents took off had been harrowing but mostly…confusing. The only clue among all the silence had been their nervous energy. "So is that why you bought the oldest car you could find? Because it has no radio?"

"It was a gift."

"From who?" I couldn't keep the surprise from my voice. He didn't seem like the type to allow someone close. With one glance, I knew he was a lone wolf—like me.

"Doesn't matter," he muttered. "He's dead."

"That's pretty morbid." He tried to shrug but grimaced, clearly forgetting his wounded shoulder. "How are you not in pain right now?"

"You're distracting me," he said, almost like an accusation.

"I'm sorry. Should I let you concentrate?"

His lips twitched before he muttered, "Smartass." His tone was amused, almost whimsical—as if he were already used to me. The snow started falling harder, so he pushed the lever that controlled the windshield wiper and tried to hide his wince from using his injured shoulder.

I bit my lip and shoved my hands under my legs to keep from wringing them. "Do you need me to do something?"

His head cocked curiously. "Like what?"

"I don't know...try to stop the blood?" *Anything to get your hands on him, right, Lou?*

"It's just a graze. Looks worse than it is."

"Oh."

"You were pretty quick." It almost sounded like he was in awe.

"A lot of good it did." I felt my cheeks heat at the worry in my voice.

Especially when he said, "I'll be fine." His tone was gentle and assuring. A far cry from the way he'd spoken to me when we met.

I simply nodded, but it didn't stop the ache in my chest. I barely knew this kid. And he *was* a kid albeit a dangerous gun-toting one who someone clearly wanted dead.

"Why were those guys after you?"

"Fuck if I know," he spat. I wasn't buying it for a second, though.

"If we're going to be friends," I said with more confidence than I felt, "we can't lie to each other."

He glanced at me then through wide eyes. "Who says I want to be your friend?"

"I saved your life. You've yet to return the favor, so until the debt is paid, you're stuck with me."

"Or I could just kill you right now and be done with you."

His gaze never strayed from the road as he threatened me for the third time in half an hour.

"But you won't," I said confidently, and I felt my heart warm in confirmation. I had no idea how I could be so trusting after what I'd just witnessed, but I knew nothing Wren said or did would make me believe that he would ever hurt me.

I'd had just about enough of my hormones for one night.

This time, his gaze lingered when he looked my way. "You think I'm a good guy?"

I studied him long and hard. Beads of sweat trickled from his hairline, over his sculpted cheek, and down his clenched jawline. He was clearly in pain but was too macho to admit it. "I think you're not as bad as you think."

He suddenly seemed uncomfortable and looked away. "Jesus, you're stupid," he spat. "And naïve."

I forced a laugh to hide the feeling of being punched in the gut. "Nice try, but I'm not going to cry and run the other way because you hurt my feelings."

"Whatever," he mumbled, and I found myself hiding a smile. The longer we talked, the more his attitude seemed adorable rather than intimidating. A few minutes later, we pulled into the driveway of a two-story brick home. The small front yard was overcome by a trampoline, a big wheel, a pink bike with training wheels, and other toys.

"Who lives here?" Had he brought me home? Did he have siblings? Would his mom like me? I covertly ran my fingers through my hair to straighten it.

"You ask a lot of questions."

"You don't think I should? I met you five minutes ago."

"It's been longer than that," he smartly retorted before hopping out.

I rolled my eyes before following him to the door. I waited quietly although nervously as he knocked rather obnoxiously.

"They could be sleeping."

"So?" He knocked again even louder.

Seconds later, the door was whipped open, and a hulking man with a bald head and a scowl that rivaled Wren's stood on the threshold with a gun in one hand and a cigar in the other. I took small steps back until I was hovering behind Wren and clutching his jacket lightly in my fist. Dude looked like Colonel Kurtz from Apocalypse Now.

"What the fuck do you want, Harlan? It's late. My kids are sleeping."

"Those gremlins you call children aren't sleeping, you dense fuck. I bet anything Georgia is sneaking cookies out of the kitchen right now."

Sure enough, a little girl sporting pigtails and Minnie Mouse pajamas ran from the kitchen with a fist full of crumbled cookies.

I was prepared for the man to shoot us both right then and there. Instead, he turned and shouted at his giggling daughter to go to bed as she ran up the stairs. He then walked away without inviting us in, and when Wren moved to follow him, I quickly released him. I didn't get a chance to say "I'll wait in the car" before he grabbed my wrist and dragged me through the open door.

"Who's the girl?" the colonel questioned as he plopped onto the couch, reaching for the remote.

"No fucking clue," Wren answered.

"And you brought her to my home?" he roared. I could have sworn I heard the plastic crack under his meaty fist.

"I need you to fix my shoulder," Wren explained although he didn't sound the least bit sorry.

"It had better be life or death," he threatened.

Wren shrugged his uninjured shoulder and headed for the bottle of rum on the wooden coffee table. I was still standing in the foyer, feeling seriously out of place, when the bear of a man stomped over to me and demanded my name.

"Leave her alone," Wren said before I could answer.

The man grunted and stuck out his hand. "Call me Shane."

I shook his hand and started to offer my name when I caught the subtle shake of Wren's head. Since Shane had his back turned, he didn't witness Wren's objection, but the warning was clear.

Don't trust him.

"Pleasure," was all I said.

Shane growled his displeasure, eyed me up and down, and then disappeared upstairs, probably to silence the pitter-patter of little feet coming from above.

"Why don't you—"

"No," Wren interrupted.

My lips snapped shut, increasing my frustration. If Wren didn't trust this guy, why come here? "Well, can I ask for a glass of water, at least, or will that get my head blown off, too?"

Wren's nostrils flared before he shot up from the plush couch and stalked into the kitchen. I smiled as I listened to him open and slam cupboards and drawers and then, eventually, there was running water from the faucet. When he returned, I couldn't hide my shock when he handed me a tall glass of water *and* a peanut butter sandwich.

"Thanks."

He walked away without a response, and I followed him into the living room where he watched me closely as I ate. Shane returned just as I was taking the last bite of my sandwich. It only took a few seconds since I couldn't remember the last time I had something to eat or drink.

Shane ordered us to follow him into the kitchen and set a large case on the table. When he popped open the lid, I saw all kinds of medical instruments and medicine. It wasn't your typical first aid kit, that's for sure. I might have assumed he was a doctor if he hadn't answered the door with a gun in his hand looking like he'd use it and sleep like a baby afterward.

And I doubt they'd swear as colorfully as Shane did when he peeled the jacket and shirt from Wren's body. I gasped as a sense of foreboding crept up from fingertips until it seized my entire body. All I could do was gape as my mind raced to understand, to accept, and then to plan a fucking escape. The nasty wound on top of his shoulder didn't turn my stomach nearly as much as the tattoo etched into the skin of his nape—a bold X with the number nineteen in the left angle, an eighty-seven in the right, and the notorious motto underneath.

I am not led.

Exiled.

Wren was Exiled.

And everyone in the city knew what that meant.

I didn't know how to even *begin* from here. I'd already guessed that Wren was dangerous. Those guys wielding automatic weapons meant business, which told me Wren was no angel.

But *this*...this was a death sentence. And I was guilty by association.

Wren glanced over his unwounded shoulder, and I could feel him watching me, waiting for my reaction. I didn't give him one. I pretended my wide-eyed horror was for his wound even though the bullet had only grazed him just as he said. He lied when he claimed it wasn't as bad as it looked. A shudder shook my body as I imagined how much pain he must be in. How he'd been able to pretend otherwise, I'd never know, but right now, he looked seconds from passing out.

When Shane finished cleaning the wound, he dropped the bloody cloth on the table, and I noticed Wren paled and turned his head in disgust.

"Don't tell me you don't like blood," I blurted with equal parts hostility and incredulity.

He stared back at me but didn't respond.

"Makes him queasy," Shane supplied. "Last time, he threw his guts up all over my floor. Bethany bitched for a week."

"Last time?" I squealed. "You mean he's been shot more than once?"

"This makes three," Shane informed with a misplaced sense of pride.

I swayed on my feet as if someone were pointing a gun at *me* right now. Wren had been shot three times? But he was so young. Why would anyone want to hurt him? Was it because he'd hurt them first? Sorrow, fear, anger…it all overpowered my girlish infatuation.

"You're going to need stitches," Shane grumbled as he set about sterilizing supplies.

Wren simply nodded, and I realized he was still watching me even as he took a swig of rum.

Despite my inner turmoil, I couldn't stop my feet from moving or explain why I grabbed his hand, but when he held mine for dear life, I knew there was no way I was letting go. His warmth comforted me as much as mine must have soothed him.

I didn't miss a single wince or clench of his jaw as Shane sewed his flesh back together. My stomach turned at the same time my heart pounded with worry. Wren's pain felt like my pain. I only wished I knew why.

After Shane finished dressing the newly stitched wound, he pressed a couple of painkillers into Wren's hand and ordered him to take them when the alcohol wore off. Wren defiantly popped them both in his mouth and swallowed. Shane chuckled and shook his head as he cleaned up. I wanted to scream at this monstrous man who'd taken part in corrupting him, but Wren's hand squeezed mine, effectively keeping me silent.

"You and the girl can take my spare for the night."

"We're leaving," Wren announced.

It was all I could do not to run for the door. The danger of icy roads and hypothermia was probably ten times safer than a night spent under Shane's warm roof.

"Not in this storm, you're not. That's an order," Shane quickly added before Wren could object.

Wren glared at Shane and freed his hand from mine as he stood. "Fine," he said.

I wanted to scream that it was not fine. With a jerk of his head, Wren ordered me to follow him. I did, slowly, while wondering if anyone would object if I left to brave the storm alone. I never got the chance to ask.

The moment we left the kitchen, Wren, as if reading my mind, looked over his shoulder and trampled my hopes with three words.

"You're not leaving."

Upstairs, he led me to the guest bedroom at the top of the stairs and flipped on the light. It was stylish yet simply decorated with flowing dark green curtains, a queen bed covered with a comforter to match the curtains, white nightstands on each side, and a tall white dresser with a TV mounted on the wooden surface.

"This is…cozy." I thought being alone in a car with him had been stressful. Spending the night, sharing the same bed, however, was…nerve-racking. My body didn't seem to mind, and I told myself I was too tired to care. No way could I still find him irresistible after what I had just learned.

Wren didn't respond, and I began to wonder if he considered all conversation rhetorical. He pulled the comforter and a pillow off the bed, and I watched, feeling perplexed yet a little relieved, as he began making a pallet on the floor. After freeing his gun from his waist, he placed it under his pillow.

"What are you doing?"

"Going to bed," he answered without sparing me a single glance.

"But your shoulder won't survive on the floor. Take the bed. I'm used to sleeping on the ground." That wasn't exactly true, but he didn't need to know that. I couldn't exactly spend the night alone on a park bench and expect to survive the night unmolested. It forced me to take risks my homeless peers didn't have to, so I got creative. Sometimes, I'd spend the night right under my foster parents' noses inside a neighbor's shed. The older school buses were easy to break into, and sometimes, I crashed with Miles during the rare times his parents weren't hovering.

Wren paused, and I would have thought he might be considering my point except he looked pissed as fuck. Lying down, he grimaced as he searched for a comfortable position.

"You're going to be doing that all night if you don't take the bed," I observed.

He stood to his feet quicker than I would have expected, gripped the front of my shirt, and with little effort or care, he tossed my ass on the bed. Eventually, I stopped bouncing enough to see him watching me with his arms crossed. His eyes dared me to move from the bed.

"Now go the fuck to sleep."

Stalking across the room, he shut off the light.

"I'm dirty, and I smell," I admitted shamefully. The bedding looked too pristine. I shuddered to think what my dirty clothes were doing to them.

"Yeah, no fucking kidding," I heard him mutter before he lay back down on the pallet.

Flushing from my greasy hairline to my still frozen toes, I lay perfectly still until his breathing deepened before it evened out. I scooted from the bed, careful not to make a sound, and shed my backpack before peeling the clothes from my body. I refrained from tossing them across the room like I would if I were alone. Keeping them close meant easy access. I could put them back on undetected before Wren woke up in the morning.

With my dirty clothes safely crumpled in a pile next to the bed, I slid under the cool, clean sheets and snuggled deep. It had been a week since I slept in a bed and even longer since I slept in one this comfortable. Regardless of the circumstances and the company that came with it, I planned to savor it. Who knew how long I'd be on the streets this time. I'd been caught enough times to know it was inevitable.

"Hey, kid?"

At the heart-dropping sound of Wren's voice so perfectly lucid, I yanked the sheets to my chin, clutching them tight and swallowing my squeal.

That asshole had been pretending to sleep! Had he watched me undress? Against my will, my toes curled at the possibility. I decided to ignore them and focused on my outrage. Realizing he'd called me 'kid' again helped out a lot.

"Yes?" I snapped.

He hesitated and silly me, I held my breath. However, it was nothing compared to my reaction to what he said next. "I owe you one."

My heart, no longer content to canter, sped into a full gallop until it felt like I was soaring. "Is that a thank you?"

"It's whatever you want it to be," he muttered evasively. I had a feeling he wouldn't have given me even that much if he knew how far my imagination reached. When he didn't say more, I assumed he was pretending to sleep again, but then he said, "If we're going to be friends, I'll need to know what to call you."

Smiling in the dark, I retorted, "Who says I want to be your friend?"

"It's like you said," he drawled, and I could hear the smile in his tone. "I haven't returned the favor and saved your life. You're stuck with me."

Despite feeling like I was flying, I debated giving him my name. He had warned me not to trust Shane...did that mean I shouldn't trust him, either? After a few uncomfortable seconds ticked by, I gave him a name that wasn't mine. "Lucy."

My heart began to pound so hard I feared he might hear and know I'd lied. The worst part was that I wouldn't even be able to explain why.

"Lucy," he echoed, and my stomach twisted brutally with regret. "I like it, Lou."

Hearing that name, I glared at the ceiling, forgetting all about my guilt. I must have been the only person in the world who detested it. Even my parents had called me Lou. I swallowed down all the abandonment issues bubbling up and sternly repeated, "*Lucy*."

Of course, he didn't respond, and a minute later, I knew why when I heard snoring coming from the foot of the bed.

Giggling softly, I hugged my pillow, and even though he was probably faking again, I let my eyes slowly drift shut.

"Wake up."

I jolted awake at the command, and my eyes slowly cracked open. The first thing I noticed, however, was the freshly laundered scent of the pillow my face was shoved into. Panic speared my empty stomach as I wondered where I ended up last night. Groaning, I flipped onto my back and blinked a couple of times to clear my cloudy vision before searching the room for the source of the voice I knew I hadn't dreamed.

Across the room, I found Wren leaning against the closed door, fully dressed and looking better rested than I felt. He was watching me, and the moment our eyes connected, it all came flooding back. "Is the house on fire?" I grumbled and then inwardly cringed at the raspy croak of my voice.

"No."

Relaxing again after stretching, I closed my eyes. "Then do me a favor. Find the nearest cliff and walk off it for me, will ya? I'm sleeping here."

"I guess you're not a morning person," he remarked, amused.

"I'm not a *people* person."

"What if I told you we're going shopping?" he asked, switching tactics. "Would you like me then?"

My eyes popped open, but I couldn't meet his gaze. "Um… no thanks."

"That's too bad."

Sitting up, I finally met his gaze. "Why is that?"

"Because I wasn't asking."

We stared at each other for a long time, something passing between us that I couldn't understand. "I have a feeling you rarely do."

He didn't respond as he crossed the room, and the closer he got, the more I became aware of how little I wore. I clutched the comforter closer to my chest when he reached the bed, but none of the scenarios happening in my head occurred in real life. Instead, he snatched my dirty clothes from the floor and tossed them on top of me. They were still damp from the snow, but right now, they were a godsend.

"Get dressed," he ordered.

I nodded and waited for him to leave.

He didn't.

The bastard retreated across the room, perched both elbows on the dresser behind him and crossed his ankles with a hint of a smile.

"Some privacy?"

"You're a pretty heavy sleeper," he remarked. "Who says I haven't already looked?"

I ignored the wild beating of my heart and said, "Should I add pervert underneath gangbanger then?" Mentally, I patted myself on the back for not melting into a puddle.

His smile widened, but it didn't reach his eyes. "So you did see."

My gaze fell to the bed. "It was pretty hard to miss."

"Then you know that you can't ever talk about last night." Although a warning, his tone was surprisingly gentle. I wanted to believe he cared, but I knew he was only looking out for his own ass.

"Don't worry. There's nothing about last night I care to re-live." In fact, I was counting the seconds until I could get out of there. Hot or not, Wren was bad news. I knew that now and was thinking clearer thanks to a good night's sleep. "Now can you leave so I can get dressed?"

I blinked a few times, losing some of my nerves when the smoky gray of his eyes slowly became a stormy blue. However, I'd only gotten a glimpse before he turned his back.

"I meant for you to leave the room."

Silence.

Unbelievable.

I quickly hopped up from the bed and cursed when the cold morning air touched my skin. Didn't these people believe in heating?

After I finished dressing, I took the time to study him while his menacing gaze was averted. He was tall—definitely over six feet. And the muscles he possessed were subtle, but he was definitely on the right track to being a modern Adonis in just a few short years. His hair wasn't as dark as mine. My own was nearly pitch black while his hair reminded me of delicious chocolate. My gaze trailed lower, touching every part of him, including his sculpted ass encased in jeans that hugged his thighs just right. When the long fingers on both hands suddenly flexed, curling and uncurling, I studied them too and wondered just how much blood was on them.

"You done checking me out?" he questioned with a laugh.

"What are you talking about? I wasn't checking you out," I lied even as I felt my skin flush. I bent to tie the laces on my black combat boots. The heels were four inches high and almost as thick as my arm—not to mention they were unpractical, but they made me feel empowered.

"I can see your reflection in the TV screen."

My hands paused from looping my laces, and I glared at his back. "You mean you were watching me this whole time?"

He turned around with a satisfied smile. "Yup."

I looked away but felt my lip curl as I finished tying my laces. "I guess chivalry is dead after all."

"If chivalry were dead, baby girl, your cherry would have been mine last night."

I shot up from my crouched position and propped my hands on my hips. "Who says I'm a virgin?"

His gaze trailed from my face to my neck to the top of my breasts exposed in the low-cut cami. "Only virgins blush like that."

"So you're an expert?" At seventeen I doubted it, but it was clear Wren knew more than I did. My palms begin to sweat at the mere possibility of sex while Wren looked perfectly at ease. He shrugged, and I realized I hated his arrogance as much as his indifference. "Yeah, well, sex is off the table. We're friends, re-member?" I had no intentions of being his friend, but it was the only card I had to play. If he pushed the issue, he'd soon find out how eager I was to spread my legs for him. Just this once before I never saw him again.

"Friends fuck."

Between my thighs, I felt those words fall from his tongue as if he'd purposely placed them there. "Not us."

He slowly smiled. It was seductive and full of promise. "You might regret those words later."

There won't be a later. "Not before you do," I said and blew him a kiss.

His eyes fell to my lips and held steady even as he said, "Care to make it interesting?"

"How so?"

"Whoever begs for it first can never have it with anyone else." I was ready to laugh, to agree, to decline—I didn't know—when he added, "For as long as they live."

"That's a pretty big promise. What if you're bad in bed?"

"What if I'm not?" he countered.

Our gazes connected and held for so long my body felt hot enough to combust at any moment. I knew then that I was will-ing to take that risk for one night with him. "Deal."

He nodded unceremoniously, blinked until the lust I knew

I hadn't imagined was gone, and said, "Good. Let's go," as if we hadn't just finished discussing fucking one day.

"That's it?"

He paused on the threshold of the door. "I'd go down on you to seal the deal, but I'm not touching you until you have a shower." He looked me over and said, "Maybe two or three."

"Fuck you."

"Oh, you're gonna." My stomach fluttered, and he must have seen something in my eyes because he suddenly frowned and said, "There will never be more between us than a fuck. I'm not someone you want to get too close to." At my dumbfounded look, he added, "Do you understand?"

Hell no. I didn't understand.

Why care if I ever fucked anyone else if he didn't want more? Why offer friendship and then tell me to stay away?

I felt like I had whiplash. I also wasn't buying it.

Before I could lash out, however, I stopped and wondered if *I* even wanted more.

"I understand," I agreed. We both heard the doubt in my voice, but thankfully, he didn't speak on it. Suddenly, I felt out of my depth. I was too young to be having this conversation. I didn't know the first thing about sex, and until Wren, I hadn't considered finding out anytime sooner.

Although a boy himself, I had the feeling Wren would be a patient albeit demanding teacher. Maybe we'd even learn together?

Wren said he'd meet me outside before disappearing. I listened to his thundering footsteps until they faded before I grabbed my backpack and ducked into the bathroom. Even though I was out of clean laundry, the shower beckoned. Hearing Wren's comments echoing around in my head, I blushed as I shed my clothes and hopped inside. I scrubbed my skin as hard as I dared under the hot water and even took longer than usual brushing my teeth and detangling my hair. When I finally made it downstairs, I found Wren standing by the door, catching a key ring that Shane threw to him with one hand while holding his cell phone to his ear with the other.

Noticing me, he sharply ordered "Just get here" into the phone before hanging up.

I offered a hesitant good morning to Shane, who didn't bother returning the greeting and, instead, stared at me as if I were already on a witness stand. Clattering was coming from the kitchen along with the sound of a little boy and girl screaming for French toast.

"I better get in there and help Beth," Shane grumbled. He then pointed a thick finger at Wren and added, "I want a full report of what the fuck happened last night. Thanks to that prude he keeps around, the boss is already in a crabby mood. You hear me, boy?"

Wren nodded halfheartedly before focusing on me. He jerked his head toward the door, telling me that it was time to go, but I couldn't make my feet move. What if he'd been lying about shopping—although I still didn't know for what—and he was actually taking me somewhere to kill me? Would they ever find my body?

Of course not, Valentine. He's Exiled.

Growing impatient, he crossed the room, took my hand, and led me out into the cold morning. To my credit, I didn't kick and scream although I really should have. The houses on the block were close together, which meant *someone* would hear me. Unless they were too afraid...

There were about six inches of snow on the ground, and it seemed the entire neighborhood was out shoveling snow from their walkway or scraping ice off their windshields. Wren approached a running silver Toyota Tacoma and ordered me to get in.

"You're taking me somewhere to kill me, aren't you?" I asked in a hushed tone over the hood.

He stopped and turned to me with his eyebrows bunched. "What?"

I clutched the straps of my backpack tighter. "I'm a loose end, so you have to kill me. It's in the gangster handbook." The blank stare he gave me didn't make me feel any better. I frowned. "Don't you guys have like a code or something?"

His head cocked to the side. "If you believe I plan to kill you, why do you care if the neighbors know about it?"

"Why the hell would you think I cared?"

"You're whispering, mouse." I could tell he was holding in a laugh, which only added to my humiliation.

"Oh."

"I'm not going to hurt you," he said after a long, uncomfortable silence.

My gaze fell to the ground, and I sounded heartbroken when I said, "I don't believe you."

I heard the snow crunch, and then his large booted feet appeared in front of me. A cold finger lifted my chin, and then my teary gaze met his stormy one. "I promise."

My next breath and "Okay" rushed out of me.

He stared at me for a few seconds longer, and I had a feeling he was looking for any remaining doubt. Finding none, he moved around me, opened the passenger door, and waited for me to hop in before closing the door. I watched him walk back around the truck to his side, and the expression he wore told me he wasn't happy with himself. My gut told me it was because he'd made a promise he shouldn't keep.

"So," I said as I buckled in, "what are we shopping for, Renny?"

His head whipped around, and he frowned. *"Renny?"*

"You dishonor my name, I dishonor yours."

His eyebrows wrinkled. "What's wrong with Lou?"

"What's wrong with Renny?"

"It's stupid."

"I concur." I smiled innocently.

He winced and backed out of the driveway. Neither of us spoke until he pulled into a shopping center ten minutes away.

There were a ton of people already out, probably scavenging for last-minute supplies. What we got last night was mild, although it would have had those pussies in the south running for the hills or boarding up their houses. I silently cursed when I counted the days until spring and realized we still had six more weeks of winter.

He hopped out, and I followed him across the parking lot. I grew self-conscious of my appearance when we walked into a clothing store, and I noticed the dirty looks directed my way. Wren seemed oblivious as he headed for a rack of coats in the women's section. I had trouble swallowing as I wondered about the girl he was buying a jacket for. A foreign feeling washed over me, and I knew it had to be jealousy. If he turned around right now, I wouldn't be able to hide it, and the part of me without pride wanted him to see it.

Would he break it off? I couldn't help but hope that he would, and at that moment, I learned three things about myself I hadn't known before.

I was possessive, selfish, and completely irrational.

Then again, maybe these feelings had been born rather than freed. I'd only known Wren for less than a day, and already, I could feel myself changing, and I wasn't entirely sure it was for the better.

I had only just managed to school my features when he glanced over his shoulder. "You going to help or not?"

As casually as I could, I asked, "Shouldn't you call your girl-friend—or whoever you're buying that for—to help you?"

He turned away from the rack with a scowl so fierce that I involuntarily took a step back and then cursed myself for cowering.

"Girlfriend?"

"Or whoever," I repeated.

His expression evened out, and then he chuckled as he rubbed his lips with his forefinger. "I was just talking about fucking you not even an hour ago. What makes you think I have a girlfriend?"

"Men are dogs," I pointed out with a shrug.

"Not. Me," Wren growled as if I should have known.

I stared back at him in disbelief while wondering if I'd offended him or if 'pissed off' was just his default. "I just met you."

He looked me up and down and not in the slow, appreciative way I pretended not to like. "So you did." Turning back to the rack, he angrily ripped an olive green coat from it. A lady in the next aisle gasped when the hanger flew over her head from the force and landed two aisles over. I tucked my lips in to stifle my laugh at the way her already magnified eyes had grown even larger thanks to the bifocals perched on her nose. She was still blinking rapidly in disapproval even after Wren mumbled an apology and turned to me.

"Let's go," he said between clenched teeth.

I eyed the coat strangled in his fist as he stalked away. It was even uglier than the orange one, and I giddily hoped whoever Wren was shopping for was as hideous as that coat.

I struggled to keep up with his long, determined strides to the cash register. Once we reached the front, I stood silently as he grabbed a gray ribbed beanie with a black and gray fuzzy ball on top from a bin along with a thick, black scarf and matching gloves. I nodded my approval and decided to keep them for myself the moment he wasn't looking.

The cashier cheerily greeted us both. Of course, Wren only rudely managed a nod while remaining tight-lipped. I offered a halted wave, and my smile was even more awkward as we waited for him to ring up the items.

"That will be $114.99," the cashier stated. Wren reached into his pocket for his wallet and paused when he came up short.

Shit.

"What the fu—" His eyes cut to me.

I considered denying stealing his wallet to satisfy my jealous heart, but his hard expression told me there wasn't a chance he'd believe me.

Shamelessly, I reached into my pocket, removed two hundred

dollar bills from his wallet, and handed it to the suddenly nervous cashier.

"When did you—"

"While we were getting shot at."

The cashier paused from counting my change, but neither of us paid him much mind.

"You save my life, and then you steal from me?" Wren questioned in a low tone. I should have been afraid, but he'd vowed not to hurt me, and I had the sense he didn't break his promises easily—certainly not over a few bucks.

"No, Renny. I saved your life *so* I could steal from you."

The cashier interrupted Wren's reply by stuttering the amount of his change. I snatched it before Wren could even react and tossed him his wallet while pocketing the cash. I then bounced out of the store thinking how well I'd eat with eighty-five bucks plus the Benny I'd already pilfered.

I hadn't even remembered taking his wallet until I'd dug through my rucksack after my shower, hoping to find a cleaner shirt. I couldn't help wanting to know as much as I could about him, so before I came downstairs, I rummaged through it. Sadly, other than cash, there had been nothing inside but his license and a picture of a young dark-haired woman so beautiful it almost hurt. She wasn't alone in the photo, either. A little boy, maybe eight or nine, with almost identical features was sitting next to her. It didn't take a genius to know the boy was Wren and the woman he'd been smiling up at with such love and adoration was his mother.

His license was interesting, too, though not nearly.

Wren Joseph Harlan had brown hair, blue eyes (sometimes), and was born August 31st...1995.

My stomach twisted into knots almost as tight as it did the first time I did the math. He'd be eighteen soon.

I didn't like that the age gap between us was more than I'd thought. I'd only turned fifteen a few days ago. I wondered if

Wren would have made that pact with me if he knew just how much younger I was or that I wasn't even old enough to drive much less have sex.

"Give me my money back," Wren demanded when he finally joined me on the sidewalk.

"Why? You obviously don't need it. You're just upset that I bested you," I boasted with a wink.

"Lou…"

"Renny."

He blew out air, and without a word, stalked across the parking lot with the shopping bag in hand. Once we settled inside the still-warm truck, I studied him. He didn't look as pissed as he was a second ago. In fact, he seemed completely relaxed.

"You know she's going to hate it, right?"

"Hate what?" he said as he started the truck and backed out slowly.

"The coat. It's ugly as all hell."

"Good," he said with a smirk. "Because the coat is for you."

I tried to speak and choked on my tongue instead. "For me?" I squeaked.

"For you," he confirmed.

"Well…" *Say thank you!* "Why'd you have to pick the ugliest one?" I grumbled instead. I knew I sounded ungrateful as hell, but it was better than swooning, for fuck's sake.

He peered over at me in disbelief. "You're a little shit, you know that?"

"Would you rather I lie?"

At his black look, I shrank back into my seat. He quickly closed his eyes and silently cursed. When he opened them again, his eyes were blue, but the scowl was gone. "Please don't."

I felt my eyebrows bunch and my heart crack just a little. "You have problems with trust, don't you?"

"Everyone does. Some have trouble giving it, and some have trouble keeping it. We all learn that the hard way."

I laid my hand on his arm and felt the muscles bunch underneath. "I have the feeling this will be the start of a beautiful friendship."

"Why's that?"

"Because I trust you."

I didn't miss his wince or the way his hands strangled the steering wheel, but I chose to chalk it up to grumpiness. Maybe he didn't really want a friend, but he could sure use one.

Neither of us spoke the entire way back to Shane's house. It had started to snow again, and I wondered—no, panicked at the thought of spending another night trapped in his house. When Wren turned down the street, my heart skipped a beat when I noticed the police cruiser and an all too familiar white Ford sedan with blue writing on the side.

Wren didn't miss a beat as he pulled into the driveway.

"I have to get out of here," I whispered. He must not have heard me, though, because he put the truck in park.

I looked around anxiously trying to figure out a route of escape. Seeing none, I turned helplessly once more to Wren and paused at the guilt I saw lining his profile. I knew right then that he had been the one to call them.

Sighing, he shut off the truck. "You really shouldn't, Louchana."

My eyes bulged at the sound of my real name even as my entire body shook with rage. *He knew? How?*

"Shouldn't what?" I spat instead. It didn't matter how he'd learned my name. What mattered now was what he'd done with it.

"Trust me."

Snow continued drifting from the sky, and the silence that followed seemed heavier than the blanket of falling white flakes. Ms. Laura Strickland—my social worker—and two officers exited their cars at the same time and locked eyes with me through the windshield.

"Noted."

"Now you just remember, young lady, we expect you back in this house by four and not a minute later."

I shouldered my backpack and nodded while Eliza Henderson, my foster parents' daughter, smiled reassuringly.

That smile quickly fell when her father added, "And Eliza, you *will* let us know if she's late, won't you?" The Henderson's both worked for one of the prisons—I could never remember the name—and worked long hours that frequently extended into the night. And when they weren't working, they were at the church down the street, at Bible study or running one of the many programs I refused to attend.

"Eliza," her mother snapped when she hesitated.

Eliza reluctantly nodded while avoiding my gaze. I shrugged, not blaming her for the corner her parents had backed her into, and headed for the door. Besides, I didn't think Eliza would snitch. I had a bus to catch that I didn't want to miss because the alternative was a ride to school and more time for lectures.

The Hendersons were good people, but my parents had been good people, too.

Eliza, who was a year younger than me, had tried desperately to befriend me, but I refused to budge.

I didn't like getting too close to people.

In the two and a half years since my parents ditched me, I had succeeded—until Wren fucking Harlan. In less than twenty-four hours, he had taught me a valuable lesson.

Trust no one.

No matter how much I desperately wanted to.

It had only been a week since he gave me up. Surprisingly, the Hendersons were willing to do what no other family had—they accepted me back into their home, which was more than I deserved. A good placement was like winning the lottery, and I'd unknowingly hit the jackpot when I found this kind family.

The only real problem in the multimillion-dollar equation was me. It was only a matter of time before I ran away again. I knew it, the Hendersons knew it, and my goddamn social worker knew it. But she was patient and kind too. Anyone else would have thrown me into a group home or juvie and been done with me a long time ago. It's happened before, and I could count on my fingers and toes, and all of my many caseworkers' too, how many times I'd gotten into a fight at group homes. The only good that came from it was that I was now pretty scrappy. It served me well whenever I decided I'd rather live on the streets than subject myself to warm, family dinners or perverted men. You name it, I've lived it. It's been a hard couple of years, but I wised up fast.

"Hey, wait up!" I heard Eliza shout.

Ignoring her request, I didn't stop until I reached the bus stop.

She was panting when she caught up to me. "You know I'd never rat on you, right?"

"I hear ya."

"Seriously." She tugged my arm until I faced her. "I want to be friends."

Where have I heard this before? Oh, right. From a certain dark-haired gangbanger with eyes that changed colors, and who had a reoccurring appearance in my dreams. "Well, I don't."

"I know you want me to think you're a total bitch, and if I'm honest, sometimes you're *really* convincing, but I already know you're not. I heard about what you did to that girl who called me a porker."

Eliza was on the heavier side—a size eighteen she'd gleefully gloat—but that only added to the fact she was beautiful as fuck. She had red hair that fell to her thick waist, green eyes, big and round enough to make Bambi envious, and lips so pink and pouty even I'd wondered a couple of times what it would be like to kiss her. Hell, if anyone could convince me to give up boys, it would be Eliza.

All the girls at school knew she was a babe, and so did the

boys, which is why she got more shit thrown at her than anyone else, *including* me. I was homeless, orphaned, and a loner. Wherever the totem pole ended at my school, I was ten feet below it. Eliza, simply because she was beautiful inside *and* out, had been forced even lower.

"I don't know what you're talking about."

"Of course, you do." She huffed. "People are saying Cora Peterson will need plastic surgery if she wants her nose straight again."

I shrugged while inspecting my nails. "Cora has a bad habit of not watching her step. I warned her before, but she's so clumsy that she tripped anyway."

"Into her locker?" Eliza questioned with a raised brow.

"It broke her fall."

Thankfully, the loud rumbling of our bus stole her attention, and we both watched as it slowly approached the stop sign across the street. It hissed as it rolled to a stop and blocked my view of the cars that were parallel parked. But not before I glimpsed the sun beaming off the hood of a 1966 Chevy Impala. My legs suddenly turned to jelly, and if they shook any harder, my knees would be knocking together. The bus started forward, hissing and rumbling as it turned and rolled toward our stop, continuing to block my view. Once the bus doors opened, everyone pushed forward at once, and since I was standing in the middle of the small crowd, I was herded up the steps. I anxiously made my way toward the back of the bus, shoving aside the ones slow to take their seat, and peered out the emergency door's window.

The spot where the Impala had been was now empty.

As hard as I tried to convince myself, I knew I hadn't imagined it. I was warm all over, not to mention I felt like my blood was rushing and every pleasure point my body possessed had been awakened. I couldn't quite catch my breath. Dazed, I sank into the empty seat next to Eliza and ignored her curious glances as my mind continued to race.

Why had Wren come? What could he hope to gain by stalking me? And most importantly, why the hell was I so excited by the possibilities?

I could think of nothing else. The entire day passed by in a blur, and I couldn't recall a single moment beyond spotting Wren's car. During the bus ride home, my eyes kept scanning the street and every parked car, but I didn't spot the Impala hiding in plain sight.

Did he know that I'd seen him? Would he come back? Did I want him to?

I didn't go straight to the Hendersons' as I'd been instructed. Instead, I hopped another bus against Eliza's warnings and spent the next few hours spinning in circles, figuratively and literally.

Roll Down was a roller disco and a weekly tradition for my parents and me, along with weekend trips to our favorite dessert bar—where they served the tastiest macaroons—and summer bike rides through Central Park.

Bike riding was always my mom's idea. She had this vintage mint-colored bike that she loved with a basket in the front that she decorated with fresh flowers whenever I wasn't riding the handlebars. I'd hurriedly snap pictures before the moments I knew I would want to relive could pass me by. I'm not sure when I fell hopelessly in love with her bike, but she would often promise that one day, it would be mine. My mom loved everything vintage, from retro diners and drive-ins to rotary-dial telephones, vinyl record players, and Mary Janes. She collected so much that stepping into our home had been like stepping into the past.

Now it was all gone and so was she.

Dad's only passion was running one of the many bodegas clustered in our old neighborhood. Viva Las Deli was a piece of home for those who had hailed from Vegas and was the best sandwich shop and convenience store on our block. My dad made a mean hero, and people would drive across the city in a hail storm just for one of his mouthwatering subs. When I was growing up, the bodega was one of my favorite places to be during the summer because it usually meant all the cherry popsicles I could eat. And when I wasn't ruining my appetite, as Mom would scold, I was running around the neighborhood chasing memories.

Photography for me wasn't about the art—I didn't know shit about lighting, angles, or which high-end camera performed best. It was about my need to possess all the things beautiful so I could admire them later. It was like catching butterflies.

At least, that's how it began. The night I'd met Wren was the first time since my parents left that I felt that long-forgotten urge.

When I finally walked through the door a little after seven, Eliza jumped up from the kitchen table covered with her. "Louchana! Are you trying to give me a heart attack? My parents will be home any minute!"

"You're a little young to have a heart attack, aren't you?"

"Hey, man, I watch *House*," she said, referring to the medical drama whose reruns she couldn't get enough of.

I snorted, and she giggled in return. "I think you just have the hots for Hugh Laurie."

"What's not to like? He's tall, handsome, and his character can get me out of gym class. I'll even put up with his grumpiness if he can save me from sixty minutes of Coach Brown's screaming."

"Coach will choke on that whistle before that happens."

Eliza sighed and got this look in her eye as if imagining it. "One can only hope."

I joined her at the table where she goaded me into helping her with her Algebra homework. I had a knack for math that Eliza exploited every chance she got.

"I wish you wouldn't skip school," she fussed as she packed up a couple of hours later. "You're easily the smartest kid at our school. You could go to Harvard."

"A couple of A's doesn't make me a genius."

Eliza waggled her finger and tsked. "Humble *and* smart...

forget Harvard. You could rule the world, Louchana Valentine. Or at least be president." Her eyes suddenly widened, and I knew she wasn't done. "You could date Nick Jonas!" she squealed as if that were better than being president.

I shook my head, amused and unable to hide it, and she returned it with a frustrated frown.

"I saw your transcripts, Lou. You've never dropped below an A. Not even for a single B."

The front door opened, and Cathleen and Dan walked through with a smile and carrying a box from Sal's that turned Eliza's frown upside down. I was happy for the distraction but not nearly as much as I was for pizza.

"Hey, kids. We brought cheese."

"With pineapples?" Eliza said hopefully.

"With pineapples," her father confirmed and ruffled her hair. He reached to do the same to me and failed to hide his hurt when I stood up from the table, subtly dodging his hand.

"I thought we could all eat together," Cathleen suggested as I headed for the door.

I could hear the hope in her tone and hated myself when I said, "I've got homework but save me a slice, will ya?" I didn't stick around to hear her answer and ran up the stairs.

I burst through my bedroom door, fighting the clog in my throat and didn't bother with the light as I peeled my jacket from my body and toed off my ratty boots.

"Took you long enough," a deep voice taunted. I was in the middle of pulling my shirt over my head when light flooded the room. "I was beginning to think you were avoiding me."

I didn't scream or bother to turn and confront the intruder until I had my boot in my hand. I flung it across the room and smiled when it bounced off his forehead and fell to the floor. Wren didn't get a chance to recover before I pulled a razor out of my hair and swiped at his stomach.

"Jesus, Lou," he whispered. "Fucking stop!"

I liked hearing the desperation in his voice and took another swipe, but this time, he anticipated my move and grabbed my wrist, squeezing until I cried out into the hand he'd clapped over my mouth, and I dropped the blade.

"What the hell is your problem?" he demanded once I was defenseless.

"Hey, I've got a better question. What the hell are you doing here, and why are you stalking me?"

He dropped my wrist and glared as he rubbed my dusty boot print from his forehead. He'd probably have a bruise by morning thanks to my wicked arm. "I was making sure you stayed put."

"That's not your business," I sassed as I made my way to the old stereo the Hendersons loaned me and turned the volume up high. Cathleen and Dan were patient people, but I had a feeling finding a boy in my room was crossing a line.

"Yeah, well, I made it my business," he retorted arrogantly. "What are you going to do about it?"

"Nothing." His expression became an adorable mixture of astonishment and suspicion, and I smiled. "You'll be dead or in prison soon," I explained. "Why waste a perfectly good manicure?"

"Are you willing to risk it?" he questioned, sounding confident once more.

"You're Exiled. What other outcomes could there be?" I searched his eyes for the answer, but he gave none. The confidence in his voice, the playfulness of his smile, the amusement in eyes…it was all gone in a flash.

"I could walk away," he suggested.

"Would you?" I shot back. I shouldn't have been surprised that he was one of them. Exiled recruited lost boys who grew into broken men. The younger the male, the less they understood the world and even less about themselves. They were often hormonal teenagers simply looking to rebel against their parents and themselves, and so Exiled promised them freedom only to give them a prison instead. There was no walking away. He *had* to know that. Which meant…

"You're toying with me," I announced without emotion because he deserved none.

"No more than you toy with me." I didn't miss the anger brewing in his gaze.

"When have I—"

"Fates change every day," he spoke sharply. "You give one power over the other when you speak on it."

"I didn't peg you for superstitious."

He looked away while swallowing hard. "I'm not, Lou. Not really."

"Then how can you believe that I would or could will you to be dead?"

Leaning his head against the wall, he closed his eyes. He didn't speak for a while, but when he did, he tore my heart in two. "The last time I can remember dreaming was six years ago. I woke up in the middle of the night, crying and sweating from a nightmare. My mom had a knack for convincing me that I was not only brave but so full of goodness that the monsters in my closet should be afraid of *me*. So I got out of bed, and I ran to her room, but I didn't go in."

"Why not?"

"I heard her whispering. She never liked being interrupted while she was on the phone, so I thought about going back to bed, but I couldn't. I had to tell her about my dream. The door was cracked open, so I peeked inside, and I saw her pacing back and forth. She was holding the phone to her ear, and she was crying, saying how she didn't have a lot of time left. At least that's what she told her best friend. She said she was going to die, and she spent the next three days believing it. She didn't sleep, didn't eat…she wasn't my mother."

"What happened on the third day?"

His face contorted into a grimace, and I wished at that moment that I could take his agony away. "She was killed. A hit and run."

My legs suddenly felt too weak to stand, so I crossed the room and sank onto the bed. "You're an orphan, too?"

His eyes popped open, and his eyes were blue as he stared back at me. "Yeah, I guess I am."

"Is that why you joined Exiled? Because you wanted a family?"

His gaze searched mine for a long, long time. "How much do you know about Exiled?"

I looked away and busied myself picking at the bedding. "Only what everyone else knows. That you're bad news." Exiled sold anything they could get their hands on—drugs, guns, *and* women. And when they weren't peddling their illegal wares, they were extorting the innocent people who ran legitimate businesses. My parents had lived in constant fear of one day falling on the mercy of Exiled. The detectives investigating their disappearance, however, had ruled out any foul play when they discovered their bank accounts depleted and the purchase of two one-way tickets to Paris. Mom had always dreamt of living there.

A picture of them safe and sound with a new life, arguing over frivolous things as they stocked the shelves of their new bodega entered my mind. Despite my hurt over them leaving me behind, I couldn't help smiling.

"You're wrong, kid, and that's nothing to smile about," Wren said interrupting my daydream. "I'm the *worst* kind of news."

"Will you stop with the 'kid' bullshit? You're not old enough to vote, get married, or even play the lottery. You're just a kid yourself."

He shook his head. "I lost my childhood a long time ago."

"That makes two of us." We'd both grown up prematurely, and there was nothing we could do about it now. We couldn't turn back time or forget the things we'd learned. The other kids our age didn't know how good they had it or that all the emotions they were currently juggling were only a portion of what was to come.

"Except no one took it from me, Lou. I torched that mother-fucker myself. That's the difference between you and me."

I shot up from the bed and balled my fists. "You don't know shit about me."

"Besides the fact that I can still smell the baby milk on your breath, I've got a whole fucking file on you, and I've read it from cover to cover. What it doesn't say, I'll find out eventually because I'm not going anywhere," he warned.

I crossed my arms to appear stern and also hide the evidence of what his threats had done to me. I cursed myself for not wearing a bra today. "You told me not to trust you."

"And I meant it."

I stared back at him incredulously. "And they say women are confusing creatures," I muttered. I threw my hands up and said, "Well, as you can see, I'm safe and sound. Let me show you the exit." I crossed the small room to the open window where he had, no doubt, gained entry. *I really need to learn to lock this thing.*

"Not so fast." I stopped but didn't turn around. "You're *fifteen*," he announced as if I weren't aware. It almost sounded like an accusation. As if I were the betrayer and not the betrayed.

I turned to face him, and I wore a smug smile. "And?"

"When I said I'd fuck you, you didn't think to tell me your goddamn age?" he roared.

I winced even as my ire rose.

"Will you keep it down? Besides, you knew I was young."

"And that's where I fucked up," he agreed and closed the distance between us. "I was *hoping* I was wrong. When you made that deal, I assumed I was."

"Boo fucking hoo."

His hands seized my waist without warning, and then he lifted me in the air before angrily tossing me on my bed. I'm pretty sure if he had a table, he would have flipped it over instead. Chest heaving, he stalked after me ready to pounce, but the moment I scrambled away, he stopped, closed his eyes, and swore. I then watched wide-eyed as he stormed to the window and, without a word, jumped over the sill in one swift motion.

I was still panting when I heard him grunt followed by a string of curses after he landed on the cold, hard ground. I could only imagine the shock the impact had sent to his knees.

Good.

In fact, I hoped he broke something.

A knock on my door mere seconds later, however, had my heart thundering for a different reason.

"Lou?" Eliza called out, and I released a sigh of relief that it wasn't Cathleen or Dan at my door.

"Yeah?" I answered as I hopped up from my bed and tiptoed to the window. One quick peek confirmed that Wren was gone. I was searching the street for signs of his car when I realized Eliza hadn't responded. Crossing the room, I ripped open the door. If only I'd considered my tousled and flushed appearance before I did so. Judging by Eliza's wide eyes and blush as she repeatedly glanced over my shoulder, I knew what she was thinking.

"My parents sent me to check on you. We heard an awful racket."

"I was working out."

She frowned as if she'd never heard of such a thing. "Working out?"

"I heard it relieves stress," I offered lamely. "What's up?"

"Um, right." She then held up my backpack and a plate with two slices of pizza. "You left your homework." Remembering my excuse to get out of having dinner with the Hendersons, I accepted both with a guilty twist of my gut. When I offered no excuse or apology, she huffed and said, "You know my parents really like you. *I* really like you. We all want you to feel like part of this family." Her cheeks turned pink when she added, "Maybe you could try with us?"

I had trouble swallowing as I looked away.

"Lou?"

Inwardly, I cringed. Every time I heard that name, I felt crushed under the person's heel. My parents had given me that nickname, and each time I heard it, I was reminded of the fact that they were gone.

"Thanks for the pizza." Stepping back, I shut the door in her face, and I didn't move until the sound of her footsteps and her crying faded.

I told myself I had no reason to feel bad. They brought this on themselves. My parents had the sense to get out while they could. It was only a matter of time before the Hendersons did, too.

As I was leaving for school the next morning, I found Wren's Impala boldly parked in front of the Hendersons' home. And this time, I knew it wasn't just wishful thinking. He was in plain view, leaning against the passenger door, looking bored and a little agitated. He also seemed oblivious to the curious but wary stares he was drawing from the neighbors. As my stomach fluttered and my center warmed, I silently prayed I wasn't one of those girls who found stalking attractive.

"Back for more?" I taunted as I sidled down the short walkway.

"You're late," he retorted with his usual nonchalance.

Feeling as bold as he did, I was now standing toe-to-toe with him. "You're stalking me."

"In my defense, you did say I was stuck with you."

"Yes, but not at the hip."

"*You* don't have hips."

Before I could offer a comeback, the front door opened and Eliza, who had been avoiding me, rushed down the steps, probably thinking I was already gone. She was still zipping her brand-new coat closed and hadn't noticed us, but when she finally did, she came to a dead halt at the sight of Wren. I groaned knowing that she'd have questions about Wren I couldn't and wouldn't answer.

Ignoring my obvious irritation, they both spoke at the same time.

"Who is that?" Eliza questioned as her eyes flitted curiously between Wren and me.

"Is she wearing the coat I bought for you?" Wren said as he snapped to his full height.

"He's nobody," I said to Eliza while ignoring Wren completely. "The bus will be here any minute. Let's go." I grabbed her hand, pulling her after me. Thankfully, Eliza didn't protest and, surprisingly, neither did Wren. We made it to the stop just in time and had to wait at the back of the line while everyone loaded onto the bus.

"So is he who I heard in your room last night?" Eliza whispered.

I made sure to keep my gaze straight ahead even though I wanted to look back and see if Wren had stuck around. He was hunting for something, and I had a feeling I was the prey. "There was no one in my room last night."

It was finally our turn to hop on, but as I started forward, the doors suddenly snapped close. Confused, I knocked on the door, and when my gaze met the bus driver's, he shook his head and drove off.

"Um…what just happened?" Eliza asked, sounding as dumbfounded as I felt.

Before I could answer, the Impala suddenly appeared where the bus had been just a moment ago. I watched through narrowed eyes as he leaned over and rolled down the window. "Let's go."

I had a strange sense of déjà vu, and I quickly remembered what occurred the last time I got in the car with him.

"What did you say to our bus driver?"

The corner of his mouth lifted. "I told him you'd be riding with me today."

"No, I won't, you fucking lunatic!" I turned to grab Eliza again intending to haul ass, but she was already pushing past me and climbing into his backseat. *What the hell?* "Eliza, what are you doing?"

"It's like thirty degrees," she whined as she buckled her seat belt. "Do you really expect us to walk all the way to school?"

Wren smiled and said nothing as he sat back in his seat and shifted the car into drive. He already knew he'd won because I wasn't about to let my fri... um... Eliza ride alone with him. I sighed and slid into the passenger seat. Wren took off before I could even get my seat belt fastened. I threw a dirty look over my shoulder at Eliza who smiled apologetically.

I started to scold her but then Wren beat me to it by scolding me instead. "Leave her alone. You're just upset because she has more common sense than pride."

"Wouldn't it be better to have both in equal measure?"

"Not always." He took his eyes from the road and met my gaze. "Not when it counts. For instance," he continued, focusing back on the road, "common sense tells me to stay away from you"—his hand tightened around the steering wheel as if the thought enraged him—"but my pride won't let me."

"What does your pride have to do with it?"

"You think you don't want me around, and I'm determined to prove you wrong."

"I'm still not seeing how that's supposed to be a good thing."

His eyes were mesmerizingly blue when he glanced my way again. "You will."

I had no ready response. There were only the butterflies awakened by the heat blooming in my stomach.

"Besides," Eliza cut in, reminding us both that she was in the car, "we all know you weren't going to walk. You'd freeze your tits off."

Wren laughed at her comment, but I had a feeling it was because he knew it would piss me off. I ignored them both and stared out the window.

When he pulled up to our schools, which were right across from each other,, he ordered me to hang back before letting Eliza out on his side. I obeyed solely so I could give him a piece of my mind and pretended not to notice how deeply Eliza blushed when Wren wished her a good day. I snorted and crossed my arms while pretending interest in my schoolmates hanging out on the lawn. The moment he climbed back inside and shut the door, I let him have it.

"This little 'agreement' that you're taking *way* too seriously is off. Stay away from me, Wren."

"You need a friend, and I need a distraction. What's the problem?" he asked with more patience than the situation allowed. How could he be so casual when his actions were far from sane? More importantly, why was I tempted to get closer and find out?

"You're dangerous and not just because of what you do for them," I said, referring to Exiled, "but because of what you do to *me*. I'm not sure I like who I am when you're around."

"I'd never ask you to be someone you're not, and I'd never hurt you. As tough as you think you are, the world is tougher. It's a tenacious bitch, and you need someone watching your back."

"But why do you care?" I pressed. "It can't be because you're so benevolent."

"Did you not hear me say I get something out of the deal?"

"What exactly do you need distracting from?"

His nostrils flared, and he sighed. "Does it matter? It won't ever cost you a damn thing." When I didn't respond, he added, "Do we have a deal?"

I stared into those perplexing eyes of his, drawn to the flame I glimpsed within them. Against my will, my lips said "Sure" even as my mind screamed no.

Wren nodded and looked away.

I could tell he wasn't as confident about the seal we'd just placed on our fate as he'd like me to think, but like me, he was too far gone. Something invisible, unbreakable, and incurable had a hold on us, drawing us in like moths to a single flame. Could we one day break free of it, or would it choose to break us instead?

Clearing his throat, he said, "So be it."

I slowly reached for the handle unable to understand why I was reluctant to go when he spoke again.

"Wait."

I sat back and forced myself to relax while he reached into the back seat. A second later, a silver gift bag appeared in my lap with blue stuffing paper, and whatever was hidden inside felt pretty heavy.

"Happy Valentine's Day, little Valentine."

I continued to stare at the bag like it was a bomb. "What is it?"

"The idea is for you to open it and see."

"No. Tell me," I demanded more forcefully.

"Open it, Lou." I met his gaze, and a silent battle of wills ensued. Off in the distance, I heard the school bell ring, and I knew he heard it too when he said, "You're late, and I've got nowhere to be."

"I find that hard to believe. After all, there's no shortage of innocent people in need of terrorizing."

"Very funny."

"Yes, I thought so." I peeled aside the gift paper and peered inside. Frowning, I reached in and pulled out the transparent glass sphere depicting snow falling over the city. "A snow globe? But I'm not a tourist."

"Besides the clothes that you couldn't be bothered to fold or hang, your room was noticeably bare of the things that led you here...to me. There were no memories, Lou."

"They're gone," I said after a long heavy silence.

"What's gone?" I couldn't see his frown since I was watching the snow falling, but I heard it in his tone.

"The memories. My parents took them when they left."

I let him lift my chin and brush away the tear I didn't know had fallen. "Then we'll make new ones." I felt his other hand cover mine, the one holding the globe. "And we'll start with this. To remind you of the night we met."

The flame in his eyes danced as he stared back at me, and only now when it was too late did I realize there *would* be a cost to letting him get close.

My heart.

The price I paid one day would be my heart.

CHAPTER
ONE

The Moth

Two Years Later

"C HECKMATE."

I took a sip of my drink as my opponent giddily tallied up her points.

"Twenty-two points," she announced before marking them on the notepad next to her.

"You're cheating," I seethed.

The sharp look Kendra gave me could have cut through steel. "And you must be sore from all the losing."

Kendra was not only an escort but one of our most popular, and my personal favorite although not for the reasons anyone might assume. She had the smoothest dark brown skin, almond-shaped eyes, full lips that beckoned, and jet-black dreads that curled around tits that must have been molded by God himself. However, it was the humor, wit, and mettle the other girls in Fox's stable lost to drugs and abuse a long time ago that drew me to her. She started escorting for Exiled a few weeks after my initiation, and our first meeting nearly five years ago hadn't exactly gone well.

Swallowing the sour taste the memory left on my tongue, I grumbled, "You don't get to brag when you're only ahead by ten points."

"Winning is winning," she boasted with a sly smile.

I ignored her wagging tongue and arranged the tiles to spell devotion before frowning at the board. The last three words I'd played had been desire, denial, and agony.

"Oooh," Kendra said with an exaggerated wince. "Twelve points." She marked my points down, and after playing her turn, she stared at me. "Something bothering you?"

"No," I lied. "Why?"

"Because I can tell you're a million miles away, and it's making you suck at Scrabble more than usual."

I took the time to spell out duty before answering her. "I told you we should have played spades."

"Eight points," she mumbled while writing it down. "And you suck at cards, too."

I rotated my shoulders in agitation and refrained from getting up to pace the room like a caged lion, which was precisely how I felt—bound and hungry.

"Baby, you're really tense," Kendra cooed. She stood from her chair—the red silk robe I'd gifted her falling open to reveal her naked body—and came around to stand behind me. I felt her breasts against my back as she leaned into me and ran her hands from my fists resting on the table, up along my arms until, finally, she gripped my shoulders. My head fell forward as she began manipulating the tense muscles there. "How's that feel?"

The only response I could manage was to release a groan loud enough to be heard anywhere in the large two-story house. At that moment, I didn't give a shit about anything but her small hands kneading away weeks, months, two years of tension.

That lasted until I felt teeth nipping at the shell of my ear and heard the flirtation in Kendra's voice when she said, "You know well by now that there's more where that came from."

"Don't start something we can't finish," I flirted back while wearing a crooked smile.

Those magical hands fell away, and I looked back in time to see her prop them on generous hips. "And why not?"

"Because it's bad for business," I said, knowing it was a lame excuse. Fox allowed Exiled to indulge as long as the men paid in full and kept their fists to themselves. In fact, he insisted on it. It was his idea of keeping up the morale, and the men were more than willing to take advantage. Their only concern when they walked through those doors after a long day was their cocks. Keeping the girls safe never entered their minds, which left me as the sole defender of their well-being. Kendra had been an amazing teacher, but for her and the other girls' sake, I could no longer allow sex with her to distract me.

I'd come by as often as I could for as long as I could to ensure things were running smoothly and the girls were treated well. Not only did the johns sometimes get out of hand but so did the round-the-clock guards we kept here to make sure that didn't happen. I can't recall how many broken ribs and kneecaps I've dealt in exchange for the black eyes and busted lips given to the girls. Kendra, in particular, had been on the receiving end of many disgruntled customers' fists. She had a way with her mouth that gave men immense pleasure only to bruise their ego when she finished. If she didn't make us more money than she cost us, Fox would have disposed of her a long time ago. That didn't stop me from warning her repeatedly to keep her head down, though. Fox was neither tolerant nor merciful.

"Or maybe," Kendra teased, pulling me from my thoughts by palming my cock through my jeans, "you're not as worried about business as you are of that gorgeous little monster finding out about us."

At the mention of Lou, I stood rather abruptly, almost toppling the chair and knocking Kendra over in the process. My cock was straining against my zipper, threatening to break free, and I told myself it was because of the woman offering herself to me and not the girl I couldn't have. Turning, I leaned down and kissed her forehead. "There is no us, and she's none of your business."

She scoffed while tying her robe together. "You can't be that possessive and protective *and* expect anyone to believe you don't have feelings for her."

I groaned, regretting the day I'd foolishly allowed Kendra to find out about Lou. I'd been in the middle of one of my visits when Lou video called. I had let it ring, intending to return her call when I finished conducting business. However, Lou, refusing to be ignored, had rung incessantly until I finally gave in and answered. I must have scolded her for ten minutes straight, knowing everything I was saying was going in one ear and out the other.

Kendra had naïvely stepped in to save a helpless Lou from my tirade by snatching my phone and introducing herself, but the reception she received had been...chilly. Lou wordlessly stared back at a smiling, unsuspecting Kendra until she got the message and awkwardly returned my phone. I could tell the encounter had flustered Kendra and wished like hell I could have warned her before she set herself up for failure. Lou, on the other hand, pretended nothing happened and chattered about everything under the sun, rarely stopping to take a breath.

"She's my friend," I explained for what might have been the hundredth time. "That means my protection comes with the territory." Besides, Kendra had already learned the hard way that however possessive I seemed, Lou was ten times worse. She was a far cry from the girl who couldn't wait to get away from me two years ago.

"*We're* friends," Kendra argued, waving her hand back and forth between us. "You're in so deep with her that you don't even know how far you've fallen, but you're smart enough to know you can't ignore it forever."

"My mistake. I must have forgotten to mention that she's my *best* friend." After two years, I knew I was beginning to sound like a broken record and that soon, my ears would be bleeding. In the beginning, I wanted Lou to the point of distraction, but the closer we grew, the better I was able to exorcise those thoughts from my mind.

Mostly.

I knew I wasn't completely cured, and now that the bandage was beginning to peel, I wondered how long it would be before my heart was an open wound again. It was nothing compared to the pain Lou would feel when she eventually discovered the truth about me.

I was a monster, after all.

She didn't approve of my fealty to Exiled, and her feelings have only grown in the time since she'd convinced herself that some good still resided inside of me. If she only knew that Fox, Exiled's leader, wasn't the one to recruit me, but that it was me doing the corrupting all along.

Three years after my mother's death, I signed along the dotted line and accepted a life that was mine to inherit from the moment I took my first breath.

"If only everyone had a best friend who becomes as rabid and bloodthirsty as you do if someone so much as blinks at them wrong," Kendra mused. "It's hard not to feel slighted. *We* were friends longer, but you call Lou your best friend."

I could only shrug in response. Some friendships became threadbare, holding on for as long as they could, while others never stopped pushing for a stronger foundation. Lou challenged me to be a better person. Kendra only reminded me that I wasn't.

Noticing my nonchalance, Kendra smiled and tilted her head. "It's no wonder Lou sunk her teeth in you so deep you couldn't possibly walk away without leaving a piece of yourself behind."

I frowned and chose to focus on the part that didn't threaten my sanity or make my heart beat out of control. "You don't think I'd kill for you?"

She gave me a look that said she was on to me. "Maybe, if it was the right thing to do, but you'd not only kill for *her*—you'd *die* for her and wouldn't think twice about it."

I felt exposed as I stared back at Kendra while fighting to conceal my guilt. It was as if she'd run her finger under every line of my conscience, reading me as easily as an open book. Somewhere along the way, I'd made a vow. I wouldn't take life and forfeit my soul. Not without exhausting all options. Not for Fox and not for the men I called my brothers.

But for Lou?

I'd gladly leave it wrapped with a shiny red bow at hell's door.

"You shouldn't romanticize," I advised as I headed for the door. I needed to get out of there fast before I did something stupid like begging Kendra for advice on how to make Lou mine.

"I'd hate to break your heart."

I already had one foot out the door, eager for a quick escape, when I heard her mumble, "It's not *my* heart you should be worried about."

My grip on the doorknob tightened until I threatened to rip it off completely.

"It's always a pleasure," I threw over my shoulder before slamming the door behind me. As Kendra's cackles trailed me down the hall, I began to understand how men could be driven to violence in her presence. She never fucking let up.

Downstairs, I headed for the kitchen, following the enticing smells permeating the air. Most of the girls were able to fend for themselves and were pretty decent cooks, but there was only one who could create something this mouthwatering.

I stepped inside the modernized kitchen and found Irma hovering over the flattop stove. Her dark hair was in a messy bun high on her head, and the strands that escaped stuck to her sweaty nape. The stylish red frames perched on her thin nose were mostly fogged from the heat, making me wonder how she could see what she was doing.

"You're just in time," she said without looking up from whatever she was sautéing. "I fixed you a plate."

Ignoring the plate of steaming roasted chicken, rice, and carrots waiting for me on the island, I walked over to the stove and kissed her flour-dusted cheek.

"Don't toy with me, young man. You'll give this old woman hope."

I laughed and copped a squat on one of the stools, drooling over the food she'd prepared. It was quite a spread for the middle of the day. "Age is only a number," I flirted.

"That's it," she said as she turned and pointed her spatula at me. "No dessert for you."

"What if I told you forty-five was the new thirty-five and that *you* don't look a day over twenty-five?"

"I'd say you have two slices of my lemon meringue coming your way." She winked before turning off the stove and wiping her hands on the bright blue apron wrapped around her waist. "Your mother would be proud, you know," she gently said, and I was glad my mouth was full of her tender, juicy chicken, saving me from having to respond. "Before you, there was no one to look out for us." She palmed my cheek when I couldn't hide my surprise at the emotion in her voice and finally met her tearful gaze. "No one to care as much as you do."

"It's nothing," I said, shrugging as if that proved my point.

"You don't believe that. I know you must wonder, just as I do, that if someone had been here to stand up for us all those years ago, your mom might still be with us today."

"Enough," I snapped. Wiping my mouth with a cloth napkin, I regained my footing while holding Irma's gaze. "There was nothing you nor I could have done to change what happened. It was an *accident*."

She looked away just as a lone tear escaped her eye. Irma had been my mom's best friend and another one of Fox's escorts until he deemed her too old to turn a profit. Most women would have taken their freedom and ran for the hills, but Irma had refused to leave the girls and became their unofficial house mother instead. Before Kendra, Irma was Fox's top girl, but even she had been expendable. My mom…she lost some of her value when she fell in love with the wrong man and had his baby.

"Stop that," I said before pulling Irma into my arms. "She wouldn't want you blaming yourself or getting upset again."

"Oh, you're right." She wiped her eyes and stepped away. "Finish your food," she ordered once she'd regained control of her emotions. "I'll get your room ready and put fresh sheets down."

"Don't bother," I told her as I dropped down onto the stool. "I'm not staying."

Irma insisted on keeping my mother's old room free for whenever I chose to stay a few nights. The unspoken reason had to do with me losing my shit the day I met Kendra. I'd caught her not only escorting a john from my mother's room but wearing the robe I'd saved up my allowance to surprise her one Christmas. I hadn't reacted well, and Kendra being Kendra hadn't docilely stood by while I raged and, in return, spewed venom of her own. I apologized the next day by gifting her a silk robe three times more expensive, and Kendra had graciously accepted my apology by relieving me of my virginity. The next day, she moved out of my mom's room despite my protests, and Irma has been sure to keep it empty ever since.

"Then you be sure to tell Winny that I said hello," she ordered, referring to my grandmother, who lived out in New Jersey.

"I will," I promised, not bothering to correct her on where I was actually headed.

Satisfied, Irma floated from the kitchen, likely on the hunt for someone else in need of mothering.

I was busy scarfing down the rest of my food when my phone buzzed in my pocket a few minutes later. Deciding whoever it was could wait, I continued eating. Five minutes later, my phone buzzed again, followed by a third, fourth, and fifth, each spaced less than a minute apart. Shoving aside my nearly empty plate, I released a string of curses as I yanked my phone from my jeans.

There was only one person this eager, or rather impatient, to get a hold of me.

And I knew she'd shamelessly ring my phone back to back until the battery eventually died if she had to. A part of me wanted to believe she did it because she was frantic with worry, but I knew the little shit just didn't like being ignored. Besides, she would never admit to being worried about me anyway.

As I left the kitchen and headed for the front door, I bypassed reading the texts she'd sent and stabbed the video call button. After only a couple of rings, a fuzzy picture of a gray tiled ceiling appeared. A second later, the focus changed, and I was staring at a stony-eyed Lou. Her dark hair was haphazardly piled on top of her head, emphasizing her youth and making her look angelic.

I could only sincerely accuse her of the former.

Tearing my gaze away, I peered into her background, attempting to determine her location. A bulletin board covered with papers and the narrow wooden door next to it were my only clues.

"I'm in class," she confirmed through clenched teeth.

I smirked, remembering that it was the middle of a school day and satisfied to have gotten under her skin. It was only fair since she seemed to live underneath mine. I checked to make sure her earbuds were in before asking, "Is your school on fire?"

"No."

I sat on the hood of my car, planted my feet on the bumper, and rested my elbows on my knees. I was strangely content as the rest of the world and all the bad inside it melted away. There was only Lou.

"Then what's the emergency?"

She paused, and I knew that if she weren't trying to hide the fact that she'd taken a call during class, she'd be screaming in my ear.

"You didn't read my texts?"

"I must have forgotten to." And then I smiled, making her scowl deepen.

She adjusted her position, and I narrowed my eyes at the writing on her chest. Surely my eyes were playing a cruel trick on me.

"What the fuck are you wearing?"

"What?" She glanced down at her tank top in confusion. "What's wrong with my shirt?"

"Nothing if you're trying to send a message." My voice lowered to a whisper. "Are you sending a message, Lou?"

"Get a grip, Harlan. I've had this shirt since I was nine."

I highly fucking doubted it. The fucking thing read 'Take me to bed or lose me forever.' The only thing keeping it from being a complete fucking come-on was the brown teddy bear next to it—unless you were into that sort of thing.

Then another thought—one that had me shooting up from the hood of my car—occurred to me. "I want to see the rest."

"Pardon me?" she questioned, feigning modesty. Her wide-set eyes, however, did nothing to deter me. There was no way I could dismiss what she was wearing, and I had a feeling she expected no less from me. She probably planned it to get my attention.

"Pan the camera down now. Let me see you."

She hesitated for all of three seconds before she did what she was told, and I pretended my cock didn't take notice. I cursed when my suspicions were confirmed. Lou had been telling the truth all right. Judging by the way her breasts strained against the cotton and the sliver of skin peeking from underneath the hem, she'd also outgrown the shirt.

How the hell had she'd gotten away with it? Didn't the school have some kind of policy? I asked her as much.

"I've been wearing my jacket all day," she whispered before rolling her blue eyes.

"Put it on."

She blinked twice. "What?"

"Put. It. On."

"But it's hot," she whined, forgetting she was in class. A moment later, a woman was standing over her shoulder with her arms crossed, and I didn't get to hear much before the call ended, but I did catch a glimpse of the sly grin on Lou's face.

She thought she'd won.

Running my hand down my face, I tried to talk myself out of what I was about to do. Twenty minutes later, after breaking every traffic law written, I stalked the halls of West Bridge High, hunting my best friend.

CHAPTER
TWO

The Flame

"MISS VALENTINE," MY TEACHER SAID THE MOMENT I HUNG up on Wren, "the bell doesn't dismiss you. *I* dismiss you." I was thinking up an equally clichéd response when she added, "In your case, it seems you couldn't at least wait for the bell."

"I'm really sorry, teach. That was my daddy." A few of my classmates snickered. "He gets a little growly when he's worried."

"Miss Valentine, I am fully aware of your situation and know very well that wasn't your father on the phone. However, in the note I'll be sending home to your foster parents informing them of your detention, I'll be sure to include the school's office number in the case of an emergency."

"Detention?" My head jerked back. "But it's the last day of school!"

A chorus of sympathetic groans and not-so-sympathetic laughter erupted. She silenced them with a warning look before refocusing on me.

"I'm sorry, Miss Valentine. It looks like your summer vacation will be starting a little late." She touched my shoulder gently before walking back to the front of the class and resuming the lesson that she wouldn't bother grading.

I sighed, relieved that she hadn't taken my phone, and texted Wren.

I got detention. I hope you're happy.

Twenty-minutes later, the bell rang, and I still had no response from Wren. As the teacher wished us a good summer, we all filed out to head to our last class of the year.

The volume in the hall was louder than usual even though there was significantly less traffic. The seniors all skipped and most of the lower classmen with them. Even goody-two-shoes Eliza had faked a cold and stayed home in bed. My attendance today, including my perfect attendance over the past few weeks, was one of the conditions of my advancement to senior year. If it weren't for Wren, I would have dropped out a year ago. He insisted I stay in school, and as always, I couldn't find it in my heart to resist him. If only...

I shook the thought off just as I felt a punishing grip on my arm. I didn't get a chance to see who it was until they pulled me into the nearest empty classroom.

"What the hell is your problem?" I ripped my arm away and rubbed the spot knowing there would probably be a mark. I wasn't as worried about the bruise as I was explaining it to an already irate Wren. I knew he wouldn't waste the opportunity to come around barking orders after the conversation we'd had. After staying away for two weeks, raising his blood pressure was the only way to get his attention. He was stubborn, but I was determined.

"Why haven't you returned any of my texts?"

I hid my blush behind a glare. Dean Daniels was the entire hot guy package—blond, blue-eyed, chiseled jaw, and charming smile. He was also rumored to be the school's first pick for quarterback next year. With those arms and pecs, it was easy to see why. Dean looked and acted like your average boy next door only way hotter and way cooler. And...he had a huge crush on me. No one knew why, least of all me.

Crossing my arms over my chest, I casually leaned against the door as if my heart weren't racing. "It's a little impossible to return what I didn't get."

"You expect me to believe that?" he shot back.

"Do you see me giving you any other choice?"

He glared at me for a few seconds longer before dropping his gaze and smiling shyly at the floor. "I'm sorry for being a dick. It's just that you confuse me, Lou. Girls usually treat me like their world revolves around me. You don't seem to care if I exist in yours or not."

"I…care."

"Really? You don't sound too sure."

I frowned knowing he wasn't just insecure. Dean was nice, crazy hot, and he didn't hurt innocent people for a living. I *should* have been one of those girls who drew hearts around our names in my notebook or sighing every time he passed me in the hall. Why wasn't I? It wasn't as if his attention had zero effect on me. I'd have to be blind. However, all I truly felt was flattered. Unfortunately, flattery wasn't enough to get him in my pants. *Thank God.*

"I don't want to get my hopes up," I said placatingly. "You just broke up with Cora, and you've been with her forever. Are you sure it's over?" Besides the fact that Cora still blamed me for her slightly crooked nose, I wasn't in any rush to give her more ammunition to hate me by dating her ex-boyfriend. I wasn't the least bit afraid of her, but I preferred keeping my head down. A lion on the hunt wouldn't let their prey see them before the kill.

Just as the bell rang, Dean reached out and pulled me close. Dropping my arms, I let him press me against his chest, and I tilted my head back since he towered over me. He was even taller than Wren, making me wonder why he didn't go for basketball instead of football. At his height, he could probably just drop the ball in the basket.

"She's catty, self-centered, and not all that bright. Trust me. It's over."

He leaned down, and I knew right then he was going to kiss me. Suddenly, my hands were shaking as they fisted his letterman jacket. He'd be my first. Did he know? Did I even want him to be?

Sadly, I didn't get the chance to find out. I blinked in stunned surprise at the large hand that came out of nowhere and gripped Dean's face like those facehuggers from Alien before he was pushed—no, *thrown* across the room, crashing into desks on his way down.

My first thought was that a teacher had discovered us and had one *hell* of an overreaction. However, that theory was quickly laid to rest when Dean's assailant turned, and I was held hostage by blue-gray eyes.

"Wren?" I gasped. And then my shock cleared, and I screamed, "Are you out of your mind? What the hell are you doing here?"

"I could ask you the same." He jerked his head toward the door. "School's over. Go wait in the car."

I propped my hand on my hips and stood my ground. Behind Wren, Dean groaned as he struggled to stand. I wanted to run over and help him, but I knew that would only make things worse for Dean. "School isn't over for another hour."

Wren stalked the two or three steps it took for him to stand toe-to-toe with me. "It is for you, so go wait in my fucking car."

"Yeah, curse and growl at me. That will make me move faster."

He smirked. "Fine." He took a step back. "Have it your way, little Valentine." Turning, he headed straight for Dean. His hand was reaching behind him for the gun I knew was at his waist.

He wouldn't.

Surely, he knew he couldn't.

It was beyond reckless and cruel—even for Wren.

"When it comes to you, Louchana, I can't be reasoned with. You make me lose control."

Those were the words he said to me after he found me getting slapped around by some guy whose wallet I didn't even remember stealing. The guy had obviously remembered me, though, judging by the split lip he'd given me. The broken jaw he limped away with had definitely cost him more than a few stolen bucks, though.

I shoved aside the memory and rushed to grab Wren's hand. "Wait!"

He paused just a foot away from Dean, who was already on his knees looking seconds from pissing himself. When Wren looked over his shoulder expectantly, I mumbled, "I'll go, asshole. Just leave him alone."

I squeezed his fingers when he simply stared back, and he sighed. "Now, Lou."

With one last apologetic glance at Dean, I reluctantly headed for the door, more than certain he'd never speak to me again. Dean wasn't the first guy Wren had run off, but he had, by far, incurred the worst of Wren's wrath.

Another one bites the dust.

Stepping into the empty hall, I wondered at my smile that had somehow slipped free. I told myself that it was just his determination to protect me that caused it. No way was he jealous and no way was the fluttering in my belly butterflies.

Wren didn't take long to follow. Seated in the passenger seat of the Impala, I had my headphones in, happily humming along to 'You're My Best Friend' by Queen when he emerged from the school. Hopping in, he cranked the car until it roared and drove away without a word.

Wren didn't immediately take me home. Instead, I perked up when he pulled into a familiar parking lot, and I saw the sign for Roll Down. I hopped out the moment he'd parked and was already making a mad dash for the door when I felt his hand grip my arm gently but firmly…as if he knew *exactly* how to touch me.

Wren - 1

Dean - 0

Not that I was keeping score because, of course, there was no actual competition. Wren was my best friend, and the line that hadn't been present the night we met was firmly drawn.

"Not so fast. Where's your jacket?"

"I told you," I said as I stomped my foot, "it's too hot."

His gaze narrowed, and I quickly shifted my own. "There was no jacket, was there?"

"Of course!" I said as I looked any and everywhere but him. "Why would I lie?"

"Then where is it, Lou? I don't recall seeing you with one."

I pursed my lips. "I must have lost it during all the drama you caused."

I could feel him burning a hole in the side of my face but refused to meet his gaze. After a few seconds, he turned on his heel without a word and stomped back to his car. I impatiently waited where he left me and watched as he popped open the trunk and produced one of his many plain white T-shirts. Walking back over to me, he held out the shirt. "Put this on."

"I can't wear your shirt, Wren. That thing will swallow me!"

"Then it's too bad you can't shrink this, too."

My jaw nearly kissed the pavement. "I did *not* shrink my shirt."

"Well, it didn't shrink itself. You barely look like you can lift your arms."

"Because I grew boobs, you jackass!"

His gaze fell to my chest, and the look in his eyes made my body temperature hot enough to boil lava. "I'm well aware."

Tossing me his shirt, he stalked for the entrance of the skating rink. Knowing there was no chance in hell he'd let me skate without the cover of his shirt, I huffed and yanked it over my head. However, the moment I caught a whiff of his scent and realized the shirt smelled like him, my grumbling came to an immediate halt. I was transported to nirvana. Completely exalted. I wanted to roll around in it until I was covered in his scent.

Unfortunately, I had to settle for lifting a handful of the shirt to my nose.

Wren didn't wear cologne, yet he always managed to smell so damn good and manly. If his scent was ever bottled, I had the perfect suggestion for a name—Forbidden Fruit.

Incidentally, that sobered me up quickly.

The minute the euphoria faded, I looked around for Wren, hoping he hadn't seen me sniffing his shirt like a bitch in heat and realized he must have already gone inside.

I sighed. One of these days, I'd have no choice but to relieve the tension building inside me. And Wren…well, he'd just have to step aside and be okay with that.

Inside the building, I shivered at the cool air blasting on full power and wished I *had* brought a jacket. I looked around the dark skating rink, the only light coming from the colorful spotlights above and spotted Wren on one of the black leather couches shoving on a pair of black skates. My eyebrows touched my hairline in surprise. Usually, I'd have to beg and beg Wren to skate with me, and the answer was almost always no.

"You're skating?" I redundantly asked as I approached him on cautious feet.

He shrugged without looking away from the laces he was busy tying. Feeling awkward and frustrated at the same time, I plopped down on the bench next to him and shoved on the much smaller white pair he knew I loved. I used to have my own, but that was a long time ago. Wren stood after he finished lacing up his skates, and I half expected him to start without me, but he didn't. Instead, he knelt in front of me and took over lacing mine up when my stupid hands wouldn't stop trembling. The moment he finished, he stood and held out his hand. I slid my hand into his warm palm just as the first strings of 'After You' by Meg Myers began playing through the speakers. He skated backward, leading me past the low barrier, and the moment our skates touched the maple floor, I started to pull my hand away. My stomach dipped when, instead of letting me go, he gripped me tighter, and I watched the colorful lights dance around his face as we skated around the empty rink. Neither of us said a word or looked away.

"Are you mad at me?" I finally asked after the song ended.

"I'm mad at myself."

"Why?"

He shook his head and blew out air. "It's complicated."

"I promise I can keep up."

His hand fell to my waist, and he pulled me closer, and I knew it was a reflex when he said, "It's also dangerous."

"I'm not afraid."

His eyes seemed to glow, and I told myself it was the lights. "You should be."

"Why would I be afraid when I have you to protect me?"

"Because someday, it might be me you need protecting from."

My eyebrows knitted. "Did something bad happen…" I looked around before saying, "At work?"

He shook his head. "No more than usual."

I was careful not to let my relief show. "Then you have nothing to worry about. You're not as easily corrupted as you think, Wren Harlan." I gripped his shirt and stood on the tips of my toes until my lips brushed his ear. "Neither am I."

Pushing away from him, I began skating in earnest, drawing figure eights and twirling until I felt the weight gradually lift from my shoulders. Wren trailed after me, watching every move I made with a fascinated gleam in his eyes. I also knew he was watching like a hawk for anyone who came or went and made sure I didn't frolic too far away.

I felt protected and free while, at the same time, I felt overwhelming sadness for Wren. No matter how much I hoped, he might never be free of the corruption, paranoia, and guilt.

When was the last time Wren felt like a kid, lived without such a heavy burden on his shoulders? He was only nineteen, and so far, he'd seen and done more than people twice his age and not all of it good. At that moment, I wanted nothing more than to bring warmth and light in his cold, dark world. To remind him there was more to life, more to *him* than death and cruelty.

Across the rink, I caught Wren's eye and smiled. His gaze turned suspicious—a testament to how well he knew me. A moment later, I skated toward him at full speed.

"What the hell are you doing?" he shouted. I could hear the panic in his voice, and my smile grew.

"Catch me!"

"Goddammit, Lou!" he roared as he raced to meet me halfway.

I shouldn't have enjoyed the frantic look on his face or his desperation to keep me from getting hurt as much as I did, but a satisfying heat bloomed in my belly anyway. Wren cared more than a best friend probably should. Maybe like a brother?

Whatever the reason, I wanted more of it—of this and him. I wanted Wren to feel alive, and I wanted him to live. For himself as much as for me.

We both reached the center at the same time, and I didn't give myself a chance to reconsider before I launched myself into the air and into his arms. Strong, capable hands caught me just like I knew he would, but then he seemed to lose his balance and went crashing to the floor, taking me with him. My shriek was cut off by the impact of his body breaking my fall. The sound of Wren hitting the floor echoed over the music, making me cringe. He grunted and then groaned, and I could only imagine the pain he was in.

"Are you okay?" I lifted as much as I dared without hurting him further. "Did I break you?"

He froze and then stared into my eyes for so long I forgot that I'd even asked a question until he answered. "Not yet."

Those words seemed to mean more than he intended, causing me to squint as if he'd just posed a difficult math question. "What do you me—"

"Hey, are you guys okay?"

Tearing my gaze away from Wren's was harder than ripping off a Band-Aid, but he left me no choice when he looked away, and I could have sworn I saw a flash of guilt in his blue eyes. Eric, the freckle-faced redhead who worked the counter, stood over us anxiously waiting for a response. Neither of us had even noticed him approaching. Frankly, I was surprised he'd seen our fall given his red eyes and the heavy smell of weed clinging to his uniform. I was pretty sure he'd even ratted me out to Wren a couple of times in exchange for a few ounces.

"We're good, man," Wren supplied.

I said nothing as I carefully lifted off my best friend and busied myself brushing the invisible dust off my body to avoid eye contact.

Wren was quicker than he should have been to regain his feet, and I realized why when he snatched his vibrating phone from his pocket and answered with a clipped, "Harlan."

I watched the light flicker and then fade from his eyes as he listened to whatever the caller was saying. "I'm a little busy. Can't it wait?" I inched closer in time to hear a lot of yelling and swearing. Wren's nostrils flared, and I knew there would be steam coming from them if possible. "Fine. Give me an hour."

Not again. My quaking heart crumbled at my feet. *I just got him back.*

I nearly dislocated my shoulder squeezing into that top this morning, and it looked like all my efforts to gain his attention had been for nothing. As if hearing my thoughts, his gaze found mine.

"Make that two."

I smirked despite my frustrations. At least Wren was smart enough to know that I wasn't going to let him run away that easy.

Wren ended the call in the middle of the caller's tirade and grabbed my hand before pulling me to him and pressing me to his side. His head dipped, and he said, "Congratulations on becoming a senior," so quietly and solemnly that had I not been intently focused on his lips, I wouldn't have known what he said.

"I might not be since you made me leave, and I probably won't be allowed back."

He paused as if only now remembering the conditions of my advancements before saying, "I'll take care of it."

I rolled my eyes. "Of course you will."

He buried his face in my shoulder, and I felt his lips move along my collar bone. "Not now, Lou. Please not now," he pleaded.

"What's wrong?" I cried, feeling my gut twist painfully. Something was eating him, and if he couldn't tell me, his best friend...I tried not to think of the horrifying possibilities.

"Nothing."

"You mean something?" With his arm around my waist, he squeezed me tighter. It was a warning and an effective one. I could feel myself giving in but not giving up. When it came to Wren Harlan, that was just something I couldn't do. "One of these times, they're going to split you apart until you shatter, and I'm afraid..." I took a deep breath and willed my emotions away. "I'm afraid I won't be able to piece you back together again."

He lifted his head and quirked a brow. "I'm not easily corrupted, remember?"

"Yes, but you're already broken." He frowned, clearly insulted, so I pressed my hand against his chest right where his wavering heartbeat was. "There's a rift here. It's tiny, thin, and almost impossible to find." I let my hand fall to my side and sighed. "Unless you know where to look."

And everyone knew how quickly one tiny crack could splinter and become a gaping hole. Would I even be enough to fill it? We only had each other, after all.

Exiled was a taboo subject between us—almost as taboo as the idea of us ever being more than just friends—so in typical Wren fashion, he shut down. Stepping back, the muscle in his jaw ticked as his arm fell away. "Noted."

"Are you mad?" I prodded with a curl of my lip.

"No."

I might have believed him if he hadn't looked away defiantly.

"You sure? You seem a little salty to me."

His hand shot out, gripped my chin, and pulled me in until I was swimming once more in his ocean without a boat, a paddle, or an ounce of hope. "Drop it."

"Make me."

His flaming gaze dropped to my lips, and I quickly tucked them in wondering if he was thinking what I thought he was thinking.

No. It couldn't be.

Although…

Wren had been attracted to me once before. Was it too far of a stretch to believe he could be again? Did I want that? I couldn't be sure of what I wanted, but I knew what I didn't want, which was the ruin of our friendship. I would never allow myself to survive without Wren. Call me weak, but Wren was the only one I was willing to be this vulnerable for, and I still haven't forgiven him for making me feel this way.

"Trust me," he said, his voice thick with something I couldn't put my finger on, "you don't want that as much as you think you do."

"You don't have a clue what I'm thinking," I sassed.

"Oh, yes, I do."

I propped my hands on my hips and huffed. "Why are you so sure?"

His voice dropped an octave when he said, "Because maybe I'm thinking it, too." Pushing me away, he skated for the exit.

My mouth hung open even as I told myself I was reading into things. Wren wasn't bold or reckless. He was careful and calculating. He'd never make such an admission out of the blue like that.

When he peeked over his shoulder and smirked, I growled, knowing that he had been screwing with me.

"You're an asshole!" I screamed the moment I caught up to him.

He was busy shoving on his shoes when he smiled. "I give as good as I get, Lou. Remember that." He winked and once again, it felt like a come-on, but this time, I knew better.

"All right, you won this round, but when you go to prison, don't be surprised if I don't visit you. I'll be too busy having the last laugh."

He peeked at me over his shoulder. "You're pouting," he gleefully observed.

"Am not."

"Are too."

"I. Am. Not."

He stopped tying his laces to trace my lips, which were indeed poking out. His voice was softer and full of wonder when he spoke again. "Are too."

My lips fell open in a gasp, but he had already turned away as if nothing had happened. As if he hadn't just threatened to turn my world upside down. "Stop doing that!"

"Doing what?"

"Flirting! It's against the rules."

He looked at me with a frown that seemed genuine. "Whose rules, Lou?" He waited for my response, and the sounds that emerged from my throat resembled a stalled car that wouldn't start. When he flashed that smug, satisfied smile, I knew he'd gotten me again.

I wisely chose to ignore him this time and traded the skates for my sneakers. I still had an attitude by the time he dropped me off home, but he didn't seem to mind when he kissed my cheek before telling me to behave. The Impala roared as it sped away, and I smiled as I watched from the sidewalk. He and I both knew there wasn't a chance of that.

CHAPTER
THREE

The Moth

I WATCHED LOU THROUGH THE REARVIEW MIRROR AS I DROVE AWAY and wondered what she'd do next to provoke me. I gritted my teeth as anticipation flowed through me like an electric current. I felt alive knowing that I had something to look forward to. It took me longer than I liked to remember why I came running in the first place.

That damn T-shirt had to go.

Lou's breasts had grown at least two cup sizes, and before today's stunt, I had been blissfully unaware. I could barely keep my mind or my eyes off them, forgetting for brief moments that they were attached to my best friend. My onus.

The reminder was usually enough to sober me. At least until I saw her again. It wasn't unheard of to be attracted to a friend, but when the stakes were this high, I'd have to be a fool to do something about it.

And cruel.

And if I had my way, which I intended to, Lou would never know why.

We were connected to the very last stitch. Letting Lou go would be like severing a limb. She belonged with me.

An hour later, I found myself in a hotel room sitting across from Jacobo Jiménez—the infamous cocaine supplier that Fox so hungrily coveted. Right now, it was more of a face-off since we'd not only kidnapped him for this impromptu meeting but we'd also been indirectly stealing from him all these years by stealing from Thirteen. Jiménez was younger than I expected, having accomplished as much as he had. His reputation certainly preceded him. Jacobo Jiménez was not only cunning and ruthless but also a shrewd businessman. And Fox was salivating at the jowls for a chance to do business with him. So far, we'd been getting by on the scraps we'd managed to commandeer from Thirteen, but that was no longer enough for Fox.

"My brothers tell me you're ready to negotiate."

"They did a good job assuring me I had no choice," he returned in a thick Colombian accent.

I looked him over ensuring that he remained unharmed. Fox would have had us all killed for ruining his deal if Jiménez had been hurt. We'd treated him better than any captive, stashing him inside this lavish hotel suite in the middle of Manhattan for the past week. It took a week of reconnaissance during one of his rare visits to the States before we snatched him from his town car out in Miami. It had been a long two weeks since my mind never left New York and Louchana Valentine. I knew she'd be pissed about my absence, but she also knew I didn't have a choice. In a better world…well…let's just say a lot would be different.

"So let's talk."

"As impressive as you've proven to be," he drawled, "you're a little beneath the pay grade to converse with me."

Shane shifted irritably while I took the insult on the chin and relaxed against the cushioned armchair. We were positioned catty-corner to the pale blue tufted couch Jiménez sat on as if he were actually in control, and maybe he was. There was a reason he'd climbed so high in a world so low. Shane continued to stir in the chair next to me, not looking the least bit hospitable. Even though he ranked higher than me, his people skills were nonexistent, so we both agreed I'd do the talking. The terms and what we were willing to offer were predetermined, anyway. The only thing left was Jiménez's cooperation.

There was only one way he was walking out of this room alive, so one way or another, he wouldn't be supplying Thirteen anymore.

"I'm afraid you'll have to make do."

"In doing so," Jiménez responded casually, "I'll have to assume your boss thinks he's too good to speak with me. That doesn't bode well for whatever deal he's pursuing."

"Did you meet with Father?" I shot back, referring to Thirteen's leader. I already knew he hadn't. Very few have seen his face, but *no one* knew his name. Growing up, I'd heard the men whisper their speculations about our founders' past affiliation. Whenever a new Father ascended, he shed his identity— most likely by faking his death—and became what anyone would rightly assume to be a myth. After all, how the hell could anyone remain this invisible?

While Fox lived in exile, he at least had the luxury of showing his face to his men every blue moon. Usually to reinforce his authority when the men grew skeptical.

"Ah, there's the fire I could sense burning under all that cool control."

I ignored Shane's disapproving glare and leaned forward. "No more games, Jiménez. Will you supply us or not?"

"I will," he said, and I could feel every man in the room relax. "Under one condition."

"Which is?"

"I'm bound by a noncompete clause with Thirteen." I held his gaze, waiting for the punchline. "Before we can do business, I require the contract to be broken."

"Let me guess…you want Father dead?"

"Is that a problem?"

"Not at all," I assured with ease even as my stomach turned. I had a mean poker face perfected over the years in this world. I'd learned from the best, and the best turned out to be a gifted liar.

"Then we have a deal." Jiménez stood and held out his hand, but I just stared at it, not caring if I appeared rude.

"You've been Thirteen's connect for over a decade. One would think a relationship that exclusive would be harder to sever."

"It would have been…if Father hadn't been demanding lower and lower prices to recoup the losses his enemy—that's you— caused. I've been losing money for years, so I think I need to re-evaluate my loyalties rather than my profit margin. Satisfied?"

I stood and forced myself to shake his hand, ignoring the crawling sensation creeping under my skin. "For now."

Then again, it wasn't really up to me. No way should we trust this guy, but Fox would always have the final say.

"What the hell are you doing?" Lou's sharp whisper could have cut me in half.

I stood in the middle of her bedroom ready to do the same to that godforsaken shirt she'd been wearing earlier. After the meeting with Jiménez, I had made a beeline back to Lou. This afternoon hadn't been nearly enough to make up for the time I spent away. Lou was the fix I needed to dull the rest of the world and feel alive again.

"I'm making sure you don't lose your senses again." I gripped the hem in both fists and started to rip it down the goddamn middle when she shrieked.

"You can't! My pa—they bought me that shirt!"

I paused seeing the frantic desperation painting Lou's face. These were one of the rare moments Lou wasn't pretending not to care about anyone other than herself. I often wondered if she was like that before she became an orphan.

"If I catch you wearing this again, I won't give a fuck if the Virgin Mary sewed it by hand. We clear?"

She nodded eagerly, her eyes glistening. I felt like a monster, but I refused to give in. I allowed Lou to have her way too much as it was. I offered her the shirt, and she snatched it from me with a glare that should have had me lying dead.

"A wise choice," she said once the shirt was safe from me. "I would have keyed your car."

"I believe you."

"Good," she replied tartly.

I watched through narrowed eyes as she carelessly tossed the shirt on top of the dresser she barely used. Lou was a slob, but it worked for her. She seemed to know where everything was.

"Mr. and Mrs. H home yet?"

She whirled around and faced me with her arms crossed. "Mr. and Mrs. H?" she mocked with a tilt of her head. "You know they can't stand you, right?"

I shrugged. It didn't matter to me just as long as they continued to cooperate. "I'm sure whatever the reason is, you're to blame."

"I'm an innocent, *impressionable* young lady, and you're the hot, mysterious bad boy who's corrupting me."

Not surprised in the least, I snorted. The Hendersons likely suspected that whenever Lou ran away from home, it was to be with me. That was only mostly true. Sometimes, she ran away to get my attention if only to assure herself that I was still alive though she would never admit to it. Lou knew I'd always go hunting. And even though she never said it, I knew Lou also ran away whenever she was beginning to feel content. She didn't want to let her guard down only to be abandoned again. Regret knotted in my throat, making it hard to breathe.

Remorse was an even harder pill to swallow.

"Like I said," I retorted after shaking off the useless feelings, knowing I couldn't change her past...or mine, "I'm sure you're to blame."

She blinked those big sparkling blues at me in disbelief. "For being innocent?"

"For convincing them that you are," I replied although it wasn't entirely fair. Despite the scars hardening her heart, Lou's soul remained unblemished.

"Trust me," she scoffed. "It's the last thing I want *anyone* to think. I might as well put a 'kick me' sign on my back."

I lifted a brow. "You're worried about not looking cool?"

"Why, of course," she replied good-naturedly. "I have a rep to protect." I watched her plop down on her bed and lean back on her elbows with a smile. I knew she was full of shit. Lou never cared what anyone thought of her. She was happy to let people judge her as long as their assumptions kept them far away from her.

No, Lou was worried about being vulnerable.

"Get up," I ordered her.

"Why? I'm comfortable."

Of course, she then flipped onto her stomach, giving me an unobstructed view of her pert little ass in those tiny white shorts. They molded to her hips and thighs so well they might as well have been white cotton panties—the crest for virgins, a symbol understood by any red-blooded male, no matter what language he spoke.

I looked in time to see her peeking at me over her shoulder, and my cock went rogue, stirring in my jeans at the sight of that coquettish smile.

Jesus, fuck. I felt sweat beading around my hairline. Did she have any fucking clue how inviting she looked?

"I need to shower." And thanks to Lou, it would have to be a cold one.

She frowned, and I saw genuine confusion etched all over her soft features. "And you need me to…what? Wash your back?"

I palmed my face, letting my hand slowly slide down. How could I even for a second think this girl wasn't innocent? She had no idea what that kind of offer sounded like to a man with a hard dick and blue balls.

If she got in that shower with me—if she *touched* me at all—I'd forget the fact that she was my best friend, underage, and a virgin. I'd push her against the wall and pound the shit out of her until the tile broke and the water turned to ice.

And even then, I might not stop.

"If the Hendersons come home, it's wise if they think you're the one showering."

Her mouth formed a perfect O as color filled her cheeks. "You want me to come with you?"

"That would be wise."

"Wise?" she echoed. "I'm not so sure about that." She seemed to think it over before whining, "Can't you just shower when you go home?"

"What's the big deal, Lou? I'm not asking you to jump in with me."

"You'll be naked, and I'll see," she squeaked, sounding just like a mouse. I bet if Lou were under the covers, she'd be clutching them under her chin as if she were the one naked.

"Don't you have curtains?"

"What about when you undress? Or when you get out?" she interrogated.

I didn't answer her because I'd already lost my patience. Stalking across the room, I ignored her squeal as I bent low and tossed her ass over my shoulder. "Quiet."

She had no choice but to do as I said when I opened her bedroom door and stepped out into the empty hall. The house was small, and the walls were thin, so I usually waited until they'd all gone to sleep to sneak inside Lou's bedroom, but after two weeks of being away, there was no way I could wait for night to fully fall.

Creeping down the hall on silent feet, I didn't dare take a breath. The Hendersons would be home any minute from work or Bible study or whatever the hell it was that kept them gone and out of my hair. I let out a deep exhale the moment we were safely shut inside the bathroom. I was more than eager for the day Lou would be on her own, and I could come and go as I pleased.

Maybe I'd get us a place, and we could—

I paused and blinked a couple of times wondering where the hell my head had gone just now.

"Don't you think you're being a little paranoid?" Lou questioned once I set her on the sink.

"It's a necessary evil."

"If you say so," she muttered.

I leaned over and locked the door before reaching behind my neck and gripping my T-shirt. It was gone a second later. Neither of us commented on the fact that I was still standing between her legs when I reached for my belt buckle.

"I do." I then toed off my shoes before shedding my jeans and boxers. I heard her gasp, but when I straightened once more, she had firmly fixed her gaze on the wall behind me. I chuckled.

"You're being cruel," she said with a pout.

"Am I? You can look if you want. I don't mind."

She rolled her eyes. "I don't want."

"Hm...I'll try not to take offense."

Lou crossed her arms and lifted her nose in the air as if she didn't care one way or the other. I padded over to the shower and ran the water before she could change her mind. I didn't want to be caught red-handed with a hard-on.

"Can you hurry up?" she griped.

I peeked over my shoulder and found her bouncing her right leg. She was clearly agitated, which was only fair given my current state. "That wall isn't nearly as interesting to stare at as my butt, is it?"

Lou's mouth tightened, and she shifted her gaze away even further. "It's cold in here."

"I'll warm you up."

No longer able to hide her interest, her head whipped

around, and she stared at me in shock but didn't dare let her gaze travel south. "What?"

"I'll warm you up," I repeated. "The steam from the shower should kick in any minute now." She was still gawking when I disappeared behind the shower curtain with a grin, and as usual, fucking with Lou after she challenged me was indeed the highlight of my day.

I also lied about the steam because the water pelting my skin was icy cold, making me even more miserable, but at least it did the trick in cooling me the fuck down. For a while, I closed my eyes and just let the water wash over me, drenching my hair and my face.

I didn't realize how much time had passed until she said, "There's no steam."

I smiled at the timidity in her tone, knowing she'd been tamed. At least for now. Lou had unintentionally wandered into territory she didn't yet understand, and it made her nervous. Cautious.

"Give it a few minutes."

"It's been five," she pointed out.

My eyes popped open, and I silently cursed before hurriedly turning the knob. Immediately, the water began to warm, and after a couple of minutes, I heard Lou sigh as steam began to fill the small bathroom.

"Better?" At least for one of us, it would be.

"Yes, thank you," she whispered, and then I heard her shift.

Peeking through the sliver of the curtain that I'd carelessly left open, I saw that she was now straddling the corner of the counter giving me a view of her creamy thigh, softly sculpted calf, and one of her dainty-ass feet.

I almost punched the tile when my cock slowly started to rise again.

Fuuuuck!

I grabbed my dick and squeezed. Normally, I wasn't so hard

up, but there hasn't been anything normal about my actions since meeting Lou two years ago. I shut my eyes, but her leg—one I'd seen a million times before but never while my dick was in my hand—was already etched vividly in my memory.

The simplest solution was the most obvious one, but I didn't see anything simple about jerking off while my best friend, a girl I swore to protect from monsters like me, sat two feet away. And I wouldn't just be beating my dick. I'd be getting off to thoughts of *her*, innocent little Lou.

While my head fired warnings to turn back now, my cock had no such reservations about crossing this line.

She'd never have to know.

"Please hurry, Wren."

My grip on my cock tightened, and I groaned in agony even as my hand slowly began to move, giving her what she wanted. She had no idea what those words did to me. To us.

Fuck it.

Just from the few tugs, I already knew the pleasure would be worth all the loathing and shame I'd feel once I came so after pouring some of her body wash in my palm for lube, I closed my eyes and gave in.

I was already damned, so what was one more offense? At least this time, I'd be getting something out it. No amount of money or power could hold a candle to the fantasy playing out in my head—Lou spread out before me, eager, wanting, and mine.

I'd start with those adorable toes of her. Kissing and bathing every digit before I moved to her ankles, her legs, her thighs— massaging and caressing.

In my fantasy, I left no part of her untouched because I knew I'd never get the chance again. The sounds I imagined she made as I worshiped her pushed me further toward the edge. Soft whimpers and wanton cries, or maybe she'd moan, and it'd be my name on her lips. My stomach clenched, and I groaned wanting it all. My strokes became jerkier, more desperate.

I pictured her wearing that shirt and ripping it from her body, baring her breasts. I licked my lips as I imagined pulling her nipples into my mouth and sending her writhing beneath me for more.

"Wren?"

The sound of my name sounded so vivid and crisp. I squeezed my eyes tighter and felt myself grasping for something, but I didn't know what.

I was between Lou's thighs now ready to drive inside and fuck us both to death when I said, "I know, baby. I'm coming."

The gasp she let free when I started to enter her sounded even more real. So real that I came that instant with a gasp of my own. Cum poured over my fist but was immediately washed away by the water still raining over me. I felt like a bitch when my knees wobbled, but what was even more disturbing was the absence of regret or shame I had anticipated. Instead, I felt lighter.

Until I heard Lou ask, "What the *hell* are you doing in there?"

"Masturbating," I answered honestly. "Want to give me a hand?"

"Ha. Ha. Very funny."

"I'm curious," I told her as I grabbed the neon pink loofah I'd taken her to buy. Then I squirted some of that fruity green apple shit that drove me crazy onto it. "Which part did you think was a joke?"

"Obviously, you aren't jerking off while I'm sitting here, and even if you were, you wouldn't tell me."

I smiled at that. "You're right," I lied. "I wouldn't." I scrubbed the day away and then quickly rinsed off the suds before ripping open the curtain without warning. The water was still running so Lou was caught off guard when I stepped over the lip of the tub.

Her eyes nearly fell out of her head, and then she quickly slapped her hands over her eyes missing my grin. "Jesus! Wren!"

"My bad. I must have forgotten you were here."

"Clearly!"

I looked around the bathroom for extra towels but didn't see any. "Towel?"

"Why should I help you, asshole?"

"Because your foster parents will be home any minute, and you don't want to have to explain to them why I'm naked, do you?"

She huffed and grumbled, "Fine," before hopping off the counter and stomping toward the door. All the while, her gaze never strayed. Not even once. If I hadn't known her so well, I might have fallen for the act and believed she wasn't curious. "But after you get dressed," she continued, "we need to review the boundaries of friendship."

I laughed at her attempt to gain control. "Sure thing."

I saw the stiff set of her shoulders and waited for her to call me on my shit. Instead, she wordlessly stepped into the hallway. The second the door slammed behind her, I braced my hands on the counter and hung my head. The euphoria was gone, and I felt like shit. I really should have known better than to think I wouldn't feel remorse. I wasn't just Lou's best friend. I was her protector.

I also needed her more than she needed me.

It took her a little longer than I expected to return, but when she did, she was flushed and holding a fluffy pink towel. I didn't get a chance to ask her what was up before she tossed it at me and said, "The Hendersons are home. I'll go downstairs and distract them while you get dressed."

She was gone before I could respond, and after I redressed, I stood there contemplating what to do. I could go back to her room and spend the night on her floor as I'd planned, or I could stay the fuck away from Lou until I got my mind right.

Closing my eyes, I saw fantasy Lou lying spent with a lazy smile on her lips and staring at me from under lowered lids. She already wanted more, and I was powerless to resist. At that moment, I knew what I needed to do.

I got the fuck out of there.

CHAPTER
FOUR

The Flame

I WATCHED THROUGH THE STORE'S GLASS WINDOW AT GRAND Central Terminal as my mark searched through his wad of cash for a bill small enough to pay for his items. The moment he left the mini convenience store, I trailed him, but his long strides were making it difficult to follow without drawing attention from the officers and their large dogs. I was ready to give up and find a mark that wasn't in such a hurry when he finally slowed and stopped to check a directory.

Closing in, I appeared casual as I stood next to him and slipped my hand in his pocket while pretending to check the directory. He shot me a pleasant smile, which I returned as a garbled voice spoke over the station intercom.

I was already backing away when I bumped into a hard wall and heard "So it's picking pockets you prefer to a good home."

Even though I hadn't seen or heard from Wren in the month since he taunted me with his naked body and disappeared out my bedroom window, I didn't need to turn to see who spoke those words. Unfortunately, the man whose wallet I'd stolen had also heard him.

Wren's hand circled my nape before I could get out of there while his other dug inside my waistband to grab the wallet I'd hidden under my sweatshirt. The mark's skin turned a deep red when Wren returned it to him.

"Why you little—"

"Walk away," Wren cut in, making it clear to the guy whose side he was on.

I flashed the irate man a cheeky grin but refrained from sticking my tongue out at the feel of Wren's hand tightening around my neck—an unspoken warning.

You're not out of the woods yet.

The minute the flustered man scurried away, I shoved against Wren's chest as hard as I could. Of course, he didn't move an inch, so I got in his face until we were toe-to-toe.

Never mind that he had almost a foot on me or that we were drawing attention. One of those guided tours walked by, and none of the patrons seemed to be listening as they eyed us. They were probably hoping for a scene so they could record it and post it online.

I was almost giddy at the thought of Wren becoming an internet sensation. That would piss him off more than I ever could.

Wren seemed to have similar thoughts because he smoothly wrapped his arms around my waist making it look like we were a couple.

"What are you doing here?" I hissed.

"Looking for you, of course."

I wanted to smack away the cocky smile he tried to hide. "How did you find me?"

"Your only friends are all homeless and hungry. How do you think?"

"They're not my friends."

"Because you don't need anyone?" His tone warned me to tread carefully, but like Wren once said, I'd always been hard of hearing.

"Bingo!"

His eyes seemed to darken, and unconsciously, I took a step back. Noticing my fear, he laughed, which just pissed me off even more.

"You're not as tough as you think, mouse."

The look I gave him would have withered lesser men. Wren, of course, would never allow himself beneath anyone, least of all me. Ignoring the longing that was warming my belly, I propped my elbow on my wrist and inspected my nails. "And you aren't as sane as you think. Stalking isn't something friends do to one another."

He had me hemmed against the station directory before I could blink—although, to outsiders, it may have looked more like a lover's embrace. Not that any of the travelers noticed or even cared as they hurried to catch their trains. Their absentminded frenzy was the reason rush hour was the perfect time for picking a wallet or two. On the days I was feeling frisky, I'd steal as many as four.

Still, I looked around hoping to catch the eye of some Good Samaritan. Perhaps the dark-haired man who desperately needed to shave. Even though he had to be twice Wren's age, he certainly had the physique to give him a run for his money. He looked lethal, like a predator lying in wait, as he leaned against one of the pillars diagonal from us. It became obvious the longer I stared that he was watching us. A moment later, I knew I'd be getting no help from him when the corner of his mouth turned up in amusement, and he melted into the shadows like he was Jason Bourne or something. *Douchebag.*

"Neither is running away," Wren retorted, drawing my attention back to him and shoving the stranger from my thoughts. He was seething, yet instead of fear, I felt an adrenaline rush—an urge to tip the scales and feel the full force of his anger. So many times, we'd unwittingly waltzed on the boundaries of friendship. It was only a matter of time before we danced across them. "I watch your back, and you do what I say. That was the deal."

My nostrils flared even as another part that I was forbidden to share with him gushed. "That doesn't sound like friendship to me. Seems more like ownership."

For a moment, his eyes seemed to lose focus as he leaned in. "Well, then you're mine."

My lips parted, and any second now, I expected to tell him how absurd he sounded, but all that came out was a breathless gasp. How could it feel this natural to be claimed by him?

More importantly, had Wren felt it, too?

This feeling as if a piece we'd overlooked had finally fallen into place.

A moment later, I got my answer when I read the silent swear on Wren's lips and measured the distance between us after he took a cautious step back. It was as if he needed the space but was hesitant to give me too much.

Maybe he was afraid I'd pounce if he ran.

"We clear?"

His tone was clipped—authoritative—the swift slam of a briefly opened window. I wondered if I'd imagined it—a trick of the mind like the blue flame creeping from the edges of his usually gray irises. Wren would say it was just a reflection of my own emotions. My gut told me otherwise.

Not so eager to be burned by those embers, I looked away. The attention we were starting to draw had my heart galloping for a different reason. Dad had always warned me to choose my battles wisely, and instinct told me this was one of those times.

Submit to rebel another day.

"Crystal."

His eyes narrowed when I batted mine.

He was smart not to trust me.

"Can we go?" I whined when he looked ready to scold me some more. "I'm starving, and you ran off my mark."

"Hunger didn't seem to bother you when you ran away. Again."

My lips pursed. "A gentleman would offer to buy a girl a sandwich."

His chuckle sounded forced. Like it was an effort to mask how tempted he was to wring my neck. "I'm no gentleman. That's why you hate me a little less than the rest of the world."

"Just a little," I admitted with my forefinger and thumb pressed close together. "My tolerance for you above others can be measured with a pinch of salt."

The jab seemed to ricochet off his chest and slam into me with the force of a Mack truck when he winked. So simple yet so effective. My empty stomach was still doing cartwheels even after he turned and walked away.

Like an obedient puppy wanting more, I followed.

The sun was shining high and bright when we stepped outside the station. Wren immediately reached for his shirt collar before looking down with a frown. To his credit, he didn't even bother searching the ground or his pockets before his gaze cut my way.

"I'm the wrong person to steal from, mouse."

"And I thought you would have learned by now." Lowering the aviators now covering my eyes, I peered at him from the top of his shades. "There's nothing mousy about me."

His gaze dipped, and the lazy perusal of my body made me feel both powerful and insignificant at the same time. Because underneath his dismissive gaze, I glimpsed the interest he tried so hard to hide.

"Well, I thought gutter rat was a bit harsh."

I was ready to jump on his back and claw his eyes out when he seized my hand—his warmth and strength a cocoon I never wanted free from. I let him pull me down the street where he parked off Park Ave, and when we reached Wren's Impala, I started to round the car. I didn't make it past the taillight before I was swept off my feet and planted on the trunk.

His hands stayed put.

"Before I take you home, we need to get some understanding."

"Wasn't that what we were doing inside?"

He simply squeezed my hips in response.

"I can't always be around, Lou." The clench of his jaw

made me wonder if it bothered him more than he let on. "I have to trust the Hendersons to keep you safe. I have to trust *you* to stay safe."

It was my turn to feel frustrated as my leg bounced. "I'm never going to be the girl who waits like fine china to be dusted off and played with, Wren. I know what I'm doing out here. I won't break."

One of his hands left my hip and pressed into my thigh. "It's not just about staying alive," he argued through gritted teeth. "When you run from them, you run from *me*." The fingers still curved around my hip were now digging into my bone, but I hid my wince and welcomed the pain. It gave me an inexplicable sense of comfort to know I affected him. Perhaps more than a best friend should.

"What can I say? Some girls want to be chased."

"You are not *some* girl. You're—"

His mouth pressed into a tight line, and I knew his hesitation wasn't because he struggled with finding words. Wren was a man of few words because he always chose them with care and purpose. He knew exactly what he'd been about to say, and so did I.

My girl.

He almost said I was his girl.

Feeling triumphant, I decided to throw him a bone. "You can't be too upset with me. I let you find me, didn't I?"

"You *let* me?"

"You can't catch me by surprise if I know you're coming."

"Then why run?" His frustration rang loud and clear.

"I told you…sometimes a girl needs to be chased."

He went completely still. "So this is about you feeling ignored?"

"Neglected," I corrected. "It sounds less unreasonable."

He stared at me for a long, long while. "If we weren't in a public place, you'd be over my knee right now."

"You're the one who wanted understanding."

"Lou, I was working."

"I know. You were doing bad things for a bad man."

"I was Exiled before I met you, and I'll be Exiled long after you're gone."

I frowned feeling like he'd struck me. "Where would I go?"

His head lowered but not before I saw the light blink from his eyes. "To greener pastures."

Cupping his cheek with my palm, I forced his gaze to meet mine. "Not without you."

I let Wren take me home where he made me shower after claiming he found me so quickly because he could smell me a mile away. I squealed—mouse, indeed—and fled before he could see my red cheeks.

Upstairs, I let the shower water warm until it was nearly scalding. For thirty minutes, I scrubbed, and when I thought I was clean, I scrubbed some more.

Downstairs, I emerged wearing my comfiest pajamas with water still clinging to every strand of hair. The Hendersons were probably at the church or out to dinner, which left me maybe a couple of hours to ease the tension lining Wren's broad shoulders.

I considered offering him a massage but realized feeling those muscles for too long would only make *me* tense.

Drinking it is.

I'd ply him with the stash Mr. Henderson kept hidden from his wife and hope that he'd be too plastered to drive home. I knew he'd stay if I simply asked him, but where was the fun in that?

"Eat," he ordered after setting a steaming bowl of mac and cheese with bits of bacon mixed in just the way I liked it.

He didn't wait to see if I obeyed and started cleaning up. "Aren't you going to have some?"

"I don't eat pork."

My fork paused at the entrance of my mouth. "You Jewish or something?"

He grinned but shook his head as he tested the water for warmth. I was glad one of us found this funny. He never told me. I said as much.

"You never asked," he shot back, and it was unfair. So fucking unfair. If this was payback for running away, then consider me punished and then some.

Flogging would have been more merciful.

He was too focused on his task, frowning as he scrubbed cheese from the small stockpot, to notice what his accusation had done to me. My fork clattering to the table drew his attention, and he stared at it before turning his scowl on me.

"Are you saying I'm self-centered?"

"I'm saying it's not a big deal, so don't make it one." He rinsed the suds from the stainless steel and moved on to the wooden spoon Mrs. Henderson often used when mixing cookie batter. Seeing him so domesticated did something strange to my insides, but so did his nonchalant regard for my feelings.

Images of us having angry, hateful sex on the counter and then the kitchen floor after flashed in my mind. If only we had become lovers instead of friends that stormy night…

I shook away the madness clouding my mind.

Any other ties would have unraveled a long time ago because Wren and I were too alike.

Aggressive. Controlling.

Sensual nights would have become battles for dominance.

I picked up my fork, silently conceding, and dug in. It took me a while to realize Wren was watching me with lips tucked in and blue eyes gleaming.

"What's so funny?"

"You have macaroni on your chin."

I felt around for it, and just as I grew frustrated enough to leave it, he took pity on me—the calluses on his thumb scraping my skin as he wiped the cheesy shell away.

His rough yet gentle touch jumpstarted my clit until it purred.

It's better this way.
It's better this way.
It's better. This. Way.
"Thank you."

He only nodded—his eyes darkening to a shade of blue I'd never seen—before moving away to finish the dishes. When he finished, he took out the trash, and I tried not to seem too eager for his return. However, it became impossible after only a couple of minutes. I forgot all about shame as I listened for his footsteps and watched the open entry. By the time five minutes had passed, I was on my feet and headed for the front door.

I had already sworn in the few steps it took me to reach the door that our friendship would be effectively over if he'd left without a word.

But when I ripped open the front door, I suddenly wished he had left. Instead, he stood with the bag of trash still in his hand as some jogger wearing hot pink spandex pawed at him.

Her smile said she wouldn't think twice about blowing him right there on the street, and the wide smile Wren returned told me he'd welcome it. I didn't recognize her, so I assumed she lived somewhere close by.

Not for long.

Intending to find out where the bitch lived so I could burn her house down, I stalked toward them on quiet feet. Wren sensing my approach, peered over his shoulder, drawing the whore's attention.

Wren's expression became wary when I flashed her a welcoming smile.

"Hi, I'm Lou!" I held out my hand, and she took the bait, shaking it with a firm grip.

"Alex."

"Wow! What a lovely name for such a handsome man," I flirted. And then I smiled in secret glee at the nearly silent "fuck" Wren uttered under his breath.

"Excuse me?" she squealed. "I'm a woman!"

"Oh!" My hands flew to my mouth as I pretended to be horrified. "Oh, no. I'm so sorry! It's just that your Adam's apple was throwing me off."

I didn't make out most of the threats she'd screamed because Wren had already swept me off my feet and hurried me back inside the house. The moment the door shut behind him, I laughed my ass off until he swatted it.

Hard.

I was still in shock long after he'd set me on my feet.

"What the hell was that?" he demanded. Before I could answer, he threw up his hand, halting me. "Don't answer that because I shouldn't be surprised. I really shouldn't."

I rubbed my sore cheek after the initial sting dulled into an ache. "Yeah, well, you're welcome."

"And what should I be thanking you for? My blue balls?"

"No, from the train wreck waiting to happen. Alex was so not the man for you."

"Cut the crap, Lou. That was a woman, and you know it."

"Could have fooled me." I headed for the kitchen to grab a bottle of water, and when I returned, his eyes were moving back and forth, desperately trying to recap the encounter.

I snorted.

Men.

"There was no Adam's apple," he said as I uncapped the bottle and took a swig of water.

He sounded less sure this time, and when I only shrugged, steam practically blew from his ears. Alex had indeed been a woman. Beautiful and lithe and a hell of a lot more Wren's speed than any of the others.

Bitch had to go.

"Fine. Then go after her."

But he wouldn't. I knew he wouldn't.

And it wasn't because I made him question her gender. Wren

had been hit on by men before, and just like the many women he found no interest in, he was always gracious when he turned them down. No, he wouldn't go after her because he would have done far worse in my shoes. I'd die a virgin if Wren had any say.

The look he threw me said he knew I was bluffing. Sighing, he did the only thing he could. He rubbed his forehead and stared at the floor.

"Why are you so upset?" I asked as I sipped at my water. "Alex is one woman. There is plenty of fish out there." I knew I'd been cruel, regardless of the reason, and if I ever saw her again, I'd apologize profusely...and then I'd warn her to stay the hell away.

"Yeah?" He lifted his head, and our gazes connected. "Then tell me why I've been fucking my fist ever since I met you."

I choked on my water.

He held me hostage with his stare, showing no mercy as I fought to catch my breath. I blinked away moisture pooling in my eyes and rasped, "I didn't need to know that."

Regardless, it lingered in my mind, poking and taunting, daring me to do something about it.

"Really? I thought you'd be happy to know."

"Why would you think that?" I squeaked.

"Because you've been cockblocking me for two years, and I want it to stop."

I didn't need to question if he was serious. I may not have known he didn't eat pork, but I knew that tone and that sniper-focused intensity. Still, I heard "I'll stop if you stop" and knew that sultry voice belonged to me.

He went so very still, his eyes now a telling blue as the temperature in the room dropped dramatically. Gray meant he felt nothing, while blue...blue meant he felt *everything*.

"What did you say to me?"

His sharp whisper had me taking a step back even as my nipples threatened to pierce my camisole. I hadn't realized he was closing in or that I hadn't stopped backing away until my back was against the wall and he was caging me in. His forearms were on either side of my head, ensuring I couldn't escape. With nowhere to go, I did the only thing I could. I lifted my chin and met his gaze.

"You want sex?"

Heat shot from my belly to my core at what sounded like an invitation—a promise to fulfill my every need or desire no matter the cost to our friendship.

"I—" Sinking my teeth into my lower lip, I kept whatever I'd been about to say from escaping. Unfortunately, it also drew Wren's attention to my mouth.

He was still staring at my trembling lips when he said, "Speak up, Lou. I can't hear you."

I tried, but the words became lodged in my throat. As if sensing this, Wren's right hand curved around the column of my neck where he caressed my skin.

I felt each sweep of his thumb in every nerve and the warning behind it.

"Look at you…virgin pussy ripe for the picking, and you're just dying to hand it over to some undeserving guy. And the icing on the cake, or should I say the cherry on top, is that you can't even admit it to your best friend. Why is that?"

Because the undeserving guy is my best friend.

And there was the undeniable truth, out in the open—at least in my mind. I could never go back to a time when I was blissfully unaware, and I hated him for it.

"I don't know, Wren." My voice was cold but clear. "Could it be the same reason you've allowed me to stand in your way?"

I saw the guilty shift of his eyes, felt his thumb pause, and wondered if he could feel my galloping pulse. "I guess we'll never know." Regret laced every word, but we both pretended not to notice. "You're tired. Go to bed."

It took a moment for the command to register—especially since he made no move to put much-needed space between us.

"It's the middle of the day."

"Think of how well rested you'll be when morning comes." He jerked his head toward the stairs. "Go."

I didn't argue again when I realized he was giving me an out. With all these 'not so new but no longer dormant' feelings stirring in my gut, putting distance between us was ideal.

"Good night, Wren."

"Good night, Lou."

I dipped underneath his arm and headed for the stairs. Once I reached them, I looked back and found him with his hand still braced on the wall, his head dipped low and his chest heaving as if he'd just run a marathon.

I ran up the stairs before I could say something brash…like showing him everything I was thinking and feeling. Inside my room, I collapsed on my bed, and as Wren predicted, I was out within minutes.

The summer was winding down, and so was my patience. I promised Wren I'd be a good girl and stay put—his exact words—and in exchange, he'd come around more, but so far, I'd been the only one holding up my end of the bargain. Okay, so he'd managed to keep his word for like a month and a half, but for the past three days, he'd been missing in action, and no amount of phone calls or texts would gain his attention.

If that was the way he wanted to play it, then so be it.

I'd been 'missing' for less than a day when he suddenly appeared in my camera lens. I'd been preparing to take a shot of Leo performing a Sex Change and ended up capturing Wren's face instead. Incidentally, it turned out to be a pretty good picture. It captured his seething anger in *vivid* detail.

I wasn't surprised that he'd found me so quickly since I hadn't made it difficult. I'd been hanging out all day with Miles and Leo at Astoria, one of the local skate parks in Queens. It was only a few blocks from where I lived with the Hendersons.

Lowering my camera, I feigned innocence with a smile. "Hey, bestie!"

Rather than return my greeting, he crossed his arms and pinned me with a glare. "Why didn't you go home last night?"

I shrugged. "I was waiting for you to give me a ride."

"Jesus fucking Christ," he swore before exploding. "Running away from home because I won't cater to your every whim is fucking childish and stupid, Lou!"

Some of the skaters came to a screeching halt at the sound of Wren's roar, and I could feel them watching. Miles and Leo were also tuned in as they approached with cautious steps. Still, I was calm and very much used to Wren yelling. I expected it. Hell, sometimes I even got a thrill from it.

"And not taking two seconds to pick up the phone and tell me you're alive is fucking selfish and cruel, Harlan."

He stared at me for a long while as if considering my point, but I knew before he spoke that I wouldn't get through. We'd had this argument countless times before. No matter how fast we'd grown up, there were times like these when I was reminded of how young we still were. Our emotions and how we handled them said it all. We both knew we lacked the maturity to deal with a connection this intense, and the wise choice would be to take a step back, but we were also so very stubborn.

"Let's go."

"I promised Miles and Leo I'd get some shots for their Instagram. If you want to take me home, you'll have to wait until I'm done."

His eyes narrowed, and he stepped closer until I could see nothing else but his chest. "Did you hear me giving you a choice?"

"No." I lifted my chin until our eyes met. "But I have one... whether you like it or not."

He chuckled and then leaned down until his lips touched

my ear. "You're right. You do have a choice. You can leave here on your own two feet, or I can carry you." His hands then found my hips and squeezed. "Don't fuck with me right now, Lou. I promise you that me causing a scene will be the least of your worries."

I was about to tell him exactly how I liked my ass kissed when I heard someone call his name. We both turned our heads, and I saw some guy who looked like Sung Kang from The Fast and the Furious movies approaching.

"Wren, bro, is that you?"

Wren let me go with a look of surprise. "Sonny?"

"Jeez, man, I thought you died or something!"

Wren laughed, and for once, it wasn't a sarcastic or pissed off one. I blinked a few times because, at that moment, I hardly recognized him. The guys shared a manly embrace before Wren answered him. "Nah, I'm not dead yet. What have you been up to?"

"I should be asking you that!" Sonny chortled. "Me? I've been doing much of the same—fucking and skating," he said with a shrug.

"You're like thirty-five. You haven't settled down yet?"

"Nah, man. These girls, they're smarter now."

"You mean they know you're full of shit?"

"*Exactly.*"

Miles and Leo were standing next to me now, and I felt one of them nudge me—most likely Miles—but I couldn't look away from Wren and Sonny. As Wren talked with his friend, he seemed younger, lighter, more playful—as if he'd been transported back in time.

"So what are you doing here?" Sonny inquired. "Please tell me you're here to give me some competition!"

I frowned, wondering what alternate universe I'd been transported to. Wren didn't skateboard. At least, not the Wren I knew.

"I don't skate anymore," Wren announced, shocking the hell out of both Sonny and me but for different reasons.

"What?" Sonny shrieked. "What happened to you being the next Tony Hawk, Bam Margera, Rob Dyrdek? *Actually*, what I believe you said was that you'd be better."

Wren rubbed his chin and winced. "Yeah, well, I talked too much back then."

"Hey, there's nothing wrong with having a dream, *especially* when you have the guts and talent to make it a reality." Sonny shook his head and sighed as if Wren not skating anymore was truly a tragedy.

Considering what he'd given it up for, maybe it was.

"So what are you doing now?"

And just like that, Wren shut down, and I recognized my best friend once again.

"Working odd jobs," Wren hedged. "Staying busy."

I rolled my eyes. *Odd jobs, indeed.*

"Yeah, I was sorry to hear about your mom," Sonny offered sheepishly.

"Yeah, thanks, man. It was good seeing you again." Wren turned to me, seemingly dismissing Sonny altogether, and when I saw the empty look in his eyes, I wanted nothing more than to fill them again. I felt his fingers gently curl around my arm, and I placed a tentative palm on his muscled bicep.

"I want to see."

His brows furrowed as he stared down at me. "See?"

"You skate. You never shared that part of yourself with me."

"Because I don't believe in looking back, Lou. It's not who I am anymore."

"And *I* don't believe that. You're bossy, temperamental, and sometimes cruel, but you're not a coward." I shot him a skeptical look. "Are you?"

"Is that a challenge?"

"You're also intelligent," I answered with a smirk.

He looked away and exhaled loudly through his nose. "I don't have a board."

"You can use mine," Miles immediately offered. I was surprised by his eagerness and generosity considering Wren and Miles hated each other. Miles blamed Wren as the reason I wasn't susceptible to his charms while Wren believed I was. Maybe Miles was just eager to see Wren make a fool of himself. Thanks to Sonny and all his excitement over witnessing Wren skate again, a large crowd had formed and every eye fixed on Wren was skeptical.

Even I wished I'd kept my mouth shut when Wren reluctantly accepted Miles's board. Wren thanked him, and Miles nodded graciously, but the smirk he shot to Leo once Wren turned away had me shooting daggers at him. Miles went wide-eyed and shrugged with an expression that said, "What did you expect?"

I turned my attention to Wren, who had the board trapped under his foot and was gazing down at the bottom of the bowl, his expression blank.

I touched his fingers, and he flinched as if I'd electrocuted him. "Are you sure you can do this?"

He seemed amused when he met my gaze. "It's a little late to have second thoughts, mouse."

"Just admit that you're excited, Harlan. Maybe even a little thrilled?"

He chuckled and then looked around at the crowd before saying with a wry twist of his lips, "I'm not ready to let you off the hook just yet."

And with that, he went soaring over the lip of the bowl.

CHAPTER
FIVE

The Moth

LOU DROVE ME CRAZY, BUT SHE ALSO MANAGED TO BRING A LITTLE more color into my world with each encounter. She didn't know that I stayed away so long for her sake, but I also know if she did, she wouldn't care. She wanted what she wanted, and for some reason, she wanted me. Lou would remind me often and passionately that I'd been the one to demand friendship as if the distance made me care for her less. If only I could tell her what staying away did to me. Doing so would open a door I wouldn't want to close, and I'd made a vow not to ruin her any more than I already had.

Mr. Henderson had called me this morning, weary and concerned when he discovered Lou hadn't come home from school. It was the arrangement we had to keep the state from throwing Lou's belligerent ass back in a group home or worse...juvie. Either she didn't realize how much the Hendersons cared for her or she didn't care. Lou was pretty perceptive, so I knew the answer was likely the latter, and it made my guilt much harder to bear.

"That was insane!" Sonny cheered. "I'm not even surprised that you've still got it after all these years."

I wiped the sweat off my brow and grinned. My heart was still racing, and for a while, I'd completely forgotten what I'd become. Lou was even looking at me like she'd never seen me before.

"Yeah, you really got some moves," Leo said in awe. And then he sheepishly added, "Do you think you could show me that last one?"

I spent the next couple of hours doing demonstrations all the while keeping a close eye on Lou. I wouldn't put it past her to sneak away while I was distracted, and I also wanted to make sure the little prick with a permanent hard-on for her didn't try anything. It didn't escape my notice that he never left her side for a second. The only reason I hadn't lost my shit was that the entire time I was out there, Lou only had eyes for me.

Miles was closer in age and probably had more in common with Lou than I did, and I didn't like that one bit. Was I jealous? Fuck yeah. But who the hell wasn't possessive of their best friend? Why should I share when others didn't? It had absolutely zero to do with the fact that Lou got my cock hard. Or that ever since that day I allowed myself to jerk off in the shower to visions of her, I hadn't been able to stop. Two years I'd been good and kept my thoughts pure, and I guess that a fist full of cum every night was my reward.

Jesus fucking Christ.

"It's getting late," I told her when I was finally able to break free. She didn't respond, and I could tell something was eating her but decided to suspend my curiosity until we were alone. My gaze reluctantly slid to Miles, and I handed over his board. "Thanks."

He cleared his throat, and he looked like he'd just swallowed nails when he said, "You're pretty solid."

"Thanks, man. My ollie isn't as good as yours, though."

"When did you see him do an ollie?" Lou interrogated before Miles could respond.

I just stared at her until her eyes narrowed with understanding, and Miles shifted uncomfortably.

Of course, I watched her for a while before I actually approached her. She'd been in her element, happy and carefree. As pissed as I was, I'd been even more reluctant to disrupt her peace.

It reminded me that one day, she'd find someone worthy of her, living in a home that could never be broken, and…I'd be forced to let her go. That's if I lived long enough to see her wed and happy. My lifestyle didn't exactly promise a long lifespan.

A part of me hoped I was long dead before the day came when she would take another man. That pain would be worse than any death could bring. She wouldn't be mine anymore, but I'd always be hers.

"You're right," she agreed with a sigh. "It's late." She said goodbye to Miles and Leo and promised after almost five minutes of badgering, negotiating, and whining, to catch up with them later. I pretended not to notice Miles's hostile glare when I finally had enough and grabbed Lou's hand, pulling her away, but I sure as shit felt it on my back all the way to my ride. It made me look at Lou curiously, wondering what she was doing to him when I wasn't around—knowing Lou, not a damn thing.

This girl was a magnet.

I hoped for my sake she didn't learn how to wield this power she didn't know she had anytime soon. I knew if she used it on me, I wouldn't stand a chance no matter how wrong it was.

"Sonny had some interesting stories about you to share," Lou announced once we were alone in my ride.

"I'm sure he did." Just as I was sure that no amount of short responses would deter Lou—she was like a bloodhound on a trail.

"What I don't understand is why you didn't tell me any of this yourself?"

"I told you," I said with a sigh, "I don't believe in looking back."

"But you're not looking forward either. You're hiding."

"If you say so."

"Why did you stop skating, Wren?"

"I didn't have a lot of time for fantasy after my initiation."

"But it didn't have to be a fantasy!" she screamed, losing her patience. "I saw that with my own two eyes. Why can't you?"

"Because I was already under Fox's thumb, Lou. I had a choice to make and not a lot of time to make it."

"He made you work for him?" And I was lucky I did. The alternative, as son of a traitor, would have been for Fox to take pleasure in killing me rather than corrupting me.

"No...I convinced him."

She blinked, and I could feel her disbelief washing over me like crashing waves. "*Why?*"

"I never told you, but...my mother was a prostitute, Lou." I felt shame heat my cheeks, and I couldn't help but wonder what Lou would think of me. "She wasn't that much older than you when she started working for Exiled. It's how she met my father."

"He was a-a John?"

I shook my head and took a deep breath before saying, "He was Exiled." It was only part of the truth, but I couldn't risk telling her the whole truth and having her look at me differently. I glanced at her and saw her watching me, and the look on her face told me her eyes were wide open in more ways than one.

"You said you were already under Fox's thumb. Is...is *he* your father?"

The look of utter revulsion etched across her face had my stomach turning. At that moment, I knew I could never tell her the truth. I'd lose her.

"No."

That much wasn't a lie. Fox wasn't my father, but she had no idea how close my father had been to Nathaniel Fox.

Her loud sigh of relief had me gripping the steering wheel.

"Where is he now?"

"He's dead."

I could practically hear the wheels turning in her head. "Your father was the one who gave you this car, isn't he?"

I nodded. "I didn't meet him until I was eleven. After my mother died."

"If they both worked for Fox, how could that be?"

"My mom kept me far away from her lifestyle. It was mandatory that she live in the stable, but it was no place for a child, so she left me in the care of a widow out in Jersey. Before my mother died, I had no idea my father even knew of my existence. When she found out she was pregnant with me, she left the stable. I guess I wasn't enough for her to turn her life around, though, because after I was born, she went back. To him. When she died, my father claimed me. He made me a part of his life, and then he died, leaving me alone in it. I wasn't given a choice when I became a part of this world, but it was *my* choice to stay in it."

From the corner of my eye, I saw her frown as she fought to understand. "So you became a menace to get back at your parents?"

I laughed, but it was bitter. "Most of the guys who join Exiled are just kids looking to rebel against their parents, Lou. What makes you think I'd be so different?"

She was silent for a long while, and I could hear the disappointment in her voice when she said, "How did your father die?"

"He betrayed Exiled, and Fox punished him for it."

"Hold on a sec!" she shouted as she gaped at me. "You're working for the man who killed your father?"

"My father betrayed me too, Lou." I clenched my teeth so hard I was surprised when I didn't chip a tooth. "He's the reason my mother is dead."

"But you said your mother's death was an accident."

"Getting hit by that car was an accident, but the reason she was there in the first place wasn't. Fox made sure I knew about my father's infidelity when he told me what my father had done."

"And if you could turn back time and change one thing?" she asked me.

The light in front of me turned red, so I slammed on the brakes and faced her. "I'm not sure I'd be strong enough to go through with it."

"Why?"

"Because it means I'd never have met you."

She frowned. "You don't know that."

"Maybe not, but if things were different, the way they should be, you wouldn't need me. And you sure as hell wouldn't want me in your life."

She frowned, and I could tell she was confused. "But isn't becoming Exiled the thing you'd change?"

"No," I admitted quietly, and she looked genuinely shocked by that. "There's something else I regret more than that."

"Tell me," she gently demanded. And then she must have sensed my reluctance because she added, "Please."

One word from her and I was tearing down the wall I'd spent years building so that she could see my heart beating for her on the other side. "I regret everything that's been taken from you, Lou. I regret you ever being hurt. And I regret...I regret not being able to stay away from you."

She looked away, and when she turned back, her blue eyes glistened. "So you're saying...you're saying you wish we'd never met?"

"Yes."

She flinched as if I'd raised my hand to strike her and cried, "Why?"

"Because maybe it wasn't just a coincidence that we met in the first place."

"What else could it be?" she pushed through clenched teeth.

"A cruel twist of fate," I mumbled.

CHAPTER SIX

The Flame

"HEY, PHIL!" I THREW A QUICK WAVE AS I RUSHED PAST HIS perch behind the counter. Mrs. Henderson had sent me to the store for eggs, and since I was still grounded for staying out overnight a week ago, she was giving me fifteen minutes to return before she reported me missing, and she didn't care what Wren Harlan had to say about it. I'd fled as quickly as I could for fear of the warmth thawing my heart. Those damn Hendersons were determined to show that they cared about me, and I was determined to show them why they shouldn't.

"Look who it is," Phil greeted. "You know, I'm surprised to see you!"

"Why?" I shouted back as I grabbed the carton of eggs, my usual bag of Chester's hot fries, a Slim Jim, and a Ding Dong for Eliza.

"I've heard rumors."

"Oh?" I couldn't have sounded less interested as I tossed my snacks on the counter and slapped some money down.

"There's been talk…about the company you keep."

"What about it?"

"The name Wren Harlan mean anything to you?"

"Doesn't ring a bell," I lied easily. There was no real reason for me to lie. It wasn't as if I ever bothered hiding my friendship with Wren, but it remained to be seen why it was any of Phil's fucking business.

"I'm sure it doesn't," he retorted sarcastically. "You should know, though, that he's bad news. People cross the street when they see him coming, and everyone knows he only comes around here for one thing." His expression turned accusatory, and then he reached under the counter and brandished a shotgun. "He's also the reason why I keep Martha close."

"A little extreme, don't you think?" I remained unimpressed when he cocked the shotgun although anger simmered in my gut. A fanciful part of me thought of Wren as invincible—my own superhero—but that didn't stop me from wanting to protect him from douchebags like Phil who judged what they didn't understand.

"Three bodegas on this block are now paying Exiled for protection," he informed me as he bagged my items.

"From what?"

"Exactly."

"I think you might be paranoid," I teased, never letting on that my mind was racing. I already knew that Wren was Exiled, but until now, I'd never been forced to consider what that meant.

Wren wasn't good to many, but he was great to me. Which only made the truth that he was a bad guy a hard pill to swallow. I also had to bear the guilt of knowing that there was nothing Wren could have done or had yet to do that would ever make me give him up.

"You just be sure to tell your boyfriend to stay the hell away from my shop," Phil ordered.

"Bye, Phil."

Stepping outside, I ripped open my chips with more force than necessary, spilling half the bag. Completely forgetting Mrs. Henderson's deadline, I was in no rush to get back. The entire way, I was deep in my thoughts as I munched on what was left of my chips. I was halfway through the bag and still drowning by the time I reached my foster home, but then I heard his voice break through the water like a hand on my shoulder, pulling me back to the surface.

"Penny for your thoughts?"

I scanned the street until I found the source of my troubled thoughts watching me from the driver's seat of his car. The tinted window was lowered only enough for him to speak through it. With Phil's accusations still swirling around my mind—not to mention the festering wound from Wren calling me a cruel twist of fate—I got as close as I dared. It seemed like all we did lately was argue and spew venom. There was this unspoken tension between us that hadn't been there before, and for some reason, neither of us dared bring it up.

"What are you doing here?" I didn't sound the least bit welcoming, but if he noticed my mood, he didn't let on.

"Surprising you."

I gave him a mocking smile. "Don't you have innocent people to terrorize?"

His brows drew together, and then he was stepping out of the car and towering over me. Not only did he smell really clean and masculine but he also looked deliciously formidable as ever in his usual simple attire of dark jeans and a white T-shirt. During the warmer months, he usually opted for sneakers instead of boots and the faded black hoodie he currently wore instead of his brown distressed leather jacket. Or as many of his admirers preferred, no jacket at all. The way his muscles pushed against his T-shirt left little to the imagination, not that it kept his fans from dreaming anyway. For most of us—them—it was all they'd ever have.

"Problem?" he asked me.

"Do you hurt them?"

"Who?" he demanded as if I were the one under the line of fire.

"The people you take money from."

If possible, his eyebrows dipped even lower. "Who have you been talking to?"

"Does it matter? He didn't tell me anything I didn't already know."

Callously, he stepped back and leaned against his car as if he truly didn't have a care in the world. "Then what's with the attitude?"

"Just because I know what you are doesn't mean I'm okay with it!"

"A little late to be self-righteous," he remarked, his tone and his gaze dismissive.

"Screw you."

My attempt to storm away, however, was swiftly thwarted by his hand gripping my arm. He dragged me close, nostrils flaring and breathing fire until he had me pressed against his hard chest. "Don't you fucking walk away from me."

All pretense of nonchalance had been swept away.

"Or what?" I challenged.

"You really want to peek behind that curtain?"

He pressed closer, and it was then that I felt his other hand—on my hip—squeezing. I wasn't sure he was even aware of it—as if it had naturally fallen there. My lips parted as my heart sped up and the urge to press my legs together mounted.

Maybe I did.

But like always, as quick as the thought formed, I brushed it aside. Wren and I weren't the types of friends to share anything more than our time and loyalty. I didn't know all of his secrets, and he didn't know mine. The fact that we were content to keep this wall erected between us ironically was what made us the best of friends. It was a load-bearing kind that would turn our friendship into rubble if we ever tore it down.

I didn't look away, didn't dare cower. If I had, I wouldn't have seen the plea in his stormy blue gaze.

"You and I both know," he snapped as he gripped me tighter, "that I'm not the only one afraid of what's behind there."

I snatched away when I felt the sting of his rejection all over again. "And I distinctly remember you being the reason."

He looked ready to grab me again, but at the look I sent him, he plowed his fingers through his hair instead. "You were *sixteen*, Lou. What was I supposed to do?"

"I don't know, but you weren't supposed to lie to me!" I wanted to scream some more, but the surge of anger I felt quickly faded away as my shoulders sagged and a tear escaped. "You weren't supposed to make me look like a fool."

His lips parted, but when he said nothing, I turned and ran away, leaving him standing alone on the street.

CHAPTER
SEVEN

The Flame

One Year Ago

"YOU'RE LATE!" I SCREECHED OVER THE SOUND OF POURING rain and thunder.

A soaking wet Wren winced at my shrill tone as he climbed through my bedroom window cloaked in black from head to toe. My stomach turned because I knew what the dark clothing meant, but I chose not to fixate on it. Tonight was the season two premiere of *The 100*, and I didn't want to miss a second of Bellamy Blake. I was convinced there was no one like him, so broken yet he gave and gave and gave.

"I was getting the damn milkshake you asked for. *At the last minute.*"

My irritation dissipated at the sight of the chocolate shake in his hand. Without an apology or word of thanks, I snatched the shake from him and began devouring its yummy goodness. How he managed to climb up here with it, I'll never know and didn't bother to ask.

"Quit your bellyaching, bestie. It was on the way."

"And just my fucking luck the shake machine was broken, so I had to drive to another White Castle to get it."

I flopped back onto my bed and turned up the volume to drown out Wren's grumbling. Bellamy was going to be on screen any minute. "Uh-huh."

"It was twenty minutes in the opposite direction."

"That sucks."

"You're not even listening to me, are you?"

"Of course, I am." I couldn't believe the real name of the actor who played Bellamy was *Bob*. Bellamy was dreamier. I couldn't imagine myself in a million years screaming "Harder, *Bob!*" while in the throes of passion.

Wren finally gave up trying to make me feel bad and peeled his soaking wet hoodie off before sliding onto the floor where he rested his back against the foot of my bed. Ten minutes into the show, I heard what sounded like a bear yawning and realized it was coming from Wren's stomach.

"Jesus, is that you? Didn't you eat?" It sounded like he hadn't in days.

"There wasn't enough time."

I was about to remark that he could have gotten food at White Castle when I remembered he hated it. Finally, shame came.

"Want some of my shake?" I offered the cup, but when he looked over his shoulder with a frown, I remembered that he hated chocolate, too. *Psychopath.* Who doesn't like chocolate? As far as I was concerned, it should have been a major food group. With a shake of his head, he refocused on the television.

The show went to commercial, and I used that time to run downstairs. Five minutes later, I guiltily returned with a plate of the roast Cathleen had made for dinner. I tried not to think about how many Bellamy scenes I'd missed. Thank fuck for reruns, I guess.

"Here you go. It's not much." The budget in the Henderson household was strict, and not even the stipend they received for fostering me helped much, but once upon a time, even a roast had been out of the question. Neither one of the Hendersons had received a promotion or raise, so where the extra cash came from, I didn't have a clue.

He only glanced at the plate before holding my gaze long

enough to make me squirm. Finally, he took the food with a smirk that confused me, and dug in.

My eyes widened when the plate full of roast and rice was gone in under a minute. I wasn't sure even a wild animal could be capable of such a feat.

"Want some more?"

"Nah," he said with a burp and a smile that made me giggle. "I'm trying to watch my figure."

My laughter died when I eyed the muscles stretching his shirt and jeans. Wren was far from the lanky teen I'd met. At nineteen, he was still a teen, but he was no longer lanky. And he *certainly* had nothing to worry about. We may have been friends and nothing more, but not even I could deny that he was pure hunk.

"I think you'll be fine." I reached out for the plate, and when he handed it over, I ran back downstairs. For a brief moment, I didn't care about the show or Bellamy Blake. I just wanted to take care of my friend.

Thankfully, tonight was Bible study at the church, which meant we were all alone. It occurred to me then that there hadn't been a need to make Wren climb through my window. At least there was less chance of the nosy neighbors seeing. Wren was a bit of a hot topic among the neighborhood, which I hated even more than he did. Especially since Samantha Davis, the leggy neighborhood slut was always sniffing around him. It wouldn't have bothered me as much if I hadn't glimpsed the interest in his eyes whenever she came prancing around in tight low-riders that showcased her tramp stamp. She'd noticed too and had become even more smug than usual.

It wasn't that I was jealous...like I wanted Wren for myself... sexually.

It was that Trampy Bambi pretended like they were a couple, the world was their house with a white picket fence, and I was the goddamn dog.

I can't count how many pats on the head I've received since

she photobombed our friendship, but I did know the next one would probably end with me breaking her bony wrist.

What did Wren even see in her long legs, twenty-four-inch waist, and perky DDs, anyway? If she could just find a runway on the other side of the world and leave us the hell alone, that would be great.

I spooned food onto the plate and trekked back up the stairs, but when I made it to my room, I found Wren preparing to leave. He was typing on his phone and hadn't noticed me yet.

"Where are you going?"

My stomach turned as I silently prayed it wasn't Exiled.

"Sam's. She said her parents aren't home."

I swallowed down the bile threatening to rise when I realized there was a worse alternative to Exiled.

"So what, are you like her boyfriend now?"

He grimaced as he continued to type on his phone. "I'm going to fuck her, Lou. We don't need a label for that."

The plate nearly slipped from my hand. Wren's mumbled words felt like a band around my throat cutting off my next breath. He didn't even notice me slowly dying. He was probably describing all the dirty things he wanted to do to her while I was already a forgotten, insignificant blip in his past.

This was the part where someone would tell me to shut up, that I was overthinking, being dramatic, and a tad silly.

But it didn't feel that way. My fears were very real. For as long as I'd known him, there had been no one else, and now out of the blue, I was expected to share him with little resistance?

Not a goddamn chance.

She'd only ruin the parts of him that were still beautiful.

I couldn't allow that to happen.

"Why do you like her?"

He glanced up then, more than likely detecting the jealousy I tried so hard to hide. "Why does it matter?" he shot back with a confused frown.

"Because it's getting serious, don't you think?"

He snorted. "Hardly."

"But you want to have sex with her, so that means it's serious!"

He stared at me for a moment before tossing his head back and laughing. "God, you're naïve."

A growl so fierce ripped from my belly that it vibrated my entire body and shook the plate in my hands. "Just answer the question, Harlan."

His laughter died as quickly as my composure had unraveled.

"Jesus…" he swore with narrowed eyes. "What the fuck is up with you, Lou?"

A valid question. What had come over me? I'd always been possessive of our friendship but not like this. It was as if someone had flipped a switch and woken up a part of me I didn't recognize.

Neither did Wren, judging by the way he was looking at me right now.

"I just…" I inhaled and slowly released. With every breath of air, I felt more in control. To be safe, I set the plate down before I could do something rash…like hurl it at his head. "I don't trust her."

He shrugged and pocketed his phone as if my revelation didn't matter. "I'm not in love with her, Lou. I want to fuck her because she's sexy sure but also because she's not…"

"Not what?" I demanded when he hesitated.

He looked pissed off, and I could tell he was reluctant to answer me when he pushed the words through his teeth. "Jailbait."

I felt like I'd been kicked in the stomach. All I could do was watch him go when he turned on his heel and flung his body through my open window.

The wind howled and blew the curtains on my window. I was still frozen in the same spot when it dawned on me that he was running away.

From me.

To *her*.

Spinning around, I raced down the stairs, my heart reaching out for the troubled boy it craved while pounding a mile a minute. I barely slowed enough to throw open the front door. The sky had opened up in the seconds it took me to run outside, and just then, a lightning bolt cracked across the sky, illuminating his shadow moving through the pouring rain.

It was beating down on his back, soaking through his clothes, but his steps were quick and determined. Not to get to her, I realized, but to get away from me.

"Wren!"

Thunder rumbled at that moment, drowning out my voice. The small part of me that was still unsure how much of him was really mine told me it was a sign to turn back now. To let him go.

But I couldn't.

I knew us too well.

"Wren!" This time, my voice carried, and when he turned around, I realized I didn't know what the hell to do or say. His eyes were pleading as he stared back at me through the dark and rain. He wanted me to let him run away.

"Go back inside," he shouted over the rain.

"No."

"Go back inside!"

"No!"

He was glaring now as he stomped back across the street, but I didn't care because as soon as he was within reach, I launched myself off the small stoop and into his arms. Wrapping myself around him, I held on tight and savagely sank my teeth into his sculpted jaw.

"Fuck, Lou." He tried like hell to untangle me, but I only bit down harder, earning his grunt of pain. There was no way I was letting go if it meant sharing him with Samantha Davis. Or anyone.

I still couldn't put together the reasons behind my actions. I was simply reacting out of instinct, and it urged me to fight like hell.

He was still wrestling to free himself when an annoyingly sultry voice called out. "What the hell…Wren?"

Peeking over his shoulder, I saw Samantha standing on her stoop, sporting serious camel toe in red satin shorts with lace trim and a matching cami.

I felt my dinner rising in my throat.

I couldn't compete with that because I could never give him that.

Wren and I shared a bond deeper than Samantha could ever hope to have with him. Sex would only ruin it. Not that I wanted to…with him.

"Are you okay?" she shouted as she descended the steps.

Wren spun around until he faced her.

"What is she doing to you?" I heard her question.

It was then I remembered that my teeth were embedded in his skin. I realized how deranged I must have looked, but if the shoe were on the other foot, Wren wouldn't have reacted any saner.

He simply had no understanding when it came to protecting me. Why couldn't I be allowed to feel the same?

"Go back inside," he ordered her. "I got her."

"But she's—"

"Go!" Like a whipped puppy, she scurried back across the street. Or at least I assumed she did. "Lou," he cooed as he smoothed a hand down my back. "You've got to let me go."

I shook my head, and when he winced, I finally let go, not wanting to hurt him further. My arms and legs were still wrapped around him, but he no longer seemed so eager to get away.

Laying my head on his shoulder, I whispered, "Stay with me."

His hands tightened around my hips as if he wanted to do just that. "We both know why I can't, Lou."

His tone was level and without emotion, but I knew better. I lifted my head needing to look into his eyes, and just as I suspected, blue had completely taken over.

"We both know you want to."

He sighed. "I wasn't a virgin when we met, Lou."

Nodding, I forced myself to swallow. "I know that."

"I haven't been a virgin since we met, either," he clarified with a raised brow.

"I…know," I responded a little less enthused.

"So what's up with the cockblocking?" His gaze was unflinching as he waited for an answer.

Fearing that he'd see too much, I unwrapped my arms and legs from around him. His hands were there to steady me once I was back on my feet, but suddenly, his touch felt too intimate. His frown only burrowed deeper when I moved away from him.

"Lou?"

"I don't know why, okay? It just feels different."

"Different how?"

"For starters, you've never flaunted them in my face before. I know there are girls who…do stuff…with you…but I never had to know who they were or what they looked like. Trampy Bambi lives right across the street! I have to see her face every single day, all smug and sexed, and I *hate* her!"

"But why? What did she do to you?"

She reminded me that I couldn't have all of you.

"Nothing. It's just…you trust your gut all the time. This is me trusting mine." Only I had nothing to go on except jealousy.

Wren stared down at me for a long time, his gaze hard and unyielding, and I knew he was just trying to stare me into submission. When a full minute passed, and I still hadn't changed my mind, his nostrils flared, and this time, he was the one to pull away.

But then my heart dropped when his feet kept moving, carrying him across the street, and I helplessly watched as he entered her home and shut the door behind him. For a while, I felt too numb to move. Too numb to feel the rain. But then I realized the rain had stopped and the sky had cleared, and so had my mind. Coming to my senses, I slowly trudged inside and headed straight for the shower. I needed to wash away my shame and hope some of my dignity remained. One day, I'd look back on this day and cringe. Hopefully, it wasn't sixty or seventy years from now because I'd probably stroke and die from embarrassment.

I could still smell him when I shed my wet clothes, so once I was under the pounding hot spray, I made sure to scrub my skin extra hard. His scent always had a way of clinging to me even after the briefest touch, and I never minded before, but this time was different. For the first time, it felt like it didn't belong. Right now, he was across the street imprinting on someone else.

The most frustrating part was that I knew Wren was no monk, but I'd never actually been subjected to seeing him with girls. Once upon a time, I could have been that girl, but we'd fooled ourselves into thinking we were better off as friends. I never forgot the bet or the way he looked at me when I agreed. I just…pushed it away. We both did.

After ten minutes of scrubbing, I could no longer feel him on me, so I stepped out and with only a towel covering me, I headed to my room and tried not to hope that she'd give him herpes.

The 100 was still playing when I got to my room, but I wasn't in the mood. With one last lingering look at Bellamy, who suddenly didn't seem quite so captivating anymore, I shut off the TV and immediately plunged the room in darkness.

Unwrapping my towel, I let it fall to the floor at the same time light flooded the room. A yelp escaped me as I dove for the towel. Meanwhile, Wren stood frozen to the spot with eyebrows damn near touching his hairline, his mouth forming a perfect *O*, and his hand still on the switch.

When the shock wore off, anger quickly took its place. "What the hell are you doing?" he had the nerve to yell.

"Excuse me?"

"Why are you naked?"

"I took a shower, genius!" He continued to glower even after I finally managed to secure the towel around me. "What are *you* doing? Shouldn't you be banging headboards with Bambi?"

"Who?"

"Samantha!"

Rolling his eyes, he stepped inside the room, grabbed the remote, and much too casually reclined on my bed.

"Wren?"

"That's over," he muttered. He never even took his gaze from the TV as he channel-surfed.

"Well, you didn't have to stop on my account."

"Actually, I did," he quipped with a curl of his lips. "You can fuck anyone, Wren. Just not my neighbors."

"You sure about that?"

My heart skipped a beat. "What?"

His focus zeroed in on me, and for several seconds he just stared. "You heard me."

Turning away, I rummaged through my dresser in search of more barriers. In my heart, I knew that if Wren touched me, not even a bulletproof vest would be enough protection.

"When you eventually got bored with her, she'd be a thing of your past, but she'd still be my neighbor."

"So that was the only reason you cared?"

"What other reason would there be?"

I held my breath waiting for his reply, but he was quiet for so long I gave in before he did. Sucking in air, I grabbed the first shirt and pair of shorts I touched and bolted for the door. Unfortunately, he decided to give chase and caught me with a hand around my throat before I could cross the threshold. His hold wasn't harsh or threatening, but then Wren never needed either to have me right where he wanted. Forcing my back against the door, he moved in, stopping just short of his body pressing against mine. I'm pretty sure all hell would have broken loose if it had. His eyes seemed to be glowing when our gazes locked.

"You're too young."

"I know that." And I did. The problem was that I didn't care as much. "I also know that I won't be sixteen forever." The moment the words left my lips, I was shocked by them, awed by them. I'd never meant to utter them.

"Jesus Christ, Lou!" Wren pushed away from me and shoved his fingers through his hair. "This is never going to happen. We're friends. *Just* friends. That was the deal."

My gaze fell to my feet. "I-I think you should go."

My heart tore in two when I heard his sigh of relief. "Fine."

"And I don't think you should come back." I was staring at the floor when I said that, so I didn't see his reaction, but I felt it. His shock, his anger, his confusion…it was all the things I felt but *more*. This wasn't our first fight or even our worse, but it was the one that hurt the most. He wasn't even the one to blame. It was my jealousy that caused this.

I should have just let him fuck her.

It wasn't as if I truly believed he'd fall for her or anything. I just couldn't bear the thought of knowing she could have him in ways that I couldn't.

"What the hell are you talking about, Lou?"

"Don't come back, Wren. I swear you better not come back."

"Or what?" he challenged. He'd taken a threatening step forward, and when I met his gaze, I could see that he wasn't going to back down. It shouldn't have surprised me. Wren had always given me what I wanted except space.

"Or nothing. I just won't talk to you."

He chuckled with disbelief and a little genuine humor. "Silent treatment? You're threatening me with the *silent treatment*?"

I twisted my lips with a shrug. What could I really do? Wren had my foster parents under his thumb, and whenever I ran away, he always managed to find me and bring me back. Short of killing him, I was stuck with him.

Unless I could convince him.

"Come back...and I'll fuck Miles."

"What?" Time stood utterly still as we both waited for the other's submission. "What the fuck did you just say, Louchana?"

I was about to speak when I heard the unmistakable sound of the front door opening and closing.

The Hendersons had returned from Bible study, and I knew it meant I had won this round—for now.

"You better go," I taunted and nodded toward his only exit.

Wren looked at the window, and then with a smirk, made an about-face. Before I could stop him, he was jogging down the stairs. I could hear the Hendersons startled surprise when he cheerfully greeted them. A moment later, the front door opened and closed.

"Lou?" Mr. Henderson called up the stairs.

My voice shook when I answered him. "Yes?"

"Could you come down here, please?"

I started down the stairs until I remembered that I only wore a towel. *Shit!* After hurriedly dressing, I rushed downstairs to receive my punishment.

I was grounded for a month.

While the Hendersons tolerated Wren, they had strict rules about entertaining him alone in their home. I wouldn't be seeing anyone for a long time, not Wren and certainly not Miles.

Well played, asshole.

After spending nearly half an hour assuring them that nothing inappropriate happened, I excused myself upstairs and wearily slid into bed.

It didn't take long for the tears to come, and once I started, I couldn't stop. I never thought I could hate and love someone equally, but with Wren Harlan, anything was possible.

My next sob was caught in my throat when I heard the window being shoved open. My back was to it, but I didn't need to see. It could only be Wren. I hurriedly wiped away my tears even though I knew he couldn't see them.

Thankfully, the carpet muffled the sound of his feet touching the floor. I had a feeling the Hendersons would ground me for life or worse—send me back to the group home—if they caught Wren in my room twice in one night. I listened as he removed his jacket and then his shoes and shirt before my bed dipped under his weight. I then sucked in a breath when I felt strong arms slide around my waist and pull me against a wall that was hard, hot, and familiar.

Trying my best to sound unaffected, I released the air I was holding and said, "I told you not to come back."

His arms tightened around me as if he were afraid I'd run. "I never left."

Too tired but mostly too relieved to fight, I sighed and snuggled deeper inside his arms. "Stalker."

His chest shook from laughing, and I felt myself smiling.

"Lou?"

"Yeah?"

"I can't lose you, too."

My heart nearly burst from my chest at the vulnerability in his voice. "You won't. Best friends for life."

The next morning, I delivered the news that I was grounded and kicked him out of my room. He then recited an address—Miles's address—before gently kissing my forehead and climbing from my window.

As I watched him go with a frown, I wondered if he meant what I thought he meant. Just as I began to think I was wrong, he stopped and shot me a meaningful look over his shoulder.

Message received.

It should have troubled me, but all I felt was the ache in my belly easing, knowing that he returned my jealousy.

In the window's reflection, I saw a smile that didn't leave my face the entire time I got ready for school. But then I stepped outside and found Samantha waiting.

And right there on the Hendersons' stoop, she shared every little detail of their dirty deeds.

When I confronted Wren, he had nothing to say.

He never even bothered to deny it.

CHAPTER
EIGHT

The Moth

Present

"A MARRIED COUPLE LIVES ALONE IN THE HOME, AND MY SOURCE says they're old as shit. It will be like taking candy from a baby," the informant boasted. Harry was our latest mole in Thirteen's operations after the last one was discovered and sent back to us in pieces. At the moment, Harry was attempting to sell us on a heist that sounded too good to be true, and from the looks of the men hanging onto his every word, he was succeeding. I should have been more invested, but I couldn't stop replaying the argument with Lou earlier today.

I knew one day I'd regret the decision I made a year ago, but I knew my little Valentine better than she knew herself. Lou wasn't the kind of girl who crushed. She was the kind who fell. Letting her believe I fucked Samantha kept that from happening, and if I were honest, the moment Lou batted her lashes my way, there had been no hope for Samantha.

Or any other girl.

"How much coke are we talking?" Shane asked with an eager glint in his eye. Other than me, he was the only one who had our leader's ear. Nathaniel Fox was as paranoid as he was cruel, and for the former, he had every reason to be.

Fox was cast out of Thirteen for allegedly murdering their former leader, and conspiring with Crow, Exiled' cofounder, to succeed him. The formation of Exiled cemented the accusation. With a hefty bounty on his head, Fox had zero chance of surviving, not without help and an army to hide behind him, so with the help of Crow, he initiated a rivalry that spanned nearly three decades. No one could be sure of what was true because much like the present, our past was shrouded by too many secrets.

Fox himself was a mystery to those who served him. Few of us had seen him and even fewer who knew where he kept himself hidden. After Crow's death, Fox retreated into the mountains, truly living in exile. He wasn't too far away that he couldn't manage his operations—delegating played a key role—but he was far enough to remain hidden from his enemies. Nothing lasted forever though. We now controlled New York, but it had taken us three decades, and a lot of blood spilled to make it happen. Thirteen had the entire East Coast on lock, and by taking control of New York, we had become a thorn firmly embedded in their side. But it wasn't enough. We needed to behead the beast.

"Twenty kilos."

Eddie, who kind of looked like a much younger Michael Peña, whistled. "That's half a million dollars. Boss is going to shit a brick. Literally."

He laughed at his joke and Siko—who got his name for resembling the actor, Joseph Sikora—joined in until I silenced them both with one look. Siko and Eddie were reasonably new to the crew but had both impressed Shane with their ability to procure information and eliminate threats without blinking an eye. However, if it weren't for the fact that they had supplied the mole, they wouldn't have been allowed in the room.

"How sure are you of this information?" I grilled even though I knew any argument I made at this point would be ineffectual. Exiled cultivated greed and recklessness and often paid the price, and Fox...he didn't care how many men he sacrificed as long as he reaped the rewards.

"Cross my heart," Harry said as he did so, "and hope to die."

"If you're wrong, that can be arranged," Shane casually threatened as he chewed on his toothpick.

Harry tried to hide his nervousness as the atmosphere in the room became grim. The wheels in my head were turning faster now as my gut burned. Something was off, and if I couldn't prevent the train from leaving the station, I'd make damn sure I was there to derail it if it went south.

"I wouldn't let you down, boss."

Shane turned to me without giving Harry's claim any credence. "We can't risk a sloppy job. You interested?"

I nodded though it seemed superfluous to offer consent. Even if I hadn't insisted on being there, I wasn't foolish enough to believe Shane was actually giving me a choice. I had authority and respect within Exiled, more than the rest, but even my leash extended only so far.

"Good. I don't want to give Thirteen a chance to distribute the product or risk them getting spooked and relocating the coke, so once boss gives the okay, we move in." He stood from the table, and in typical Shane fashion, he left the room without acknowledging or offering any goodbyes.

Harry waited all of five seconds before scurrying from the room back to whatever hole he'd come from.

Siko and Eddie were excitedly discussing how they'd spend their cut of the money. No doubt a job this size would guarantee a generous commission. I had a hard time suppressing my irritation when I ordered them back to work.

After they had left, I moved through the shotgun house making sure everything was running smoothly. This particular spot was the hub for our counterfeiting operation. We printed and sold fake money to anyone desperate, greedy, or stupid enough to buy it and made a pretty nice profit, but it wasn't even close to our largest moneymaker.

Fox's stables covertly sprinkled throughout the city brought in twice as much—not to mention the drugs and guns we callously flooded into the streets. More recently, Fox had sunk his teeth into gambling along with its reluctant ringmaster, Mickey Johnson. Mickey had his hand in everything that could be bet on, making an impressive name and profit from his efforts. And now Fox demanded a piece of the pie, finally elevating his extortion of local businesses cloistered in our city to most of the East Coast. It was only a matter of time before he set his sights even further. After all, Fox's ambitions were designed to not only threaten Thirteen's but engulf them. So far, we'd succeeded in pushing most of Thirteen out of New York, but our rival had long since graduated from being a simple street gang. The terrified whispers were beginning to utter *mafia,* and if Fox hoped to keep up with the seven decades of terror Thirteen wrought, he couldn't afford to show mercy.

Not that he ever considered it.

One of my brothers texted me about a party another member was throwing, but as usual, I turned them down and crashed at the stable, much to the girls' pleasure. In the beginning, I couldn't get enough of Exiled parties—the girls, the booze, the drugs. I never indulged in the latter, but I had more than I could handle of the former. Back then, I hadn't had all the power and the responsibilities that came along with it, but after I fucked up my initiation, Fox was determined to make me prove my worth. Five years later, I was still paying for the ounce of mercy I'd shown.

The setting sun made it hard to read Lou's expression when she stepped outside the next day, but I could tell by her body language that she was still pissed.

"I wasn't expecting to see you for a while," she mumbled when she finally stood in front of me with her arms crossed. She wore white denim shorts that were frayed at the end and hugged her thighs. I could only imagine how her ass looked in them and swallowed back a groan. The black ribbed tank top she wore was cut so dangerously low her breasts were close to spilling out, and even more frustrating was that it was cropped, showing off her belly button. My jaw clenched when I thought about the time she'd considered piercing it. I had begged her not to. I never explained why I was against it, and she never asked. For a few days, I tortured myself wondering if she knew until I finally stopped myself from thinking about it.

Even now, my mouth watered at the thought, and I forced myself to swallow.

"But you were hoping I'd come," I said with confidence, making her eyes narrow. She didn't reply and, instead, walked around me, heading for my car. I smiled at her back and followed her.

She didn't speak the entire forty-minute drive, but when I parked, she sighed, knowing she'd have to talk to me as she looked around in confusion. "Why are we here?"

"I thought I'd hang out with my best friend. Is that okay with you?" Before she could answer, I turned toward the scattered screams and hustle-bustle lying ahead, knowing she'd follow. Since it was the Friday before school started, the beach and boardwalk at Coney Island were full of people trying to catch the last rays of their summer fun.

Lou still had her arms crossed and her mouth in a flat line as she looked around with disinterest. I chuckled knowing it wouldn't be easy thawing her.

I stopped at the first food stand we came across and turned to her. "Hungry?"

She shrugged while refusing to meet my gaze, and I held back a grin. Spotting a ridiculously long, beef hot dog, an idea formed, so I ordered one. We spent about five minutes maneuvering through the crowd until we found an empty bench near the beach. I straddled the bench , and she did the same, but then I pulled her close until her bare knees touched mine, and handed her the hot dog.

Her eyes widened as she looked from me to the hot dog and back again. "I can't eat all of this!"

"I'll help you."

Her gaze turned wary, but when I made no sudden moves, she sighed and began nibbling the end closest to her mouth. I waited until her third or fourth bite before I chomped down on the end facing me. She paused, and her gaze widened again as she stared at me over the hot dog.

She hurriedly swallowed the portion she'd been chewing before asking, "What are you doing?"

"Eating my half," I answered with the obvious.

"We can just split it in half."

"It will make too big of a mess," I pointed out. Which was why I requested for it to be fully loaded.

"Well, can't you just wait until I'm done?"

"I could, but I'm hungry *now*." *And for more than just food.*

She tried to hand over the hot dog. "Then take it. I can wait."

I breathed out through my nose and pinned her with my gaze. When I spoke, my tone made it clear that I wasn't fucking around. "Eat, Louchana."

Her nostrils flared, and when I pinched her hip, not realizing my hand was still there, she took another bite. Our gazes never strayed the entire time we shared the hot dog, and I was relieved my plan had worked. I didn't want her running from me, taking parts of herself away. Just this once, I allowed myself to get lost within her eyes, and I could tell she did the same.

We were nearing the center when I spotted an exhausted-looking elderly couple looking around for a place to sit. Seeing an opportunity to get even closer to her, I quickly flagged them down and shouted, "This seat's open!"

Lou frowned when she glanced behind her. There was only room for maybe one of them, so without warning, I grabbed Lou and sat her in my lap. Problem solved.

The couple shot me grateful glances before taking Lou's vacated seat.

"What are you doing?" she said in a panic. I would have thought she was uncomfortable with her new seat if she hadn't grabbed my shoulders and immediately wrapped her legs around me as if I were dangling her off a cliff. I guess in a way I was.

"Making room for the elderly," I told her before tucking my bottom lip inside to hide my smile.

"Why are you doing this?"

I sighed seeing genuine confusion in her eyes. "I'm trying to apologize, Lou. Now if you could just shut up and let me," I grumbled.

She frowned then. "By making me sit on your lap?"

"By being with you." I inhaled the stale air and let it out slowly. "We've been fighting more lately."

Her gaze turned somber as she studied me. "I noticed, too."

"Any ideas why?"

She peeked up at me from her lashes. "You're a dick?"

Amusement shook my chest as I stared down at her. "That's one theory."

I finished off the last of the hot dog, balled up the wrapping, and aimed for the garbage can a few feet away. When it cleared the rim, Lou said with sarcasm dripping from every syllable, "Let me guess…you're remarkably skilled at basketball, too."

I winked and stood us up before taking her hand and leading her onto the beach. I found us an empty spot on the sand and plopped down, bringing Lou with me.

"We probably should have brought a towel," Lou remarked. "We'll track sand in your precious Paula."

I paused. "Paula?"

"The Im*pala*," she answered and then burst out laughing at the scowl on my face.

"How are you just going to name *my* ride?"

"Easy." She chortled. "I've been calling her Paula this entire time. This is just the first time I've done it to your face."

"What?" I roared, and she howled even louder while clutching her stomach.

Before she could recover, I pinned her to the sand with an evil grin and attacked her sides with my fingers. It wasn't long before she was begging for mercy, and by the time I finished, she lay spent in the sand. Neither of us spoke, and I wasn't sure how much time had passed. It didn't matter.

I was still hovering over her, gazing into her eyes glistening with tears from my tickling when I said, "Am I forgiven?"

Her lips parted, and as she blinked, I held my breath. I knew I wasn't just asking forgiveness for our fight yesterday.

"I'm not sure," she said in a playful tone. "I don't think I should forgive you so easily. It sets precedence." Her expression turned thoughtful. "I think a foot rub should suffice." I grinned and rolled away, and when I pulled one of her feet into my lap, she sat up on her hands and screeched, "Wait! I was kidding!"

Any other protests she might have had died when I slowly peeled the flip-flop from her foot and began massaging the muscles there. It wasn't long before her eyes fluttered followed by a groan, and then her head fell back on her shoulders.

"You're one of those dudes who have a freaky foot fetish, aren't you?" she said when I moved to her other foot.

I barked out a laugh. "Fuck no." I had to admit though, even if it was to myself, how pretty and dainty Lou's feet were. Even the dark purple nail polish coating her toes was fascinating to me. My tan was deep while her skin looked like she'd been kissed by the sun. She was soft, too, and for a second, I worried that my rough hands would mar her skin, but then I shook off those ridiculous thoughts and dropped her foot abruptly.

She lifted a brow but thankfully didn't ask questions as she sat up all the way. "Thanks," she said and grinned as she began slipping her sandals back on her feet. "You're forgiven."

"I didn't fuck her," I blurted before I could stop the words from spilling. I released a long string of curses in my head as I watched and waited.

Her smile immediately fell as her chest rose hard and fast. "What?"

"Samantha," I told her, my voice sounding calmer than I felt. "She lied."

Lou's eyes narrowed to slits when she faced me. "Why would she lie?"

"Because she was jealous." I struggled to swallow before saying. "Of you."

"That's ridiculous," she spat.

"Was it? You came on to me that night, Lou." *And turning you down was the hardest thing I ever had to do.*

"And you made it clear," Lou said with a sneer, "that she had nothing to be jealous of."

"Come the fuck on." I groaned. "I had an itch she was more than eager to scratch, but one word from you, and I chose agony over pleasure. Don't you dare tell me she had no reason to be jealous."

She shot to her feet, and I followed her. "If I cause you *so* much pain, if I'm such a *cruel twist of fate,* why the fuck don't you just stay away from me?" she screamed.

Just like that, we were once again at odds with each other.

I held her gaze, and whatever she saw in mine made her gasp. *"Because,"* I growled. And then I gripped her chin and pulled her close so I could feel her heat and she could feel my need. My arm locked around her waist, and I pressed my lips to her ear. "I'm the moth to your flame, Lou. I'd rather be burned a thousand times than be free of you."

"But you said—" she whimpered before I gripped her chin harder and cut her off.

"I know what I said. I also warned you that I wouldn't have the strength to change it." I took a deep breath, and it shuddered out of me. "I'm fucking weak for you, Lou."

I let her go, and she was suddenly shy and unsure as she avoided my gaze. "I don't know what to say."

"We say nothing, and we do nothing. Those are our only options, Lou."

"But why? Being best friends doesn't mean we can't be there for each other…in every way."

"It does for us."

She propped her hands on her hips. "Then explain it to me."

"I'm not good enough for you," I told her honestly. I sat back down, but she stayed standing.

"Try again."

I shook my head. It was the only answer she'd ever get. The whole truth would send her packing, and I'd lose her forever.

She sighed and then stared at the sand for a while before saying, "Fine."

I watched her slide her feet from her sandals and take a couple of steps toward the water before peeking over her shoulder at me.

"Coming?"

I gave her a crooked smile. "I'm not a toe-dipping kind of guy, and there are too many people around to go skinny dipping."

She blushed, and I felt the blood rush to my cock knowing at that moment, she imagined how the rest of the night might go if things were different between us and we were alone.

Shrugging, she smirked and said, "Suit yourself."

And then I felt like I'd been punched in the gut with a Louisville slugger when she sexily shimmied out of her shorts and shirt, and without any regard for the hundreds of people around, she ran to the water in just her panties and bra.

Cursing, I shot to my feet with a growl that would send a lion running for safety and took off after her.

"Are you coming up?" Lou quietly asked me as she stood in front of the Hendersons' front door, twirling her key in her hand. Her question strangely made it feel like we'd just gotten back from a date and she was inviting me up for a nightcap.

I eyed her damp hair, which had gotten wet thanks to the wave that crashed into us before I could drag her out of the water, and the rest of her still dripping water. I wanted desperately to get her out of those clothes and wrapped around me so I took a step back.

"I don't think that's such a good idea."

She frowned. "Because of the thing we're both thinking but can't say?"

I took another step back. "Yes."

I wasn't expecting her gentle smile, and it was all I could do not to kiss it from her lips. She shouldn't be smiling. She should be running scared like I was right now.

"Good night, bestie." With a wave of her fingers, she disappeared inside the house, and I could finally breathe again.

CHAPTER NINE

The Flame

"**I** NEED YOU TO PICK ME UP!" I SHOUTED INTO MY PHONE. I ADMIT I was feeling a little grumpy, but considering the fact I'd spent the entire day searching the city high and low for my best friend, I think a little moodiness was allowed. It didn't matter that I'd gone against all of Wren's warnings *never* to go looking for him. The asshole was avoiding me and not for any of the usual reasons.

Today was Wren's twentieth birthday, and as usual, he refused to celebrate. Every year, he'd say the same thing.

"How many times do I need to celebrate being born? You wouldn't dig up a person's corpse every year and bake them a fucking cake for dying."

"Why?" he breathed into the phone, and he sounded every bit as annoyed as I sounded.

Snatching the phone away from my ear, I doubled-checked the name on my screen with my nose wrinkled. Since when did Wren not jump at the chance to do things for me?

"Do you know what today is?"

"Monday," he replied, and his tone was drier than the Sahara desert. "Shouldn't you be in school?"

"My first day isn't until Thursday. Besides, I'm dropping out again."

"Lou."

"Kidding, bestie!" A warm feeling spread over my tummy

knowing he cared. My best friend would often take my breath away without even trying. "Are you coming to get me or not?"

"I'm a little busy right now." And then I heard what sounded like flesh impacted followed by a pained groan. The warm feeling went in an instant, and icy coldness took its place.

"I won't need you for another couple of hours," I said, losing some of my excitement. I didn't have to question if Wren noticed when he started speaking to someone in hushed tones in the background. I couldn't help straining to hear his surroundings while wondering if he was safe. Wren was always so secretive about where he went when he wasn't with me. Other than the nights he slept on my bedroom floor, I still had no idea where he laid his head. I didn't know if it was for my protection or his since he often accused me of being reckless.

I heard a door close a moment later, and then he sighed. "What time?"

"Seven please, and there's a dress code, so you have to wear something nice!"

"Why?" he asked sounding suspicious. "Where are we going?"

"It's a surprise."

He grunted. "It can't be if I'm driving."

"Well, for the next couple of hours, it's a surprise."

I waited for his smartass response, but none came. Instead, he asked me if I had everything I needed for school. The day after we'd gone to Coney Island, he'd taken Eliza and me shopping for school supplies. The Hendersons were begrudgingly delighted since they hated Wren but couldn't afford to put up much of a fight.

Wren continued to grill me about everything under the sun, and before I knew it, two hours had passed, and he was ringing the Hendersons' doorbell. I rushed down the stairs with the roses I'd gotten for him in hand before Eliza could have the chance to gush and blush like she always did. Judging by the romance novels she hid from her parents, Eliza liked her heroes bad. My curfew was at ten, which left me plenty of time to have Wren all to myself. When I opened the door, however, my pleasure immediately took a nosedive.

"You didn't dress up!"

Wren was wearing his usual attire—blue jeans and a white T-shirt. The only difference was that he'd thrown on a white button-up that might have been okay if he hadn't left the shirt open and worn a tie. His gaze slowly perused me before cocking his head to the side. "Neither did you."

My jaw dropped as I looked down at what I'd chosen to wear. "This is my best dress!" It was a white skater dress with an embroidered lace hem. It was nothing special, but whenever I wore it, Wren stared just a little longer than usual when he thought I wasn't looking. I'd even paired it with black wedges to make my legs look longer.

"I've seen you dig through trash in that dress."

"For the record," I defended as I crossed my arms, "it wasn't for food. I stashed a wallet I lifted in there when I ran from that beat cop."

Smirking, he gripped the front of my dress and pulled me over the threshold before closing the door behind me. "Let's go."

I dug my heels in when he tried to pull me down the stairs. Strangling the strap of my mom's rucksack, I gave him my sternest look. "Could you at least try to be excited?"

His nostrils flared as glared up at me from the bottom of the stairs. "I showed up, didn't I?"

"Sometimes showing up isn't enough."

He groaned and threw his head back on his shoulders. "Jesus fucking Christ, you're spoiled."

"And you're an asshole, but you don't hear me calling you names."

He threw his arms out in defeat. "What do you want me to do, Lou? It's too late for me to change."

That was true, and to be honest, I wasn't even upset about him not cleaning up. Wren looked good no matter what he wore, but it was just as he said. I was spoiled, and he had only himself to blame. Wren still hadn't learned to stop letting me have my way.

"Let me drive the pussy wagon."

His glower only deepened. "Nice try."

"It's interesting that you didn't deny it being a pussy wagon."

He shrugged—appearing too smug for my liking—before doing an about-face and completely missing my reaction. My feet felt like lead as I slowly followed him to his car. I couldn't even find the energy to argue when he got into the driver's seat. Getting to drive his car was a long shot but so were the desires I held closer to my heart.

"Where to?" he asked once he had the engine started.

I recited the address and stared out my window the entire drive. I didn't have to question if he noticed my mood. He made it clear with the happy tune he was whistling that he didn't care.

Asshole.

Almost an hour later, I was so far inside my head that I hadn't noticed we'd arrived until his hand brushed my knee as he reached inside the glove compartment. Pulling out a black tie, he quickly buttoned up his shirt, flipped up his collar, and slipped the tie around his neck. My lips parted as I watched him. When he'd finished, he tucked his lips inside his mouth, holding in his laugh as he eyed me.

"Oh," I breathed out.

"Yeah, oh," he echoed sarcastically.

I snapped my lips shut, refusing to apologize. I might have made assumptions, but Wren had been all too willing to play his games. He moved around the car, and after opening my door, Wren held out his hand for me to take. When he noticed me staring at his hand like it was covered in shit, he squatted and met my gaze. "Problem, bestie?"

I knew he was mocking me with that endearment. He was

just lucky I didn't crack my knuckles across his face. "Why would there be a problem?"

"You tell me."

We stared at one another, waiting for the other to bend or break.

It was almost always me.

That's why I was caught off guard when he softened and looked even remorseful. I didn't understand why until he lifted his hand to thumb away a tear I didn't realize had fallen. My cheeks heated, and I quickly looked away, feeling silly. Noticing my embarrassment, he quickly unbuckled my seat belt and pulled me from the car. After slamming the door, Wren pressed my back against it and forced me to look him in the eye as he caged me in.

"Wren—" I started to protest, but he cut me off.

"Sometimes I forget that letting me take care of you meant you'd be taking care of me, too."

I couldn't do anything but hold back more tears. I didn't even understand why I was so emotional. It wasn't that big of a goddamn deal!

He glanced down, noticing the roses I'd pick up from the corner store. "These are for me?" He freed them from my clutches without waiting for a response and sniffed them with a boyish smile. "I'm happy as fuck that you care about my birthday…even if I don't."

I gasped. "So you *do* know it's your birthday!" I know my surprise seemed ridiculous, but with Wren, I could never tell when he was bluffing. He had a damn good poker face.

He sighed. "Yeah, Lou."

"Why don't you care?"

He shrugged. "I just don't. There doesn't have to be a reason."

Refusing to let it go, I said, "But you make a big deal when it's my birthday."

"Because I know you'd put bleach in my drinking water if I didn't."

I couldn't help snickering because he had me pegged. "I wouldn't kill *you*. Just your car."

His head jerked back, and he looked more afraid for the hunk of metal than he did his own life. "That's a little extreme, don't you think?"

"I'd feed it candy bars," I insisted with a straight face.

The sound of a throat clearing interrupted his retort, and my entire body turned red this time when I saw a man standing a couple of feet away waiting to get inside his car. I didn't even realize how close Wren and I were standing until now. Even though we weren't touching, we couldn't have looked like two platonic friends. To my immense mortification albeit secret delight, rather than stepping aside to let the man pass, Wren moved even closer. I gasped at the feel of his hard body pressing firmly against mine. It felt different than the brotherly hugs he'd given me in the past although I'm not sure he meant it to.

The man mumbled his thanks before quickly hopping inside his car.

I expected Wren to put space between us immediately. Instead, he patiently waited for the man to set up his GPS, adding to my torture. I couldn't be sure with my brain short-circuiting, but it felt as though Wren had pressed even closer when the man began backing out of the parking spot. He was hard everywhere, and my body was yielding without much of a fight.

I felt Wren's heated gaze and wanted to avoid the challenge I knew I'd see in them, so I watched the taillights until they faded. Coincidentally, that was the moment Wren stopped holding me hostage.

"We should go inside," he said while checking his watch.

I was busy staring at him like he'd grown a second head. How could he pretend that we hadn't just crossed some line? That we hadn't been crossing many of them all summer long?

"I hope you didn't make reservations."

He finally looked at me just as I managed an indifferent expression.

"I did, but you can just threaten the maître d'." The reproachful look he gave me made me smile which only deepened his scowl. "Hey, if you're going to be a menace, you might as well enjoy the perks."

Shaking his head, he led me into the restaurant. Of course, I picked the nicest one available. I'd snatched quite a few wallets and pawned some valuable watches in anticipation of this night.

We were fashionably late, but luckily, we were shown to our table without anyone having to shit their pants first. I slid into the booth, and as usual, Wren followed me, sitting close enough for our thighs to touch. It was no wonder we had a hard time convincing strangers that we were friends and nothing more. I'd need his hands and mine to count how many times we were told what a lovely couple we made.

"My name is Derek, and I'll be serving you tonight." The waiter recited the specials and raved about their best wine—even though neither of us was old enough to drink—before asking what we wanted.

Like always, I ordered for us both while Wren checked his messages. "Two Pepsis and mozzarella sticks for the table please."

"Is Coke okay?"

My smile immediately fell. "If I wanted watered-down Pepsi, it would be," I grumbled.

Wren looked up from his phone with a smug expression. "You're just mad because no one ever asks how Pepsi is doing."

"I know a guy who was a Coke salesman," I bullshitted. "He quit his job because it lost its fizz."

"Pepsi is kind of like a hand job," Wren mused. "Never my first choice, but I'll take it anyway."

In perfect sync, we regarded the waiter with blank expressions, and after stuttering in confusion, he hurried away to fill our order.

"And a glass of water!" Wren shouted after him.

I made a mental note to double the poor guy's tip. Grinning at each other, we both ignored the dirty looks we received and perused the menu.

Wren was a creature of habit. He'd order his usual medium rare steak with fries while I attempted to wow myself with a spontaneous choice.

Just as I predicted, he took a quick scan of his menu before setting it aside. The waiter returned with our drinks, and Wren immediately took a sip of his to test for flatness. I didn't like the ache I got in my belly from watching him do such a simple act, so I quickly grappled for a diversion.

"Do you think if I eat enough oysters, I'll eventually shit pearls?"

My question had the desired effect when he choked on what might as well have been diet cola. The moment he regained his composure, he looked at me with crazy eyes.

"Well...do you?" I prodded. The longer he stared at me, the harder it got to keep a straight face, but somehow, I managed.

Never taking his gaze away, he snatched up one of the carefully folded napkins and dried his mouth. A giggle escaped me, and in the blink of an eye, Wren went from looking angry to pleased. And almost a little excited.

Amusement gave way to confusion, and then he was whispering in my ear, "I almost forgot about the spanking I promised. Thanks for reminding me."

After I'd shed my clothes for all to see on Coney Island Beach and Wren pulled me from the water, he told me ever so bitingly that I needed to spend some time over his knee. My heart began beating faster as my mind raced, but I forced myself to appear unbothered even as my deepest fantasy manifested.

"I recall it sounding more like a threat."

"Then consider it a promise now."

"And I told you," I said, my voice like sharp steel, "you're not my father." That wasn't exactly true, though. Wren was my father, brother, and best friend rolled into one, and I still wanted *more*.

Thankfully, our waiter returned with our appetizer before Wren could deliver the retort I saw burning in his gaze.

"Are we ready to order?" the waiter haltingly queried. I guessed he'd noticed the tension or maybe we weren't as funny earlier as we'd thought.

Wren ordered his steak, and I thought it best for everyone that I didn't get the oysters, so I ordered the lobster. As the waiter took down our orders, my mind turned over the implications of our conversation. I didn't expect him to follow through with his threat, but what did it mean that he'd made it in the first place?

I was holding my breath in anticipation of being alone and picking up where we'd left off, but when the waiter finally left, Wren simply said, "We should eat these before they get cold."

I stared at the platter of untouched mozzarella sticks while Wren unwrapped his flowers and casually dunked them in the glass of water.

I shouldn't have been surprised that he'd chosen to pretend nothing had happened. He'd give just a little only to take it all back.

It could have been that he was playing a private game for his own amusement, but I knew he wasn't capable of being that cruel. At least, not to me. That left only one possibility, and according to Wren, it was forbidden. I crumpled my napkin in my fist. If Wren were harboring secret thoughts and pretending otherwise, then it was time he tasted his own medicine.

We didn't speak as we devoured our appetizer. My appetite was gone, but I was just happy for the distraction. Wren answered a few calls, and I didn't bother ear hustling because he always kept it short and cryptic.

By the time he finally pocketed his phone, only one mozzarella stick remained, and we both reached for it at the same time. Wren was quicker and bit into the appetizer triumphantly. To my surprise, he even taunted me by wiggling the fried mozzarella between his teeth, and just like that, the tension was broken. If only he knew it was the opening I needed to exact revenge. Clearly, we'd both underestimated how daring I could be because, when I leaned over and bit the protruding half, his eyes widened in shock as my own heart skipped a beat. The joke ended up being on me, however, when our lips brushed. My stomach fluttered as I quickly sat back and clapped my hands over my mouth afraid of how he'd react.

To my dismay, he gave no reaction at all.

His expression turned blank, but he didn't turn away. A lifetime seemed to pass before he excused himself to the bathroom. I watched him go before spitting the suddenly tasteless mozzarella stick into the cloth napkin. Sometimes I believed I was a fool to feel what I did, and other times, I knew in my heart I wasn't wrong. Like when I glimpsed the sizable bulge in his pants when he got up from the table.

I allowed myself a moment of doubt, believing his body reacting to mine was pure biology, but then I decided to open my eyes and bet on my gut. The same desires building within me were also stirring in Wren, but only one of us was running scared. It was hard to feel remorse when he had only himself to blame. He should have never pursued me even if it was platonically.

The waiter returned with our food, and I snuck a couple of Wren's fries. I was still nibbling when he came back ten minutes later, but this time, he sat across from me.

"Everything okay?" I asked, forcing the hurt from my tone.

"I just realized I haven't eaten all day," he said with a sigh.

"Do I have to start packing your lunch every day?" I teased. My smile slowly fell when he didn't laugh and avoided my gaze altogether. The rest of dinner passed in tense silence until the waiter came and cleared our plates. Reaching inside my messenger bag, I stared at the gift Eliza helped me wrap, wondering if I was about to make another colossal mistake.

"What's that?" Wren asked, taking away the choice I'd been leaning toward—shoving it in my bag and never letting it see the light of day.

My hands shook as I slid it across the table and mumbled, "Your birthday present."

He looked up in surprise, and I sucked in a breath. I'd never gotten him a gift before.

"Breathe, Lou."

I shook my head and continued holding my breath.

"Fuck!" Sensing what I needed, he hurriedly ripped the wrapping paper away, and I let out all the air in one whoosh when he stared down at the framed photo. I watched his Adam's apple bob and his breathing turn shallow before he finally spoke. "Fuck."

This one was different than before. As if I'd knocked him on his ass.

"Why?" he choked out.

I shrugged. "You shared your passion with me, so I thought it was time I shared mine with you."

Wren always asked to see the pictures I took with the camera he bought me, but having no confidence in them, I always denied him. This was my first time showing him one of my 'butterflies.' Six months after we'd met and we'd both fallen into the routine of being friends—strictly platonic friends—I'd taken my Polaroid camera and used my very last shot to capture a picture of him. I'd been saving that final exposure for something special. It turns out I cherished the shot of Wren sleeping more than I did the last gift my parents had ever given me. He had no idea just how young and vulnerable he looked while he slept. I knew him well enough to know he wouldn't *want* to know. The stubborn ass would never sleep again.

"Do you like it?" I asked nervously.

He swallowed before carefully setting the frame down on the table. "Yes," he eventually replied.

But it was too late. I didn't believe him.

"Jesus, you're an asshole even when you're trying to be nice. If you don't like it, give it back!" I reached for it, but he snatched it up with a glare.

Our waiter returned with the check, and we both reached for it, but since he was still holding my gift hostage, I beat him to it and shoved more than enough cash inside the leather envelope.

"It's your birthday," I explained, feeling smug over my small victory. "I should pay."

"You shouldn't be wasting your money on me. The next time you run, I don't want you snatching more wallets to feed yourself."

I regarded him with a tilt of my head. "I'm pretty sure your money is dirtier than mine, Harlan."

He stared at me over his glass as he took one last sip of his drink. The look in his eyes when he set his glass down had me gushing in my panties, but with one sweep of his lashes, it was gone.

"Let's go."

I sighed and let him pull me from the booth.

Paula rolled to a stop outside my foster home, but Wren didn't shut off the engine. I knew he wasn't planning to stick around, and hiding my disappointment wasn't as easy as I had hoped.

"Thanks for dinner," he said after a long silence.

I tore my gaze away from the Hendersons' front door and found him watching me.

"You're welcome," I replied. More silence followed until it was broken by his ringing cell phone. I watched him pull it out and curse when he saw who was calling. Unfortunately for my stomach, I also glimpsed the name on his phone's screen.

With every fiber of my being, I hated the man who offered Wren only darkness. Nathaniel Fox was a man whose acquaintance I'd never met, but I knew despite Wren's vehement disapproval, one day I would. I'd make sure of it if only to give that man a piece of my mind. Wren had only been a boy when he came into Fox's service, and Fox probably hadn't thought twice about using Wren to pursue his evil desires while he remained safely in the shadows.

"I have to go," Wren announced. He was suddenly tense and agitated, and as much as I hated the thought of him going off to do bad things for a man who didn't deserve him, I couldn't bring myself to add to his stress. Not when I knew it would distract him and possibly get him killed.

Placing my hand over his larger one, I felt his warmth and began counting the seconds until I'd feel it again. "I know."

I couldn't tell if he was more shocked or relieved at my acquiescence, but at that moment, I wanted to make it clear that I accepted who he was, not what he did. In Wren's case, the two weren't mutually exclusive. Before I could think better of it, I heard myself asking, "Do you know the age of consent in New York?"

His eyes slowly closed, and he looked in pain as he struggled to swallow. "Seventeen," he answered hoarsely.

When my hand slid to his thigh and squeezed, his eyes flew open, and I smiled seeing that they were blue. I no longer had to wonder if these desires I felt were one-sided. "Come back to me, Wren."

CHAPTER
TEN

The Moth

NOT FEELING LIKE SCALING THE SIDE OF THE PALE BLUE HOME, I dug in my pocket and pulled out a key that none of the residents knew I had. I never used it while they were home, but I couldn't be bothered with the cloak and dagger bullshit. It had already failed me once tonight.

I flexed my fist and had the urge to turn back and mete out proper punishment. But even as my need for vengeance filled me, so did reason. Because I knew when my fist connected with Danny Boy's pretty face, instinct not cowardice had propelled him to drag me out that door to leave our brothers behind. Still, guilt plagued me. I hadn't actually *seen* Siko and Eddie die.

I stood frozen under the porch light, trying to convince myself not to go back. It'd been a couple of hours since the heist in Long Island. The bodies would have already been disposed of, and if Thirteen were even half as thorough as my crew, Siko and Eddie's corpses would never be found.

Shoving in my key, I let myself inside the quiet home bathed in darkness. By now, I'd learned which floorboards creaked and carefully avoided them as I made my way up the stairs. The house was larger than it looked on the outside, and every inch of surface and wall space was filled with knickknacks and family photos —a true home. When I reached the second floor, I stared at the large cross hanging on the wall at the end of the hall. I felt His stare and heard His question, but having no excuse or explanation for my actions, I offered him only a one-shoulder shrug before pushing inside the small bedroom.

I expected her to be asleep given the time, but there she was, curled on her side, wide awake and staring at the floor. I considered backing out and leaving. She'd sense my anger, and I didn't have the patience to answer her questions. Before I could escape, however, her soft voice filled the dark space of her bedroom.

"I thought it was going to be a few weeks before I saw you again." Her eyes never strayed from the frayed carpeting. It had only been three days since my birthday, but the time had seemed to stretch for me, too.

"Do you want me to go?"

She was sitting up and across the room faster than I thought her capable. She moved around me, and I listened as she slowly shut the door, and then I felt her hands on my shoulders, tugging my shirt up and over my head.

"You're where you're supposed to be," she whispered as she tossed my shirt at our feet. She then took my hand, and I let her pull me to her bed where she pushed me down with a warm hand on my chest. I watched her as she pretended that touching my bare skin didn't affect her as she knelt and began tugging the laces of my boots.

"What are you doing?"

"Taking care of you," she answered matter-of-factly. "Like you're always taking care of me."

"I don't recall ever undressing you."

"Yeah, no kidding," she mumbled. Her hand paused from tugging the knot of my laces free at the same time I froze.

Leaning down, I pressed a finger under her chin and lifted her face. As always, she was an open book, letting me read every page. The desire I saw there almost made me look away, but I was a glutton for punishment. I was also selfish, wanting to drink up the need shining in her bright blue eyes to the very last drop.

"What was that?" I'd heard her clearly even though she hadn't meant me to. She didn't know that I was aware of everything she did and said—more than I should be. She breathed in deep, and I did the same. While I wanted to hear her say the words, a part of me hoped she never would because I could never deny her.

"Say it, Lou. Don't be a coward." I knew my taunting hit its mark when her gaze turned defiant.

"I said to lift your foot."

My smile was victorious, hiding my relief as I lifted my foot. Lou was unnaturally stubborn, which ironically made her easy to manipulate. A paradox, indeed.

She yanked my boot from my foot and let it fall to the floor with a thud. She repeated the action with my other boot before closing her eyes and taking another deep breath to compose herself. Her eyes remained closed when I reached down and lifted her into my lap, but she didn't fight me. With a sigh, she cradled her head on my bare shoulder. When her lips brushed the skin of my neck, I just barely stifled a curse. I didn't just feel her touch there but in my fingers and toes and even my goddamn kneecaps. Neither of us spoke for some time, but Lou had never been good at keeping her thoughts inside—at least with me—so, of course, she was the first to break the silence.

"What happened?"

"What makes you think something happened?"

"Because your eyes are blue today."

"Blue?"

"Most of the time, you're a robot, but I always know when your soul is open." She lifted her head and stared back at me. "Your eyes become an ocean, and sometimes I wonder if I'll drown."

I found it hard to swallow as my grip on her tightened. "It's just your own emotions reflecting back at you."

Her gaze turned hard. "I'd believe that if I wasn't beginning to know better."

I cursed and almost shoved her off my lap. We were heading into forbidden territory, and I was starting to feel cornered. Carefully laying her on her back, I ordered her to get some sleep.

"I can't sleep until I know what's wrong."

"You mean you won't," I corrected from my place on the floor. She already had it set up for me, knowing all along that I'd come.

"Whatever gets you talking faster."

I was staring at the ceiling, replaying each moment from the time we stepped into that house tonight when I heard myself say, "I lost two men today."

I heard her shuffling around and her bedding rustling until out of the corner of my eye, I saw first one dainty foot and then two touching the carpet. She was lying next to me a second later, cradling against my side before I could tell her to get back in bed. My hands itched to pull her closer. I wanted to hold her, and I knew she wanted it, too.

"I'm sorry," she whispered, and I knew she was sincere even though she despised Exiled and everything we stood for. What *did* we stand for? I'd forgotten a long time ago.

"Me too."

"Were you close with them?"

"No, but it doesn't matter. They died under my watch."

"You can't take responsibility for everything bad that happens in the world."

"No? Well, what about the bad that I cause?"

"It doesn't have to be this way. You can leave it all behind."

"There's no such thing as leaving Exiled. My father learned that the hard way." Fox had called him a deserter. My father wanted out and was willing to kill for it.

"Tell me his name."

I counted to ten before speaking. This wasn't our first time having this conversation. "I can't."

"Because it hurts?"

"Because it won't change a goddamn thing." I turned my head, which was a mistake because it brought our mouths impossibly close. "And because I don't want his name on your lips."

My heart thundered in my chest, and I stopped breathing entirely when she threw her leg over my waist and straddled me. I wondered if she felt it under her small hands. Though they were planted on my chest, it was her burning gaze that held me hostage. "Don't treat me like china," she ordered through clenched teeth. "I'm not one of *those* girls."

"Which girls are those?"

"The delicate flowers easily trampled. The girls who clutch their pearls and faint at any sign of distress. I don't even own pearls."

"You don't? We'll have to fix that."

She viciously dug her nails into my bare chest, and I wondered if she could feel my cock hardening beneath her. "Don't you dare buy me pearls."

My hands found her barely-there hips, intending to return her gift of pain, but instead, I explored. She'd certainly filled out in the two years since I had met her, but I usually liked my girls with a little more curve. If she only stayed off the fucking streets, I was sure she'd have more meat on her bones. Somehow it hadn't mattered. My cock only answered to Louchana fucking Valentine.

"Who's going to stop me? You?" I lifted a brow.

"Buy them, and I'll trade them for a happy meal the next time I run away."

My hand shot out and found its way around her neck, and then she was on her stomach underneath me, shooting a smile over her shoulder that pissed me off and turned me on at the same time. Leaning down, I pressed my lips to her ear, careful not to let any other part of me touch her. "That spanking I promised is still on the table."

The smile on her face disappeared. "You're not my father."

"Damn straight and do you know why?" I was already

answering by the time she shook her head. "Because I wouldn't let you leave me no more than I would leave you."

"And I'm supposed to believe you?"

"You already do."

She snorted, flipped onto her back, and when she held up her pinky finger, there was a vulnerable glimmer in her eyes. "Best friends forever?"

I stared back at her pinky with a raised brow and slid my fingers through hers instead until our palms met. "Yeah."

The next morning, I jerked awake, but a soft, warm body pressed against mine hindered my ability to move. Blinking until my vision cleared, I frowned when I confirmed it was Lou barely clothed and curled around me like a second skin. I'd sent her back to her bed last night, and like a thief in the night, she'd climbed back into mine.

It had taken a lot of begging and reasoning to get her from under me and back where she was safe from me, but as usual, Lou had to push back. I lay perfectly still as her breathing changed and she began to stir, and by the time she was fully lucid, my expression was blank and carefree.

"You snore," I said before she could have the first word. At least now I could direct the conversation into a safe zone.

"You never minded before," she replied with zero shame as she stretched lazily before snuggling deeper under my arm.

I had trouble swallowing as I wondered how the hell it had gotten around her in the first place. Had I sought her out even while unconscious as she had done me?

"Because you never snored directly in my ear before."

"Ugh! You're such a grump this morning. What's the matter? Didn't get enough beauty sleep?" She peeked up at me from under naturally long lashes. I hated how much more innocent it made her look.

"You're not in your bed."

"It's uncomfortable," she whined. The sound went straight to my dick.

"Funny," I said with a sarcastic curl of my lips. "That's not what you said six months ago when you claimed the new one hurt your back."

"I was wrong to let it go. It knew just what my body needed, and if only I had given it a chance, I know it would have made me feel so very good."

I jackknifed into a sitting position and was quickly on my feet. There was no way in hell she had been talking about mattresses just now.

No. Fucking. Way.

"Wren?"

"Get dressed for school."

She checked the time and frowned. "It's still early. Besides, it's only the second day. No one cares enough yet."

"Yet you already have one tardy. Or did you think I wouldn't know about that?"

"You need to get some business, and stay out of mine," she grumbled.

I chose to ignore her as I pulled on my shirt and boots. I should have been the one with the fucking attitude. Lou was becoming about as subtle as a nuclear bomb, and it all started the night of my birthday. I'd brought her home after dinner, and out of the blue, she asked me if I knew the age of consent in New York. I could still remember her slow, sensual smile when I answered her.

Lou was seventeen. Which meant that at this very moment, I could lock the door, throw her down on that bed two feet away, and no one would be able to do anything about it.

I wouldn't. No matter how hard it was getting to hide the fact that I wanted to.

She was still too goddamn innocent. Too innocent to

understand or accept the things I had to do. The trespasses I made against her and so many others. No matter the need keeping me awake most nights, I couldn't use her that way. So I used her another.

Lou was my onus. My light. The very last tether to my soul.

I couldn't risk losing her. It was out of the question. She meant so much more to me than a hot, dirty fuck. I *needed* her, more than she needed me.

I'd been echoing that fact so much lately that it was becoming my mantra. The reminder I needed to keep my hands to myself.

Out of the corner of her eye, I watched her check her phone and curse. "Cathleen and Dan are already up. You're going to have to go out of the window."

I didn't miss the way her skin flushed or the way her teeth sank into her bottom lip. The last time I came through that window, my first attempt to scale the side of the home ended with me fucking up my knee. I couldn't even blame it on alcohol because I hadn't been drinking. I had just been that eager to get inside. It had only been a day since I'd seen my little Valentine, but I couldn't wait until morning.

Lou had sweetly knelt between my legs, pushing my control to its breaking point, and iced my knee with a frozen bag of peas even after I growled and told her not to fuss. I was trying to hide how fucking much I'd missed her. I was able to see the anger and hurt in her eyes, but her concern for me won out. Spending even a few hours away from her always left me feeling hollow and the hole only grew the longer I stayed away.

"Fine." I checked my watch and cursed as she had a moment ago, earning her a giggle. I long ago stopped being surprised at how much we rubbed off on one another. "I've got a run to make, but I'll be back in a couple of hours."

Her smile fell. "What kind of run?"

Hearing the panic in her tone, I stopped mid-stride in my trek to the window and whipped around. "What?"

She shifted nervously but held my gaze. "You aren't going to seek some kind of vengeance for last night, are you?"

I felt my nostrils flare and regretted my loose lips. Lou wasn't the type to learn her place. "Why is that your business?"

"Are you kidding me? You're in mine all the time!"

"Yours won't get me or you killed." I made it to the window before she spoke again.

"Don't you think last night was a sign that you should walk away from Exiled?"

I slammed my hand against the wall, not giving a fuck about her foster parents catching me in her bedroom, and faced her one last time. No matter what, I was jumping out of that goddamn window.

"Give it up, Lou. It's not happening."

"But it is! Sooner or later, you're going to have to choose!"

"Choose?" I didn't realize that I'd taken a step toward her until she stepped back.

"Yes. Between Exiled and your soul, Wren. You won't be able to hold onto them both forever."

"What do you know about my soul, Lou?"

"I know it doesn't belong to Fox."

"Yeah? Then who does it belong to? You?" I wanted to fling myself out of that window when I caught wind of the quiet rage building inside me. She didn't deserve my anger, but there was no one else around to take my frustrations out on.

She flinched but quickly recovered as her shoulders squared and confidence entered her gaze. "*Stay.*"

My fingers dug into the molding around the window, keeping me in place when I felt my body—no, the very soul she was so desperate to save—gearing to lunge toward her.

My gaze slowly traveled over every inch of her, not sexually but desperately, taking in her beauty and innocence, and I wished I had her camera so I could capture how fierce and how 'mine' she looked right now before meeting her gaze. I knew it would be a while before I saw those arresting blues again. I didn't kid myself into thinking I'd ever stay away. I was a moth, and she was the flame burning only for me.

Without another word spoken, I turned and launched myself out of her window but not before I heard her cry of alarm. I landed on my feet, and the shock that shot up my legs hurt like hell, but I didn't look back as I walked away from the blue home and Lou.

At least for now.

Deep within the mountains, I walked through the front door of a secluded cabin and found him already waiting for my arrival. He stood on the balcony overlooking the foyer with his hands braced on the railing and a tight expression. Shane stood off to the side, looking like he'd just gargled piss. I knew they'd be pissed that we'd lost the score, but *I* was pissed that we'd lost brothers. Last night had been a setup, and I wouldn't stop until I found out who was responsible. It was my job, after all, so I'd start with Harry, the goddamn mole who'd sold us the information. Shane enforced Fox's rule while I posed as just another lieutenant, someone who only called shots on a mission when, in fact, I was so much more. I was Fox's eyes and ears and, ultimately, the person solely responsible for keeping him alive. Most of Exiled would be foaming at the mouth for that honor, but Fox giving it to me was a stroke of cruelty, not generosity.

"I hope you're well rested," Fox greeted in his signature calm tone that I knew better than to trust. "I, on the other hand, don't recall sleeping a wink. How could I?" he continued when I wisely remained silent. "My workers aren't flooding the streets with the cocaine I was promised."

"It was a double cross. The informant—"

"The informant has already been dealt with." At that moment, not a single ray of light could be found in his eyes.

I scowled, forgetting who stood before me...or maybe I no longer cared. "Before I could question him?"

"You might have been granted the chance had you been present. Care to share what kept you?"

"Not really." There was no way in hell I was telling him about Lou. Fox didn't view any threat as idle, and I prayed he never knew just how dangerous Lou was for him. Every second I spent with her was a temptation to become the man she naïvely thought me to be.

He glanced at Shane with amusement that I knew was a ruse and muttered, "Kids."

The blood in my veins boiled though I gave no visible reaction. It was true Fox had taken an active part in making me who I was today, but I hated the idea of him thinking that he'd been an actual father to me. My mother had played the most important role before she died. She was the reason I was so torn between this life that came with money and power and the life that could be, a life filled with normalcy and peace.

I remembered feeling alone and confused, especially when her accidental death became a murder the second the driver of the car that hit her kept going. The case was all too quickly reduced to just another file discarded in a dark, overflowing basement. Eight years later, I was still restless with thoughts of her death. I'd been too young at the time, but as I grew older, the less I'd come to accept the explanations of her death. It felt too much like it was swept under the rug.

When Fox's focus returned to me, he paused, and I quickly shoved the thoughts of my mother aside. "Where are my drugs, son?"

The deceptive calm in his voice was gone and in its place a pitch that warned me to tread carefully. "We never got to them. It was too risky to try."

"You made this decision?"

I hesitated, and no doubt Fox noticed, but I couldn't open

my mouth to tell him it was Danny Boy who decided to leave the coke behind. Fox would only insist I present the kid to him for questioning. And for some reason, I didn't want him on Fox's radar any more than I did Lou. I couldn't explain or understand the feeling of being bound to that prick. I'd become aware of it the second we met. Had he felt it, too?

I might have asked except I didn't trust him. The men I called my brothers have always been easy to read. With a single meeting, sometimes a glance, I'd know what it was they desired most in the world, but Danny Boy? He was a steel vault that I couldn't crack.

"It was my call," I confirmed.

"Then I'm making you personally responsible for recouping our losses and evening the score."

I wanted to point out that the drugs hadn't actually been ours to consider a loss, but I knew it would only get me a bullet in my kneecap. Just last month some wise-ass recruit had learned that lesson for all of us.

"It's done," I vowed despite my uncertainty. I hadn't fucked up a mission in five years. Not since my initiation. My fingers flexed as I imagined driving my fist into Danny Boy's face again. I had him to thank for this fuckup, but since he was also the reason I was still breathing, I'd spare him this once.

Not for the first time, I considered Danny Boy as the culprit who tipped off Thirteen. The surprise and anger I glimpsed from him had been genuine but so had the other emotion I couldn't quite pinpoint. Sorrow? Regret? Guilt? I figured it had to do with him leaving Eddie and Siko behind, which was why I hit him. He didn't get to make those kinds of decisions and then regret them.

He made his bed. We all did.

Anger that I didn't anticipate surged through me at the thought. Something pulled at my mind, tugging on a distant memory, telling me he didn't belong in this world. I itched to get him far away from it, and I told myself it was for the sake of Exiled.

"Good. We have other matters to discuss," Fox demanded. He was about to order me into his office when a vision in cream satin cascading down her slight figure and flowing around her ankles appeared next to Fox. The long, dark hair that had barely kissed her shoulders when she arrived four years ago was clipped high on her head while her olive skin glistened in the morning light.

Fox eyed her lustfully while she held her shoulders back and pretended not to notice. Brown eyes so light they were almost gold landed on me and softened although they remained wary. I don't think I've seen her look anything else since arriving.

"It's good to see you, Wren."

"Grace."

"You're well?" she quizzed, and then her gaze cut warningly toward the man at her side as if she would protect me from him if necessary. As if he weren't her captor as much as her lover. It made me wish I had been there to warn her that day she'd crossed his path. No one walked away from Nathaniel Fox.

"As expected."

She studied me carefully before saying, "I was just about to make breakfast. What would you like?" It wasn't a request but an expectation that I share a meal with them. A demand only a mother would dare make. It made me wonder where she'd come from and who she might have left behind. No one knew anything about her other than the fact that Fox never let her stray far from his sight. I also wasn't convinced that it was infatuation that made her his prisoner. Maybe she was his prize, the spoils of some secret war he'd waged.

"He won't be joining you," Fox dictated before I could politely turn down her offer. "But I can never resist your cooking. Save a plate for me, will you?"

I watched her wince and then stiffen when he grabbed her ass. It wasn't anything I hadn't seen before between them, but what made it strange this time was when I found his gaze firmly fixed on me. It's true, I wanted to roar and rip his arms from their sockets, but for whatever reason, I knew he was expecting that. Grace was as good as a stranger to me, but it didn't stop me from wanting her far away from him. Defending her honor, however, would be a grave mistake for both of us.

None of it mattered a moment later when she tactfully kissed his cheek and stepped from his embrace with a teasing smile that didn't reach her eyes. She could have frozen hell over with that icy gaze of hers. Luckily, Fox hadn't noticed because he still only had eyes for me as I stood stoic and silent as the ever-loyal soldier. I knew he was baiting me, and I knew his anger over the failed mission last night had nothing to do with it.

"Of course, dear." Grace descended the stairs, and as she passed me in the foyer, she laid a soft hand on my arm and squeezed. Instantly, the tension left me as she floated into the kitchen.

"Quickly," Fox directed with an impatient wave. "Before any more distractions. Royal and Scarlett will be down in a minute."

I smiled at the mention of his teenaged twins. They gave him hell every chance they got. And just like everyone else Fox encountered, he had earned their resentment, Scarlett more so than her brother since she was without a cock and, therefore, served no real purpose to her father. It was Royal who would ensure an heir worthy enough for Fox's dynasty. It all seemed so sixteenth century to me but to each his own.

I followed Fox and Shane, who had been remarkably silent the entire exchange, into his office where we discussed operations and my efforts to weed out Thirteen's spies. Every so often, one would infiltrate our ranks to seek out Fox. Thirteen wore marks the same as us, so I proposed full-body searches of all recruits, but it was a temporary solution at best. It was only a matter of time before Father caught on, and they found better ways to conceal themselves.

The reality was that Fox's days were numbered if we didn't find and eliminate Father first. And now, with Jiménez demanding we take out Thirteen's leader before he even considered supplying us the pressure to do so was becoming insurmountable. Thirteen was older, larger, and better connected. We paid a few cops to look the other way and intimidated anyone who didn't see things our way, but Father had entire cities and politicians in his pocket. The line separating the once humble street gang from mafia were blurring every day.

Thirteen was trafficking anything they could get their hands on—drugs, guns, and even humans. Meanwhile, we were reduced to the crumbs of crime—gambling rings, prostitution, and extortion. It was a miracle Thirteen hadn't already crushed us under their shoe, but it was only a matter of time.

My heart rate sped up at the thought of Thirteen bringing Exiled to an end, and as always, I wondered if it was hope or dread that I was feeling.

CHAPTER ELEVEN

The Flame

MY STOMACH'S GROWLS GREW EVEN MORE INTENSE AS I DREW closer to the Pizzeria. It was a popular tourist spot, and I knew the perfect mark would be waiting inside with a pocket full of cash. The money would only be wasted on some corny souvenir, which would just be stowed away and forgotten once they returned home, so I didn't feel the least bit bad about robbing them. It was up to me to spend their money better—maybe on a nice juicy steak—so why not?

Wren said I had to be the worst 'homeless' person in history.

I honestly didn't get his beef. Sure, a steak was a splurge, but at least it wasn't drugs.

And in Manhattan—the central hub for tourists—there were plenty of pockets to pick.

Like the group leaving the Pizzeria now.

I could practically smell the money. It overpowered even the scent of the pizza making my stomach growl. They all looked my age, maybe a year or two older, so I figured they were skipping school for some kind of double date. A guy with reddish brown hair and tattoos *everywhere* abandoned the girl he'd been flirting with by the door and joined them. He didn't fit like a fifth wheel, so I figured he was the group's resident playboy. I didn't get a good look at any of their faces, but I didn't need to. I only cared about what was in their wallets.

They walked a short distance before one of the guys stopped

in front of a shop overflowing with souvenirs and ducked inside. His friends, the one covered in tattoos and the other with an impressive set of muscles, followed after him while the girls stood on the sidewalk talking. Well, the petite one with dark brown skin and doe eyes chatted. Her friend, sporting a messy dark blonde ponytail, brooded while only pretending to listen. I liked her already.

The guys were flashier, so I had been hoping to lift one of their wallets, but I guess their girlfriends would have to do. The broody one was distracted, too deep in her thoughts to see me coming, so I chose her as my victim. Picking up my pace and making sure to keep my head down, I purposely bumped into her, and while she was busy fighting to stay upright, I slipped my hand into her pocket, mumbled an apology and kept moving with her wallet and her cell phone in tow. The cell was just a beat-up flip phone, and her wallet only had forty bucks. I was cursing my bad luck and had half a mind to turn back and give the shit back when I heard someone roar my name.

I knew that voice, and right now, I *loathed* that voice.

I knew he would be looking for me.

That morning a month ago when Wren jumped from my window and didn't look back, I decided I wouldn't, either. When he'd texted that something came up and he wouldn't be able to drive me to school, after all, I knew he was avoiding me. It was the same song and dance, and I should have been used to it by now. What pissed me off the most is that I'd waited for him anyway. Every night, I lay awake waiting for my window to slide open and for him to fill my room as easily as he'd done my heart, but he never showed. On the morning of the third week—the longest he'd ever stayed away—I walked away from the shelter the Hendersons provided.

That had been a week ago, and I'd left everything behind. The cash he always seemed to leave lying around, the phone I knew he was tracking, and my foolish, broken heart.

I should have known it wouldn't last.

Even in a city with over eight million people, he always managed to find me. We might as well have been the only two people on the planet.

Before I could run, my feet briefly left the ground when he grabbed my hood and yanked me into him. "Give it back," he growled.

I wrestled to get out of his hold when his scent and heat began to cloud my judgment. I wanted him to kiss me even if it was hard and punishing. I had a feeling that sex with Wren would hurt so good. "How did you find me?"

He ignored me as usual and shoved his hands in my pockets searching. I huffed when he found the wallet and phone I'd lifted. I didn't get why he cared so much. He was a member of the most brutal gang in this city and had done things much worse than pick a few pockets.

Our names should have been Pot and Kettle. We were constantly at each other's throats to be better when neither of us would listen.

He dragged me down the sidewalk, and like a dick, he made me face the girl I'd stolen from. Now that I was getting a better look, I started to debate if she was rich at all. Not only were her plain clothes worn but she lacked the vibe that said she was better than everyone else. She seemed wary as her worried gaze flicked between Wren and me, and I could tell she was debating if I needed rescuing. I snorted. No one else in this world could handle Wren as I could. I crossed my arms and waited, not the least bit sorry.

"This belongs to you," he said as he held out my wallet.

Her attention shifted to her tattered wallet—another red flag that I'd misread my mark—and her big brown eyes became almost black.

"Thanks," she said tightly. "How did you know?"

I just barely refrained from smiling when he scowled down at me and said, "She does this a lot."

I knew he was thinking about the night we'd met. We had both almost died, but it didn't stop my foolish heart from painting the memory as a magical night that could have only been bettered by one unfulfilled promise. The thought of his touch sent a tingle down my spine while heat spread upward from my toes, melting by bones and turning my legs to jelly while igniting the ball of tension in my stomach. Not wanting them to see my girlish infatuation, I sneered at the girl whose pocket I'd picked.

"Big fucking deal. I'm homeless, and I have a better phone, and her wallet only had forty bucks. What kind of rich kids are you?" I cringed when I realized I sounded like a brat, but at least I didn't sound like a horny brat.

"Lou," Wren said warningly.

The girl's anger faded when she seemed to study Wren closely, and although I didn't see interest in her gaze, I was ready to scratch her eyes out anyway.

"Her mom was a hotel maid," the girl with whiskey eyes and brown skin remarked. "And my dad coaches high school football. What makes you think we're rich?"

"Been trailing you since the Pizzeria. If you're not rich, your boyfriends definitely are." And as if I'd conjured them up, their guys stormed from the little souvenir shop. I smiled knowing Wren's day just went from shit to diarrhea shit. A little explosive and a whole lot of messy. "Here they come, bestie, and man, do they looked pissed, but you can take them." All three stepped from the store, a unit moving as one as they tactfully surrounded us. The pretty muscled one with light brown hair and the greenest eyes was the first to speak. The tattooed one was grinning and rubbing his hands together like he had been served a buffet. He was so damn tantalizing I was caught off guard when I felt moisture pooling inside my mouth. Still, it was nothing compared to the tsunami, earthquake, rain, and hellfire Wren stirred inside me with just a glance.

I turned away.

"What's up, Danny Boy? You look…different."

"Harlan," the infamous Danny Boy greeted with a nod.

I'd heard his name come up more than once when Wren thought I wasn't listening. I never thought I'd meet the thorn firmly embedded in Wren's side. I certainly didn't expect some preppy-looking god, but I guess it made sense why Wren so obviously didn't like him.

I was fantasizing about how many steak and lobsters I could buy with his wallet when Wren said, "Aren't you going to introduce me to your friends?"

I was taken aback by the rising hostility in his tone. Sure, Wren didn't seem to like him very much, but his loyalty to his brothers was unwavering. Right now, he looked like he wanted to rip Danny Boy's gorgeous head from his body and play kickball with it.

Danny Boy positioned his body in front of the blonde with a million questions in her eyes, blocking her from view. "Why would I do that?"

Wren simply leaned around him and asked the girl for her name. If she were smart, she wouldn't answer. I knew he would never hurt her, but Danny Boy didn't know that, and Wren didn't want him to know. I couldn't see what was happening, but her silence was telling. Wren stood to his full height, and I recognized the approval in his eyes as he said, "You trained her well."

I blinked a few times wondering where my best friend had gone. I didn't recognize the boy standing next to me.

"We're going now," Danny announced. They all moved at the same time, walking away with tense shoulders and quick steps.

"I'll see you soon, Danny Boy!" My eyebrows rose at Wren's petty taunt. I'd never known him to stoop and wondered even more about the boy who had gotten so far under his skin.

Wren's eyes were bluer than ever when his attention shifted to me. "Let's go."

I fell into step next to him, knowing it was useless to refuse him. "So what was that all about?"

"Business," he answered curtly. "Where have you been?" He didn't seem interested in the answer, however, as he glanced over his shoulder.

"Oh, you know," I said with a shrug. "Around."

He signaled for a taxi, and I yelped when I felt his painful grip on my arm. He shoved me into the back seat, gave the cabby cash, and the Hendersons' address before turning those stormy blue eyes back on me.

"Do not pass go. Do not collect two hundred fucking wallets. Go straight the fuck home, Lou."

I crossed my arms and pouted. "I don't have a home."

He grabbed my face with gentle hands, and for a second, I thought—I hoped—he would kiss me. "Your home is with me. Don't run away from it again."

"I didn't—"

"You ran away to get my attention," he said, cutting me off. "You have it."

I didn't bother denying it knowing he'd read me like a first-year novel. "You ran away first," I said shyly.

I thought he'd deny it, but he didn't. "I'm sorry." And then he kissed me. Lips that I yearned to feel brushed my forehead before he pulled away, slammed the door shut, and pounded the roof. The cab jerked away, and I watched through the back window as he sprinted through the crowd in the opposite direction. There was only one reason he wouldn't see to it that I followed his orders.

I sat back and sighed.

Danny Boy.

CHAPTER
TWELVE

The Moth

LOU HAD CALLED MY BLUFF.

My heart had been in my throat for a fucking week, and now that I'd found her, I could finally breathe again. She knew exactly what I'd do if she walked away and played me as easily as if my notes were written on a music sheet. I didn't have time to be ashamed about that as I raced through the crowd. I'm not sure I even could be. I would abandon all reason just to follow her to the ends of the earth. Sometime during my search for her, I decided I wouldn't run from her anymore. I still had no intentions of giving her my cock, but I could no longer risk being on edge around her. I already had plans to visit Kendra this week and finally pick up where we'd left off when I met Lou.

She'd never have to know.

And even though my stomach turned at the thought of lying to Lou, more than I already had, I knew taking her to bed would be a worse offense.

I managed to catch up to Danny Boy and his friends since they'd parked about twenty blocks away. I flagged a cab as they entered a parking garage and waited with a direct view of the entrance. There was only one way in and out. Not even five minutes later, the driver's window of a red Jeep rolled down and the tattooed punk I caught eyeing Lou with a little too much interest for my liking swiped his ticket before speeding into traffic.

"Follow them," I ordered the cabby. One thing I loved about this city was that there was no shortage of weird shit happening, so he didn't bother asking questions before trailing the Jeep.

When we arrived in some ritzy town I never even knew existed, I decided I'd seen enough. I directed the cabby back to New York.

I'd always known Danny Boy wasn't who he claimed to be, but I hadn't expected some rich prick looking for a thrill. For a second, I suspected him of being just another Thirteen spy. He was just too damn good at being bad to be anything else.

I chuckled and told myself I wouldn't be back.

Unfortunately, I already knew it was a lie.

Danny Boy wasn't who I thought, but the current pulling me toward him didn't abate. It only grew stronger.

Lou didn't awaken when I climbed through her window, weary and angry, late the following night. My prediction had come true. I'd gone back to Blackwood Keep, and against my better judgment, I confronted Danny Boy.

Or rather Ever McNamara.

Heir to a multibillion-dollar hotel empire.

And the only son of Thomas McNamara.

Surprisingly, what bothered me most wasn't Danny Boy or his double life. Something about his father had seemed familiar to me. As if I'd known him in another lifetime.

I shook my head as I toed off the black and white striped Adidas Lou had picked out, swearing the sneakers almost made me look normal. I snorted, and with a moan, she shifted in her sleep causing the sheet covering her lower half to slip dangerously low. Before I could rethink it, I ran my fingers over the curve of her naked hip now bare to me. Thoughts of Ever McNamara fled to the recesses of my mind as I marveled at the smoothness of her skin.

It was a surprising contrast to her hardened demeanor, but I always knew it was a front. She was a pillar, no doubt standing tall and appearing strong, but one day, her cracked foundation would crumble, and I'd make damn sure I was around to pick up the pieces.

Even if she didn't want me to be.

There were times when she didn't appreciate just how seriously I took my role as her best friend. She claimed I acted like her father rather than her friend. If that was what she called making sure no one ever hurt her again, then sure—I'd daddy the fuck out of her.

Another moan slipped from her lips when my fingers reach the edge of her frilly blue panties, but this time, it was the sound of my name on her lips. For a second, I panicked, thinking she'd caught me perving on her, but when her even breaths continued, I realized she was still very much out of it, and a smile slowly formed as my fingers dipped lower.

"What are you dreaming right now, Lou?"

Her breath seemed to catch as I continued to toy with the seam of her panties.

"Are you dreaming of me?"

She sighed in response.

"You are, aren't you?"

A low whine escaped her.

"I know what you're after, little Valentine. I've known all along." We both seemed to stop breathing when my fingers dipped beneath her panties and I felt her smooth skin. "How can you be sure you can handle me when I haven't even kissed you yet?" I swallowed, cursing myself but then decided to allow myself honesty. At least this once.

She was writhing now, attempting to relieve the ache I knew was building, but we both knew it was useless. Nothing short of getting me inside her would ever do.

"You want to come." It wasn't a question but a statement

of fact. "But you don't get to come. You've been bad, Lou. This is how I'll punish you." I freed my fingers from her panties and stepped back. As if I'd snapped my fingers, breaking her from my spell, she jackknifed from the bed, breathing hard and looking around in confusion. When her gaze pierced the dark and found me, I remain perfectly still, my hands already in my pockets, pretending my fingers weren't burning with the memory of her soft skin.

"Wren?"

My eyebrow rose. "You expecting someone else?"

"Oh, I don't know," she said as she began playing with the ends of her hair. "Miles said he'd stop by."

She peeked at me from under her long lashes, and my teeth gnashed together as a smug smile broke apart her sleepy pout. She knew exactly how I felt about that prick who was always sniffing up her ass.

"Did you warn Miles that I'd have a bullet waiting for him if he does?"

Her smile turned coy as she peeked at me through the hair falling over her eyes. "Jealous?"

I didn't answer her. Instead, I snatched the thick blanket neatly folded at the end of her bed and began making my pallet on the floor. When I turn back for the pillow that I'd come to think of as mine, I found her on her back watching me with her legs wrapped around the pillow and her cunt pressed against the pillowcase.

It was a trap only a fool would fall for.

Sighing, I took a step toward the bed as she fought another smile. I was struck, and for a moment, I wondered if I'd still be considered a fool if I fell for it willingly. Only the sight of her blushing prettily brought me hurtling back to reality. Reaching down, I yanked free the pillow her head was resting on. Her head bounced off the mattress, and I laughed when she was momentarily dazed.

"That's mine!" she protested as she sat up in bed.

Shrugging, I tossed her pillow on the floor. "You seem to like the one you're riding, so by all means, have at it."

"You can have it back," she whined.

"No thanks. You keep it." Her scent was probably all over it by now, so there was no way I'd get any sleep and, frankly, neither would she. There's only so much a man can resist before taking what was so brazenly offered to him.

"I don't understand why you sleep on the floor anyway. There's plenty of room up here with me."

I lifted my shirt over my head and let it fall to the floor. "It's a twin bed, Lou."

"Then I guess you'd have to hold me."

I took a deep breath, but it wasn't enough. My control began to splinter right down the middle. Turning to face her, I saw Lou had abandoned the pillow and was now kneeling on the bed, her taut belly visible thanks to the crop top, and I could tell she wasn't wearing a bra because the top was so sheer I could see her dark nipples peeking through. And her frilly panties... God, those fucking panties. My cock rose as swiftly as my anger. Fortunately, for me, anger won.

"I won't be doing that now or ever, Lou." My eyes narrowed to slits when she attempted to step from the bed. "Do we understand each other?" My tone quickly had her rethinking her next move, and she was back to kneeling.

I watched as her sexy as fuck lips parted, and her eyes quickly filled with tears I knew she'd never let herself shed. A second later, she dropped onto the mattress and turned her back to me.

I stood there for a moment longer watching her, but she didn't make a sound or move a muscle. Tiptoeing over to the bed on silent feet, I grabbed the sheet at the foot of the bed, and she stiffened when I covered her with it.

"You're a coward," she said through clenched teeth. Her body trembled with the exertion it took not to cry.

"No, Lou. I just know I'll never be the man you deserve. One day, you'll see it, too."

It was hard not to crawl into her bed and soothe her the way I knew she wanted. She didn't respond, and I told myself it wouldn't have mattered. Nothing she did or said would make me touch her. She was too young, and I was too damaged.

My jaw clenched, and I wanted to punch a hole in the headboard when blood rushed to my dick anyway. I scoffed and finally walked away. As I dropped onto my pallet, I realized I had only myself to blame.

Lou was spoiled as fuck.

A monster of my own making.

My cock nearly burst through my jeans at the thought of corrupting her more.

"Did you find him?" she said in a small voice after a silence that lasted too long. I knew she wasn't asleep. We'd never been able to sleep much at all when we were upset with the other. Small talk was always her way of reaching out to me.

"Find who?"

"Danny Boy. I know he's what kept you away."

"I found him."

"Did you hurt him?" I heard the hitch in her voice and hated the thought of her losing faith in me even though I wished she would. Eventually, I'd disappoint her once and for all.

"I didn't hurt him."

"Why not?"

"Because—" I stopped short, not wanting to speak the truth out loud even though I felt it in what remained of my heart. I listened to her shift and knew when her gaze found me in the dark. I could feel her wrapping me in her cocoon.

"You're safe with me," she whispered, giving me the courage to speak what was in my heart.

I was lying on my back, so I let my head roll to the side so I could see her, too. "Because I-I think I'm meant to protect him."

At that moment, it felt like someone had taken hold of my soul as if it were my hand and squeezed.

Yes.

I heard the confirmation and felt the determination to do so rise. I bit back a curse.

I always knew Danny Boy didn't belong in my world. I'd been keeping my eyes open for any opportunity to get rid of him. I never suspected the world he did belong in, however, and it pissed me off to no end to know that he risked his life for a fucking thrill. My mind raced, unable to accept the answer as fact. It just didn't fit. He was too goddamn smart.

"Why?" Lou questioned.

"I don't know why. I just…know."

"Is it the same feeling you had when you met me?" There was no jealousy in her tone, only curiosity. She'd cut out her tongue before admitting it, but I knew Lou hated sharing me with anyone as much as I hated sharing her. We only had a limited amount of time to spend in this life, and I wanted every second of hers.

I averted my gaze until I was staring at a hole in the ceiling. "It's different."

"How?"

I took a deep breath, knowing I was about to step back on dangerous ground. *Too late to turn back now.* "Because even though I know you can take care of yourself, I'd never let you."

I listened to her release a breath before her timid voice broke through the dark. "Why?"

Against my will, my gaze found hers again. "You know why."

My tone left nothing for her imagination to figure out. Judging by her wide eyes and gasping lips, I knew my eyes had conveyed more than I'd intended. I was just grateful the dark concealed my painful hard-on and the hand I used to grip it as I, hopefully, stroked it back into submission. I, however, didn't miss the full-body shiver she tried to hide under the soft light of the lamp bathing her.

And just like I'd always known, she retreated, not as ready for the full force of my desire as she believed herself to be.

"Good night, bestie."

"Good night, little Valentine."

She was dead to the world when my quiet groan pierced the silence, and I used my T-shirt to clean away the evidence of what she had done to me.

CHAPTER THIRTEEN

The Flame

OKAY, SO, WOW. AND BY 'WOW' I DO MEAN *HOLY FUCKING SHIT*!
I was starting to believe Wren when he said I was too innocent for him.

I couldn't get the way he looked at me out of my mind. A week later and it was *all* I could think about it. It was searing hot, anxious, and full of promise. The image I had of him ripping the clothes from my body for the unfettered access his lips and hands would require still plagued me. It was so vivid, enthralling really. Better than high definition porn.

"Are you okay?" Eliza questioned warily as we walked home.

School had let out early today so teachers could have extra time for professional development. I had no idea what that meant, but I had to be the only one in my entire school *not* happy about it. That was just two hours without distraction from my thoughts. Although, if I were capable of being rational right now, I'd accept that it wouldn't have mattered. School or no school, Wren and the hard cock he'd tried to hide a week ago were the only things holding my attention at the moment.

"Fine," I lied. Horny as hell wasn't exactly a medical condition. Just a frustrating one. "Why do you ask?"

"Because you're sweating in the middle of October, and you're breathing hard even though you're a pencil."

"Hey!" I barked, a little miffed.

"A very *sexy* pencil," she assured me with a wink. "Definitely hotter than a number two. And lead pencils got nothing on you."

"Now that's better," I grumbled even as I laughed at her ridiculous analogies.

"So what's up, buttercup? I know something's on your mind," she prodded. She even put away the book she'd been reading to give me her full attention. The guy with sweaty abs on the cover gave me a pretty good idea what it was about.

Wren's are better.

"Nothing major. I haven't seen Wren in a couple of days, and he's not answering my texts. I could be dead for all he knows."

"I'm pretty sure the texts assure him you're not."

"Well then, *he* could be dead for all I know since he won't respond," I griped.

She looked at me then like she didn't know what to do with me. "Do you really believe that?"

"No," I said with a sigh. "He's too badass." I stubbornly believed Wren could kick Superman's ass if he wanted to, no matter how many times he warned me he wasn't invincible.

"Then relax. You know as well as everyone else with eyes that he can't stay away. He'll be back."

"What are you talking about?"

"The only thing the two of you have in common is that you're both dicks. You don't seriously believe you're just friends, do you?"

"We're just friends," I lied.

"Oh, please!" she scoffed and waved me off. "You're dying to get his cock in you, and you know it."

I blinked in surprise, not expecting this little church mouse to be so crude, and then I narrowed my eyes wondering if Eliza was as innocent as she seemed. "Believe what you want, but it's not going to happen."

"Because you don't want it or because you believe you shouldn't?"

Oh, I definitely want it.

"Both," was what I dared say aloud. We'd danced around the subject—come so dangerously close—but never, not since the winter's night we met, had we ever admitted our desires outright. I think we both feared doing so would permanently wreck the bond we've clung to for two and a half years. There were too many what-ifs to eradicate them all, and only one of them worked in our favor.

What if everything worked out between us?

What if it didn't?

The latter was enough to keep us both on our leashes. Right now, I was the only one tugging at mine anyway.

"That's bullshit, and you know it," Eliza argued with more vehemence than I believed necessary. I shouldn't be surprised though. She'd been team Wren since the moment she climbed into his back seat two years ago. I just figured that, like me, Eliza was harboring a secret crush although I doubt hers consumed her day and night. We weren't the only ones afflicted, either.

Unintentionally, Wren had become a popular fantasy among my peers and a reoccurring nightmare for their parents. Everyone at my school and in my neighborhood knew of him. The boys marveled while the girls adored. He had bulldozed and trampled his way into every aspect of my life and was now more my guardian than the Hendersons. Not even they dared to exorcise him from my life. I think to them he was more a relief than a usurper anyway since I was pretty sure that Cathleen and Dan were the reason why Wren always knew when I ran away. Duty would have required them to notify Laura, my social worker, immediately, but Wren was more than cunning enough to keep the Hendersons happy and me off social services' radar. I was just grateful her heavy caseload kept her home visits infrequent. My social worker was drowning in orphans, and I wasn't even close to being her biggest headache. I ran away a lot, but I never hurt anyone like many of the kids thrown into the system. For them, it was the only way they knew how to survive because there wasn't anyone to teach them better.

Wren wasn't exactly a squeaky-clean influence, but some would say he was my guardian angel. I almost laughed at the notion. There was nothing angelic about Wren Harlan. He was too powerful. Too fierce. Too potent. He could have been my white knight, but his armor didn't shine. It was shrouded in darkness, and it was only a matter of time before it swallowed him whole.

Over my dead body.

"What's bullshit is that you won't let it go," I retorted.

"Fine." Eliza's eyes suddenly turned hopeful. "Since you don't want him, can I have him?"

I was ready to rage and explain how that will never happen when I spied the smile she tried to hide and the mischievous twinkle in her eye. I was about to confront her when I stopped short, spotting Paula parked in front of the Hendersons.

"Looks like you spoke him up," Eliza gloated gleefully.

Excited, I made my way to his car, but Wren was nowhere in sight. Cathleen and Dan were both still at work, and even if they'd been home, I couldn't imagine them all sitting down for mid-day tea. The most obvious answer was that he was waiting for me but then…where was he? Against my will, my gaze drifted to the brick home across the street, and I could have peeled the red paint from the door with my glare.

I told myself that he wouldn't.

He couldn't.

He'd *promised.*

CHAPTER FOURTEEN

The Moth

"FUCK." I GROANED. MY EYES FLUTTERED CLOSED BEFORE I forced them open again and sat up in the bed.

Lou's bed.

I hadn't intended to stick around after dropping off film for her Polaroid and a new memory card for the digital camera I'd gotten her for her birthday. She preferred vintage, but I was hoping she'd consider pursuing photography one day—maybe investigative journalism since she was a nosy shit. She needed to expand her horizons, and I was determined to steer her in the right direction.

I'd let myself in with the key she still didn't know I had with plans to drop her shit off and get the fuck out of dodge, but I'd found myself sitting on her bed to clear my head. That had been two hours ago, and I'd woken up feeling groggy as hell. Once the fog of sleep cleared, I began to panic as I checked my phone for the time.

Seeing that it was two hours before school let out, I sighed in relief and stood from her bed. Her sweet scent drenched the sheets, which was probably what lulled me to sleep in the first place. I groaned as I headed for the door feeling pathetic. How could such an innocent girl disarm me so easily and often? I should have seen all her moves coming from a mile away, but she brought me to my knees at every turn.

Opening the front door, I stopped short at the sight of Eliza shaking a near catatonic Lou while calling her name with increasing panic. The only sign of life from Lou were the tears falling from her eyes. And I knew instantly that I'd caused them.

"Lou."

My voice broke through her stupor, and when her eyes found me standing in her doorway, I saw relief in them just before her shoulders sagged, and she began to tremble.

Cursing I rushed down the stairs. "What happened?" I growled at Eliza.

"Dude, how'd you get in our house?" she questioned rather than answer me.

I shot her a look that sent her fleeing for the safety of her house and took her place in front of Lou.

"Did something happen?"

I felt a surge of violent energy at the mere thought of someone causing her even the smallest harm. Lou was a bit of drama queen, but none of that mattered because when it came to Lou, I didn't take chances.

"Nothing," she croaked and then sniffed. "I was just wondering where you were."

My gaze zeroed in on the tears staining her cheeks. "You were crying."

"I had an eyelash stuck in my eye. Eliza helped me fish it out." She hiccuped before rushing around me for the front door. I watched her go, wondering if it was wise to stop her and demand answers. My idea of comfort would only damn us both. She took the decision away from me when she whirled around on the middle step. "What are you doing here?" she questioned as if it just occurred to her where I'd been.

"Two days ago, you texted me asking if I could 'talk' your teacher out of giving you detention, and then you told me you also needed more film."

Her laugh sounded forced as she crossed her arms. "So you thought breaking and entering was more logical than waiting for me to get home?"

I paused at the hostility in her tone. "I didn't have time to wait for you to get home," I explained warily.

"Then why are you still here?"

My phone chimed, saving me from looking her in the eye when I said, "I took a nap on your bed and overslept."

I heard her scoff and looked up from reading the message from Shane. Her arms were crossed, and I could tell she was annoyed but also a little…suspicious?

"Well, I hope you didn't wrinkle my sheets."

I knew then that something was seriously wrong. Lou wasn't exactly the neatest person. Sometimes, she made me feel like her mother.

Make your bed, Lou.

Pick up your trash, Lou.

Why is there a bra hanging from the ceiling fan, Lou?

"I was surprised to find there were sheets at all," I retorted, keeping my tone light.

She rolled her eyes even though she knew I was right. It took her forever to remember to wash her sheets, and whenever she did, it took her even longer to put them back on. Perhaps she was content to sleep on a bare mattress because she'd slept in worse places. I wondered if it weren't for my nagging or Mrs. Henderson taking pity on her now and then if she'd forgo them altogether. If anyone ever asked, she'd probably claim a minimalist lifestyle.

"Well, I won't hold you up," she said after an awkward silence. "Thank you for the film." She turned to leave, but I found I wasn't ready to let her go just yet.

"Not so fast," I said while pocketing my phone. "Why did you get detention?" It wasn't the question I wanted to ask, but I didn't have time to explore Lou's ever-changing emotions.

She frowned. "Don't you have somewhere to be?"

"It can wait," I growled. That sleeping bear she was poking at was now fully awake, and if she didn't tread carefully, we'd both be in trouble.

"It's like this," she said with a sigh, and I knew right then she'd make me sorry for asking. "Some girls were gossiping, and it was interfering with my daydreaming, so I told them to can it, but then my debate teacher accused *me* of being disruptive and decided to call me out."

"How did he call you out?"

"He asked me to weigh in on the topic."

I lifted a brow, knowing she made the teach sorry too. "Did you?"

"I didn't want to, and when he insisted, I told him it wasn't anyone's busy if he had a tiny penis, but to be safe, he should wear looser pants. Turns out it wasn't the topic he meant."

She immediately braced for my scolding, but I was a statue. I had no idea what to think. Knowing Lou, she could be telling the truth, or she could be lying, so after a few seconds of indecision, I spun on my heel without a word and walked away. It was the smartest decision I'd made since the moment I decided to look after her two years ago.

I felt her watching me as I headed for my car as quick as my feet would carry me. I shouldn't have looked back, but she was a magnet, and I was powerless to her call. She looked remorseful, but I knew better than to think it was sincere. I smiled, a promise, and it hit its mark, unnerving her.

Hopping in my car, I sped away before I could turn back. Lou was playing with fire, and it was only a matter of time before it engulfed us both.

CHAPTER FIFTEEN

The Flame

I WAS HUMMING *FIREWORK* BY KATY PERRY AND STUDYING MY PAINT-chipped toenails against the fluffy blue bathroom rug when my phone chirped. I knew by the chime who was texting, so I fished it out of the jeans pooled around my ankles and eagerly read the message.

Wren: This isn't over.

I smirked even though he couldn't see. It had been a couple of hours since he'd left, but I was clearly still on his mind.

Then why'd you run away?

Wren: Priorities, mouse.

I poked my lip out. I thought he'd forgotten all about his little pet name.

I'm not your priority?

I held my breath as I watched the three dots move for some time only to be disappointed. He'd changed the subject.

Wren: Where are you?

Home.

Where you left me.

Wren: More specific than that.

My heart took a few leaps of joy even as I frowned. The question had no relevance, which could only mean one thing. I'd unnerved him.

Smiling, I texted back.

Bathroom.

I watched the dots move some more before I got a reply.

Wren: Since when do you shower at night?

My smile grew, feeling girlishly flattered that he knew my routine. It was true I preferred morning showers to showers at night, but some days required both.

Not showering. :-)

Wren: So you're texting me while peeing?

Not peeing. :D

There was more dot watching.

Wren: TMI, Lou.

I shrugged as if he could see me.

Besties tell each other everything.

Just then, I heard Mrs. Henderson calling me for dinner.

I now had a dilemma.

If I ended the conversation first, Wren would think I was up to no good and barrage me with endless questions. Sometimes, I wondered if it was a ploy to keep me talking because he was too macho or afraid to admit when he needed me. When my phone chimed and I read his reply, I saw the perfect opportunity.

Wren: We're not those kinds of friends.

Does that mean we're the other kind?

Wren: ?

I gritted my teeth, knowing he was being coy. It didn't matter when I was playing games of my own.

The kinds with benefits.

My heart was pumping a mile a minute when I hit send. Setting my phone down, I quickly cleaned up all the while listening for the chime signaling his reply.

Just as I predicted, it never came.

Wren's natural response to any challenge was to fight, but when it came to our friendship, he always fled.

Sometimes, I wondered if I'd mistaken curiosity for interest the night we met. The stalking that followed hadn't helped matters, but perhaps I'd been naïve. Wren's speed was someone like Samantha who had more legs and experience to offer than I did.

By the time I made it downstairs, I'd completely lost my appetite.

The ache in my stomach only worsened when I caught Mr. and Mrs. Henderson eyeing me nervously during dinner for the third time. When Mr. Henderson took a deep breath, I knew I wasn't going to like hearing whatever was on their minds.

"I have wonderful news," he cheerfully announced. Mrs. Henderson couldn't contain her sudden excitement, making it clear she'd already heard the news. "I've been offered the position of warden."

While the Hendersons celebrated, my mind raced as I waited for the other shoe to drop. A promotion meant more money, which they could certainly use, but it wasn't a cause for the worry I'd glimpsed. Perhaps it meant the extra money the Henderson's received for fostering me was no longer needed.

"Does this mean I'm getting a raise in my allowance?" Eliza squealed, confirming part of my suspicions.

Why keep an extra mouth around to feed if that mouth was always causing trouble? More than once, I'd put them in danger of facing severe consequences whenever I ran away, and they didn't report it at Wren's behest. In the five years since my parents abandoned me, I'd stayed in many shelters—some good, most bad—but living with the Hendersons had come closest to feeling like home. I'd built a wall around my heart, and while Wren held no qualms about forcing his way in, the Hendersons had been gentler and patient. *A lot of good it did them.* I'd had enough of being handled with kid gloves. My parents were also patient. I had enough of that, too.

I no longer trusted kindness. How many people were kind because it was their true nature and not because they feared the consequences that honesty brings? How many have offered compassion only to rip out hearts when no one was looking?

It's the assholes who aren't appreciated enough. At least you could count on them to look you in the eye and tell you what's what.

Despite my fears, I was happy for the Hendersons. They were good people who deserved more but found it in their hearts to be content with the little they had. No matter where I ended up, I wished them the world.

"We'll discuss that later," Mr. Henderson patiently deflected. "There's more you should know." Mrs. Henderson reached across the table, and they joined hands. "The promotion requires that I relocate."

Eliza's happy smile quickly fell as her forehead wrinkled in confusion. "Okaaaay…so how far are we talking? Brooklyn? Long Island?" Light suddenly entered her eyes again. "Manhattan?" she squealed happily.

"No, sweetie. Your father's new job is in Austin."

"We'll be leaving at the end of the year," Mr. Henderson announced. There was a finality to it.

"Texas?" Eliza yelled so loudly that even I was startled from my stupor. "But that's on the other side of the country! I have a life here!"

"Eliza, you're only sixteen," Mrs. Henderson chillingly reminded. "The life that your father and I gave you is a figment, which will end right here at this table if you continue to scream at your father in my house."

I was both impressed and a little shaken by Mrs. Henderson. She showed remarkable poise in the face of her daughter's rage while Mr. Henderson was more contrite. He always had trouble telling Eliza no, whereas Mrs. Henderson was sterner in her rule.

"I know you're reluctant to leave your friends behind, but this move is good for our family. I'd no longer have to question if I'd be able to send my child to college," he passionately argued.

"But what about Lou? You'd just abandon her? And have

you forgotten what God thinks of money? *For the love of money is a root of all kinds of evil*," she recited.

My gaze cut her way, but she was too busy hurling Bible verses to notice. I knew deep down Eliza cared about what happened to me, but unlike God, I didn't appreciate being used as a weapon.

"Yes," Mr. Henderson said, changing gears and addressing me with solemn eyes. "Lou, the decision to move did not come easy. We have come to care for you very much even though," he said with a small smile, "you've made it clear that you do not welcome our affection."

Guilt made me look away, but then Mrs. Henderson spoke, drawing my attention once more.

"We spoke with your social worker about our options," she informed me. "Taking you with us was our first choice, but Laura didn't think it was the obvious choice."

"Or even possible," Mr. Henderson added. "We'd have to adopt you legally, and because your parents may still be alive, the hoops we'd have to jump through would be considerable."

"But we're willing to do it," Mrs. Henderson rushed to add, "if you are."

The lump in my throat grew larger as the fist around my heart squeezed tighter. I had been wrong about losing a home, but I *never* expected this. I didn't trust the hope I felt swelling in my chest, which was why I blurted the first thing that came to mind. "Why would you go through the trouble? I'll be eighteen in four months."

"Because it's not about delaying your independence," Mrs. Henderson said. "It's about having a family to call your own."

"For the *rest* of your life," her husband added.

I couldn't take the hopeful look in their eyes, so I looked away. Unfortunately, my gaze locked with Eliza's, whose overjoyed expression matched her parents. She seemed to have forgotten her anger over being uprooted.

"We'd be sisters, Lou!"

"Oh…" I was thrown off guard by Eliza's sudden excitement. "Um…this is a lot to take in. Can I think about?" I requested while keeping my tone polite. They didn't need to know that I'd already made up my mind. There was no way in hell I was moving across the country. I had a family once, and they abandoned me when I needed them most. My heart wasn't capable of giving another family a chance to do the same. Even if I could find it in me to forgive my parents and move on, everything I needed was somewhere in this city—losing his soul at that very moment.

The Hendersons were sound asleep when I crept down the stairs in the dead of night. The weight of my mother's rucksack on my shoulders didn't compare to my heavy heart, but I reminded myself I was doing this for them, too. Until tonight, I hadn't realized how much I was hurting them by keeping my distance, or maybe I hadn't been capable of caring until now. Starting tonight, I would no longer be a burden, and that was the best gift I could give to repay them for their kindness.

I'd left a note this time—when I'd never bothered before—telling them not to wait for me. There was so much more I wanted to say, but I couldn't risk giving them false hope. Instead, I finally gave them the push they needed to walk away. It wouldn't be their fault. This was all on me.

Reaching the front door, I didn't dare breathe until I stepped into the cold night. Wren wasn't going to be happy when he learned I ran away, but for once, I was going to save him the trouble of hunting me down.

Unbeknownst to Wren, I'd learn his phone's passcode recently and began accessing his location history, notating his more frequent destinations. I knew without a doubt that Wren was unaware of the feature, not only because his interest in technology was nonexistent but also because he would have deactivated it.

With the lifestyle he led, he couldn't afford to take chances. As his best friend, duty propelled me to enlighten him, but knowing it would come in handy one day, I selfishly withheld the knowledge. I just hoped it didn't cost him one day.

For now, I patted myself on the back for talking him into getting the iPhone. Before me, he had been content with his last phone—an ancient Android that could barely snap a decent picture.

Fishing the wrinkled slip of notebook paper from my pocket, I studied the list of addresses I'd written down. It was easy to narrow down where to start since two of the listings belonged to the Hendersons and my school. The most peculiar, however, was the addresses out of the state. There was a town in New Jersey called Sunset Bay that he'd been visiting like clockwork every Sunday. However, the address in Connecticut was new. Every day for the last week, he'd gone to some town called Blackwood Keep, and my gut told me these visits were what kept him away.

I studied the other three locations he frequented the most. The barbershop where we'd met was the only one I recognized. The second address was on Long Island while the last one was a mere blip in the mountains that drew my brows together.

Figuring the barbershop was a long shot and the mountains too far to travel this time of night, I settled on Long Island.

"It's too dangerous, Lou. All it would take is you being in the wrong place at the wrong time."

Shrugging off Wren's warnings, I set off. Maybe I'd find trouble, or perhaps I'd finally find answers to the burning questions I had about Wren.

CHAPTER
SIXTEEN

The Moth

I LOOKED OVER THE GROUP OF FRESH RECRUITS WHO WERE HANGING onto my every word with a mixture of fear and awe. Their ages ranged wide with the youngest being no more than ten or eleven. I barely held in my curse when he was brought in to be branded. They were getting younger every fucking year and rarely lasted a month before they were picked off by Thirteen or one of us when they outlived their usefulness or did something stupid. It wasn't often that they were lucky enough to be arrested and either returned home or thrown into juvie. I, myself, had only been fifteen when initiated, but I wasn't new to the way of life. My father had unwittingly shown me the way after my mother died and he mercilessly plucked me from my bed and the only home I ever knew in the middle of the night.

When the kid was called to get his brand, I watched as he slowly stood and trudged toward the chair. It was the same one I sat in to be marked, and unlike this kid, I never once questioned if I belonged.

The moment the kid settled, Larry readied the needle, and the kid immediately began welling up, earning a few sneers for his tears. Seeing my opening, I rushed over and snatched the kid up by his collar before shaking him hard enough to turn his brain into a ping-pong ball.

"What the fuck are you crying for?" I didn't wait for an answer before I started dragging his ass. The sound of the other recruits snickering echoed around the shop as I made my way to the door with the kid in tow.

"No one moves," I said warning the recruits. I knew they'd all rush out to see me beat this kid senseless. When they all nodded, I resumed my quick strides. The kid could barely stay on his feet, but I showed no mercy as I forced him into the unforgiving cold.

The moment we were out of sight, I stood him up straight and let my real anger take over. "What the hell are you doing here, kid?"

"I-I-I-I don't know," he cried, pissing me off even more. There was nothing bad or broken about this kid. How had he ended up here?

"Where are your parents?"

"Don't got none." He sniffed and looked toward the shop. "Is it going to hurt?"

"Yes," I said, refusing to bullshit him. "But you know what hurts worse?" He shook his head no. "Bullets. And it doesn't sting a little like that needle in there. It pierces, and it burns. And if you're really unlucky, it kills you. You want that?"

He shook his head even harder this time.

I quickly pulled my gun and held it at my side. It was abundantly cruel, but I knew it would get the job done. His eyes were impossibly wide with horror as he trembled. "Then get the fuck out of here. If I see you again, I'll save my enemies the trouble and blow your brains out myself."

I watched him run away as fast as he could, but I didn't allow myself to feel relief. He wouldn't be the last, and I knew there was no way I could save them all. Exiled grew its numbers by targeting troubled youth at their most vulnerable with the promise of rebellion and freedom from leadership. These lost souls accepted our brand and wore it like a badge of honor, completely unaware that they were signing their own death certificate. To leave Exiled was to welcome death—the only way out.

I knew there would be questions that no one would dare voice when I went back inside, but I didn't give a fuck. Exiled may have had no qualms destroying lives, but I did, and anyone who had a problem with that could see me.

As I started back inside, my phone rang, and for the first time, I debated answering.

"Harlan."

"There's a snake in my grass that I need taken care of," Fox greeted in code.

"I'll call maintenance," I answered, referring to our team of hitters. I had no idea why he was bothering me with this shit when Shane was his enforcer, but questioning Fox wasn't something I did often. I learned early and painfully to pick my battles carefully.

"That's already been taken care of," he said, earning my frown, "but this is a delicate situation, and it requires a personal touch."

I sighed, knowing my day had just been highjacked. Fox rarely stepped out of hiding, but when he did, my presence was always required. I was his eyes, ears, and his human shield if it came to that. "When?"

"Now," he said before hanging up.

I started for my car parked around the corner, not bothering to offer my team an explanation. Craven and Jackal, two of my foot soldiers, could handle the recruits.

By the time I hit the corner, my game face was firmly in place. However, my phone rang again, and the moment I read the name on the screen, it felt like someone had punched through my chest and seized my heart in their fist. I quickly answered, knowing it wouldn't beat again until I had answers.

Even though I already knew the reason for the call, I somehow still feared the worst.

"When did she leave?" I snarled while my strides became longer, quickly carrying me to my car.

"Last night," Mrs. Henderson rushed to answer. "She left a note. She never leaves a note."

"What did it say?"

"She told us not to wait for her."

"Jesus." I stopped short. My feet became heavy like lead, and it felt like someone had snatched my heart right from my chest. "What the fuck happened?"

She went on to tell me about some job in Texas and their offer to adopt her into their family. I'd already checked out of the conversation. I knew without a doubt that Lou had no intentions of going back and that scared the hell out of me because, for the first time, I wondered if I'd even be able to find her. I'd drag her back even if it meant I'd never see her again. Did Lou know? Did this mean she was running from me, too?

I swallowed down the string of curses rising in my throat, knowing the woman babbling frantically on the other end wouldn't approve.

Lou was too blinded by the pain her parents had inflicted to see what could be. That was where I came in. My insistence on doing what was best for her, however, meant never completely having her trust, and *that* fucked me up more than any of the bad shit I'd done. It was also the reason I indulged her recklessness more often than I should. I couldn't handle it if she ever turned away from me.

"I'll find her," I promised, but it felt empty. When I finally reached my car, my will was torn between what it needed to do and what it had to do. However, when I settled behind the wheel, all doubt was erased.

CHAPTER SEVENTEEN

The Flame

AS THE MORNING STRETCHED, THE SUN ROSE HIGHER AND brighter in the sky, making the day a beautiful one. For me, it only ignited my frustration. I now had a new appreciation for Wren. Hunting him down wasn't as easy as he made it seem. My feet hurt, I was hungry, sweaty, chafed, and tired. Of course, Wren had a car while I only had my legs and public transportation to carry me from place to place.

The house on Long Island turned out to not only be a dead end but a brothel. An older woman sporting an elegant dark bun and red cat-eye frames had answered the door, and when I asked for Wren, she couldn't contain her surprise. To her credit, she didn't bother denying she knew him, and after assuring me that he wasn't there, invited me inside anyway. In hindsight, I wished I'd turned her down, but Irma's offer of fresh coffee after a long night and my persistent curiosity made the invitation too tempting to resist. Irma was curious too, but she didn't pry—much— and when she offered some of the roasted chicken she'd made, I'd been ready to accept. Until a beautiful dark-skinned girl, who I'd only seen once but never forgot, sauntered into the kitchen with a sensual grace I knew I would never possess.

"You're Lou, aren't you?" she asked knowingly the moment our eyes locked. Her gentle smile was hesitant, and I didn't bother returning it. She was the first to fold and looked around the kitchen with a frown. "Where's Wren?" she asked no one in particular. "I didn't see his car out front."

"Lou came alone," Irma explained when I remained noticeably silent.

My conscience was begging me to get over my jealousy and be kind, but I couldn't. My gut told me Wren had been with this girl. To me, that was more than enough cause to hate her forever. She'd taken something from me. Something I knew I could never have back.

Wren said he'd been celibate since I stopped him from screwing Samantha, and I believed him though I didn't know why. Kendra was beautiful, and if I had her at my disposal, I'd definitely be hitting that and often. As always, pleasure and relief flowed through me knowing that Wren had been mine all this time even if neither of us realized it.

I didn't stick around long after that. Kendra had tried unsuccessfully to thaw the wall of ice I'd built around me, but I remained impenetrable. Not wanting to spit on Irma's hospitality further, I made a quick escape.

Now I stood in front of the same barbershop I'd huddled under for shelter the night I'd met Wren. I hadn't been back since that night, and recalling my near brush with death, my legs shook a little when I stepped inside. The parlor had an over-the-top masculine touch with tiled stone floors, brick walls, brown leather barber chairs, and black and silver accents decorating the walls and surfaces of the shop. It also smelled heavily of cigar smoke.

And standing alone inside was the tallest man I'd ever seen with a wild mane of golden hair brushing massive shoulders and a full, unkempt beard covering the lower half of his scowling face.

"A-are you Bear?"

"What was your first clue, kid?" He set down the clippers he was cleaning and picked up another, barely sparing me a glance.

"Oh, I don't know," I answered returning his sarcasm and forgetting to be afraid. "The fact that you're huge and hairy?"

He grunted, and I wondered if that was his idea of a laugh.

"When you're old enough, you'll appreciate the sight of a real man."

My nose wrinkled as I studied the man before me. Wren had been a scrawny teen with muscles just beginning to bloom when I met him, and as promised, he filled out so deliciously well over the past couple of years. He had enough to appreciate for a lifetime without going overboard. Some women were into men who looked like lumberjacks, but I didn't think I would ever be. "Don't count on it."

Tossing down the clippers, Bear turned and lowered his hulking frame into the brown leather barber chair before slouching low. "What can I do for you"—he squinted menacingly—"besides throwing your scrawny ass out of my shop?"

"I'm looking for Wren."

He froze and then stared long and hard enough to make me squirm. "You Lou?"

"Yeah…" I frowned as I shifted on my feet. "How did you know?"

"I've known you for two minutes, and I already want to put my fist through that wall." He pointed to the one behind me and then looked me up and down. "It makes sense."

Crossing my arms, I lifted my chin. "Do you know where he is?"

It turned out Bear did know how to laugh. Loud enough, in fact, I could have sworn I felt the ground shake beneath me. "I now understand why my godson has been so crabby lately. You're the little monster turning his balls blue."

I didn't react at first as I replayed the little bomb he casually dropped over and over. "*Godson?* You're his godfather?"

Bear shrugged and stuck a toothpick in his mouth, lazily twirling it around while staring as if he were bored with me already. "Unofficially. I knew his father."

"You're Exiled?" I unconsciously took a step back. His gaze narrowed, telling me it hadn't gone unnoticed.

"Do I look like the type who needs another grown man telling me what to do?"

"Wren is Exiled," I pointed out.

"And I wish to God I'd been there to stop it. His father would probably kill me if he were still alive."

I scoffed at the notion of Wren ever having a positive male role model in his life. From where I was standing, they'd all failed him. "If his father didn't want him to be part of his world, why did he bring him into it?"

"After Pam died, he didn't trust anyone but himself to keep his boy safe. Anything else?" he asked me a sneer.

Yes. "No." I had a million questions swirling in my brain, but I doubted Bear would be willing to answer them all. Besides, the only person I cared to hear the truth from was Wren.

"Good. Now get out of my shop," Bear rudely ordered as he regained his feet with a grace I didn't expect.

My bladder chose that moment to protest, so I said, "Can I use your bathroom first?"

His only response was to toss his thumb over his shoulder in the direction of the bathroom before disappearing behind another door. When I emerged from the bathroom, Bear was nowhere to be found. I was heading straight for the door when something shiny caught my eye. There was only a second of indecision. But my sore legs and feet and the fact that I still had more places to search won out over worry of Bear's wrath.

After all, how hard could it be to drive a car?

Bear's 'car' turned out to be a monstrous black pickup with a tint so dark I couldn't see inside and a huge grill on the front. It was intimidating as hell, but it was too late to turn back now. I was proven right when I witnessed Bear storm from his shop seconds after I began carefully pulling away from the curb. Shrieking in fear at the savage look on his face, I slammed my foot on the gas, and the truck shot into traffic, narrowly missing the car parked in front of me. I screamed the entire time it took me to get the hang of the peddles. The truck would shoot forward only to jerk to a stop a second later when I hit the brakes. All the while, Bear chased me down the street shouting obscenities and threats.

Once I'd put enough distance between Bear and me, I pulled into a gas station and studied the list of locations I'd written down. All that was left was Sunset Bay, Blackwood Keep, and the mountains. And while the logical choices were obvious, my gut and curiosity chose for me.

A few hours later, and after getting lost a couple of times, I pulled alongside a small lake that shimmered under the sun, and for the first time since I started my search, I didn't regret waiting to talk to Wren in person. I only insisted on doing so because he usually found it easier to tell me no when we were apart. He thought me naïve, and maybe I was, but I was also beginning to recognize the power I had over him and didn't feel the least bit guilty wielding it.

If I had called Wren and told him what the Hendersons had planned, he would have let me go and made sure that I never saw him again. In his mind, it would have been all for me, but a little bit would have been for him, too.

But if he had to face me, he would never be able to say goodbye.

Hopping out of Bear's truck with my camera in tow, I looked around in awe. The trees with their gold and red limbs were so tall that they seemed to touch the sky, and the grass was still a vibrant green even though it was the middle of October. As if suddenly reminded, I shivered against the cold seeping into my bones, but for once I didn't mind. The air seemed cleaner up here, and the quiet was calming when it'd never been before.

Across the lake, I spotted a sizable cabin peeking through the trees and lifted my camera to get a better look. People were my chosen subject and Wren my favorite muse, but this was all too gorgeous not to capture.

I'd never known such peacefulness.

Unfortunately, it was shattered a moment later by a piercing scream.

CHAPTER EIGHTEEN

The Moth

I'D JUST HUNG UP FROM MY FIFTEENTH ATTEMPT AT REACHING LOU IN the last hour when I heard, "You need to get your shit together."

Looking up, I spotted Fox's true pride and joy leaning against the doorjamb of the guest room. "Now isn't the time for your shit, Royal. I'm liable to fuck up that pretty face."

Rather than heed my words, he chuckled and stepped inside the room but not before checking the hallway and locking the door behind him. My antenna rose, but I said nothing as he moved across the room.

"Do me the favor, I beg you," he griped. "At least Scarlett was lucky enough to look like our mother."

I sighed and rubbed my throbbing temple with my thumb. I wasn't in the mood to listen to him bitch about his father. At sixteen, it was normal to hate your parents, but in Royal's case, he had every reason, so I took a deep breath and prayed for patience.

"Relax," he said, reading my mind. "I'm not here for another therapy session. I have information...and questions."

Hearing that didn't ease my tension. Exiled and all the shit that came with it was the last thing on my mind. Lou had been missing for two days now, and it was getting harder every second not to think the worst.

"Go, bother Shane." I was already stabbing Lou's name and placing the phone to my ear.

"I'm pretty sure that's the last thing you want." His suddenly grave expression had my blood running cold as I listened to Lou's voicemail pick up for the sixteenth time. My stomach clenched at the sound of her mockingly sweet voice telling me to leave a message.

I'd left several. All of them threatening.

I was tempted to hurl the phone across the room and watch it shatter and crumble against the wall much like my heart was doing right now.

Something was wrong. I fucking knew it.

The minute I surrendered to instinct, I felt a calm wash over me as I plotted the murders of the faceless culprits. And if I found Lou alive, God…

She was never leaving my sight again.

"Wren, man, I need you to listen to me." Royal's voice brought me out of the dark tunnel I was sinking further and further into.

"I'm listening." And I was, but I couldn't guarantee I'd hear a word he had to say.

"I overheard some of the men talking. My father's on a rampage. Apparently, he's pissed at you, too. Why didn't you show up to the cabin the other day?"

"Something came up," I bit out as I stabbed Lou's name again. At this point, I knew she wouldn't answer, but I kept calling anyway so that I could hear her voice. My eyes drifted closed as I listened to her recorded message for what might have been the hundredth time before hanging up and focusing on Roy.

Fox had been pissed all right. So much so that he stuck me on babysitting duty when he had an army of guards protecting the twins around the clock.

For most of the year, they were stowed away in this penthouse apartment and homeschooled. It became the Royal and Scarlett's gilded prison since Fox barely allowed them to see the light of day. Until we eradicated Father, he wasn't taking any chances on his heir becoming meat for Thirteen. That didn't stop Fox from preparing his son for his future reign especially since Royal was such a devoted student. Although he hated his father, Royal was hungry for power, and that gleam in his eyes grew brighter every day.

As for Scarlett, I shuddered to think of the plans Fox had for the daughter he made clear he had no use for.

"Yeah, well, I don't know how you're going to get out of this one, man. He's got everyone combing the city looking for some girl who saw him off a cop."

"Girl? What girl?"

"I don't know. They think she was a camper, but they didn't find a campsite when they looked. Only tracks from the truck she was driving."

My phone rang, and my heart leapt, thinking it might finally be Lou, but my relief was short-lived when I saw t was only my godfather. He'd been calling me nonstop for two days, but I didn't have time for his shit either, so I hadn't bothered picking up.

Sighing, I accepted the call and braced for another lecture. I didn't know who was worse, Lou or Bear. "Yeah?"

"Where the fuck have you been, boy?"

"I'm in the middle of some shit. Can this wait?" Usually, I had more respect for the man who tried his best to fill my father's shoes, but these weren't normal times. Lou was missing, and she'd taken my sanity with her.

I didn't understand most of his response because he shouted it so loud that even Royal was startled. I'd caught a few curse words and what sounded like Lou's name, but I told myself I was hearing things. According to Bear, Lou had stolen his truck after she'd gone to his shop looking for me. I didn't hear anything else he'd said after he told me some men claiming to be cops showed up the next day looking for her. They probably were real cops. Who else could have run the plates and traced the truck back to Bear...

By the time the last puzzle piece snapped into place, I'd stopped breathing.

The men who showed up on Bear's doorstep had indeed been cops—dirty ones under Fox's payroll. I hung up on Bear, calmer than I should have been, and turned to face Royal, who was watching me warily.

"What kind of truck was it?"

He didn't hesitate, and before he finished rattling off the exact make, model, and color as Bear's truck, I was running for the door.

Not wanting to turn shit to tsunami shit, I stupidly allowed Fox to send me here as punishment. He didn't appreciate loose ends, and the moment I befriended Louchana two years ago, she became a gaping hole. It was only a matter of time before Fox figured out exactly who Louchana was—and she discovered what I'd done.

PART TWO

FOREVER

CHAPTER
NINETEEN

The Flame

MY LUNGS WORKED HARDER THAN I THOUGHT POSSIBLE WHILE the sweat pouring into my eyes blinded me from seeing that the alley where I sought refuge was a dead end. The two men following me did, and they cackled with glee as they closed in fast, eager to do their worst.

After three days of being on the run, they had finally cornered me. With nowhere else to run, I did the only thing I could. Lifting my camera, I snapped a few photos, garnering the reaction I'd hoped for. They stopped short and glanced at each other in confusion. Taking advantage of their momentary distraction, I ejected the memory card and with nimble fingers, slipped it inside the wide leather band around my wrist. Eventually, they would find my body, and the police would have the evidence they needed to put Fox away for life.

And Wren would finally be free from his influence.

I'd never been very religious, but I thanked God for that much.

Fox's bullies, who looked like older versions of Butch and Woim from *The Little Rascals*, now stood directly in front of me, blocking my view of the street and any chance for escape. After I fled the mountains, I'd stupidly ran back home or at least as close to home as I dared. I didn't want to put the Hendersons in danger, and for once, I'd made the right call. After what I saw up there, I knew Fox was more than capable of murdering an innocent family.

"Give us the camera," Butch demanded, "and we won't hurt you."

My back was literally against the wall, but I still refused to cower. "It's enough that you're going to kill me. Don't insult my intelligence too." If Wren were here, he'd probably growl at me to keep my mouth shut even while his eyes shone with pride. Then again, if he were here, he'd kick their asses.

"Have it your way," Woim conceded right before he lunged for the camera.

I made a show of trying to fight him off, even though it wasn't much of a struggle. Once he'd taken the camera, I found myself staring down the barrel of his partner's gun.

"Fox sends his regards."

"I bet he does."

To my surprise, Butch and Woim chuckled. "Maybe I won't kill you just yet," Butch teased while eyeing me lustfully. "I like my bitches feisty."

"So does your future cellmate."

His smile quickly dropped, and with it, the idea of sparing me. It was just as well since I'd rather die than let him touch me.

"Have it your way."

Preferring not to see death coming, I let my eyes drift close as my heart raced, and my hands shook. I never thought much about the end or cared for that matter how or when I would go, but now that it was here, all I could do was think about all the things I didn't have the courage to do.

Like stealing a kiss from the boy I loved.

I had so many chances, and my only regret was that I didn't seize the day.

Even though I knew there was no way out of this, I couldn't resist vowing to take what was mine if given a chance.

As if accepting my vow, the sky opened up a moment later.

Instead of a ray of sunshine, however, there was a chorus of whooping laughter followed by wheels rolling down the paved alley. My eyes popped open, and I watched as the guys from the skatepark Butch and Woim chased me from as they crashed my execution. Leading them was Leo and Miles.

They quickly circled Fox's cronies, and the rest of the crowd followed suit, putting distance between my executioners and me. Butch and Woim began to panic as they struggled to pick a target, and I prayed that whatever plan Leo and Miles had cooked up worked. The only thing worse than your own demise was being the cause of someone else's.

"Now would be the time to run, Lou!"

After only a moment's hesitation, I took advantage of Woim's distraction, rescued my camera, and got out of dodge. However, when I reached the end of the alley, I couldn't help looking back and worriedly meeting Miles's gaze. He jerked his chin, a silent order to go, and I smiled. Mouthing a quick thank you, I took off down the street with the hope that they got away from Fox's men unscathed.

I also knew that I wasn't totally out of the woods yet. The city belonged to Fox, and after finding me so easily, he'd just made it clear that it was no longer safe for me.

Even though I had nowhere to run, I was eager to get there, and when I was out of breath, and my legs were weak, I planned to run some more. At least, that was plan until I was snatched from behind a mere block away. I tried to fight, but my captor was too strong. Stronger than I would have believed either Butch or Woim to be. I screamed when I couldn't break free, but that was cut short when I was turned around.

The moment our eyes met, that relentless sense of familiarity returned, and against my better judgment, I relaxed in his arms. Even though I could probably trace his entire face from memory, he was a stranger to me. Still, he couldn't have been worse than the men I'd just escaped. I was just glad he stepped in to save me this time.

The first time I saw him leaning against that pillar in Grand

Central, I wasn't close enough to see his eyes. If I had, I would have warned Wren. The second time I glimpsed him he'd kept his distance then, too. When I couldn't think of a logical reason that I would remember the face of a stranger in a crowd, I told myself I'd imagined things. If only I'd realized sooner that it was because I'd been staring at its likeness almost every day.

I knew at that moment it was Wren's father holding me. What else could explain the stormy blue invading this man's cool gray eyes at that very moment? Certainly not my emotions, as Wren would claim. If that were true, this man's eyes would resemble a kaleidoscope since I was feeling a million too many right now.

I was even starting to feel a familiar ache low in my belly the longer I studied him. It didn't hold the same heat or intensity, but there was no denying its presence. This would be Wren in twenty years, and I had to say that despite the rags he wore, I wasn't the least bit disappointed. Besides, I knew very well that he wasn't the homeless man he was disguising himself to be.

Looking down, I studied exhibit one with a raised brow. Underneath the filth covering his shoes were treadless soles and creaseless black leather. Even the fingernails digging into my arm were evenly clipped and free of dirt, not to mention the ratty clothing covering his clean skin smelled like spring. Whenever I spent time on the streets, Wren often attributed finding me so quickly to his ability to smell me a mile away. How did a seemingly homeless man manage to keep himself so impeccably groomed?

Well, maybe not impeccable.

The salt and pepper beard covering his lower face was unkempt, but it only made his masculinity more rugged.

The Ghost of Fathers Past pulled something from his pocket and pointed. When I heard the unmistakable chirp of a car unlocking, it occurred to me that I should be struggling. He was Wren's father, not mine.

"Hey, mister! One more step, and I start screaming!"

Of course, he didn't even pretend to take my threat seriously and without missing a single step, continued pulling me toward a black BMW.

Definitely not homeless.

He hit another button on the remote, and this time, the trunk popped open. My eyes widened at the sight of a long rifle with a scope and the shovel lying next to it. I started screaming 'stranger danger' as loud as I could. Unfortunately, no one came to my rescue before I was thrown inside and closed in complete darkness.

An hour after my abduction, I sat huddled in the corner of some ramshackle motel room watching Ghost, as I not-so-affectionally dubbed him, rummage through my mother's rucksack. It was clear he was looking for something, but there was nothing I owned that he could have possibly found useful. The only thing I took with me when I left the Hendersons' for good was a few changes of clothes, my cameras, and the globe Wren gave me to remember the night we met. The only thing left to take for myself had been Wren. There was nothing else I cared about. After about five minutes, he gave up and set it aside. "Where's your cell phone?"

"You could have just asked me. I might have saved you the time and told you that I lost it."

He shot me an indignant look before sitting down across from me. I trembled a little under the full force of his attention. "Why is Exiled after you?" he interrogated.

"You mean Fox?" I mocked. "Your old running buddy?" He gave me a look so black that I was reminded of Wren whenever I pushed him too far. "I saw something."

"What did you see?"

"Murder."

My voice sounded heavy with grief for people I didn't even

know, and I could feel my eyes tearing up. I couldn't stop seeing it no matter how much I pushed the memory away. Ghost didn't react at first, but then he nodded once as if I'd told him the sky was blue, and he stood up.

I watched him pull his shirt over his head as he crossed the room, and my heart skipped a beat. The muscles bunching on his back with his every move were definitely impressive, but what truly held my attention was the huge black bird, perhaps a raven, circling high above frightening woods and the two little songbirds—one blue, one gold—who looked lost inside them.

Unzipping the black duffel he'd brought in with him, he pulled out a black T-shirt, and a moment later, the tattoo was gone before I could figure out its meaning.

"Aren't you going to ask me who he killed?"

"You don't know who," he answered with confidence. "All you know is what you saw, and that's more than enough for Fox. He'll kill you and anyone who tries to protect you."

I lifted my chin. "I guess you should let me go then."

He let out a short, bitter laugh. "I'm not talking about me."

My nostrils flared when I realized who he meant. "I see Wren gets his brooding personality honestly."

Ghost had been peering out the window, appearing deep in thought when his head whipped around, and he stared back at me in surprise. After a few seconds, however, his expression became guarded. He probably decided I didn't know anything and was only fishing.

I decided to put him out of his misery. "I know you're his father."

He cursed and started pacing before he stopped to glare daggers at me. "Don't tell him."

"You don't have to worry about that," I said as I crossed my arms. "I don't want you in his life any more than you want to be."

The air in the musty room turned cold as he took a

threatening step toward me. I sat up straight, ready to put that defensive move Wren taught me to good use.

"How the hell would you know what I want?"

"Simple. He thinks you're dead, and you're clearly not."

"No, kid, I'm not, but I love my son."

I scoffed. "Could have fooled me." When he said nothing, I felt my heart break for Wren. "Why would you lie to him?"

"The only reason he's still alive is that Fox thinks I'm dead."

"But you've been stalking him all this time. Why didn't you ever approach him? It's not like you didn't have plenty of opportunity."

"Because I can't be too sure when and what eyes are watching," he argued. It sounded like complete bullshit to me.

"I think you'd know for sure by now if he was being watched. No offense, but you're not all that great at the cloak and dagger thing. Even I spotted you."

He laughed, but this time, there was some humor in it. "You saw me because I wanted you to."

I rolled my eyes. "Why? Weren't you afraid I'd say something to Wren?" He shrugged, and when he turned away, my eyes narrowed on his back. "You were hoping I would, weren't you?"

"I had a few moments of weakness," he grumbled, and I wondered if maybe it hadn't been as easy for him to stay away as I assumed. "I'm just glad you know how to keep your mouth shut."

I laughed then. "Your son wouldn't agree."

Ghost's smile was small as his eyes shone with pride and longing, and I realized we shared something in common. We both loved his son.

Still, I couldn't forgive him for leaving my best friend alone in a den of wolves, and Wren would tell me not to trust him, so I looked away. I heard what might have been a sigh from Ghost and then his footsteps as he crossed the room. Forcing my gaze away from the ugly-ass painting on the wall, my heart sped up as I watched him head for the door.

Was he leaving me here alone? Did I want him to?

"Stay here," he ordered.

"Oh, phooey. I figured I'd go for a stroll through the park."

I could tell he was fighting a smile when he frowned at me over his shoulder. "You're not my son's type," he said, and it felt like I'd been kicked when I was already down until he added, "but I can see why he chose you. You're good for him. You'll keep his hands full."

"You're wrong on two counts. Wren and I are just friends, and I'm no good for anyone."

He chuckled as if I had told a joke. "That's the basis of human nature, kid. We crave the things we can't have. Knowing we shouldn't just makes our desires that much more enticing."

He didn't stick around for a rebuttal. The moment the door slammed shut behind him, I collapsed against the headboard and curled into a ball. My eyes never strayed from the door as I anxiously awaited Ghost's return. An hour passed before my eyes drifted shut, and when they finally opened hours later, it wasn't Ghost I found standing over me.

I screamed.

CHAPTER
TWENTY

The Moth

I WASN'T SURE HOW LONG I STOOD THERE WATCHING LOU SLEEP LIKE some creep, but when she opened her eyes and started screaming bloody murder, I was at last convinced that it was her and not a mirage. She was safe if...not all that sound. I felt the tension in my muscles melt away when I quickly slapped my hand over her mouth to mute her screams and felt her soft skin.

She's real.

After days of no contact, I'd begun to lose hope. And when I got the call from the front desk clerk that I had a package waiting for me at a motel I'd never been to nor heard of, I assumed I'd gone insane.

Nevertheless, I vowed not to leave any stone unturned, so I came here half expecting it to be another wild-goose chase. If it weren't, then she'd surely be dead. Bear had found his truck haphazardly parked outside his shop just hours after the cops on Fox's payroll questioned him. Despite the extensive damage he'd mentioned finding when he called me, he'd been more concerned with Lou's well-being. The reports that followed were even more harrowing. Not even Miles and Leo knew where she'd gone after they saved her from Fox's men in the nick of time. She'd completely disappeared.

"It's me, little Valentine."

She tore away from me, and my brows drew together when she scrambled across the bed.

What the hell? I followed after her wanting to pull her into my arms and comfort her, but she let loose a panicked cry, stopping me dead in my tracks. "Lou?"

"S-st-st-stay away from me." Tears streamed down her face as she held her hand up, keeping me at bay.

"What the hell is wrong with you, Lou?" All this time, I'd feared my sanity when I should have been worried about hers. What the hell had she seen up there, and why was she treating me like I was some monster hiding under her bed? *Maybe I am.* I'd never hurt Lou, but right now, she was making it clear that she wasn't convinced. Had she ever been?

I took a step back and then another until my back hit the wall. Only then did she calm down. My hands balled into fists, but I tucked them inside my jacket pocket so she wouldn't see. Getting angry wouldn't persuade her into trusting me.

The only sound for the longest time was her occasional sniffle as she rocked herself back and forth in a ball on the bed. I wanted to kill Fox for doing this to her. This girl cowering before me wasn't my Lou.

"Are you going to hurt me?" she whispered after almost an hour had passed. Her gaze, however, remained fixed on the bedspread.

"No, Lou." I kept my voice gentle when I wanted to rage. Two. Years. I'd given her two years of me, and she still didn't see. I thought she had. She'd even begun to convince me that I wasn't a monster.

"Are you going to let him hurt me?"

My voice was hard and full of determination when I spoke. "Never."

Finally, she looked at me, but her blue eyes burned with mistrust. "Why should I believe you?"

"You don't have a choice," I said losing my patience. "Without me, you'll die, and I'm not about to let that happen."

"I can take care of myself," she coldly asserted.

"I won't let you."

For a moment, both of us seemed to stop breathing.

And then she lunged. Quicker than I'd ever seen her move, she grabbed a lamp from one of the nightstands, and I had only a second to duck before she sent it soaring through the air—right for my head. It hit the wall behind me, and by the time the shattered pieces finished falling to the shag carpet, she was out the door.

I caught up to her before her feet could even touch the gravel and was grateful for the empty parking lot.

"Let me go!" she screamed the second I snatched her up.

"Stop this." I squeezed my arms around her in warning, but she was so far gone she continued to fight me. When her chest heaved up and down, and her body temperature rose at an alarming rate, I knew she was in danger of passing out at any moment. Still, she fought, but I wouldn't let go.

"I hate you!" she roared just before she collapsed in my arms.

With my heart in two and my mind relentlessly replaying those three words, I carried her unconscious body to my car.

My fault. This was all my fault.

After making sure Lou was settled safely in the passenger seat, I trudged back inside the room and spotted her bag sitting in the room's only chair. She once told me it belonged to her mother, which explained why I never saw her without it. Memories were important to Lou, and I bet if I looked inside, I'd find her cameras and the moments she'd captured. It was everything she held dear.

I lifted her bag by the strap, and as I turned to go, something slipped through the open flap and fell to the carpet with a heavy thud. Turning, I was immediately brought to my knees when I saw what had fallen from her bag. With a trembling hand, I lifted it, and for a long while, I could only stare at the fake snow falling over the miniaturized city and recall the promise I made to protect her.

I gritted my teeth knowing she'd put her faith in that promise, and I failed her. Utterly.

Getting Lou out of this alive was the only way to fix my broken promise, and if I managed to survive it, I'd make sure that she never saw me again. Even in the face of my guilt, my heart rebelled at the notion of walking away, but once she found out what I'd done, Lou, without a doubt, would, and I'd have no choice but to watch her go.

CHAPTER
TWENTY-ONE

The Flame

THE FIRST THING I NOTICED WHEN I CAME TO WAS THE SMELL OF salt carried on the cool breeze caressing my skin. I sat up with a start and stared out the window in alarm. Where the hell was I? Night had fallen, and there wasn't much else to go on. Just trees and more trees on either side of the two-lane road. After about a minute of watching nothing but foliage go by, I found the courage to look to my left.

A seriously tense Wren gripped the steering wheel as he stared straight ahead, and I had the feeling he was forcing himself not to meet my gaze.

"You're awake," he greeted tightly.

"So I am." And then I blinked when I tugged at my memory but couldn't recall how or when he found me. "Where are we?" Before he could answer, I glimpsed a large sign in my peripheral. "Sunset Bay," I read aloud. My curiosity piqued when I recalled the name of the town Wren visited every Sunday. Suddenly, everything came flooding back—the Hendersons, my stupid determination to track Wren down and beg him not to let me go, and the brutal slaying I'd witnessed in the mountains. Everything that happened after that was completely shrouded. "Why are we here?"

"You need to lie low until I can convince Fox not to kill you."

I returned to staring out the window as my entire body went numb. I watched but didn't really see any of the shops and people we passed as we drove through the small town. "We both know that's not going to happen."

"It might if you tell me why he's after you."

My head whipped back around. "You mean you *don't know?*"

When his only response was to clutch the steering wheel tighter, I shook my head, pulled my camera from my bag, and after popping the memory card back in, I searched through the last photos I'd taken.

The last photos I'd ever take.

This particular memory had ruined all 'memories' for me. "This is what the man whose orders you so blindly follow is capable of."

Wren glanced over, and what he saw made him slam on the brakes, angering the driver behind him who honked their horn loudly. Wren didn't seem to notice the commotion he had caused as he swiftly pulled into the parking lot of a Wawa and snatched the camera from me.

"I know this guy," he said while inspecting the photo closely. "He's a cop. One of the only good ones left in the city." There was respect in Wren's tone and...sadness? Had Wren truly not known?

"And do you know the woman lying next to him?" Before he could answer, I said, "What about the two children next to her?" I took a deep breath, and it shuddered out of me. "He killed them, Wren. He set them on fire and watched them *burn.*"

"Jesus, Lou." He reached out for me, but at the last minute, I pulled away. I saw the hurt he wasn't quick enough to conceal, and my pain mounted. Any other time, I would jump at the chance to be held by him, but it felt wrong for him to comfort me when he was one of *them.*

"So no," I continued, sniffling, "you can't convince Fox not to kill me because I'm not going to let him get away with this."

Compassion fled as he stared back at me in disbelief. "You

can't be serious. Fox won't just kill you. He'll go after everyone you care about."

"Then there's no reason to worry because there's no one I care about."

"Really?" he scoffed. "Cathleen? Dan? Eliza?" he questioned, referring to the Hendersons. "What about Miles and Leo?" There was a pause, and I knew he was ready to ask if I cared about him, but then his nostrils flared, and he looked away. "I refuse to believe you're as heartless as you pretend," he said when my silence stretched too long.

"Heartless?" I echoed. "Your boss *tortured* that family, and you think *I'm* cruel?" Of course, he didn't respond, and I swiped at my tears as I released a bitter laugh. "Maybe I am heartless, but I never took you for a coward." I grabbed my bag and was out of the car before he knew what was happening. I made it two or three steps before he grabbed, spun, and sat my ass on the hood. "You'll smudge the paint."

When he stepped between my legs and cradled my face in his hands, I forgot to be mad. "You're fucking right I'm afraid, Lou, but you're *dead* wrong if you think I'm afraid of Fox for my sake."

I wanted to melt, but I couldn't be weak. Not now. Not even for Wren. "I'm not backing down."

His forehead touched mine, and he closed his eyes before inhaling deeply. I could feel him pleading with me even before he said, "Is this really worth your life?"

"Am I worth yours?" Afraid of the answer, my voice trembled.

I felt him flinch. "Are you asking me if I'd die for you?"

"I'm asking if I can trust you."

He froze at the same time I did. I wanted to take back the words, but I knew I never could. Wren treated my trust as a precious gift, and I'd just callously taken it back from him.

He lifted his head and met my gaze. "What did you just say?"

The black look he gave me warned me to back down, but the memory of Fox slaying that innocent family wouldn't let me dare.

"You heard me."

Wren had the power to make me do anything he wanted by force or finesse although he hardly ever bothered with the latter, so when he didn't do either, I knew without a doubt that I had hurt him.

"Get back in the car."

I did. Neither of us spoke a word or dared to breathe too loudly as he pulled the car back onto the road. The camera holding enough evidence to put Fox away for a long time, if not forever, was resting in his lap. I didn't take it back even though I knew he wouldn't stop me.

Ten minutes later, he pulled into the garage of a two-story stone and vinyl home where the smell of salt was even heavier in the air. I wanted to ask who lived here, but Wren was already out of the car and stalking toward the door by the time I'd built up the courage.

He didn't wait to see if I'd follow as he pushed open the unlocked door attached to the garage and crossed the threshold a second later. My confusion only mounted because I knew without a doubt the home didn't belong to Wren. If Wren had his way, his dream home would be completely secluded. Perhaps underground or in a cave, and you'd have to wade through shark-infested waters or wrestle a bear to gain access.

With a sigh, I unbuckled my seat belt and followed him.

Inside, the smell of cinnamon assaulted my nose, making my stomach growl. I followed the sound of beeping and found Wren inside the kitchen, removing a plate filled with cinnamon rolls from the microwave. The kitchen had pastel pink walls, dark blue granite countertops, frilly white and pink striped curtains decorating the windows, and white cabinetry. Our gazes instantly met across the center island, but then, just as quickly, he turned away and removed an old-fashioned milk jug from the fridge.

I watched him take the jug to the head and drain half the container before stopping. Heat bloomed in my stomach as I watched him move around in such a domestic setting. Every action he took showed how at home he felt in the space.

"Who lives here?"

Picking up a cinnamon roll, he bit into and chewed thoughtfully as if considering answering. "Does it matter?" he said after swallowing. "You're safe here."

Before I could argue, he swaggered past me with the rest of his cinnamon roll and disappeared from the kitchen. It hadn't escaped my notice that he never offered me one. Hoping to piss him off since he clearly didn't care to share, I snagged one from the plate. Before I could enjoy my sweet revenge, however, I noticed a handwritten note lying next to the discarded saran wrap.

Biting into my roll, I picked up the note and read it without a second thought as to whether I should.

Sweet rolls for my sweet boy.

Love,
Nana

PS. There's fresh milk. Use a glass.

A giggle escaped me, but then it died when shock and betrayal rippled through me in its wake.

Nana? As in his grandmother? As in Wren had a family?

Why hadn't he told me? I'd questioned if I could trust him because of his loyalty to Exiled. I never once questioned if he trusted me.

"What are you doing?"

I whirled around with the note in my hand, and rather than hide the fact that I'd read it, I held it up accusingly. "Why didn't you tell me?"

He shrugged as if it wasn't a big deal. It was fucking huge. All this time, I thought he was alone out in the world like me. As his best friend, I should have been happy for him, but instead, just like at the skatepark, I felt like I didn't know him at all.

"You told me you lived with a woman who took care of you. You never mentioned that woman was your *grandmother.*"

I expected him to brush me off as usual, but instead, he surprised me when he said, "I'm sorry I didn't tell you." I was even more taken aback by the sincerity in his voice.

I could only nod as I hid my surprise. "Where is she?"

"She left for one of those world cruises this morning," he answered as he grabbed another roll. "She'll be gone for a few months."

"Does this mean we'll have this place to ourselves?" I blinked at what sounded like an invitation in my tone. If he heard, he didn't let on. Sex should have been the last thing on my mind, but I couldn't help wondering if it would serve as a much-needed distraction. After all, I had made a vow in that dark alley to finally steal the kiss I'd been wanting.

Those thoughts, however, were shattered when he said, "You will. I've got to figure out how to keep you alive."

I gaped at him in disbelief. "You're going to leave me alone in a strange town and in an even stranger house to go running back to that sadistic bastard?"

"What do you want me to do, Lou? He has a price on your head that could buy anyone in the city!"

"Which means you belong here with me! You can't protect me from another city."

"Watch me."

Crossing my arms, I stuck out my hip. "If you don't have to stay, then neither do I."

He took a threatening step forward. "Oh, you'll stay. Even if I have to chain you to the bed."

"You wouldn't dare."

His dry chuckle had my lips tightening. "If you believe that, then you don't know me at all."

I gestured around the house that looked to be straight out of a Disney storybook. "Clearly, I *don't* know you at all!"

"You're staying, Lou."

"You're in for a rude awakening, Harlan."

My threat sank in, and a silent battle of wills commenced. It was all I could do not to jump in the air when he cursed and followed it with, "Two days."

"Three," I countered.

"One."

"Okay, two," I quickly conceded.

His lips twitched, and for a moment, I thought our friendship might survive until he said, "I'm surprised you want me around since you don't know if you can trust me."

And then he left me alone, feeling gutted.

Everything before waking up in Wren's car and after getting cornered in that alley came rushing back all at once, and I didn't get the chance to wonder why I'd blocked it out before shame overcame me. I'd screamed at Wren, accused him, and when hurting him emotionally didn't work, I tried to take his head off before running from him.

Wren hadn't said a word until now, and I finally understood why he was angry with me. Well, I was angry, too, so two could play that game.

I don't know how long I stood where he left me before my legs felt strong enough to use. The house was silent, making me wonder if Wren had left me here or if he'd disappeared somewhere to brood alone. My pride wouldn't allow myself to chase after him.

The open concept allowed me to see the dining and living room from where I stood in the kitchen. The large wall—also pink—adjacent to the maple dining table was a mural of framed photos and mementos, and it drew me to it.

The first to catch my eye was the photo of a beautiful girl with raven hair like mine smiling so sweetly at the camera in her green cap and gown. An older, stern-looking man stood next to her holding a sign that read Class of '93. She was flanked by a tiny, jolly woman who I knew had to be her mother. The resemblance was glaring, although she stood a few inches taller than her mother. She'd clearly inherited her height from her father.

With an urge to know who this girl was, I forced my gaze away from the photo seeking more happy memories but found an obituary instead.

Pamela Harlan had only been thirty-two when she died. I was already beginning to realize the significance of who she was and why I felt connected to her when I saw the photograph of her smiling and holding a little boy on her hip. He had dark hair, bright blue eyes that seemed to have dimmed with time, and a happy smile that rivaled her own.

I knew instantly who the little boy was.

He couldn't have been more than a few months old, but I could pick Wren out of a crowd from space.

He had chubby cheeks, and his hair was a bit curlier then, a complete contrast to his hard edge and the dark cloud that kept anyone from venturing too close. Until now, I thought I'd been the only one who dared.

There were more pictures, but none of them included Wren's father, who was still a mystery even after saving me. The next photo to capture my attention was a picture of Wren, maybe a couple of years old, holding a newborn baby. His head was bent, and the chair he was sitting in seemed to swallow his small body, but I could see the look of wonder on his face even as he held the baby tightly as if he'd never let anything happen to him.

Of course, maybe I was just being overly emotional but gazing at that picture, I knew I hadn't been fair to question where

Wren's true loyalty lay. Protecting was in his marrow and the way he took care of me…I might as well have been.

I wanted to push my pride aside. To run and find him. To fall to my knees and beg him to forgive me, and while I was there, I could show him in a more pleasurable way how much I appreciated him. If only he'd let me.

I was so caught up in my fantasy I hadn't realized he'd crept up on me until he spoke.

"I see you met my mom."

"She's beautiful."

"Yeah, she was," he agreed reluctantly. I didn't detect any sadness, but Wren wasn't exactly an open book or a myriad of emotions. He was indifferent until he wasn't, and then God help you. You'd never know how angry he was until you were already lying bloodied and broken.

"Were you there when she died?"

"I was here." And then he mumbled, "As usual," before walking away.

This time, I followed him out of the living room. I was getting sick of him dropping bombs and just walking away. I trailed him down a dark hallway and ended up following him into a bedroom. I stopped short just inside the door when I spotted the many posters adorning the wall, the cluttered desk in the corner, the five skateboards, each a different color, size, and shape, hanging above the black iron bed rail, and the dark blue and green plaid comforter atop the double mattress. This was a boy's room, and after everything I'd learned, I knew without a doubt that this was Wren's room.

He crossed the room and dropped down onto the bed until he was flat on his back with his booted feet planted on the carpeted floor. I stood there feeling awkward while he seemed perfectly relaxed. "Something on your mind?" he taunted without ever opening his eyes.

"What did you mean by 'as usual'?"

He didn't answer right away, and I could tell he was contemplating if he should. "I told you I lived here. My grandmother raised me. Pamela was good to me, but she didn't come around all that often."

"I know how that feels," I grumbled as I stared at the floor.

I could feel Wren's gaze on me when he said, "Then I guess I can understand why she stayed away."

I shrugged even though I felt anything but indifferent. "Your loss. Someone thinks I'm good for you," I pettily boasted before I could stop myself.

"Who?" he immediately demanded.

I shrugged and refused to meet his gaze. He stood from the bed and stretched, drawing my attention to his bulging muscles. I shifted against the heat and moisture pooling between my thighs, but the itch I couldn't scratch continued to build.

"Come on," he said. "I'll show you to your room." He moved past me, and I followed him to a larger bedroom with dark pink walls. I stared at the queen-size bed covered by a frilly pink quilt, which had so many decorative pillows in varying shades of pink that there was barely room to sit, before eyeing the ivory gossamer curtains. Besides the gray carpet and the white furniture, it was the only thing that wasn't pink.

"This isn't your grandmother's room, is it?"

"No." And then he frowned. "Why do you ask?"

"It's so...pink." I felt like I was trapped inside a bubble of gum.

"All of the rooms except mine are like this. I helped her paint after my grandpa died." He seemed sad as he looked around. "This was my mom's room whenever she visited."

Not wanting to think about the fact that I could be sleeping with a ghost tonight, I moved to the window. I was pleased to find that I had a view of the water and the small beach just a few paces away from the house. "When did your grandpa die?" I asked him while still facing the window.

"A heart attack took him a year before my mom died."

"I'm sorry."

"Me too." There was an awkward silence that he filled by saying, "You have your own bathroom."

I turned in time to see Wren pointing to the door I hadn't noticed a couple of feet from where I stood.

"There should be clean towels inside if you want to shower."

"Sure. Thanks." It was his turn to feel awkward although he hid it better as he continued to stand there. "Is there something else?" I peeked at him from under my lashes while trying to hide my smile. "Something you need?"

"No," he answered tightly before backing up a step, turning, and swiftly heading for the door. The moment it clicked shut behind him, I groaned and sank onto the bed. My heart was pumping wildly, but at least it was still beating. Right now, it seemed Wren's only concern was keeping it that way.

At least one of us had our priorities straight.

Half an hour later, I emerged from the bathroom, dripping wet from my long, hot shower and wrapped only in a fluffy pink towel. After searching my bag for five minutes straight, I realized with a deep groan that I was out of clean clothes. I was willing to bet Wren's grandmother had a washer and dryer, but the tired ache in my bones wouldn't even consider the thought of doing laundry tonight. The inviting bed beckoned, and after only a moment of contemplation, I undid the knot keeping my towel around me and padded to the bed with a sleepy grin.

I knew Wren wouldn't approve, but it was late, and he was in evade mode, so I knew he wouldn't be back tonight. After tossing all the tiny pillows onto the floor, I flipped back the quilt and slipped inside.

The cool covers lulled me to sleep in no time.

CHAPTER TWENTY-TWO

The Moth

I MADE MY WAY DOWN THE HALL LISTENING FOR ANY SIGN OF LIFE FROM Lou. The water from the shower had stopped almost an hour ago, but she hadn't come looking for me like I thought she would.

Lou was safe for now, but that didn't stop me from worrying, especially after the horror she'd witnessed. I wished to God that I'd been in those mountains. I wouldn't have been able to stop their deaths from happening, but I could have prevented their suffering. Something told me Fox's anger over my absence was the reason he'd resorted to such a cruel method.

"Lou?" I called as I pushed open the guest room door. I stopped short when I saw her cuddled under the blankets. For a second, not wanting a repeat of her episode back at that motel, I considered turning around and eating alone. I'd thrown some steaks on the grill while she showered, figuring she'd be hungry. There was no telling when she'd last eaten. With that thought, I crept to her bedside and called her name again. She needed to eat. When she didn't awaken, I pressed my hand on her arm and shook her. "Lou."

Her eyes cracked open a tiny bit, and seeing it was me, she immediately closed them again. "Go away," she whined irritably before turning over and giving me her back.

"Come eat."

"Sleeping," she replied as if I couldn't see that.

"I made steaks," I told her, thinking it would entice her. Lou loved steak, probably more than I did. She didn't respond, however, and when I heard her breathing deepen, I knew she'd fallen asleep again. Feeling my patience thinning, I decided to take matters into my own hands and gripped the blanket covering her. Before I could even consider the consequences, I gave it a hard yank until it left the bed completely.

Lou's eyes popped open at the same time the quilt fell from my hand and into a heap on the floor.

Shit.

Shit. Fuck. No. *Shit.*

I wasn't prepared. I felt like I'd swallowed my tongue. I'd seen Lou in various stages of undress before, but *never* had she been bared to me so completely. The curve of her ass alone had my heart beating dangerously out of control.

Before I could get the hell out of there, she sat up in the bed with her arms crossed over her ample chest. My mouth watered at the glimpse I got of her hard nipples.

"Why did you do that?" she shrieked.

"Where the fuck are your clothes?" I bellowed rather than answer her. Neither of us was right in this situation. I shouldn't have taken liberties, and she shouldn't have been naked.

Not when the last thread of my control was this frayed.

"*Excuse me?* I was covered and not to mention *alone!*" She then stood on her knees as if forgetting she was naked, and my gaze was drawn lower to her taut belly and bare pussy.

Jesus, her pussy. I wanted to reach out and feel if she was as soft there as she was everywhere else but knew it was out of the question.

"Why the hell did you come barging in here anyway?" she continued to scream. "Didn't your dear ol' nana teach you to *knock?*"

I stepped forward, itching to get my hands on her and shut her up one way or another when my short-circuiting brain got an idea.

Stomping out of the room without a word, I quickly found what I needed and returned less than a minute later. I was surprised to find even after all of her bitching that Lou hadn't taken the opportunity while I was gone to cover up. Instead, she now sat on her calves with her arms still crossed over her breasts and nothing hiding the rest of her from me.

My gaze narrowed wondering what game she was playing while hers widened with innocence. When I held out the pink cotton nightgown that would cover her from neck to ankles, she looked anything but innocent.

"Please tell me that isn't your grandmother's."

"What does it matter?" I asked, barely containing my glee over her anger.

"It doesn't because I'm *not* wearing that."

"Oh, yes, you are."

I stalked across the room, and she must have seen the determination in my eyes because she quickly scrambled across the bed to get away. Whenever I went right, she went left, and it went on for five minutes until she somehow slipped by me and ran screaming from the room. I was hot on her heels and at an advantage because she had no idea where she was going and ended up cornered in the den. She was breathing hard while I blocked the entryway, calm as ever with the gown clutched in my fist.

"Come here." I pointed to the floor in front of me, and she lifted her chin.

"Come and get me."

Her voice sounded husky and sensual, and I bared my teeth. She was starting to look like a tasty treat, and I was damned hungry.

"You'll be sorry," I warned her.

"I bet I won't."

She grinned as I took a cautious step inside while she stood perfectly still with her hands clasped behind her back. I could see all of her, and more and more, it was becoming harder to tell who the predator was and who was the prey.

"I know what you're doing," I said as I began to circle her, drawing closer each time.

She never bothered to run even though her path to the exit was wide open. It didn't matter since we both knew I'd catch her long before she made it to the door.

"What am I doing?"

"You're trying to get me to fuck you," I whispered in her ear. She shivered at my closeness while I pressed my finger gently under her chin and lifted her gaze to meet mine. "That's never going to happen."

It was a lie that I'd told myself many times, but this time, with my cock hard enough to cut a diamond pressed against her naked hip, it was impossible to believe.

Especially when she said, "Then maybe I'll fuck you."

I froze, and it gave her the opening she needed.

Lou bolted for the door, but even in my shock, she still wasn't quick enough. Or maybe I was just that determined not to let her get away. The moment my arm locked around her waist, the fight left her body, and she relaxed against me. My cock pressed against her ass, and I knew then that there was no other place she belonged. Cursing her, I tossed her over my shoulder, and my long strides carried us from the room and down the hallway.

To my room.

Storming across the threshold, I angrily tossed Lou on my bed, and her bouncing tits caught my eye as she stared up at me in nervous excitement. My mouth watered at just the thought of sucking her nipples until they were tender and swollen and she was writhing, begging to be full of me, but I didn't allow myself to stare too long. Grabbing her hip, I flipped her onto her stomach and admired the slender slope of her back.

"Wait," she said suddenly panicking. "What are you—"

My palm striking her ass cut her off, and she cried out in shock. "Shut up."

I then stepped away before I could be tempted to do it again. Lou had been begging to have her pert little ass spanked. What was one more indulgence?

Cursing again, I retreated until my back was pressed against the wall, and I closed my eyes. I wanted to fuck Lou more than I wanted to live, but Lou had become the very air I breathed. Without her, I was nothing. If I kept her innocence intact, I might stand a chance when she found out what I did five years ago.

I didn't hear Lou get up from the bed, didn't hear her coming until I felt her warm body pressed against mine and her tiny hands resting on my shoulders, easing the tension from them. My eyes opened, and without a second thought, I grabbed her waist and was amazed at how well she fit in my hands. She was slim with subtle curves—much more than she'd had when I met her. Without a doubt, I wouldn't mind feeling her with more, but sadly, it wouldn't matter if she were built like a wall or a brick house. She had the power to humble me with the bat of an eyelash. Whenever I was with her, I was little more than a thirteen-year-old boy seconds away from ruining a good pair of jeans.

"Why won't you make love to me?"

I licked my lips, and her own parted when it drew her gaze to them. "Because you think you can handle me, but you can't. I won't lay you down and stare lovingly into your eyes while I take you. I'll bend you over, Lou. I'll pop your fucking cherry and steal your every waking thought when I'm done." Leaning down, I growled in her ear. "Is that what you're asking me to do?"

She didn't respond. For the first time since meeting her two and a half years ago, she'd chosen silence. I knew better than to mistake it for compliance, though. Behind those baby blues, she wasn't considering surrender. She was plotting mine.

"I won't be gentle," I pressed almost desperately. "You know I won't."

She lifted her hand and palmed my cheek while her eyes lit with understanding. "Maybe that's why I chose you."

"Louchana...I'll ruin you."

"Good. I want to be bad." She stood on her tiptoes and said, "I want to be yours." I felt her teeth nip my ear, and the last thread of my control snapped.

"Yeah?" I asked her, and she eagerly nodded, missing the danger in my tone. "Go to my bed."

She paused as if surprised by my surrender or afraid. Maybe it was both. Regardless of the reason, I lost it.

"Goddamn it, Lou!"

She cried out when I gripped her hair in one hand and dug my fingers in her hips with the other.

"There's no time to think long and hard, little Valentine. I'm long and hard for you *right now.*"

I was sure she knew that by now. The evidence pressed against her belly, and I could tell by her trembling that she was intimated. Perhaps she was realizing for the first time that she was out of her depth. I wished like hell it wasn't too late to turn back, but I was too far gone to care about right or wrong.

The only person who could stop this now was her.

And a moment later, she did.

"Why are you doing this?" she tearfully demanded.

Pushing her away, I took a deep breath. "Because I'm no good for you, and now you know it, too."

Her nostrils flared as she hugged herself, and I could only imagine how vulnerable she felt right now. "The only thing I know is that you're afraid. Maybe even more than me."

Stalking over to my dresser, I found a clean white T-shirt, and she didn't fight me this time when I slipped it over her head. The minute she was covered, I felt my control renew.

"Get in the bed."

She hurried to do what I ordered, and I watched her crawl under the covers. The way she pulled them up to her chin, I knew she wouldn't be changing her mind about sex. At least not tonight. Leaning over, I kissed her forehead, the only placed she allowed me access before heading for the door.

Last night, after I left Lou alone in my bed, I'd gotten into my grandmother's gin, and after finishing half the bottle, I passed out on the couch. This morning, as my head threatened to split in two, I realized I was doomed to suffer the consequences of last night.

I'd been a dick and an idiot, but at least Lou was still a virgin. My conscience was clear even if my balls weren't. I couldn't even be bothered to beat my dick knowing it would never be enough. So I'd gone to sleep hard, drunk, and utterly pathetic. I had hoped for escape, but all I did was dream about taking what she so naïvely had offered.

Groaning, I tried to sit up but quickly realized there was a weight on my chest keeping me down. It took some effort to get my eyes open. Sleep clouded my vision, and the room spun, but I still recognized Lou's dark head of hair and her hand resting on my chest. Her leg was hooked around my thigh causing my T-shirt she wore to bunch around her waist. My hand found her bare ass, and the moment I felt her warm, soft skin, I was up and at 'em. My hangover forgotten as well as my honor, I allowed my fingers to slip over the curve of her ass and down to her thigh. I didn't stop. Her heat became searing the closer my fingers got to her pussy, and I licked my dry lips anticipating finding her wet and ready for me.

I'd only just grazed her swollen lips and felt the wetness pooling there when I heard, "Morning, bestie."

Those words were like a bucket of ice water, and I was grateful for them. I'd been so preoccupied with touching Lou that I hadn't noticed she had awakened. I'd almost—

My throat felt clogged when I tried to speak, so I cleared it and tried again. "What are you doing here?"

She smiled and stretched lazily. "Getting groped by you in my sleep, apparently."

I shot to my feet, and she yelped as she tumbled to the floor. I immediately held out my hand to help her, and she glared at me before shoving it away and standing.

We stared at each other, neither of us willing to say what we were thinking until I broke the silence. "I'll make coffee."

She nodded and looked away, and when I found the courage to look over my shoulder, she was gone. I was pouring coffee into two of my grandmother's mugs when she returned, clutching her rucksack. I almost lost my grip on the coffee pot when panic set in. Was she leaving? Had I gone too far?

"You're not leaving."

Her brows drew together, confusion marking her pretty face. "I'm not leaving," she confirmed. "But I do need to do laundry."

It was my turn to frown. "You've only been gone four days."

"I packed light." She then dropped her bag on the counter and grabbed one of the steaming mugs.

I sat down and watched her sip at the coffee with a look of pleasure. I wanted more than anything to keep that expression on her face. I'd work tirelessly for hours, all night if I had to.

"I'm glad to know you're good for something," she praised, chasing away my thoughts.

You have no idea. "I didn't think you were going back," I said, referring to the Hendersons.

"I wasn't," she admitted casually. "I was trying to find you so we could run away together." She winked, and though her tone was playful, I knew she was completely serious.

"I would have," I blurted unwisely. It was the first honest thing I'd said in a while. "I would have run away with you." I had no idea where we'd go or what we'd do, but I would have taken us far away from the city and the people that had stolen so much from us already. And consequently, I would have spent the rest of my life running from my past and hers.

She had no idea how deeply they were entwined.

Our gazes connected over her coffee mug, and I had the feeling she was as lost in mine as I was in hers. "I know."

Nodding, I took a quick sip of my coffee before stepping around the island and grabbing her bag. "Come on."

She followed me to the laundry room where I watched her dump a week's worth of clothes inside the machine without bothering to separate them. When she reached for the bleach instead of detergent, I quickly stepped in.

"Jesus, Lou! You're going to ruin your clothes." I removed the white T-shirt she'd shoved inside with a pair of red jeans. "Haven't you ever done laundry?"

"Of course, I have. I'm just a little distracted by your hovering."

Shaking my head, I nudged her aside and took over while she hopped on the dryer and began swinging her legs. I could feel her studying me, and after last night and this morning, I was wary of what she might be thinking. Knowing Lou, she was devising a plan to get what she wanted from me.

"What?" I growled when the heat from her stare grew too intense.

Her eyebrow lifted when I met her gaze. "You're really grumpy this morning. You know that?"

I didn't respond as I started the machine and then fled. Of course, I was irritable. My balls were full.

"Do you want to talk about last night?" she inquired shyly as she trailed me back to the kitchen.

"No."

"I'm sorry I didn't—"

I turned on her before she could finish, and she stared back at me wide-eyed. "Don't you dare apologize to me. I'm the one who knew better."

"But I—"

"You weren't ready."

Her gaze hardened before she closed the distance between us and pressed her breasts against my chest. I could feel her hard nipples poking through my T-shirt that she still wore—and nothing else.

"I'm sure it seemed that way when you were scaring me on purpose."

"And if you were ready to be fucked, Lou, I wouldn't have succeeded."

"You were a dick, and you hurt me. Are you telling me women like that?"

I shrugged and turned away. "Some do."

She huffed and crossed her arms. "Well, I don't."

I laughed and shoved aside the need to prove her wrong. "You don't know what you like, Lou. You haven't had a chance to find out."

"Gee," she retorted sarcastically, "I wonder why."

"Because you're not mine to take."

"I think that's my decision."

"And mine," I told her with a smug smile. "Since it takes two to tango."

She quickly wiped the smirk off my face, however, when she turned for the stairs and threw over her shoulder. "Not really."

CHAPTER
TWENTY-THREE

The Flame

A S EXPECTED, WREN WAS TOO SMART TO FOLLOW ME UPSTAIRS after I dropped that bomb and walked away, but that didn't mean he stayed away. An hour later, I was beginning to doze off from sheer boredom when he walked into the guest room with an arm full of my freshly washed clothes and snarled at me to get dressed. He'd taken a shower and put on black jeans and a matching black long-sleeve shirt that hugged his chest. If it were his mission to torture me, he had certainly succeeded. The clothes paired with his dangerous natural magnetism made him seem more unattainable than ever.

Before he could escape, I stood and pulled his T-shirt over my head, not feeling as shy as I might have been before last night. To my surprise, he didn't turn away. He leaned against the wall near the door and let his eyes roam every inch. He'd probably assumed I'd back down as I had last night, but the joke would be on him. I had too much riding on his surrender.

I let my gaze drop and didn't have to question if he liked what he saw. Seeing him this way pushed aside the urge to cover myself. "You still want me to get dressed?" I asked him with more confidence than I felt.

"No...but I need you to." He swallowed hard. "*Please.*"

"And what about what I need?"

I didn't give him a chance to respond before I sank back onto the bed. I wasn't sure how far I was willing to go in my seduction, but we were both about to find out. Together.

I parted my legs. Slowly. So slow that he could have stopped me before it was too late, but he didn't. He watched as I opened myself to him, and when I was done, he devoured me with his eyes. They were so blue that for a moment, I was startled, and left trembling in the wake of his emotions. Lifting my hand, I wanted to show him just how close to the edge he'd pushed me, but not quite having the courage, I placed my hand on my knee instead.

"Best friends are supposed to take care of each other." His gaze found mine at the same time my hand started to slide up my thigh. It was all I could do not to close my eyes and sever the connection. "You're always there for me…except when I need you most."

My hand was now close enough to feel the heat between my legs rising as anticipation mounted. This wouldn't be the first time I'd touched myself, but in the past, it was out of curiosity. Only now did I understand that I'd been building up to this moment. To have the courage to take what was rightfully mine.

I sighed as if all were truly lost. "I guess I'll just have to be there for myself."

"Don't," he pleaded, but it was too late. My eyes fluttered, threatening to close at the sensation my fingers were stirring. Wren's chest moved up and down rapidly as he inched closer against his will.

I knew what he wanted, so I offered him a shaky smile despite my agony and let my legs fall to the side. The moment he saw my fingers circling my clit, he groaned, and my stomach clenched at the sound.

I kept my touch light and unhurried, building my desire until the fire kindling in Wren's gaze was a raging inferno. It was enough, more than enough. Feeling my orgasm rising too quickly, I abandoned my clit with a whimper. There was no denying how much I wanted Wren. The sound of my fingers gently massaging and slowly exploring made it clear. And when the tip of my middle finger teased my entrance, I didn't think twice about filling my pussy.

He sank onto the bed to get a closer look, and I watched him lick his lips whenever I withdrew only to push deeper. At that moment, I found a way to win his surrender. My hand trembled as I moved my soaked fingers to his lips.

His eyes went wide when he saw my intent. Before he could plead some more for mercy, I traced his lips. He closed his eyes tightly, and after only a second, he opened them enough for me to slip inside and give him a taste of what he'd denied himself. The moment my fingers touched his tongue, he growled.

With my other hand, I found my clit again, chasing my orgasm while he hungrily sucked my fingers. "Do you see?" I asked shakily. I was so close. "Do you see how good it could be?"

He opened his eyes, and his voice was thick when he spoke. "I've always known."

"Then touch me," I whimpered as my fingers sped up. I was at the edge ready to fall over. "Take the hurt away. Ease the need. Make us both whole again."

He dropped his head to my thigh, and I heard him inhale deeply before he pushed my fingers away and licked me there. Just once, but it was more than enough. I threw my head back, and my toes curled as I stiffened and came with a startled cry. It was more powerful than anything I'd experienced alone. My body was locked for several seconds before I broke free of the sensations washing over me. I was still fighting to catch my breath when he spoke.

"I've tasted your pussy," he croaked, making me shiver in delight at the reminder. "I haven't even kissed you yet." And then he groaned. "There's something seriously fucked up about that."

"Then kiss me now," I pleaded. Lifting his head, I held his gaze. "And never, *ever* stop."

He looked ready to do just that before he jerked away and stood from the bed with a savage curse as he shoved his fingers through his thick brown hair. The look he gave me was dark, and I knew right then that I lost him. "That's never going to happen, Lou. I mean it."

My heart tore in half along with my composure. "Why are you doing this?" I screamed at him. It was a good thing his grandmother wasn't here, or she'd be getting an earful. "Why do you have to treat being with me like the end of the world?"

"Because it *will* be the end. Of us…of me." He began to pace. "God, if you knew what I've done," he said so softly I almost didn't hear.

"Whatever it is, I don't care. I just want you."

"You're too young to know what you want. Too fucking young to even understand what your body is telling you."

"That's not true. I'm old enough to consent."

He laughed then, and it was full of scorn. "But that doesn't mean you should."

"What does it matter if you fuck me now or wait four months until I'm eighteen? I'll be the same girl. I'll still be *yours*."

"You're just a kid," he mumbled, sounding like a broken fucking record.

I scoffed as I stood from the bed and grabbed his shirt in my fists. "You're not even old enough to drink, but you keep telling me what a kid I am. The age of consent in New York is seventeen. Do you know what it means? It means you've run out of excuses."

He freed his shirt from my fists and shoved me away so hard I stumbled. "No, I haven't, Lou. No. The Fuck. I haven't."

I was sitting on the porch swing watching the water when I heard the glass door behind me slide open. Wren had been MIA for hours, and I had no idea if he'd left me alone or was just good at hiding. My pride was too wounded to look for him.

"Are you hungry?" I heard him ask. I looked over my shoulder and found Wren filling the threshold, wearing his brown leather jacket and holding his keys. My mouth watered. I'd only just decided to give up trying to be more than friends when he showed up and called me a liar.

"Sure. Where are we going?"

"I think I know just the place." That was all he said before he led me to his car parked just outside the garage. I started for the passenger side when he grabbed my hand and dropped his keys into my palm.

"What's this?"

"You need more practice driving. I'm still getting shit from my godfather for the damage you did to his truck."

I winced. At the time, stealing Bear's truck seemed necessary. Now, not so much. "Aren't you afraid I'll hurt Paula, too?"

"She's just a car. Making sure you can take care of yourself is more important to me." He took a deep breath and said, "I might not always be around."

The sadness in his tone had me rushing forward. "Don't talk like that," I pleaded as I threw my arms around his neck and pressed my face to his chest. I'd forgotten all about this morning's disaster. "No one is going to hurt you. I won't let them."

I felt his hands at my waist, and then he pulled me closer until our hips met. "It's not my pain that I'm worried about."

I let him go and stepped back so I could see his eyes. "You won't let him hurt me, either," I said, referring to his boss.

"Yeah," he agreed, and then he looked away but not before I saw the uncertainty in his eyes.

What was Wren so afraid of? Fox was powerful with an entire army behind him, but Wren was stronger and smarter than any of them. It was Exiled who should be worried.

Unless...there was something else?

I peered up at Wren. Was there another reason he feared me getting hurt?

Before I could question him, he walked around to the passenger side and got in. I followed him, feeling weird sitting on the driver's side. Somehow, the Impala seemed larger and more intimidating. Wren, on the other hand, stretched his long body out, looking way too relaxed and sexy for my liking.

After securing my seat belt, I turned the key in the ignition, and Paula gave a fierce roar. I couldn't help grinning even as my armpits began to sweat. "Okay," I said as I eagerly reached for the gear shift.

"Aren't you going to adjust your mirrors?" Wren asked me casually. "You might want to see what's around you if you plan to get where you're going without killing anyone."

"Oh…right." I adjusted the rearview mirror and then the side mirrors before shifting the car into drive. However, when I went to press the gas, only the tip of my shoe reached the pedal. Realizing Wren had almost a foot in height on me, I went to adjust the seat, and the car rolled forward. I quickly slammed on the brake, making the car jerk to stop before throwing it back into park.

I glanced at Wren and found him staring at me with a perplexed expression. "How the *hell* did you get into the mountains alive?"

"Dumb luck?"

He snorted. "Clearly."

I huffed ready to give up on ever learning how to drive. "It would help if you told me what to do instead of just sitting there looking—" I slammed my lips shut remembering my decision to give up getting inside Wren's pants.

After a brief silence, he said, "I was under the impression that you already knew what to do."

I sighed and shrank inside my seat. "You're making me nervous," I admitted quietly.

His only response was to reach over, grab the lever under my seat, and push me closer to the steering wheel. And then he whispered in my ear, "You've got this, little Valentine," before lounging again in his seat.

Taking a deep breath, I sat up straight then looked over at him. "Seat belt," I ordered, knowing he never wore one while always insisting that I do.

He chuckled and reached for the belt behind him. "Yes, ma'am."

Once he was secure, I rechecked my mirrors and then took off. What might have been a ten-minute drive took me almost thirty. By the time we arrived, my good mood and excitement had gone to shit. Wren complained incessantly about almost everything I did.

"Stay in your lane, Louchana."

"Red doesn't mean go, Louchana."

"Watch out for that baby in the stroller, Louchana."

I was breathing fire by the time we arrived. Yanking the keys out of the ignition, I threw them in Wren's lap and hopped out. His laughter followed me across the parking lot as I stomped toward the diner that looked like an air stream. By the time I reached the door, Wren had caught up to me. His arm locked around my waist as he pulled me into him from behind.

"You can't drive for shit, but you didn't kill us," he whispered against my hair. "I'm thankful for that much."

"You're a dick," I spat. *And a tease.* His cock was growing harder by the second. Surely, he must have known I'd feel it?

"I know," he said while laughing.

I blinked, and words escaped me until I realized he was responding to my insult. He had no idea what I was thinking, but thanks to his cock lodged against my spine, I knew exactly what was on his mind. Wren didn't let me go when he walked us inside. A beaming hostess wearing skates greeted us, and I knew we didn't look anything like best friends should.

As she showed us to our table, my stomach growled loud enough to bring heat to my cheeks. They became inflamed when Wren rubbed his hand over my belly.

"Let's get some food in you," he said with a chuckle before

letting me go and stepping around me. "You're vicious enough when angry and downright terrifying when you're hungry."

I glared at his back. "I'll just eat that pretty face of yours if you don't shut up."

He threw back his head and roared all the way to our seats while I looked around in awe at the brightly colored interior and vintage décor. The black and white checkered floors gleamed while the small booths—some blue, some pink—allowed for an intimate setting. There were photos of Elvis Presley, Marilyn Monroe, Diana Ross, and James Dean hanging on the wall and there was even a jukebox in the corner. It looked like a scene straight out of the fifties, and I knew my mother would love it here.

When Wren turned and smiled, eyebrows raised expectantly, I knew he was hoping I would, too.

"Oh, God." I groaned as I pushed away the plate that once held a slice of cherry pie. The waitress had just set down a large root beer float with two colorful straws before skating away. "Go on without me," I told Wren. "I can't eat another bite."

Wren had ordered nearly half the menu, and we barely spoke a word to each other as we pigged out. The food was great, but the air between us had been...tense. I think we were both happy for the diversion since we sucked at pretending nothing had happened back at his grandmother's house. The food at least gave us an excuse not to talk about it. Not to mention I couldn't remember the last time I ate. Until we arrived, I hadn't noticed my hunger. I'd been distracted by much more demanding needs.

Wren's laugh was cut short when he reached for the cherry, and I snatched it before popping the treat in my mouth. "That was mine," he gritted.

I stuck out my tongue, showing him the cherry and worked

it like a cuckoo clock. In and out, in and out until his eyes turned completely blue. "You want it?" I teased. "Come and get it."

I wasn't prepared for him to do just that.

Gripping my jaw, he pressed his lips hard against mine until they parted on a gasp, and he stole the cherry from my tongue. I was still in shock when he pulled away and with blue eyes fixed on me, he chewed—slowly.

When he was done with the cherry, he pulled me into his lap, making it clear he wasn't done with me. This time when he kissed me it was slow, allowing me to taste the sweet syrup on his tongue as he deepened the kiss and stole the air from my lungs. My hands found his hair at the same time his fingers dug into my hips, and I pulled hard to get him closer. He grunted, but neither of us cared about the pain we were causing each other. I'd probably go insane if he stopped.

Wren had finally stolen one of my firsts, and luckily for me, I had many more to go. All for him to take.

I moaned, getting excited and forgetting we were in a public place. Wren came to his senses before I did and pulled away. His eyes were full of more emotion than I'd ever seen them hold when he stared back at me.

"I was afraid I'd never get to do that. I promised myself I'd kiss you at least once before I died. Not in my most haunting nightmares did I ever dream that I might lose you first. Don't push me," he pleaded. "Not now."

"I'm not going anywhere," I said as I held his shoulders. "So take all the kisses you want. They're yours."

He didn't say anything as set me aside before throwing down some cash. "Let's get out of here." His voice was thick.

"Are we going to bed?"

I hid my grin when he cut his eyes at me. "Yes," he said as he stood. "But to *separate* beds."

On the way home, Wren stopped at a gas station to fill up, and I wrestled some cash out of his pocket before heading inside to load up on snacks. I made sure to sway my hips, knowing he was watching and could have sworn I heard him groan.

Back at the house, he put on a movie before stretching out on the couch and leaving the comfy looking recliner for me. I turned my nose up at it before going to him on the couch and fitting myself inside the curve of his body. He tensed but didn't argue, and for a while, we both pretended to watch the movie playing. It was some movie about a married couple who went on the run together when their bosses, who turned out to be rivals, wanted them dead.

To my surprise and utter delight, Wren was the first to break when his hand began creeping up my shirt. I kept my eyes on the TV screen and didn't dare speak a word. Wren was like a skittish kitten. Too sudden a move and he'd scurry back to where it was safe. I couldn't let that happen. Not when I was so close to having him once and for always.

"What have you done to me?" He growled as he cupped my breast and brushed my nipple with his thumb. I shivered wanting more. "You give me one taste, and I'm an addict. You allow me one touch, and I'm yours. You're very cruel, Louchana Valentine."

I peered at him over my shoulder. "Men take what they think is theirs all the time. Why shouldn't I do the same?" Looking away, I whispered, "If you don't want me, you're going to have to a better job convincing me."

Turning me on my back, he kissed me softly and then deeply. "Make no mistake, Lou. There's no one and nothing I want more," he whispered fiercely. "But I can't have you. Do you understand?"

"No."

He sighed and brushed my lips with his own. "You will one day."

I broke away and stood. I wanted to lash out, but the moonlight shimmering on the surface of the water outside caught my eye. With a wicked grin, I wondered if Wren would be opposed to a midnight swim.

My best friend might be a big, bad gangster, but I had him wrapped around my finger. Now if only I could get him wrapped around the rest of me.

CHAPTER
TWENTY-FOUR

The Moth

L OU STARED OUT AT THE WATER, LOOKING FRUSTRATED AND forlorn. Well, she had no fucking idea. If today had been a test of my honor, well then, I'd failed fucking miserably. Even now, I was ready to go to her and give her what we both wanted in abundance. At that very moment, a smile spread her lips as if she heard my thoughts. Suddenly, she stepped toward the sliding glass door, and I watched feeling helpless as she pulled her shirt over her head.

She hadn't worn a bra today.

That had been a pleasant but torturous surprise. Lou was blessed with more than enough to fill my hands, so maybe it was me that had lucked out. They bounced with each step she took as she shed more clothing until she was completely naked.

"Lou, don't do this." My voice sounded hoarse, and I forced myself to get a grip. I'd been fucking long before Lou set her sights on seducing me. I knew I'd play the game better, but guilt kept me at bay. I'd taken enough from her. Stealing her virginity was out of the question. It would just be one more thing I couldn't undo.

She slid open the door and cast a smile over her shoulder as she disappeared into the night. I hesitated for only a moment before following after her. Standing at the water's edge, I watched her wade deeper, and when the water was at her waist, she turned to me and smiled.

"I won't bite!" she shouted teasingly.

I grinned back at her. "The sharks might."

"I think you're afraid of more than just fish with sharp teeth." And then she took a deep breath before dipping below the water. My heart sped up. I'd never undressed so fast in my life. The water was freezing, and I was thankful for it as I felt my balls shrivel up inside my boxers. If Lou thought she'd seduce me this way, she clearly hadn't thought it through.

It was a full minute since she had disappeared underwater and just as I was about to call her name, she appeared a mere foot in front of me.

"Come here," I growled, growing tired of her toying with me. I couldn't even muster the patience to wait and swam to her instead. The moment I reached her, I gripped her hips and lifted her. She wrapped her legs around my waist while holding me captive with her excited gaze.

"You have me. Now, what will you do with me?" Lou flirted.

I did the only thing that felt right. I kissed her. I was lost inside a black void, and she was the flame lighting the way. I couldn't resist its call. "I'm going to take you inside," I said when I finally came up for air. "I'm going to make you come." I started kissing down her neck. "And then I'm going to put you to bed." Lowering my head, I drew her nipple inside my mouth, and she gripped the back of my neck while pushing her breasts out for more. Just as she began mewling, I released her.

"Don't stop," she moaned.

"I won't," I told her as I unwrapped her legs from around my waist. "If you come back inside like a good girl." I heard her frustrated growl as I swam away and didn't have to look behind me to know she followed.

Back on the beach, she looked absolutely miserable as she shivered with her arms wrapped around herself, and I smiled. Her plan to get me inside her might have failed, but she got an A for effort.

"Come here," I said gently. "I'll warm you up." Despite her obvious impatience with me, she eagerly came into my arms and placed her head against my chest. "I've done some bad shit, and if you knew, you wouldn't forgive me. So now I have to pay the price, Lou, and my penance is never to have you."

She was silent for a long while before she lifted her head. "You're mine," she told me, blue eyes sparkling with hope. "Aren't you?"

I pulled her close and buried my nose in her hair, inhaling deeply. "Yeah, Lou. I'm yours."

Standing on the tips of her toes, she nipped my bottom lip. "Then it doesn't matter what you did. What's mine is mine forever."

I closed my eyes and tried not to let myself hope. She had no idea. No fucking clue, and I still couldn't bring myself to tell her the truth.

Back inside, and after the long hot shower e took together, I kept my promise. I kissed her all over, I touched her all over, but God help me, I left her pure.

"Aren't you going to ask me for your camera back?" I asked Lou as we lay in my bed. She hadn't used the guest room once since I'd brought her here three days ago. My grandmother would probably beat me with a stick if she knew I had a girl in my room. She was a little old fashioned, and I'd just spent the last two days breaking every one of her rules.

"After what I saw, I don't think I'll ever take another photo again," Lou answered solemnly.

At that moment, I wished Fox was standing in front of me so that I could bash his skull in. Last night, just when I thought Lou had escaped any lingering trauma, she'd woken up screaming from a nightmare. She'd relived it all over again, and then she told me with such bleakness in her eyes that she never *stopped* reliving it.

"You're stronger than you realize, Lou. I wouldn't count yourself out just yet. Besides, you haven't truly lost anything. Taking pictures of strangers was never your dream."

"Come again?"

The serrated edge of her question made me grateful that she couldn't see my face because I couldn't stop my smile. "It's something you found that you're good at, but it's not what you lay awake wishing for every night."

"Oh?"

I heard the challenge in her tone and gripped her hip as I rose to the occasion. "You want a home and a life that you can't run away from." And one way or another, I'd give it to her—even if it meant that I wouldn't be in it.

I heard the snag of her next breath and felt the pause in her toes that had been lazily sweeping mine. It happened so quickly that if I weren't already tuned in to every single breath Lou took, I would have missed it.

"Well, I hear prison is nice this time of year," she mocked, and I knew she didn't like feeling so open.

Her body jerked within the curve of mine when I pinched her side. "Behave," I warned, but it sounded more like a purr. Like I was some goddamn house cat eager for a scratch behind the ears.

She turned in my arms, and my hand found her ass when I drew her even closer. "You smell like me," Lou whispered, and then she pressed her nose into my bare chest. "I'm all over you."

She then pushed me onto my back and straddled me. The only thing she wore was my T-shirt, so I felt her warmth and wetness, both mine for the taking. I gripped my fists in the sheets so I wouldn't do just that, but then she started trailing soft kisses down my stomach.

"Lou," I called in the sternest voice I could muster, but she pretended not to hear me. I knew where she was headed, and I knew what she intended. We'd been going hot and heavy for two days, and somehow, I managed to keep my dick out of it, but Lou seemed determined to destroy what was left of my honor.

Fuck your honor, and fuck your conscience, my dick seemed to say when Lou's hand slipped inside my boxer shorts.

She wrapped a hand around me, and I almost exploded like I was twelve instead of twenty.

"Lou, don't."

She peeked up at me and held my gaze as she trailed a finger up my dick. "You got to taste me," she said, reminding me of our first morning in Sunset Bay. "Can't I have just a drop?" I closed my eyes and swore, and as if on cue, my dick began leaking pre-cum. "Hm," she said, taking notice while her finger inched closer. "Your mouth says no, but your dick says yes." She sounded truly torn when she said, "Which one should I listen to?"

My eyes slowly opened, but my mouth remained shut as I stared back at her. She looked wide-eyed and innocent, but it only took a few seconds for her to get the message, and when she reached for my boxers, I knew I was irrevocably fucked.

CHAPTER
TWENTY-FIVE

The Flame

I WAS CELEBRATING MY VICTORY FOR ALL OF TWO SECONDS BEFORE Wren stood from the bed, all-powerful and graceful like a feline. I watched him cross the room before shoving his boxers off his hips and giving his full attention back to me.

My heart skipped a beat.

I couldn't put my finger on it, but he was different. Something deeply rooted inside of me told me that I no longer had control. My belly warmed as my thighs pressed together. I didn't understand the reaction, but Wren's gaze lighting up told me he did.

"Take that off," he ordered, referring to his shirt that I wore, and I eagerly did as I was told. "Come to me."

I stood from the bed on legs that shook, but when I stepped toward him, he shook his head.

"If you want to suck me, you'll have to get on your knees."

I sank to the floor, but then I frowned once my knees touched the carpet. "But you're over there," I argued. "How can I come to you if I'm on my knees?"

His only response was to lift a brow.

"You expect me to *crawl*?" I couldn't hide the anger in my tone, but thankfully, I could hide the wetness pooling between my thighs.

He shrugged as if he were asking me for the time instead of my pride. "I've been playing this game your way, Louchana. Now it's time we played it mine."

"And what's your game?" My eyes narrowed. "Humiliating me?"

His head tilted, and when his gaze suddenly softened, I could feel myself wanting to go to him. "There's no one else here but us, Lou."

I looked around the room, assuring myself that we were alone. Even if we hadn't been, would I care if people knew that Wren had brought me to my knees? I knew without a doubt that I had brought him to his. Probably long before he or I ever realized.

Slowly, I lowered onto my hands until I was on all fours. Wren's loving gaze never left mine, and somehow, it felt like he was carrying me in his arms as I crawled to him. There was no trace of arrogance or triumph, and when I reached him, I sat back on my heels, and he leaned down to kiss me.

"You really are mine," he whispered with wonder in his voice. As if he couldn't believe it—or was afraid to.

"Yes."

He kissed me again before standing to his full height. "Then have your way with me, little Valentine." He folded his arms behind his head with a grin that would have melted my panties if I were wearing any.

With shaking hands, I reached for his cock. It was long, thick, and impossibly hard. The thick veins running down the length even made it look angry, and if that wasn't intimidating enough, the fact that I had no idea what I was doing was enough to make me contemplate backing out.

Maybe Wren knew I would.

Maybe that was why he'd given in so easily.

Feeling ravenous for more than just a taste of him, I parted my lips to take him inside, but he quickly gripped my chin.

"Tell me again," he ordered, and I knew he wanted to hear the words I spoke to him the night we trampled over the boundaries of friendship once and for all. This was our first time making it past second base, but he still made tell him every time we made out. For some reason, he needed reassurance. He was almost desperate for it.

"What's mine is mine forever."

He looked so tortured as he stared down at me. He was breathing harder than he should have been, and I knew if I placed my hand over his heart, it would be beating out of control.

"I really hope you mean that."

"I do." And to show him, I held him with my gaze as I licked the head of his cock. "I mean it now…" I licked him again, earning his groan. "Tomorrow." A drop of cum emerged, and I licked that, too. It was salty and thick, and I wanted more. "Forever…" His legs shook a little when I ran my tongue up the shaft. "And always."

The moment my mouth watered, I slipped my lips over the thick head of his cock and tried to swallow him whole. He was even bigger in my mouth than he was in my hand, and I ended up gagging and coughing as my eyes welled up. Fucking porn stars made it look so easy.

"Slow down," he chuckled, sounding a little cocky. "You'll hurt yourself."

I shook my head and held his gaze as I tried again. I gained an inch, but this time, he flinched and cursed when I grazed him.

"Teeth, baby. Watch those teeth."

Hearing him call me baby for the first time stirred something in me. I wanted to hear it again. I wanted to earn it. Pulling my lips over my teeth, I pretended his cock was one of those cherry popsicles I loved so much growing up. And when I grabbed the base of his cock to keep from getting overzealous again, he groaned. On instinct, I began stroking him, using my spit for lubrication, and Wren rewarded me with a gasp and grabbing a fist full of my hair as he began pumping his hips.

Having him so entirely at my mercy made my pussy throb until I was reaching between my legs with my free hand to relieve the ache. As my mouth worked his cock, my fingers stroked my clit.

Seeing this, his eyes became wild and unfocused. "You want to come?" he asked me in a thick voice.

Mouth full, I nodded eagerly.

"Then be a good girl and come with me, Lou." His hips began to lose their rhythm, and knowing he was close, my fingers sped up. A second later, I came with a cry that was muffled by his spurting cock. I started to pull away when he gripped my hair tighter.

"No," he barked. Wren's blue eyes sharpened when our gazes met. "Swallow."

I knew he wasn't fucking around, so after taking more of him, he threw back his head, and his abs contracted as he released a guttural groan. I felt his cum, hot and thick, ease down my throat and fill my belly. I already wanted more.

"Fuck." He fought to catch his breath, and then he kissed me. Deeply. I thought it was weird since I could still taste him, which meant he could too, but after only a second or two, I didn't give a damn and kissed him back.

He lifted me in his arms after we finally came up for air and carried me inside his bathroom where he cleaned us both up. By the time we had finished, and he carried me back to his bed, I was already plotting what we would get into next.

Unfortunately, I knew more would have to wait when he brought reality crashing back.

"I have to go, Lou. I have to go back."

I sat alone on the couch, drinking Granny Harlan's gin—I never actually learned her name—and watching reruns of *The 100*. I always ended up sneering at the television whenever Bellamy came on screen. The longer I watched, the less dreamy he seemed, and I couldn't believe I actually crushed on him. He was a selfish douchebag, and if he were real, I bet he would have been Wren's best friend instead of me.

Best friends…

I scoffed even though there was no one around to hear me. Friends don't fuck, and if they did, a *good* friend didn't let another friend go down on them and then say, "Hey, see you later!"

Only cocksuckers did that.

But oh, wait…that was me. *I'm* the one who blown Wren and then got ditched. He left the morning after, claiming he had to talk to Fox. To stand before him and *beg* for my life as if it was his to take in the first place.

That was over a week ago, and I hadn't heard from Wren since.

For all I knew, he was dead. Maybe Fox killed him just for being my friend. For wanting to protect me.

There wasn't a judge or jury alive who could ignore the evidence I had without raising suspicion. That was why Fox wanted me dead. I was a problem he couldn't pay his way out of. I shook my head. Until now, I never thought Wren could be so naïve.

But what if he succeeded?

Perhaps that was the real reason I was upset. If Wren managed to convince Fox to keep me alive, Wren would never be free of him. He'd work for him until the end of days, which could be any day now. There would be no hope left for him.

I didn't realize I was crying until I felt the tears running off my chin. I angrily swiped them away feeling pathetic. Wren didn't deserve my tears, my friendship, or my body. And it was better I told him—if I ever saw him again. I didn't want to love him anymore. I didn't want this pain. It wasn't worth it.

Tomorrow, I'd go to the police with the evidence to put Fox away for good. Wren might not forgive me, but one way or another, he would be free, and that innocent family would have justice.

Not at all at peace with my new plan or having confidence in my ability to stick to it, I reached for the gin. My eye caught the colorful flyer lying on the coffee table. Some chick my age had been handing them out when I defied Wren's orders and made my way into town a couple of days ago. Halloween was tomorrow, but unlike everyone else who didn't have a price on their head, I wouldn't be celebrating. I felt bitterness pooling on my tongue, so I drank until it didn't matter—until nothing mattered.

The world was spinning when I woke up the next morning, and with some effort, I peeled my eyes open to see that I was safely tucked in bed inside the guest room. Sitting up quickly, I clutched my head and grunted from the pain. The disorientation, however, didn't distract me from the fact that I'd passed out on the couch last night.

Before I could consider that I'd somehow drunkenly stumbled upstairs, the door opened, and Wren stood there looking very much alive if not all that well. He sported bruises that looked a few days old, and when he stepped inside, it wasn't with his usual swagger. He limped across the room, and I forgot all about my hangover as I rushed to meet him.

"Wren!" I threw my arms around his neck, and he grunted. I quickly stepped back and looked him over, wondering where he was hurt.

"I'm okay," he said through clenched teeth.

"You don't look okay to me! What did he do to you?"

"He taught me a lesson about loyalty."

"Why?" Wren was the most loyal person I knew. Incidentally, it's why I wanted to hate him. He was loyal to a man who didn't deserve it.

"Because he ordered me to bring you to him, and I told him he might as well kill me."

"And he just let you *go?*"

He laughed then, but there was no humor in it. "Fuck no. His son helped me escape." Wren's expression quickly turned troubled. "And Fox will make him pay for it."

"Fox has a son?"

He nodded. "And a daughter. You'd like them. They're little shits like you."

His eyes twinkled when I glowered at him. "Maybe he should have done us both a favor and left you to die."

Wren's eyebrows nearly kissed his hairline. "What the fuck is your problem?"

For a moment, I considered lying and walking away, but I knew he would never allow me to do either. "You left me."

"To save you," he countered.

"And if Fox had sent someone after me?" I shot back. I remembered how easily he found me and getting cornered in that alley. If it hadn't been for Miles and Leo…

"He doesn't know where you are, Lou."

"And how do you know you didn't lead him here?"

"I was gone long before Fox got wind I was, but I still waited a couple of days before coming back to make sure I wasn't followed."

"But if you hadn't left in the first place—"

"What did you expect me to do? Hide here with you forever?"

Yes. "We could go to the police."

His hand shot out, and he yanked me into him. "We won't be talking to the cops because I don't trust them," he dictated bitingly. "Any of them would sell you out." His forehead came to rest on mine, and I could feel him soften as his hand found my hip. "I won't take chances with you. That detective you saw killed was the only one who would have helped us."

"So what do we do?"

Gripping my nape with his other hand, he kissed me softly. "We run."

"Okay," I agreed all too easily. I should have been more hesitant about giving up the life I had in exchange for another, but it was as Wren said—I'd yet to find a life that I hadn't wanted to run away from. "But before we go, can we do one thing first?"

"This is stupid," Wren grumbled for the third time. We'd just found a park after searching for ten minutes and were making our way down the crowded sidewalk. In the distance, I could hear what sounded like drums followed by trumpets and other various instruments and figured the local school band had come to play.

"Will you stop worrying?" I said with a grin. "You look dashing and handsome, husband."

Wren wore a black suit and a tie that he was able to rent at the last minute, but he refused to wear dress shoes, so he paired the suit with high-top sneakers. He did let me style his hair although he bitched the entire time. And neither of us had called attention to the fact that he'd gotten hard while I ran my fingers through his hair. I'd taken my time making sure every single strand was perfectly coiffed.

I chose to wear my hair down with loose curls at the end, courtesy of Granny Harlan's curling iron. The long, fitted black dress I wore had spaghetti straps and a slit on the right side that reached my hip and showed off my garter and killer black pumps. Thanks to my bargain shopping skills, the entire ensemble had cost Wren less than fifty bucks, and when I came downstairs where he had been impatiently pacing, I could tell by his passionate reaction that he would have paid fifty thousand. It was a good thing I hadn't chosen to wear panties.

"Who the hell are we supposed to be anyway?" he griped.

"I'm Jane, and you're John." When he gave me a blank look, I sighed and said, "From Mr. and Mrs. Smith." It was the movie we'd been watching when he admitted to wanting more after kissing me for the first time back at the diner.

"I've never seen it," he claimed, and I grinned.

"That's because you were too busy feeling me up."

He sighed and refused to meet my gaze. "So where's this party?"

"It's a parade, not a party, and it's probably at the address printed right there on the flyer."

Not missing my sarcasm, he cut his gaze to me, and I hid my smile. "We should be keeping a low profile."

"Will you relax? No one knows us here."

He didn't seem to hear me, though, as he searched every face in the crowd for Fox and the goons he used to call brothers. I knew it was wise to heed his judgment since he knew Exiled better than I ever wanted to, but I was determined for us to have one more good memory to take with us before we ran.

It took us about five minutes to reach where the parade was supposed to begin, and by then, I was ready to spend the rest of the night barefoot.

Wren chose that moment to glance at me, saw my grimace, and laughed. "Your feet hurt, don't they?"

"No."

"You want to get on my back?" he asked with a knowing grin.

I almost cried out in relief, but instead, I ignored him much to his amusement.

Just before the crowd thickened, I slowed, and as if we were one, Wren stopped and turned to me as I said, "There's one more thing I need to make my costume complete."

He no longer seemed amused as he regarded me warily. "What's that?"

"Your gun."

He blinked once and then started walking again. "Forget it," he bit out over his shoulder. His long strides made it hard to catch up with him in these heels, and he must have realized it because he suddenly slowed.

"Please?" I whined. "I can't pretend to be a badass assassin without a weapon."

"You can barely drive a car, and you expect me to trust you with a gun? *My* gun?"

I stepped close enough that no one could see me grab his thigh. "If you do, I'll make it worth your while."

He barked out a laugh, and I gasped when he yanked me closer. "My dick is not a bargaining chip," he said with a growl, "and it's definitely not a toy. When I want you to play with it, I'll ask, and you and I both know you won't need persuading."

He pushed me away, and we stared at each other for a couple of seconds before I trusted my voice enough to speak. "I know all that, bestie. I just needed this."

He gaped when I held up the long, black folding blade. "How the fuck—"

"Did you forget already that I have magical hands?"

"No, I haven't forgotten," he said as his eyes turned blue. I knew he remembered this afternoon when I snuck inside his dressing room. Coincidentally, after he came in my hand, he agreed to wear any suit I wanted.

I grinned as I slipped the knife inside my garter, and once it was secured, he pulled me close again. I wasn't prepared for him to slap my ass hard enough to draw attention. I looked around, and my cheeks flushed seeing the mixture of amused and scandalized gazes.

"Why did you do that?" I snapped.

"I told you that I'm the wrong person to steal from." And then with an arrogant smirk, he took my hand and led me down the sidewalk. Embarrassed and a little turned on, I kept my head down the rest of the way.

Since we were in costume, we were allowed to walk in the parade, which the locals were calling A Nightmare on Elm Street, while everyone else kept to the sidewalk. After a while, however, it got so crowded and crazy that the lines blurred, and it didn't matter who wore what. Beers were passed around, and no one seemed to care if you were underage. Wren did. He allowed me one beer before he cut us both off.

He spent the first hour tense and paranoid as if expecting to be caught partying by his parents at any moment. And just as I began to wonder if coming here had been my worst idea yet, a miracle happened.

"I run into you twice in one year?" I heard someone excitedly shout just before a familiar face pushed through the crowd. Sonny was grinning from ear to ear as he quickly embraced Wren. "Holy shit!" he shouted when he stood back. "I'm happy you're here, man, but aren't you a little overdressed?"

"It's a costume," Wren replied, and then he tossed his head my way. "Her idea."

Sonny frowned as he looked us over. "So what...you're like a bride and groom?" He then lifted his eyebrows at me. "Shouldn't you be in white?"

I rolled my eyes when Wren faced me looking smug. "We're rival assassins who weren't supposed to fall in love, and now we're running from bad guys who want us dead."

"Right, right, of course," Sonny agreed while looking even more confused.

"And what are you supposed to be?" I asked him.

Sonny wore plain jeans and a hoodie, and the only indication of a costume was the Ghostface mask resting on top of his head. Raising the hand holding a beer, he smiled. "Drunk." He then slapped Wren on the back and said, "Let's get you two caught up."

Before Wren could tell him no, he melted back into the crowd, and reappeared a minute later with an arm full of beers.

"Follow me," he ordered, rushing in the opposite direction from where he came.

We followed him to a white van with the word *news* sloppily painted on the side and bright red paint splashed on the window to look like blood. Sonny opened the back door, and a cloud of smoke billowed from the inside revealing two guys who looked stoned out of their mind.

Sonny made the introductions before hopping onto the tail and handing Wren and me a beer. I quickly popped the tab and started chugging before Wren could say anything. Sonny whooped and cheered me on, and after finishing off half the can,

I swiped my mouth and burped while Sonny stared on in awe. "Wren, man, where'd you find this one and are there more of her?"

Wren pulled me closer to him and only said, "No," before drinking his entire can of beer. He burped when he was done, and it was even louder than mine.

"Show off."

Grinning, he pulled me close and kissed me before grabbing another beer. Before long, it was after midnight, and most of the town had called it a night except for a few stragglers. The party was more intimate but even wilder than before as some of the kids started TP-ing anything they could access, and when the toilet paper ran out, they used fire to vandalize everything that remained.

That was the moment Wren decided it was time for us to go.

He promised to catch up with Sonny later even though we both knew he wouldn't. He grabbed my hand, and we quickly made our way down the street. Halfway to his car, someone threw a firebomb inside a car, and Wren decided I wasn't moving quick enough, so he lifted me into his arms.

We had just rounded the corner onto the empty street where Paula was parked when Wren stopped short. I'd been so busy looking over his shoulder watching the crazies making their way down the street behind us that I didn't see what emerged from the shadows ahead of us.

Turning my head, I instantly recognized the man donned in the heavy wool trench coat and light gray suit. The wind blew, ruffling the strands of his thick blond hair streaked with gray. The first time I saw him had been at a distance too far to see just how incredibly handsome he was. His dark brown eyes, strong jaw, and perfect lips could make any woman shake with lust while never knowing they had darker reasons to tremble.

I was distantly aware of Wren lowering me until my feet touched the ground, but he didn't move away. Instead, he pushed me behind him.

Fox looked amused as he watched Wren's attempt to keep me safe. "That's not going to help her, son."

And before any of us knew what was happening, I was grabbed from behind, and we were surrounded by more men who had stayed hidden. Just as quickly, Wren had his gun out and aimed at Fox, but neither that nor the kicks and punches I landed on the man who grabbed me deterred the goon from bringing me to stand before Fox.

"Let her go," Wren demanded.

"You know very well why I can't do that," Fox told him in a deceptively patient voice. His sharp gaze then shifted to me, and I was suddenly grateful for the knife still tucked inside my garter. "You have something that belongs to me."

Keeping my hand pressed against my thigh, I lifted my chin. "And you have something that belongs to me."

Fox looked surprised by my boldness and then intrigued. "And what might that be?"

Without looking behind me where I knew my best friend stood ready to die for me, I answered him. "Wren."

If Fox was shocked by my answer, he didn't show it as he reached inside his jacket pocket. "Would you propose a trade?"

Before I could answer, I heard Wren growl as he said, "One more syllable and I evict your brain from your skull."

My heart fell to my stomach believing that at any moment, Fox would retaliate for the threat. When he only smiled fondly at Wren, I became even more uneasy.

"I've been waiting for this," Fox drawled.

"Waiting for what?" I snapped when Wren only stared back at him. I instantly regretted it when Fox turned those soulless black eyes on me.

"The day he'd inherit his father's ruthlessness. I look at him now, and the resemblance is almost chilling. For five years, Wren has fought against it even though he knew this day was inevitable." To Wren, he said, "Becoming a monster is your birthright, son. *Seize it.*" I held my breath when he reached out and boldly laid a hand on Wren's shoulder. "You know what to do when you're ready to return home."

Wren finally spoke, and the ice in his tone sent a chill down my spine. How Fox was able to look him in the eye was beyond me. Even *I* feared him at this moment though I wasn't the one in his crosshairs.

"I'm not coming back."

Just like that, Fox's friendly ruse disappeared, and I found myself inching closer to Wren, ready to pounce if Fox so much as sneezed in his direction.

"I think I've proven that I know you better than you think. One way or another, you will return."

Quick as lightning, Fox grabbed my wrist, ignoring the gun Wren pressed daringly to his temple. Fox just managed to press something cold and flat into the palm of my hand before all hell broke loose. The large crowd causing mayhem from the party turned the corner, and noticing the scene playing out on the dark street, they began shoving and screaming to get away. It wouldn't be long before the cops showed up.

"A token of your debt, Louchana," Fox said low enough so only I could hear. "But I doubt you'll wish to make that trade." He freed my wrist, and I immediately felt Wren's hand at my waist pulling me into him. To safety.

But I didn't want security. I wanted revenge.

"You're right to be afraid of me," I told Fox as I held his gaze. "I am a threat. But not because I have the evidence to make sure you rot in prison, but because I stole the heart of the one person keeping you alive."

"Lou," Wren said in my ear warningly.

"You're now alone because of me, exposed, and surrounded by enemies. You have nothing while I have everything." When Fox's eyes narrowed, I smiled. "You better hope I don't come for you."

CHAPTER
TWENTY-SIX

The Moth

"**G**ROSS."

Hearing Lou speak for the first time since we started heading North, I glanced over in time to see her looking around in disgust.

"What is this place?" she asked.

I looked around, too, wondering what she found so abhorrent. The trees were green and tall, the roads were clear of garbage, and because of the absence of smog, the sun shone brightly.

"What do you mean?"

"It's clean and…quiet," she answered with a wrinkle of her nose. "Where are all the rats and homeless people?"

"You mean your so-called family?" I teased her.

"There's no place like home," she chanted with a click of her heels. "There's no place like home."

"You don't have a home," I reminded. "Hence why I brought you here."

She lifted that damn camera that got us into this mess and snapped a couple of pictures. "Who did you say lived out here?"

"I didn't."

She sighed. "Why won't you tell me?"

"Will it matter?" I slowed and turned down a well-groomed path. "You don't have a choice either way."

She started to respond when a house bigger than either of us had ever seen came into view.

"Fucking shit!" she screeched.

"Language," I scolded as I parked the car. I ignored her eye roll and took a deep breath, wondering how the hell I was going to ask for help from a guy whose life I threatened almost two months ago.

"Please tell me we're robbing the place," Lou said as she bounced up and down in the passenger seat.

I didn't answer her as I slid from the car. She met me at the front but stopped short when she saw my expression. Lou knew me better than anyone and could tell that right now was not the time to fuck around.

A few feet ahead, three vehicles were parked, one of which was a vintage-looking motorcycle.

Popping her hands on her hips, she rounded in front of me. "I thought you said you were taking me somewhere safe."

I kept my gaze over her shoulder, watching the front doors of the mansion. "I am."

"Then why are you looking like that?"

"Because I'm not sure I can trust him." I felt the darkness fading away when I finally looked at her and said, "Especially with you."

She chewed on her lower lip, trying to hide the fact that she was affected. Lou and I haven't exactly been on the best terms since the night she threatened Fox. My reaction when I got her alone had been...explosive. I doubt she'd forgiven me yet. "Is he Exiled?"

"Not anymore."

"Is he a friend?"

I hesitated to answer, wondering if the truth was best. Lou wouldn't trust anyone who wasn't a friend, but she'd also know if I lied, and then she wouldn't trust me. Eventually, I said, "No."

"Then if we're not going to rob him, I say we leave," she suggested eagerly.

I knew she wasn't thrilled about getting dumped in some

stranger's lap, but we'd been on the run for almost a month, and I was quickly running out of cash and ideas. All the dirty money I'd earned over the years was currently stashed at my grandmother's house, and it had been too risky to go back after our run-in with Fox. Our only saving grace was Lou refusing to go anywhere without her mother's rucksack. It was her security blanket.

"We can't leave, Lou. There's nowhere else to go."

Before she could argue more, the front door of the house opened, and a girl who looked a little peeved stepped out wearing a blue blazer and a tan skirt. Clutched in her right hand was a helmet.

Recognizing her immediately from all the reconnaissance I'd done, I stood up straight. I knew exactly who'd be following her in three…two…one.

The door flew open, and Ever wore a vicious scowl as he emerged wearing an identical uniform. He swaggered over to Four, who was already straddling the bike and buckling her chin strap, and pulled her off the bike.

"He doesn't even fucking notice us standing here," I muttered, feeling annoyed for some reason. Ever should have been careful and more aware of his surroundings. He had no idea who might be lurking. I gritted my teeth when I felt myself wanting to march over there and *scold* him. I shook my head, shoving away the feelings. Ever was nothing to me but a potential ally.

A second later, I realized I'd spoken too soon when he glanced over, and I could tell by the promise of pain now shining from his eyes that he wasn't happy to see me standing here.

"Wren?" I heard Lou call as Ever pushed Four behind him. A heartbeat later, he was charging across the front yard. Four shouted his name, and when he ignored her, she ran back inside the house. Probably to get that douchebag that lived with them.

"Yeah, Lou?"

"Something tells me we're not welcome," she told me in a shaky voice.

I didn't get the chance to confirm her suspicions. I had only a split second to push Lou out of the way and duck when Ever swung without a single word spoken. Before I could get trapped against my car, I quickly threw my weight into Ever, sending us both crashing to the ground.

Ever wasn't pulling any punches, and neither was I. Hell, I needed to release this pent-up energy, and since fucking Lou silly was out of the question, I'd gladly settle for punching the shit out of Ever McNamara.

The sound of grunting and pounding flesh grew more intense, and I could feel my nose leaking blood, so I slammed my fist into Ever's to return the favor. After finding out who he really was, I didn't expect him to have this much fight in him. I was too distracted by kicking Ever's ass and getting mine kicked in return that I hadn't noticed when I became outnumbered.

The loudmouth with too many tattoos had somehow succeeded in pulling us apart. Remembering the way he looked at Lou when I ran into them in Times Square, I quickly caught his jaw with a mean right hook.

It was a cheap shot and my shittiest idea yet.

He countered with one of his own, but before he could come at me with more, Ever's little playmate ran between us, and we both stopped dead in our tracks. Ever was practically foaming at the mouth when he rushed to pull Four out of harm's way and immediately scolded her with his hand gripping her chin. "If they want to kill each other, let them."

"You're all acting like idiots," she shouted at him. "How could you just attack him when you don't even know why he's here?" My eyebrows rose at her level of anger. Something told me it wasn't for my health.

"I know why he's here," Ever said ominously.

Remembering Lou, who was safely watching from the hood of my car, I interrupted their bickering. "I'm not here to kill you."

Ever turned on me and seemed more pissed than when he thought I wanted to end him. "Then what the fuck?" he spat.

"*You* attacked *me*," I reminded.

"What was I supposed to think? You threatened me the last time I saw you."

Before I could answer, the douchebag who still looked like he wanted to rip me apart said, "Since no one is killing anyone, what do you say we take this inside? I need ice." With one last glare thrown my way, he stalked off for the house.

The minute the door closed behind him, Ever and I resumed our standoff until the silence graduated from tense to awkward.

"I don't know about you," Four drawled, and when I glanced at her, I realized she was speaking to Lou, "but all this testosterone is a little stifling."

Even though she was the enemy, Lou grinned back at her. *Traitor.* "It's like watching The Undertaker and Stone Cold in a staring contest. Cue the drama."

"Then we better get inside," Four suggested as she turned on her heel. "Streams are bound to cross."

She started across the driveway, and Lou hesitated for only a second before shrugging and following after her.

What the hell?

"Why are you here?" Ever gritted the moment the girls were inside.

I sighed and forced myself to pretend my tail wasn't tucked between my legs while I looked him in the eye. "I need your help."

Of all the things he expected me to say, I could tell that hadn't even come close to being one of them. He looked startled for a moment, and then he looked pissed. Very pissed.

"Come again?"

I swallowed past the lump in my throat, and still, words failed to form. How do you ask someone whose life you once threatened for help? Ever had no reason to help me just as I had no reason to trust him, but I was out of options and because of me, so was he.

"Lou was in the wrong place at the wrong time, and now Fox wants her dead. I'm not about to let that happen."

"I see…" Tilting his head, he squinted his eyes. "How the fuck is that my problem?" His tone implied that he was genuinely curious, but the lack of sympathy in his gaze told me he was anything but.

"You're the only person left in this world who I know would give a shit if Fox killed an innocent girl."

"I'm sure he's killed plenty," Ever muttered still trying to convince me that he didn't care.

"And if you help me by keeping her here where it's safe, I'm going to make sure that he doesn't get the chance again."

He blinked, and I could see he was surprised, but he quickly shook it off. "How the hell am I supposed to explain her to my father? He'll take one look at her and have the cops dragging her back to wherever she came from."

"Somehow, you got close enough to breathe down Fox's neck. Use that same cunning." I wasn't backing down. Unfortunately, neither was he. I could tell he was ready to tell me to kick rocks, so I exhaled and said, "I'll make it worth your while."

It seemed cruel to play this card not knowing if I'd succeed, but I had no choice. Ever couldn't stand me, and with good reason, so he wouldn't make this easy for me.

"You don't have anything I want."

"No…but I can get it. I can get *her*."

I was hit with the coldest stare and, on its heels, a sense of recognition so fierce that, for a moment, I believed I was looking at someone else—someone I hadn't seen in a long time. My gaze narrowed, but then whatever thought was lingering in the back of my mind faded away when he spoke.

"What the hell are you talking about?"

"I know the real reason you joined Exiled. You weren't just looking for some thrill, were you?" He didn't answer me, but his golden eyes grew darker by the second, eyes he'd gotten from Grace. Or should I say, Evelyn? I kicked myself for not seeing the resemblance before now. He looked just like her. "You were searching for your mother."

"I don't know what you're talking about," he lied, and it was clear he didn't trust me with information so precious.

"Yes, you do," I pressed. "You have Grace's eyes...and the fact that you put yourself in harm's way to free her tells me you have her courage."

"My mother's name was Evelyn," he bit out, ignoring the respect I had just offered him, but then I found hope in the faraway look in his eyes. "Grace was her middle name."

"*Is*," I corrected, and he frowned at me. "She's still alive, Ever."

"Then where is she?" he demanded, his voice thick.

"In Fox's bed," I told him easily, and he looked ready to knock my teeth out for that comment. "So do you want her back or not?"

Rather than answer, he peered at me. "You expect me to believe that you're risking your life to go against Fox all for some girl?"

"She's not just some girl. She's...she's..." When I couldn't find the words, I just stood there speechless like an idiot.

"You love her," Ever told me as if the answer were obvious.

I scratched under my chin, feeling uncomfortable discussing what I felt for Lou with him. Or anyone. "Of course I do. She's my best friend," I bullshitted. Every day, the film we kept over our friendship became thinner, and I became hungrier. Lou was taunting me, pushing me, and the only part I hated was that it was working.

I wanted Lou, but I needed her more.

If I touched her again, I'd be letting my dick ruin our

friendship, but with the way things had been going, it seemed as if the tension and frustration mounting between us would do the job instead.

Ever looked at me like I was crazy before pinching the bridge of his nose. "No, man. I mean you're *in* love with her."

Blowing out air, I felt my nostrils flare. "If I say yes, will you keep her safe?"

My tone was becoming more hostile by the second as my patience thinned. I got enough of this shit from Lou. I didn't need this pompous prick giving her false hope.

"I don't know, asshole. Do you want to say yes?" He lifted a brow, and when he smirked, it was all I could do not to start round two. The blood that dripped from his nose had already dried, but I wouldn't mind giving him a lip to match. "You should tell her," he said when the silence stretched too long.

"She knows she's important to me. That's enough."

"Wiping your ass after you shit is important to you. If you face Fox alone, you'll probably die. You don't get any more chances after that." He paused, waiting for me to give in and admit the feelings he and Lou were so sure I possessed, but I only stared back at him. "You're really okay with her believing she was only *important to you*?"

"If I'm dead, what good will her knowing how I feel do her?"

"For starters, she won't live the rest of her life in guilt thinking you gave your life for someone who's *just a friend*."

"So you wouldn't die for your friends?"

"Yes," he growled. "But only after they knew *exactly* how much they meant to me. I wouldn't dare leave them thinking they meant anything less."

"I didn't come here for relationship advice, McNamara. Will you do this for me or not?"

He paused as he seemed to consider it, but I knew he'd already made up his mind. "I'll do it on one condition," he said. I waited, not letting him see my relief as I wondered what he could want more than his mother back safe and sound. "Before you leave, you tell her how you feel."

Pushing air through my nose, I threw out my arms and shouted, "Why the hell do you even care?"

He shot me an evil smile. "Payback, motherfucker. Something tells me admitting to her how you feel would be more painful for you than any punch I could throw."

I looked at him sideways, thinking he had to be bluffing. "What about your mother?"

He shrugged. "You spoke about her as if you care for her. Seems to me like you would get her out of there anyway."

I nodded. It was the only assurance he'd get that he was right. I wouldn't dare fuel his arrogance.

"Do we have a deal?" he prodded.

It occurred to me that Ever McNamara was more ruthless and cunning than I had given him credit for. It explained how he had not only survived but thrived in Exiled even after being fed with silver spoons all of his life. I thought about Evelyn, who also managed to pull the wool over Fox's eyes for so long, and snorted.

It must run in the family.

"Yes."

"Good." Ever looked off toward the house and then back at me. The arrogance was gone, allowing me to see the stress he'd been concealing. "Because now I have a favor to ask."

I tensed. "What's that?"

"Stay for a few days."

His offer was the last thing I expected to hear. "*Why?*"

"For starters, it wouldn't be wise to leave Lou alone so soon with a bunch of strangers," he pointed out, and I realized he was right. Lou would probably slash my tires if I tried.

"And the other reason?" I prompted when he simply stared off in the distance.

Sighing, he said, "Thanksgiving is tomorrow."

CHAPTER
TWENTY-SEVEN

The Flame

A S THE BLONDE STARED OUT THE WINDOW CHEWING HER LIP, I studied her more closely, unable to shake the familiarity. With her wavy hair pulled into that messy ponytail, she looked like she'd just rolled out bed. She was pretty, beautiful even, but not in the obvious, overwhelming way that made everyone else feel inferior. She stood only about an inch taller than my five foot five, and she was slender with an ass that explained why the pretty boy was so feral over her. She must have felt me staring because she turned and suddenly the full force of her dark brown stare was on me, and I saw the challenge in them.

This girl had an edge, but I had a blade.

Smiling, I let her glimpse the wrapped metal hiding under my tongue. To my surprise, she snorted before turning back to the window.

"You worry too much," I told her.

"Are you saying I should trust that your friend won't try to hurt him?"

"Not at all," I said while laughing, "but you still worry too much."

Sighing, she let the curtain fall back into place before coming to stand in front of me. Crossing her arms, she studied me closely, and I did the same. After only a few seconds, we both said, "Have we met?"

Her eyes narrowed, and so did mine. Unfortunately, she

figured it out before I could lie. "Times Square," she said through clenched teeth. "You stole my wallet."

"And I believe I gave it back."

"Only because your friend made you."

"No, because forty bucks was a waste of everyone's time."

She barked out a laugh. "Says the girl who steals wallets."

Just then, the front door opened, and Wren and the pretty boy stepped inside looking no worse than how we'd left them.

"Everything okay, Ever?" blondie asked her brother. She immediately went to him and started fussing over his boo-boos.

I took one look at Wren and rolled my eyes. I'd seen him with worse.

I was also still raw about the way he treated me after I told his boss where he could go. He told me I'd been stupid for challenging Fox. Well, stupid is as stupid does, and I'd learned from the master.

It had been a tense three weeks with us barely speaking to one another unless necessary. Sometimes, I wondered if Wren resented me. Would he abandon me to go back to Fox? Was that why he brought me here?

"I'm Four," I heard blondie say, and I realized she was speaking to Wren.

For some reason, the friendly smile she gave him pissed me off, so I laughed rather obnoxiously. "What the fuck kind of name is Four?" I asked rudely.

In an instant, I knew by her somber expression and the way Ever suddenly looked ready to rip my tongue out that I'd committed some kind of egregious wrong. Wren quickly appeared in front of me, silently daring Ever to make a move. In just a matter of seconds, I managed to fuck up whatever kind of peace they'd established between them.

Knowing Wren would defend me even though I was dead wrong, I elbowed past him and focused on Four.

"There are worms where my brain should be." Closing the

distance while warily keeping an eye on Ever, I stuck out my hand. "I'm Louchana," I offered apologetically. *"Don't* call me Lou."

After only a moment's hesitation, she shook my hand and grinned. "Why? Does he call you Lou?" she teased, referring to Wren.

"Yes. And one day, I'll castrate him for it." Four laughed and so did her brother although I could tell he didn't want to. "So, you guys are twins?" Although they had similar coloring, they didn't look anything alike, but I figured it was because they were fraternal.

That thought fled when they both frowned, and I wondered what the hell I said wrong this time.

"Why do you say that?" Four asked.

"Your names," I pointed out. "Four? Ever? *Forever?* You're like a set, right?"

Four laughed nervously. "No, that's pure coincidence. We're not related at all."

It was my turn to frown. "But you live together."

"My mom is dating his dad."

Suddenly, it all clicked into place, and I had to say that I was relieved. Brothers didn't look at their sisters like Ever looked at Four. I had planned to corner Wren when we were alone and beg him not to leave me here with these people. I still might.

I was about to ask more questions when Ever pulled Four into him and whispered something in her ear. It was brief, and Four only nodded in response. When they started to kiss, I looked away and caught Wren's eye. He'd been leaning against the wall watching me the entire time, his eyes guarded as they'd been for almost a month now, and I wondered if maybe it was time I put pride aside and get over that damn wall once and for all.

I hadn't noticed that Four and Ever's make-out session ended until Ever sauntered by me and signaled for Wren to follow him. They both disappeared leaving Four and me alone.

"I don't mean to pry, but what was with that?" she asked me as she came to stand beside me.

"What was with what?"

"You and Wren. The tension. You could slice it with a butter knife."

"Oh." Sensing I didn't want to talk about it, she shrugged and asked if I was hungry. "Weren't you guys headed to school or something?"

She sighed as she led me through the house. "I think under the circumstances, skipping is in order. Besides, today is only a half day."

We stepped inside the kitchen and found the tattooed God who broke up the fight bent over the island, texting on his phone. He looked up, and the most wicked grin I'd ever seen split his face. "Welcome to our ridiculously non-humble abode."

I took in everything about him. The long, lean body. The pierced nose and eyebrow. The mahogany hair slicked back to show off that gorgeous visage. The bruise already starting to form on his jaw didn't even distract from his handsomeness. I knew with just one look that he was trouble.

"This is Jamie," Four introduced, and I could tell she was reluctant to do so.

"Jameson John Buchanan at your service, but you may call me Jamie and only Jamie, you lovely fuckable thing."

I tilted my head to the side. "Is calling me *fuckable* supposed to flatter me?"

"Do you want it to?" he shot back smoothly.

I was a little taken aback. "How old are you?" He wore the same school uniform as Four and Ever but he seemed older somehow. Beyond his years. And it made me wonder if this devil-may-care attitude was all an act.

He proved me right a second later when his smile turned downright predatory and sexed. "Young enough," he said with a growl that I felt down to my very bones.

The confidence that I could handle anything this guy dished was sapped from my body by that smile alone.

"Don't worry," Four said as she patted my shoulder. "He's harmless."

Maybe…but Wren wasn't.

At that moment, I realized my best friend might have just tossed me from the frying pan into the fire. Then again, if I was going to get Wren to stop running from what we both knew in our hearts, then perhaps a little jealousy could light the match.

Holding out my hand, I allowed Jamie's much larger one to envelop mine. "Louchana Valentine, virgin extraordinaire."

Four groaned in agony, but I was too busy focusing on the heat and the challenge that suddenly engulfed Jamie's brown eyes to care what she thought. "Not for long," he promised.

As I smiled my most flirtatious smile, Four palmed her face and shook her head. Oh, yeah. Wren was going to learn soon enough that he wasn't the only one determined to get his way.

After eating my fill of leftover meatloaf, Four showed me to the guesthouse out by the pool before getting a call that made her swear colorfully and disappear. I was exploring the two-bedroom house that, even in all its extravagance, seemed like a hut in comparison to the mansion when I realized I didn't have my bag or my camera.

Retracing my steps, I followed the stone path back to the main house and through the double doors leading to the family room. Four, who had grown noticeably quiet while I ate, had been too distracted by whatever was going on in her head to give me a real tour, so I stopped and looked around.

Surprisingly, it was your typical family room only twice as large. There was nothing gilded in gold or studded with diamonds. There was a large sectional that could fit an entire family and then some, a couple of comfy looking recliners, and the largest flat-screen TV I'd ever seen. Across the room, I spotted a huge fireplace. On the mantel above, framed photos sat on display. Deciding my bag could wait a few more minutes, I started across the room.

I didn't make it two steps before I heard my name. Wren stood in one of the doorways with Ever at his side, and I frowned as I paused to study them both. The two of them together tugged at my memory strings for some reason.

"What are you doing?" Wren questioned while trying to keep the suspicion from his tone. He probably thought he'd just caught me in the middle of robbing them. Those silver picture frames *had* looked expensive though it never occurred to me to lift them. I'd been more interested in the memories.

"Paula has my bag."

Wren silently lifted his hand, and I realized he had my bag and camera in both.

"Paula?" Ever inquired.

I sighed. Why couldn't anyone just understand me so I didn't have to explain?

"My Im*pala*," Wren told him, and I shrugged. I thought it was rather clever, but if Ever thought so, too, he didn't let on. I realized then that he was a bit of a prick. What the hell Four saw in him, I'll probably never know.

My gaze slid to Wren.

Then again, maybe I already did.

Ever told us his father left a few days ago to handle some crisis on the other side of the world and wouldn't be back until morning. He then asked me where Four had gone, and when I lifted my shoulders, his expression became annoyed.

"Do you think there's trouble in paradise?" I asked Wren once we were alone.

He gave me a warning look as he closed the distance between us. "Not our business."

"But I like them," I admitted with finality. "And by them, I mean Four. Ever's a dick, and Jamie's a flirt." I peeked up at him from under my lashes. "You should know that Jamie is going to try to get in my pants. He might even succeed."

The tick in Wren's jaw was his only reaction.

Feigning worry, I stepped even closer to him. "You don't have a problem with that, do you, bestie?" Of course, he didn't respond. "You shouldn't," I pressed. "All three of them are hot, which means their friends probably are, too." I smiled up at him excitedly. "We could be each other's wingman!"

I felt his strong hand at my nape before I even realized he'd moved, and then he was kissing me. Immediately, I melted into him, excited to feel his lips again after three long weeks. His hand found my ass at the same time his tongue worked its way inside my mouth. I didn't know there could be so much passion and heat in a single kiss, and I wanted more. I was practically climbing his body when he finally let me go. Opening my eyes, however, I wasn't prepared for the coldness staring back at me.

"Do what you want," he told me quietly before he dropped my bag at my feet and left me standing alone.

CHAPTER
TWENTY-EIGHT

The Moth

I WASN'T SURE HOW LONG I SPENT BROODING ON THE COUCH, BUT THE sun started setting a while ago, and Lou still hadn't returned to the guesthouse. Only my bruised ego kept me from going up to the main house to drag her ass back. Just as I began to wonder if maybe she'd been crazy enough to leave, the door opened. I shot up from the couch ready to tear into her for making me worry, but I lost all the fight in me when I saw Ever, Jamie, and their friend who'd been with them in Times Square staring back at me.

"He's got the bluuuues!" Jamie sang, or rather howled, as he headed for the kitchen carrying a couple of six-packs in each hand. I ignored him and the need to bash his face in and regarded the other two.

"We figured you could use some company," Ever answered my questioning gaze.

It was the last thing I wanted, but since I couldn't ask him to leave his own house, I sat back down and didn't say shit.

The third in their trio with green eyes and impressive biceps flopped down next to me and said, "He forgot to mention that the girls are having a man-hating meeting, and the house is no longer safe for any of us." He chuckled when I swore and held out his hand. "I'm Vaughn," he supplied when I shook it.

"Wren."

"Are you a Corona or a Bud man?" Jamie called from the kitchen. "The wrong answer might get you hazed."

"Then why do you have both?" I retorted.

"Because it's a trick question," Ever told me as he handed me a can. "Jamie doesn't give a shit who it comes from as long as it gets him wasted."

Jamie howled some more, and I wondered where the hell the off button was on him. I was in a foul fucking mood, and they were just making it worse.

"So…do you want to talk about it?" Ever asked me. I was surprised by his offer but I didn't let it show.

"No."

"Why not?" Vaughn prodded before he blew out a breath. "It can't be worse than any of our shit."

"Dude, he's right," Jamie piped in as he joined us with a beer in both hands. "*His* girl made him drive her over here so she could talk shit about him. He just stood there taking it like a chump."

"Shut up," Vaughn growled at him, making Jamie cackle louder.

"She's upset with him," Jamie continued, "because his daddy would never let him be with her. Oh, wait…Tyra doesn't know that, does she, Vaughn? She really thinks you only want sex." Vaughn's mouth tightened as he looked away. "And Ever here has his hands full juggling *two* girlfriends." Jamie tilted his head as his expression turned thoughtful. "Or is Four just your sideline?" Ever's gaze was cutting when he glanced at his cousin, but he followed Vaughn's lead and kept his mouth shut.

I wondered how they thought to give me advice when they clearly didn't know their asses from their elbows.

"Lou thinks you're a dick," I told Ever. "If your woman is really up their airing your dirty laundry, don't bet on Lou changing her mind anytime soon."

Ever's eyes widened before he shook his head. "It's amazing how fast girls band together when you fuck up," he complained. "Four *just met* Lou a few hours ago."

"Yeah, well, look at us," Vaughn pointed out.

Ever waved his hand dismissively as he sank lower in his seat to brood.

The room grew silent, and then I noticed they were all looking at me. Realizing that I was fighting a losing battle, I pushed air through my nose and said, "Lou wants me to fuck her, but… I can't." She might have even wanted to be more than friends. I ignored the longing stabbing my heart and waited for their reaction.

The silence that followed didn't last very long. "Because you think it will ruin your friendship?" Jamie asked. The humor was gone from his eyes and in its place, understanding, which I didn't expect.

Knowing it was the simplest answer, I nodded.

"It's a little late to worry about that when you've already caught feelings," Ever snitched. "At this point, *not* fucking her is what's ruining your friendship."

When I didn't respond, Vaughn turned to me. "Do you want her?"

"Yes," I growled, and all three of them stared at me with matching perplexed expressions.

"Then I don't get it," Jamie said as he scratched his head. "Were you out of condoms or something?"

"Shut up and drink your beer," Ever told him. The look Jamie gave him had me tensing up. At any moment, I expected them to come to blows, and since they could both throw a mean punch, I knew it would be a bloody one.

Fortunately, Vaughn spoke before that could happen. "There's another reason you won't touch her, isn't there?"

I nodded somberly unable to hide my guilt.

"Look, I don't know what you did," Ever said, "but its *always* better if she hears it from you."

I gave him a skeptical look. "You think it will keep her from being angry?"

They all started howling at the same time.

"Fuck no!" Ever said, still laughing. At my grave expression, he quickly turned sober again. "But it will give you a chance."

"And if your thing with her is going to work," Jamie said, "there can only be *one* alpha, and from what I heard up there, Little Lou Who is moonwalking all over you."

I knew that. Goddammit, I knew it, but there was a reason I'd always treaded carefully where Lou was concerned, and guilt had everything to do with it.

"What would you prescribe, Dr. Phil?"

Jamie shrugged. "A firm hand works wonders."

My scowl would have folded a lesser man, but Jamie didn't so much as blink. "Are you telling me to *hit* her?"

He rolled his eyes. "I'm suggesting you get your balls back from her, man."

Ever scratched his chin and grinned at me a little sheepishly. "He's not wrong...a spanking now and then wouldn't hurt."

I laughed because it had crossed my mind many times, but it required crossing a line that I'd backed away from too many times to count. "She'd probably enjoy it," I muttered.

"Yeah, but so will you," Ever countered. "More, actually."

I lifted a brow. "Are you speaking from experience?"

He sent me a sideways glance. "That's private."

Vaughn sucked his teeth. "And you don't think girls talk about that stuff?"

Ever frowned at his friend. "Four wouldn't..." He trailed off before staring off into the distance. Jamie and Vaughn both shared a looked before they started howling at Ever's expense.

"So are you going to go for it?" Vaughn asked me when they both settled down.

"I don't know..."

Jamie shook his head in disappointment before shrugging and cracking open another beer. "Maybe Lou should keep your balls," he muttered. And then he saluted me. "She certainly wears them better."

"Wren."

My eyes popped open, and my drunken gaze searched the room until I found a blurry version of Lou standing over me with her arms crossed. I could tell she was pissed, so I wracked my brain trying to remember what I'd done, but I honestly couldn't remember anything before her calling my name.

Stupidly, I grinned up at her. "Hey, Little Lou Who."

"What?" she questioned with a growl.

"Little Lou Who. That's what Jamie calls you."

I could see her glower clearly, even in my drunken state. "I don't care what he calls me."

"You should. You want him to fuck you, 'member?" It was my turn to glare. Turns out, not even alcohol could erase that little tidbit. I heard a snort and then a chuckle and suddenly remembered that I hadn't been drinking alone.

Across the room, Ever was drunkenly grinning down at an annoyed Four while she tried to get him out the door. "Come on, princess," he slurred. "I promise I'll be quick."

"I'm sure you will," Four retorted wryly. "And that's exactly why I'm saying no."

She finally managed to get him out the door but not before I heard him asking if he could eat her out instead.

I blinked, wishing I hadn't heard that. I didn't hear Four's response, but I had a pretty good idea when Ever hung his head looking as if he'd just been told he couldn't have his favorite toy. A moment later, I heard angry shouting on the other side of the spare bedroom. I recognized Vaughn's voice, which was deeper, but I squinted my eyes trying to place the feminine voice.

"That's Tyra," Lou explained. I couldn't remember if I asked or not. "She's going to miss her curfew since Vaughn's too drunk to drive. They're crashing here."

I nodded and then moaned when my head immediately

swam. *Won't be doing that again.*

"Let's go," she told me authoritatively and then waited for me to get up. I sat back on the couch instead.

"Where are we going?" I asked, grinning.

She propped her hands on her hips impatiently. *"To bed."*

"Together?" I asked, making her nostrils flare. And was that hope in my tone? I waited for the usual guilt that followed, but none came. Maybe getting wasted was all I needed to do to have sex with Lou. I snorted. I was sure she'd appreciate that.

"Yes," she hissed. "Jamie is going to need the couch."

I frowned as I looked around. Spotting Jamie passed out on the floor just a few feet away, I regarded Lou again. "He looks pretty comfortable where is," I slurred.

"He might wake up," she said.

I stood until I was towering over her and grinned. "You just want to get in my pants."

I started reaching for my belt when she said, "No girl wants whiskey dick." She turned away, and my hands fell when she started for the bedroom.

"Actually, it was beer," I corrected as I stumbled after her. "So if we do have sex, we'll just call it beer bonging."

Her shoulders jerked, and even though her back was to me, I knew she was smiling. My stomach fluttered, and my throat felt clogged as the hole in my chest filled just a little. Unfortunately, the moment we entered the bedroom, I realized that it might have just been bile all along. I made it to the toilet just as I began to empty my stomach.

I was vaguely aware of Lou rubbing my back as she sat beside me and cooed. Once finished, I collapsed on the cold tile and laid my head in her lap with a groan. She was warm, soft, and everything I didn't deserve.

"That's what you get," she scolded even as I felt her hands rubbing my hair soothingly. "You know you can't hold your liquor."

"I needed liquid courage."

"For what?" she asked curiously as she continued running her fingers through my hair. Her anger from before had faded, but my heart pounded anyway.

"I can't tell you."

Lips twitching, she held in a smile. "Best friends tell each other everything."

I searched her gaze for the longest time, and then I swallowed hard. "I don't want to be your best friend anymore."

She flinched, and I knew I'd hurt her. My lips parted to fix it, but I realized I had no idea how.

"We need to get you into a bed," she said quietly. She helped me stand only to buckle a little under my weight once I was on my feet.

"I love you," I mumbled as we stumbled into the bedroom.

She sighed as we crossed the room and gently helped me into the bed. "I love you, too, bestie."

"No…" My eyes lowered the moment my head hit the pillow. "I *love* you," I repeated. And then my eyes popped open again. It took a few seconds for them to focus and find her. "Ever said I had to tell you."

She blinked. I blinked. And then I passed out.

My eyes were still closed when I ran my hand over the empty side of the bed where Lou should have been. The sheets were cool, telling me all I needed to know. Slowly, my eyes opened, and even slower, I rose until I was sitting on the side of the bed. I felt like shit, and it had little to do with my throbbing head.

The bathroom was empty, too, when I wandered inside. I brushed my teeth and took a long shower, but afterward, I didn't feel any better. My gut was telling me that I screwed up monumentally last night. If only I could remember why.

I walked out of the bedroom and found Jamie still passed

out exactly where we'd left him on the floor. It was then that I remembered Lou putting me to bed after I puked my guts out… and the words I said to her after.

I started for the door, hoping she was up at the main house when I spotted her lying on the couch. The pressure in my chest didn't ease. In fact, it grew tighter the closer I got to her. She looked at peace as she slept, but when her eyes opened after I shook her, I knew that was a lie. Lou took one look at me, grimaced as if in agony, and turned away. I felt like a monster when she curled into herself.

Three words. I ruined her in three words.

I didn't realize I was still kneeling, still staring, until I felt a hand on my shoulder. Jamie, who looked like he could barely hold himself up, jerked his head toward the door. Sighing, I followed him up to the main house, and he led me into the kitchen. Four and Ever were already there. Four sipped from a cup while gazing smugly at Ever, who looked miserable with his elbows planted on the island and his head cradled between his hands.

"There's fresh coffee," Four offered when she noticed us enter.

Ever didn't bother to acknowledge our presence while Jamie kept going and disappeared from the kitchen.

"Thanks." I reached for the coffee pot while she hopped up and grabbed two mugs from one of the cabinets. She handed me one and set the other on the counter.

"Where's Lou?"

"Still sleeping," I told her as I poured. That wasn't entirely true, and I had no idea how I was going to fix it. Just as I finished filling my mug a thought came to me, and I poured coffee into the second mug. Grabbing both, I turned and found Ever struggling to stand. For some reason, he drank more than any of us last night. "Is he going to be okay?"

"Eventually," Four answered with a roll of her eyes. "He's just trying to make me feel bad for not putting out last night."

Taking his hand, she led him to the door. I was still watching them when Ever secretly grinned at me over his shoulder.

Shaking my head and wondering if I was actually starting to like the little shit, I started back for the guesthouse. In the family room, something small and black rushed between my legs making me stumble. The coffee that spilled burned my hand, so I quickly set the mugs down on the mantel and wiped my hands on my jeans. There was movement in the corner of my eye, and when I looked over, I saw a small black, blue-eyed lab staring back at me with his tongue hanging from his mouth.

"That's not funny."

He got excited and started running in circles as if to prove me wrong. I kneeled, and he ran up to me at full speed. The silver tag hanging from his blue collar caught my attention, so I lifted it.

"Jay D," I read aloud. He barked as if to confirm, and I had to admit he was pretty adorable. That was when a light bulb went off, and I smiled at my new friend. "How would you like to help me cheer someone up?"

Before he could agree—or not because he was a damn dog, and I was being silly—I heard Four calling his name, and then she appeared a moment later.

"There you are!" she said to Jay D, who immediately charged her. Her attention shifted to me when he started sniffing the floor around her. "He's not bothering you, is he? Ever must have kicked him out of his room when I wasn't looking," she grumbled.

I laughed at that as I wondered how the two of them could be opposite yet alike in so many ways. "Nah, he's cool," I assured her.

She nodded and knelt to scratch behind Jay D's ears. I was reaching for the coffee mugs on the mantel when one of the photos caught my eye. Forgetting the coffee, I snatched the frame, nearly toppling the others, to study the picture of the trio closer. The rest of the room faded away as blood rushed to my head, making my ears ring. Were my eyes deceiving me? Had I gone insane? Or was I truly staring at a younger version of my father? He had a light in his eyes that I'd never before seen in him.

Four looked up, noticing my silence. I knew I should play off my interest as pure curiosity, but it was too late. She was already standing by my side, wearing a frown. "Are you okay?"

"I—" The rest of my words got stuck in my throat. Whatever they were.

Four gently took the frame from my hands and pointed to the man on the far right. "That's Douglas, Jamie's father." I nodded once, seeing the resemblance easily. She then pointed to the man in the middle with light brown hair and stern blue eyes. "That's Thomas." She hesitated this time when she said, "Ever's father." My gaze was already fixated on the man to his right with dark hair, eyes that Lou would claim were only sometimes blue, and a cleft chin that, when last I saw him, he was hiding under a short beard. "And this," Four said as her finger slid over to my father, "is Sean, Thomas's best friend."

I swallowed the lump in my throat, and my next breath shuddered out of me.

Sean.

I'd only ever known him as Crow.

CHAPTER
TWENTY-NINE

The Flame

THE MANOR, AS FOUR CALLED IT, WAS IN AN UPROAR. TODAY WAS Thanksgiving, and the many hired hands rushed back and forth in preparation for the guests arriving. Mr. Hunt, the head chef, and his team of cooks had taken over the kitchen while Mrs. Greene, the housekeeper, commanded an entire army of maids to clean, polish, and decorate.

Ever's father had also returned late in the morning.

The formidable man of the house had accepted whatever excuse Ever offered to explain our presence, but that didn't stop him from looking at us suspiciously whenever we crossed his path—Wren in particular.

Four's mother, on the other hand, had barely acknowledged our presence. I didn't take it personally. Rosalyn didn't seem to hold much interest in anything, including her daughter. And other than the worried glances Four cast her now and then, the two seemed more like strangers than mother and daughter.

I lasted maybe an hour among the chaos before I fled back to the haven of the guesthouse. When I stepped inside, I found it as quiet and empty as I'd left it.

Which meant Wren still hadn't come back from his drive.

It was the only explanation I'd gotten when I asked Ever where he was. Four's failure to hide her worry, however, told me all I needed to know. Something was wrong, and Wren was attempting to keep it from me.

An hour later, I was curled up in one of the wicker sofas staring at the water from the pool when I looked up and found Four standing over me holding a dress. Jay D was at her feet, wagging his tongue and tail happily.

"Here." She held out the burgundy dress.

"What's this?"

"Something to wear for dinner. They do things kind of formal around here, so I figured you'd be more comfortable blending in. Size four, right?"

I gave the dress a once-over before meeting her gaze again. "Is that what you do? Blend in?"

Four had told me all about her former life in some bumble-fuck town called Cherry and how her mom had met Thomas cleaning rooms at one of his hotels. She may not have been fed with a silver spoon growing up, but sooner or later, she'd have to accept the fact that her life had changed. Ever would one day inherit all of his family's riches, and if their thing lasted past high school, so would she.

Her mouth tightened as if she could read my thoughts. "When I have to."

Our staring contest went on for a little while longer until I finally caved and accepted it with some hesitation. I studied the dress a little longer this time and realized it was fucking beautiful. A little couture for my taste, but beggars couldn't be choosers. Peeking at the tag, my jaw dropped at the price. I could never afford this with a thousand stolen wallets!

"And when you don't?"

She sighed and flopped down in the seat next to me. "Well, I'm dating the most popular boy in school, and no one fucks with him so..."

"No one fucks with you," I said, filling in the blank.

She simply shrugged before shooing Jay D away when he started chewing on a chair cushion. I had a pretty good idea of the kind of power Ever had. The social ladder was the same in any school. At the top were the elite who everyone wanted to either be or avoid at all cost, and at the bottom were the ones who were stepped on to reach the top. "The power he has…it doesn't bother you?"

She chewed on her lip, a tell I'd quickly learned meant she was anxious. "It used to, and, to be honest, I'm still getting used to it. We didn't exactly click when we first met, so I know what it's like to be at his mercy. The first time he unleashed his wrath on me, he convinced his father to send me to reform school…in *Europe*."

"Whoa."

"Don't worry," she said with a grin, "I got him back."

"How?"

"I made his life hell…or at least I tried to. I challenged him, and the weirdo ended up falling for me instead. The way he looked at me, the way he touched me…it made me burn for him. I fought it, but after a while, I couldn't even remember why I hated him."

"So it ended happily for you, but what about the people he doesn't fall in love with?"

"He's not a bully," she argued. When I tilted my head skeptically, she shook her head and smiled. "I guess I was the exception," she conceded. "I know it sounds lame and not at all romantic, but it's true. It's hard to get under Ever's skin and even harder to get out. He doesn't prey on the innocent, and the ones who aren't, I trust him not to go too far. The punishment always fits the crime."

"You don't think a year in boarding school was going too far?"

She cringed as if replaying a memory and peeked at me from under her lashes. "I wasn't all that innocent, either. Ever humiliated me in front of everyone at school, so I assaulted one of his teammates with a bottle of whiskey. He ended up needing stitches."

I hid my smile while thinking Four was my kind of girl after all. "Still…I'm not sure I could have forgiven him just because he batted those pretty gold eyes at me."

Four held her sides as she bent over laughing. "Trust me, it wasn't easy," she grumbled once she settled down. "I went down kicking and screaming until I realized I wasn't just hurting him but myself as well."

"And now? You're a little fish in his much bigger pond. What does he do when he wants his way, and you want yours?"

"We fight and then we fuck," she answered plainly before shrugging. "One of us usually compromises after that."

"*What?*" I chortled, and she laughed, too.

"I never said we had it all figured out!" She then shot me a devilish grin. "Either way, I always win."

"I guess you got under more than just his skin," I teased.

"She did."

I looked up, and Four's head whipped around when we heard the deep voice. Ever was leaning against the pillar just feet away, and neither of us knew how long he'd been standing there.

"She got deeper than anyone ever could."

I would have gagged if I hadn't witnessed the look in his eyes as he watched Four. She wasn't kidding about the way he looked at her. I felt like I was intruding as they gazed into each other's eyes. Slowly, she stood, and they naturally drifted to one another, but then Jay D broke the moment when he launched himself at Ever.

Ever glared down at the pup through narrowed eyes as Jay D pawed at his legs. "Cockblocker," he sneered.

Four giggled and closed the distance between them. "He's just saying hi to his daddy."

"Four, I keep telling you that mutt isn't a real baby." Much lower he said, "That comes later." It was obvious his promise wasn't meant for my ears, but even if I hadn't heard, I'd have a pretty damn good clue judging by the blush reddening Four's cheeks.

"What do you want, McNamara? You're embarrassing me."

"Gruff's here."

"What?" she screeched. I almost laughed at the startled look on Ever's face when she broke free from his arms and shoved past him with Jay D hot on her heels. She was gone before he'd even recovered.

"Who's Gruff?" I asked when the whiplashed look on his face cleared.

When he finally looked at me, I could tell he'd forgotten that I was even there. I felt a stab of envy and hoped that one day, I could be to someone the girl who made everyone else cease to exist. I lost hope each day that the 'someone' would be Wren. Last night, he told me that he loved me, and even though he'd made it clear he hadn't meant as a friend, I knew better than to believe in his drunken ramblings.

"Back home, she was a mechanic," Ever answered. "Gruff's her old boss."

"That's interesting. I always thought bosses were people you avoided until it was time to get paid."

He snorted. "He's been more of a father to her than a boss."

I noticed the tightness in his voice and said, "Let me guess... he doesn't approve of you?"

Ever sighed and he seemed to completely deflate. "If he does, he definitely won't by the end of dinner."

He was gone before I could ask him what he meant.

A startled gasp fell from my lips when I emerged from the bathroom a few hours later and found Wren waiting for me on the edge of the bed. His head was down as he stared at the floor, but it shot up, and the moment he saw me standing there, he stopped breathing. I had nothing on except the towel wrapped around me, and even though it was huge and thick, under his fervent gaze, I still felt naked. Water dripped from my hair onto the floor, and for a while, it was the only sound. I watched his Adam's apple bob as he struggled to swallow, and I wondered if he was fighting to keep whatever was on his mind from spilling out.

After an intense battle, he finally settled for a simple, "Hey."

His voice sounded heavy, and it was all I could do not to rush to him and beg him to tell me what was wrong. I was growing sick of begging Wren for anything. Last night, he told me he loved me, so maybe this sudden solemnness was the reason. Maybe he regretted it even more than I did. Many times, I've imagined the first time I would hear those words from him, and none of those fantasies ever involved him being drunk and passing out after.

"Where have you been?" I questioned as I crossed the room. The dress Four loaned me hung over the chair near the window. My back was to him when he answered.

"Had to clear my head."

I pursed my lips as if he could see. "It doesn't sound like you succeeded."

He didn't answer at first, and I realized why when I felt him press against me from behind. "No."

"So are you going to tell me what's eating you?"

He sucked in a breath. "No." And then his hand found the knot keeping my towel up, and my lips parted when he loosened it. "I'd rather eat you instead."

Before I could react, the towel fell to the floor, and there was nothing left to shield me from him. I didn't even get the chance to consider what was happening before I felt his hand on my back pushing until I was bent over the chair.

"What are you doing?" I shrieked.

"Clearing my head."

I gasped even as my pussy clenched at the thought of being used by him. It shouldn't have excited me as much as it did.

"I never did get the chance to return the favor properly." He knelt, and his hand circled my thigh. I felt his thumb sweeping my skin and then his lips skimming my ass. "May I?"

A shiver went down my spine. I knew what I wanted, but I also knew it wasn't wise. *A little late to have second thoughts, Lou.* I started this after all. I ignored his warnings and pushed us over the boundaries of friendship without any regard for the consequences. Amidst my turmoil, I felt my legs begin to tremble. Since I wasn't sure how much longer I'd be able to hold myself up, I closed my eyes and just let go.

"Yes."

I could be angry with him later.

His breathing turned ragged, and when his mouth inched closer, I felt his every exhale between my thighs, teasing my pussy until I was throbbing. Eventually, I could no longer contain the anticipation and closed my eyes when I felt it—hot, wet, and running down my thigh. And when his tongue trailed up my skin, stealing every drop, I dug my nails into the cushion of the chair and gasped.

I couldn't do this. It was too much. I could already feel myself losing control.

Before I could tell him so, he wrapped his arms around my waist, holding me in place, and buried his face between my thighs with a growl so savage I answered it with a startled cry.

His tongue swept my pussy, teasing, and tasting, and whenever he found the exact spot that made me press against his mouth for more, he'd lap at it relentlessly only to retreat when I was close.

"Wren, don't be cruel," I whined when he brought me to the brink once more. He chuckled, and the moment he abandoned suckling my clit to pierce me with his stiff tongue, I came. No sound escaped me, and other than my toes curling into the carpet, I couldn't move or speak. Not even to tell him that I was too sensitive when he started peppering my pussy with soft kisses. He seemed to get the message when I whined, and he stood.

I stayed where I was when I felt his hard cock through his

jeans. I could almost hear his thoughts as clearly as my own and knew that he was considering it.

Taking me like this.

From behind.

Bent over the chair.

Completely at his mercy.

I lifted my leg onto the arm of the chair and arched my back, opening myself more for him, and when I peeked over my shoulder, our gazes met. Neither of us moved or breathed for a few a heartbeats and then slowly, his hands went for his belt. I didn't dare look away. I heard his zipper lowering and then the rustle of his jeans as he pushed them over his hips. The moment his dick was out, swollen and veiny, he swore violently.

"I don't have a condom," he told me.

My frown cleared. "And I'm not on birth control," I said like it was no big deal. Neither of us were prepared for this, but I'd be damned if I let that stop us now.

"You could get pregnant, Lou."

"I don't care."

"Lou—"

"I don't care," I repeated, unwilling to yield. I was prepared to risk my heart, my sanity, and my future for this. For him.

When he stepped closer and pressed himself against me, the heart I was willing to put in peril, soared. I felt his cock brush against my lower lips, and my eyes drifted shut as I moaned. I was more than ready to feel all of him inside me.

But my joy quickly dissipated when he lifted me from the chair, set me on my feet, and pulled his jeans up. "We can't," he told me when he finally met my gaze.

"Would it really be so bad?" I cried, unable to hide my frustration.

"No, it wouldn't be so bad—for me. You still have your whole life ahead of you."

"With you?"

He searched my hopeful gaze, and I could see the torment in his. "If you want."

"I want," I told him in a tone that left no room for doubt, but he only shook his head.

"You don't know that yet."

"You've been my best friend—no, my entire *world* for nearly three years, Wren. There's nothing else left to know."

I didn't miss the pain in his eyes before he turned away. My hand reached out to touch his back when he spoke. His voice was barely above a whisper. "There's plenty, Lou. There's plenty."

He started for the door, but I rushed to intercept him. I was done letting him walk away from me.

"Then tell me now. Right here." I pointed to the floor before stepping close enough for my breasts to brush his chest. "And when you're done, I want you to make love to me. Condom or no condom." Reaching up, I pulled his face down until our lips met. "There's nothing you can tell me that would make me give you up." I kissed him again, deeper this time. "I've wanted you for too long."

"Lou—"

"Please, Wren," I whispered desperately as I reached for his belt. "Please fuck me. I don't care what you did." I quickly undid his jeans, and the moment I had my hand wrapped around his thick cock, he gasped as if in pain. A second later, he yanked me up in his arms and carried me to the bed.

He laid me down, and I immediately rose onto my elbows to watch him undress. He yanked his shirt over his head first, revealing those mouthwatering abs and the chest I loved so much. And then he kicked off his shoes before shoving his pants and boxers down his legs.

He didn't immediately come to me once he was naked, though. He just stood at the foot of the bed, staring, and I knew he was waiting for me to change my mind.

Holding his gaze, I let my shaking legs fall open instead. His gaze fell, and he sucked in a breath. In a flash, he was on top of me, kissing me hard and deep.

I wrapped my legs around his waist and ran my hands down his powerful back. His hot skin against mine was the most natural feeling in the world. We'd never been this vulnerable with each other before, but somehow, I felt whole.

He finally allowed us air, and my eyes drifted closed when he started kissing down my neck until he reached my breasts. Pulling my nipple inside his mouth, he suckled one and then the other until I was writhing.

"Lou…"

I slowly opened my eyes.

"I won't stop once I start," he warned.

Smiling, I dug my nails in his shoulders until he grimaced. "You better not."

He smirked as he grabbed my hands and lifted them over my head. Holding my wrists in one hand, he guided his cock to my slick opening with the other and began pushing inside of me.

He got maybe an inch or two before my pussy rejected him. He tried to go deeper, and I cried out. I knew then that this wouldn't be easy. He was even bigger than I thought.

"Fuck, you're tight, Lou." He started to pull away, and I panicked. Tightening my legs around him, I held him in place.

"Don't." I moaned.

"I need to open you, baby, or this is going to hurt like hell."

I shook my head, fearing that if he stopped even for a moment, he'd back out. "I don't care about the pain."

Getting rejected by him over and over had hurt a thousand times more.

"I don't want to hurt you," he said, pleading.

"And you will if you stop."

A silent battle of wills ensued that ended when he kissed me.

It started slow and deepened by the second. It was perfect. So perfect I never even noticed when he gripped the back of my thigh, holding me open, or when his other hand curled around my neck, holding me down. That perfect kiss swallowed my scream after he pulled his hips back only to shove inside me so brutally he broke through my virginity in one stroke.

There was no me and him after that, only us.

That was how deep he'd gotten.

He didn't stop kissing me until my whimpers died, and when my eyes drifted open, I found him watching me.

"Okay?" he asked me as he thumbed away my tears.

"Never better," I answered. My voice sounded hoarse, and there was a throbbing ache between my legs, but finally, having him inside me made it all worth it.

He grinned and kissed me before smiling against my lips. "Stubborn girl."

And then he began to move.

Carefully. Slowly allowing me to get used to feeling so full. To the need stirring in my belly. It wasn't long before I started to move, too. Driven purely by instinct, I snaked my hips and clutched him tighter. Burying his face in my neck, he groaned as he drove himself deeper, his hand palming my breast while the other gripped the sheet. He moved faster now.

Soon, my cries mingled with the sound of his heavy breaths and the bed rocking. The lewdness of the ruckus we were making only spurred us to finish. I felt him grip my hip as he picked up the pace. Neither of us gave a damn anymore that this was wrong.

Best friends forever.

It was nothing more than a broken promise now.

"Fuck, Lou, I'm gonna come."

He started pulling away, to make it last, so I tightened around him, keeping him prisoner.

"Baby." He grunted. "We can't. You—" His hips slammed into me one last time before he suddenly stiffened. "Fuuuuck!"

I held him tight, stroking his back and cooing nonsense in his ear as he came inside me. I knew the risk we were taking was huge and that he'd be pissed, but I didn't care. It wasn't like I was trying to get knocked up. I only wanted all of him. Just this once until we were both ready.

When his body finally slackened on top of mine, I slowly unwrapped my stiff legs from his waist and let them fall at my sides.

He was still planted deep inside me and breathing hard when he lifted enough for me to see his glare. "Why did you do that?"

"I wanted you to come," I told him quietly. I couldn't believe, after all that, I still found it in me to be shy. Perhaps it was the dark look he was giving me that told me I was in big trouble.

"You wanted control," he said, seeing right through me.

Before I could deny it, I was flat on my stomach with my ass in the air, and my hair gripped tightly—almost cruelly—in his fist.

My heart skipped a beat when I felt his cock lining up at my entrance. And just before he shoved his way back inside me, without regard for my lost virginity, he growled in my ear, "*One* alpha, Lou."

I let out a startled cry and gripped the sheets tightly when I felt him fill me. His cum was still seeping out of me, paving the way for him to plunder. Still, I felt tears sliding down my cheeks and didn't know if they were from joy or the feel of him hitting the spot deep inside of me that made my breath catch every time.

"I don't come until *I* say. *You* don't come until I say." Pushing in even deeper, he said, "Feel me?"

Oh, hell yeah, I felt him, and what's more, I understood him. He made sure of it as he drove his point home over and over. The sound of our skin slapping was a constant reminder lest I forget so quickly.

I pushed back into him, reveling in this side of him.

I craved it.

And if I had to push him to get it, I'd do it with open legs and willing cunt.

I wanted to be owned. To be kept. A slave to his desires as well as mine.

And if my reward for being a bad girl was a sore pussy, well then, Wren had better clear his schedule.

CHAPTER
THIRTY

The Moth

I FUCKED MY BEST FRIEND. I SHOULD NEVER HAVE FUCKED MY BEST friend. Because now I couldn't stop fucking my best friend.

As if hearing my thoughts, her pussy tightened around me, milking my cock and taking me for all I was worth. I should have been gentler, and I shouldn't have taken her again so soon, but I was smart enough to know when my brain was no longer in control.

Giving in to the pleasure, I closed my eyes, but the sounds she made as she started to come had me opening them again. Her skin was glistening with the sweat we worked up while her hair, still trapped in my fist, was in disarray. She never looked more beautiful to me.

The moment she collapsed on the bed, utterly spent, I quickly pulled out of her and gripped my cock. The first time had been an epic fuckup, and I blamed myself. I could have stopped it if I wanted to, but at that moment, there had been nothing I wanted more than to fill her in every way.

I got maybe three or four strokes in before I was coming again. Some of it landed on her back, and I growled my pleasure at seeing her covered in me. My limbs suddenly turned to jelly, and I crashed on the bed next to her as I struggled to catch my breath. Lou was so still next to me that the only sign of life was the steady rise and fall of her slender shoulders.

Her long raven hair hung down her back, and I was already

reminiscing about the way I held it in my fist like reins as I rode her. I reached out to run my hands through the silky tresses when I stopped short, a silent curse on my lips. Her hair fell more than halfway down her back just an inch or two above where I came on the small of her back.

I stood from the bed and reached for her, but the moment I touched her, Lou stiffened. My heart dropped to my stomach, immediately fearing that I'd gone too far. Had I hurt her? I clenched my teeth and cursed myself for coming back here. After my world was turned upside down and the ground swept from under my feet, I'd gone for a drive. And when that hadn't worked, I came running back to the one person who could piece me back together again. Lou had done that and more, and I repaid her by hurting her.

I reached out to her again, needing to offer her comfort.

"Noooo," she whined when I laid a hesitant hand on her lower back. "I can't take anymore. Leave me alone."

I chuckled as relief washed over me. "We need to shower."

"Later," she grumbled into the pillow she'd been biting moments ago. She sounded half asleep already.

"I—" My cheeks heated as I tried to figure out a way to tell her what I'd done. After a few seconds, I blew out an aggravated breath. *Fuck it.* "I got some in your hair."

She lifted her head and frowned sleepily at me over her shoulder. "Some of what?"

I tucked my lips inside my mouth and waited. Her eyes widened the moment it dawned.

"Ewwww!" she shrieked. "Wren!"

She tried to jump up from the bed and was immediately reminded that she'd just lost her virginity and not all that gently. I cursed before quickly scooping her up.

"Sorry," I muttered, and she lifted a brow at my apology.

"For breaking me or for jizzing in my hair?"

"Both."

She sighed as I entered the bathroom and set her on the counter. "I guess this makes us even."

She beamed up at me, but I didn't return her smile. "We should haven't done that."

"We're teenagers," she said as she rolled her eyes. "Being irresponsible is sort of our job."

I turned away, feeling my temper rising. I wasn't a teenager, which meant I definitely knew better—more than she did. I told her so as I turned on the shower.

"You were just nineteen *three months* ago. Relax, Mr. Harlan."

I shook my head and decided to keep my mouth shut. When Lou had her mind made up, there was almost no changing it. Her blatant disregard for her future only fueled the turmoil wreaking havoc in my head. We were on the run with no money. How the fuck could I possibly take care of her *and* a baby?

Unless…she didn't think we'd be around for the consequences? It was far more likely that we'd both die in a matter of days than get away from Fox forever. Peeking over my shoulder, I found her staring at the tile, a bleakness in her eyes that she didn't want me to see.

As if sensing my gaze, her head shot up, and the hopelessness cleared. "I'm sure Ever or Jamie have condoms we can use?" The smug satisfaction was gone from her voice, and in its place was that shy innocence that should have kept me from touching her in the first place.

"Yeah," I simply replied because I'd already decided that this wouldn't happen again. We might be dead soon, but at least I'd die with my conscience mostly intact. I tested the water with my hand and then turned. "The water should be warm enough for you."

"Me?" she questioned as she carefully hopped off the counter. Two steps and she was backing me against the wall of the glass shower. I held my breath as her hands slid from my stomach up to my chest. "Just me?"

"Just you," I confirmed before looking away. I couldn't take the sight of her big hopeful eyes staring up at me. "I'll shower after."

I heard the hitch in her breath and felt her hands tremble on my chest. "You're already regretting making love to me, aren't you?"

My nostrils flared as I met her gaze. "We didn't *make love*. We fucked. The fact that you don't know the difference is why I regret it."

Lou should have never trusted me with something so precious. I only touched her because I wanted to escape my past and what lay ahead—if only for a little while. I *used* her. Selfishly and callously.

And I couldn't undo it.

Pushing her aside, I stormed from the bathroom. I pretended not to hear her sniffling as I gathered my discarded clothes and fled for the safety of the spare bedroom. Needing something to occupy my mind so that I wouldn't go running to beg her forgiveness and worship her slowly like I should have done, I decided to take a shower.

Of all the things on my list of regrets, not being able to give Lou her innocence back was at the top, so I'd cherish it forever instead.

I'd been holding up the wall for the past hour watching the people crowding the room. The living room—almost twice the size of the family room that housed my father's photo—had three sets of French doors leading to the veranda. They were thrown open despite the fires lit in the hearths at each end of the room.

Lou sat on one of the bronze sofas pretending to listen to some old broad talk about fuck knows what. I could tell by the glazed look in her eyes that she was bored but was either too polite or too stubborn to walk away. I knew the latter was most likely.

She hadn't spoken a word or barely looked at me since I left her to shower alone. When she emerged from the bedroom in that red dress made of tulle and lace, I nearly swallowed my tongue. I told her, of course, that she looked beautiful, and she pretended she hadn't heard me as she headed straight for the door. All I could do was follow her up to the main house like some sad puppy who'd lost its bone.

The moment we'd stepped inside the mansion, guilt made me look around, searching for knowing gazes. None of them, however, seemed wise to the fact that I'd just finished screwing my best friend. Ever and Jamie flocked to me immediately, but after ten minutes of trying and failing to break my silence, they left me to my thoughts.

Pushing away from the wall, I drifted closer to where Lou sat when I noticed she no longer looked bored. She was tuned in to whatever the woman was saying. So much so that she didn't see when I came to stand right behind her.

"That's a cool piece," Lou complimented, nodding to the gold pin adorning the woman's dress. It seemed like a risky thing to do given the embroidered lace, so I figured it must have been important.

"Thank you." The woman beamed. "It's been in my family for a long time. I guess you could say it's our family heirloom since it's the culmination of our wealth."

I'll say. The freaking thing had rubies for eyes.

"Interesting choice for a family mascot," Lou said, and I heard her unspoken question.

"Over decades, the Mac Conchradha name has evolved, becoming anglicized and more modern. M'Concroe, M'Ecroe until it became as simple as Crowe." I frowned as my mind began to race, but neither Lou nor the woman sensed the storm building within me. "It seemed fitting that it became an emblem for my family," the woman said proudly.

"But I thought your last name was Kelly?"

"It is, dear. Naturally, my son and I took my husband's name when I married."

"I'm sorry...your son?" Lou looked around the room, and I knew she was searching for him.

The woman placed her hand on Lou's as if comforting her. "By the time I learned that my husband was promised to another, I was already pregnant. His first wife's family had money while mine did not. For sixteen years, Bart denied his son, leaving me alone to struggle." If Lou was startled by her sudden candidness, she didn't let on. "It wasn't until his wife died in childbirth along with his would-be heir that we came to an agreement and married. Our wedding was actually where my son and Thomas met and became fast friends. Unfortunately, my son was already headstrong and independent and didn't take to his father as well as he did Thomas. He'd gotten himself mixed in with some terrible people, and the hold they had on him was strong. Bart thought"—the woman took a deep breath as if gathering strength—"if he disowned our son, he would come around." In a whispered tone, almost as if it was a secret, she said, "It's been over thirty years since I've seen my son. I don't even know if he's still alive."

"That's horrible," Lou said sympathetically, and I could hear her sincerity even as the world seemed to fade away. "I'm so sorry, Claire."

"I'm over seventy years old. If he's alive, I hope I get to see my son just once before I go."

"What's his name?"

"Sean. Sean Everson Kelly." Just then, Claire looked up, and I met my grandmother's gaze for the first time. "Oh. Hello, dear. I didn't see you standing there." I felt Lou watching me now as Claire smiled at me. "You're a handsome devil, aren't you? You remind me a little of my son. Actually..." She squinted as she studied me closely, and the longer she stared, the harder it became to breathe.

Before either of us could say what we were thinking, fearing, hoping, the doors leading to the formal dining room were thrown open. A man in a large white chef's hat announced that dinner was served, and everyone moved at once.

I waited for Lou and Claire to pass before following them inside the dining room. Thomas took his place at the head of the table with Rosalyn playing the disinterested hostess at the other end. The rest of us were shown our places, and Lou was seated next to a man with a gray, bushy beard and piercing blue eyes. He nodded to her and then me, his only greeting, before focusing on Four, who was seated across from him on her mother's right. I sat next to Lou before I could be told, and Jamie sat on my left. I found it odd when Ever sat next to a girl with lush reddish-blonde hair and empty blue eyes rather than Four. Claire, the man I assumed to be my douchebag grandfather, and some tiny girl with dark skin and the biggest brown eyes I'd ever seen, separated them. And on Thomas's left, across from the strawberry blonde, sat the couple I assumed to be her parents.

In total, there were fourteen dinner guests, and most of them looked like they'd rather be anywhere else.

More people in white hats started bringing out the food. The last to be placed on the table was the roasted turkey that looked to be at least twenty pounds. Thomas stood and said a few words, and when he finished, he looked at Rosalyn expectantly.

"Thank you all for coming," she managed to say before returning to staring blankly out the window. I glanced at Four, whose face was clenched as if in pain, before glancing at Ever. He looked like he was fighting himself against going to her, and I wondered why. Glancing at the stoic beauty next to him, I suddenly had a vague recollection of Jamie mentioning Ever having two girl-friends. Surely Ever wouldn't be dumb enough to have them both here with all of their parents in attendance as well?

By the rigid set of his shoulders and the questions the blonde's parents plied him with, I deduced that Ever wasn't just dumb—he was up shit creek without a paddle. I was fighting back a grin as I wondered how he hoped to get out of this when I felt the weight of someone's attention. Across the table, Claire openly studied me and didn't shy away when I met her gaze.

Did she know?

How could she? The chances were one-in-million that we'd meet. Especially since she had no idea I existed. If it wasn't for that goddamn photo, I'd have no idea that that I was sitting across from my father's parents, sharing dinner with them as if I'd done so all my life.

The turkey was carved and the dishes served, and soon, everyone was too busy enjoying their meal to talk. The respite, I learned, was only momentary when Claire peeked at me before whispering something to her husband. He nodded and turned his gaze on me, although his eyes didn't hold the same curiosity that his wife's did even when he spoke.

"Young man, I don't believe we've had the pleasure. I'm Bart Kelly, and this is my lovely wife, Claire."

"Wren," I said, careful not to give my last name. It didn't seem to matter when I noticed Thomas's head swivel my way. What were the chances he'd know who I was when I had no clue who he was other than what I'd read online?

"Wren," Claire echoed with a soft smile. I couldn't help returning it with one of my own.

"An unusual name," Bart remarked with a frown. My smile dropped, and he tried to mask his distaste with a forced chuckle.

"Like the songbird," Claire said gently.

"Yeah," I breathed out. My chest was tight, and I had the sudden urge to stand and take her in my arms when her eyes turned glassy.

"And how do you know Ever?" Bart inquired before I could freak everyone out.

"From school," I answered automatically as I stabbed at a piece of turkey. Ever had already coached me on what to say. It only bought us a few days but one crisis at a time. Glancing at Lou, I found her already watching me. "We both go."

"Ah, the academy. One of the finest schools in the country. I wouldn't have guessed."

My fork paused mid-air, and just as Bart began to squirm under my hard gaze, I felt a small hand curving around my thigh. It was comforting and not the least bit sexual but...I got hard anyway. I didn't dare look Lou's way and risk blowing our cover by kissing her senseless. Ever's father was under the impression that Lou and I were siblings and that our parents were celebrating their anniversary out of the country. I would have snorted if I wasn't busy trying to skin Bart alive with my glare. Lou's hand squeezed my thigh, and just like that, my anger faded. I went back to eating, and so did everyone else.

The rest of dinner was uneventful, and after dessert was served, Jamie stood and raised his glass of water like it was champagne. "I'd like to make a toast," he announced with a grin.

While everyone's attention left their sweet potato pie and went to Jamie, I glanced at Ever across the table. His jaw clenched as he stared up at his cousin, and I knew whatever Jamie was about to say couldn't leave his lips. I reacted without thinking, and with stealth that I'd honed over the years for the wrong man, I had my gun out and pressed against Jamie's kneecap. The table hid what was happening and the reason for Jamie's sudden silence. I nudged his knee, indicating that he should sit the fuck down.

"Jamie?" Thomas prompted when he just stood there. "Your toast?"

I nudged his knee, suggesting that he should sit the fuck down instead. He blinked a few times before tucking his lips inside his mouth, fighting a laugh. His eyes twinkled with amusement, however, as he met Ever's gaze. "Well played," he mouthed to him, making Ever frown in genuine confusion. "To family," he said before retaking his seat.

Ever looked at me quizzically, and I shrugged my shoulders. I couldn't tell him what I did much less *why* I did it. I just knew that I didn't want anyone fucking with him. And maybe a little had to do with the fact that I just didn't like Jamie for catching Lou's eye. Miles was interested, but at least it was always one-sided.

I hurriedly took a sip of my water, cursing myself for the jealousy that made me feel like a bitch.

Once the plates were cleared, everyone scattered to the four winds, and when no one was looking, I slipped into the family room and stopped in my tracks when I found Ever standing alone in the dark. The only light came from the fireplace, and the flames allowed me to see that he was glowering as he stared down at the picture in his hand. My heart twisted in my chest. I still hadn't considered the implications of his father knowing mine, but it explained why I'd felt connected to Ever all along, and how small the world was that we lived in.

Closing the door, I met his gaze as I inched closer. I could barely keep from sighing in relief when I saw the person in the picture.

Evelyn.

"Something wrong?" he asked me when I just stood there like a statue.

I looked around the room, making sure we were alone before I answered. "We need to talk."

CHAPTER
THIRTY-ONE

The Flame

D
INNER HAD BEEN...INTERESTING. THE MOMENT THE
Montgomerys said their goodbyes and the Kellys retired
to their room, as did Thomas and Rosalyn, I cornered
Jamie outside on the veranda. "What the hell happened in there?"

Since I'd snuck up on him, he glanced at me over his
shoulder before turning back to puff on a cigarette. "Your
boyfriend is a nosy son of a bitch. That's what happened."

Even though I hated the very air Wren breathed right now,
warmth spread inside me at hearing him be called mine. "He
threatened you?"

"Oh, yeah." I thought Jamie would be upset, but when
he turned around and leaned against the white pillar, he was
grinning. "I like his style."

Crossing my arms, I shook my head. *Boys really are stupid.*
"Why did he threaten you?"

His dark eyes perused me slowly before meeting mine. "You
tell me."

I shrugged as I looked away. "I don't know."

Jamie laughed, and I knew it was at me. "Try again."

My arms dropped, and my hands balled into fists. "I don't!"

"I heard him say you wanted to fuck me, pretty girl."

"And you believed him?"

"It doesn't matter what I believe. You've already got his
attention, kitten, but he's stubborn. Batting your eyes at me

won't be enough to make him do something about it."

Huffing, I stuck my hand on my hip. "Let me guess…I should sleep with you?"

Jamie's smile was wolfish—as if he wouldn't hesitate to eat me up if given half the chance. Taking a pull from his cigarette, he blew the smoke in my face. "Not unless you really want to, my little overachiever."

I coughed and waved the smoke away. "Well, as it turns out, I don't need to flirt with you to get what I want."

He choked on his next pull, and it took him a few seconds to recover. "Damn," he said hoarsely though I could still hear his awe. "That was fast."

I shrugged. "Not really."

Jamie grinned even wider. "Been chasing that dick for a while, huh?"

"Shut up," I growled.

"There's no shame in it," he said. "Not all guys want a girl who's timid and blushes every time his dick is out."

I cocked my head to the side. "What about you? What do you like?"

He smirked as he flicked his cigarette butt over the side and pulled out another. "I don't give a fuck as long as she's willing."

"And that Barbie doll with the long legs and amazing ass? She didn't seem all that interested to me."

Jamie snickered. "How do you know she had an amazing ass?"

"It was hard to miss it in that dress." The rose gold sequin number she wore looked like it had been painted on. Jamie couldn't take his eyes off her, and although she'd kept her gaze averted, I'd known by the ramrod set of her spine that she was aware.

"You're nosy, too," he observed, and I could detect a hint of jealousy in his tone.

"What's the matter?" I teased. "Afraid of a little competition?"

Yawning, he stepped around me and headed inside. "If you can melt the ice around her heart long enough, then I tip my hat to you, little Lou Who."

"Don't call me that," I said as I followed him into the entry hall.

"Make me," he tossed over his shoulder as he started up one of the curving staircases.

I wanted to follow him and do just that but thought better of it. Instead, I hooked a right and headed for the family room where I last saw Wren sneaking inside over an hour ago.

It was only a matter of time before I got bored giving him the silent treatment. Besides, it was hard not to think about what happened this afternoon. I was sore, and I was pissed, but I still wanted more.

However, when I stepped inside the room, I found it empty. And when I looked out the window, I saw that the lights to the guesthouse were out. Maybe he'd gone to sleep?

Preferring to pretend that I'd run into him by chance instead of him knowing that I sought him out, I sank onto the couch and crossed my arms. I couldn't even find it in me to care that I was actually pouting.

I didn't notice when I was no longer alone until Four plopped down next to me with a huff and interrupted my brooding.

"Thanks for wearing the dress."

"Thanks for tricking me into wearing it," I replied dryly. Four had worn distressed blue jeans and a T-shirt that said 'Hell is a gift. Here you go.' much to her mother's immense displeasure. Thomas hadn't said a word and Ever only grinned.

She smiled and winked. "It looked better on you than it would have on me anyway."

"True."

Snorting, she curled her feet underneath her. "So that went better than I thought it would," she said conversationally.

"What were you expecting?"

"Oh, some screaming and shouting. Maybe a little blood spilled. Nothing major."

I couldn't help laughing despite my mood. *"Why?"*

"Because Jamie was there, and he lives for torturing his cousin."

"Any particular reason?"

She looked away and sighed. "No."

"Right," I said, letting her hear my skepticism. I'd learned too many hard-core lessons in my short seventeen years to be that gullible. Fuck what Wren thought.

Four had been the one to find me when Wren walked away from me yesterday, but neither of us had felt like pouring our hearts out. She ended up calling over Tyra, who had been more than willing for both of us. Still, I knew something was bothering Four, and I knew she wouldn't be able to hold it in forever.

"Claire was nice," I said to fill the silence.

"Yeah, I think it's cool that the Kellys still visit Thomas even though their son is dead."

I frowned at that. "Why are you so certain he's dead? Not even his mother knows if he is or isn't."

Four stilled before quickly sitting up. "What are you talking about?"

"Claire said she hadn't seen him in thirty years. She talked of second chances like he was still alive."

Her forehead wrinkled. "Are you sure?"

"Positive. I felt bad for her."

"But that doesn't make sense," she argued. "Why would Thomas lie to Ever about his best friend being dead if he wasn't?"

I shrugged and poked my lips out. "Maybe they fell out."

With a troubled look, she walked over to the mantel and selected one of the many picture frames. I was surprised when she handed it to me immediately after. I took it with some hesitation and only glanced at the three men posing for the camera before looking back up at her questioningly.

"Take another look," she urged. "Does anything about that picture strike you as odd?"

Granting her request, I studied the photo more closely. "Yes." My voice was calm when I was anything but. The beard was gone, and he looked twenty years younger, but I'd recognize those eyes and that cocky smile anywhere.

"And?" Four prodded.

I pointed to one of the men standing next to Thomas. "I know him."

"What?" Her gaze flitted back and forth from me to the picture. I could tell my answer hadn't been what she was expecting. "How?"

I studied the picture as the ball in my stomach tightened. What were the chances that this ghost and the one stalking Wren were one and the same?

It couldn't be. Their world was a long way from the one Wren and I lived in. It had to be a coincidence.

But Wren had said Ever used to be Exiled, so maybe we weren't that different, after all. Maybe all of our paths had crossed once before, and now it was happening again.

"That's his father," I told Four.

She perked up immediately. "Ever's?"

"No…Wren's." I pinned Four with my gaze. "Why would you think he was Ever's father?"

She gulped as she shifted restlessly. "Because it seemed odd that Ever has a cleft chin when neither of his parents do."

I mulled that over before shaking my head. "It's strange but not impossible. Bart and Claire don't have one, either."

"I know." She exhaled as if a weight had been taken off her shoulders. "I've never been so happy to be wrong in my life."

"No one can blame you. Besides, cleft chins aren't that common, and it *is* weird that Thomas's best friend *just so happens* to have one as well."

"What are you saying?"

I smirked up at Four, who suddenly looked nervous. "Probably what you're thinking."

"Ever told me that his mother walked out on them four years ago. You don't think..."

"That Thomas found out the truth and kicked her ass to the curb?" I shrugged. "If he lied about his best friend, he might lie about his marriage."

"But if Ever isn't his son, why keep him around? Why not send him away too?"

"You don't stop being someone's father after fourteen years just because a DNA test tells you that you aren't." *If only my parents had the same sentiment.* I handed her back the photo, and she returned it to the mantel.

"What do I do?" she asked me when she turned back around.

I lifted my hands and gave her a bewildered look. "What can you do?"

"Ever needs to know."

I shook my head. "But he doesn't need to hear it from you."

She shoved her fingers through her hair and started pacing. "But what if Thomas just keeps lying to him?"

I tilted my head to the side and squinted. "You took one look at that photo and knew something wasn't right. Ever's been looking at it his *entire life*. If he hasn't started asking questions by now, it's because he doesn't want to know the answer."

She whirled around to me, and her mouth formed an O. "Maybe you're right."

"I am," I said with confidence.

Four then charged across the room, and when she stood in front of me, she planted her hands on her hips. "Did I hear you say that Sean was Wren's father?"

I flinched, cursing my big mouth. I wanted to deny it, claim that she was hearing things, but the look Four gave me told me not to even try it.

So after telling Four all about my trip to the mountains,

seeing Fox murder an innocent family, and how Wren's father had later saved from me from his goons, I swore her to secrecy. I might have even threatened to slice her from temple to tit if she ever broke her silence. I still hadn't told Wren that his father was very much alive and wasn't sure I ever would.

"How long do you think you can keep this a secret?" Four prodded. "Wren saw the photo of his father. He freaked out and went for a drive."

So that was why he'd been acting so weird earlier.

Why hadn't he told me?

Ever burst into the family room before I could think of the answer. The crisp white shirt he'd worn to dinner was unbuttoned and opened wide, displaying abs and a chest that rivaled Wren's. His gaze went straight to Four. "Why aren't you in bed?"

I realized he must have gone upstairs anticipating that she'd be there waiting on him, which explained the undone shirt.

Four crossed her arms and pursed her lips. "Your bed you mean."

"That's what I said."

"Ever...it's like seven o'clock."

Crossing the room, he lifted Four over his shoulder. "Come on," he said as if he hadn't heard her. "I want to go to bed." He started for the door, but when Four mentioned that she was keeping me company, he stopped and regarded me. "Harlan's waiting for you in the guesthouse." And then he was gone with Four trying to reason with him the entire way. He clearly didn't give a damn who might see them.

Sighing, I stood and started for the door.

Time to face the music.

When I stepped inside the house, I didn't find Wren waiting for me as Ever had claimed. Instead, I heard the shower running from one of the bedrooms. Deciding to repay Wren the favor of surprise, I plopped down on the edge of the bed and waited. He emerged ten minutes later with a towel wrapped around his waist and a startled look on his face the moment he spotted me.

I knew then that Ever had been a big, fat liar.

He probably would have said anything to get into Four's pants sooner.

"Ever said you wanted me?"

He laughed and shook his head. "I told him I'd come to get you in an hour or two. I guess he wasn't willing to wait that long."

I glanced down at the carpet and mumbled, "Lucky girl." Standing, I started for the door, but an arm around my waist pulled me back, and then the door I tried to escape through was slammed shut.

"She's not as lucky as me," Wren whispered, lips at my neck.

I barked out a laugh that was dry and humorless. "Spare me the whiplash, Wren, please."

Spinning me around, he pushed me against the door and trapped my hands above my head in a punishing grip. "I'm just trying to protect you, Lou."

"Did I ask you to protect me?"

"Did you hear me ask for permission?"

I glared at him, and he glared right back. "Let me go," I said when he wouldn't back down.

"I can't," he told me. "That's the whole point. I can't let you go. I can't lose you."

My mouth fell open as my anger turned to disbelief. "Don't you know that I've been yours all this time?"

"I know...but I don't—"

I cut him off before he could finish. "Don't tell me that you don't deserve me!" I held his face in my hands. "You're not all that good, but you're not all that bad. And we *both* know I'm no angel."

I could see his desperate need to believe me in his eyes before he cast them down. "I wish it were that simple."

"It can be…all you have to do is stop fighting," I told him as my hands slid from his face down his neck and over his chest until finally reaching his waist where he knotted the towel. "Giving in felt so good…didn't I feel good?"

"Lou." He groaned, leaning his forehead on the door behind me. "Lou, don't. We can't."

His protests fell on deaf ears.

How else could I show him that our friendship wasn't a dead end or even a path that went on and on? It was a passage, and my heart was the open door that led to promising fields of green as far as the eye could see and light so bright that sometimes it was blinding.

Only Wren refused to step through because darkness was all he knew.

"We weren't building a friendship," I told him as I untied the knot keeping his towel up. "We were falling. Falling so deep we can never climb back up." I fell to my knees right along with the towel, and I didn't balk or second-guess this time around when I took him in my mouth. His hand gripped my hair tightly as I held his gaze and tried to swallow as much of him as I could. He was squeaky clean and fresh after his shower, and I wanted to dirty him back up. To taste his cock after he worked so hard getting me to come all over it. When his cum mixed with mine. As if hearing my thoughts, he pulled me up to my feet and kissed me until my legs shook.

I felt his hand at the hem of my dress pushing it up until it was bunched around my waist. My panties were ripped away, and I was snatched off my feet when he settled my legs in the crook of his arms. His cock locked in on me like a heat-seeking missile. Still, I couldn't get him inside me fast enough. He slowly filled me, and his groan mixed with my gasp once he sank himself deeply.

"Wren," I whimpered, not sure I could withstand the ache. He and I felt impossible.

"I told you." He kissed me. "I warned you." He nipped my jaw. "And now you want mercy?"

I shook my head, knowing it was the last thing I wanted and stared into his eyes. Feeling my resolve harden, I touched his cheek and whispered words I knew would send him over the edge. "I love you. That means I don't want any of you if it's not all of you. The good, the bad, the ugly and the beautiful."

He froze, blinked, and when understanding dawned, he pulled away only to plunge inside me fast and hard with a groan loud enough to shake the walls. He finally let go, letting me see how desperately he needed me, how much he craved me, and how broken he'd be if I ever walked away.

Never.

The rhythm he began as he drove me up the door was unforgiving. I grappled for something to hold onto, but there was only him. He wanted to give me slow and gentle, and I showed him it was the last thing I wanted. We'd shown enough patience, waited too long. His mouth muffled my cries even though there was no one around to hear.

"Lou…I'm not going to last, baby. I need you to come on my dick. Come on my—"

I cut his plea off when my pussy began to pulse before strangling his cock and stealing his breath. I hadn't realized he'd fallen over too until he was already spilling inside my unprotected pussy.

"Fuck!" he barked so savagely I flinched.

He started to pull out of me when I gripped his hair in one hand and his ass in the other. "I want it," I whispered desperately in his ear.

After only a moment's hesitation, he pushed deeper inside me, making me moan. I didn't let him go until he'd given me every last drop. When I finally released my grip on his hair, I yelped when he spanked my ass hard before setting me on my feet.

"Don't…do that…again." He glared down at me as we fought to catch our breath.

"I don't think it's entirely up to me," I sassed.

He shot me an indignant look then picked me up, carried me to the shower, and after he'd cleaned us up, he took us to bed.

I was lying on my side half asleep with Wren curved around me when I felt him lift my left hand and slip something on my pointer finger. I cracked my eyes open, but when I saw a ring with a sterling silver setting and oval-shaped green gem, they flew open as I blinked. I watched the green slowly turn to amber as I wondered what his gift meant. Wren wasn't exactly the jewelry-bestowing type. "A mood ring?"

"You can always tell what I'm thinking when you look in my eyes. Now we're on an even playing field."

Heat bloomed in my belly, and we both watched as the ring turned a startling violet.

"Do you know what the colors mean?"

"Yes."

I peeked over my shoulder. "So what does purple mean?"

He shot me a lazy grin as he slowly ran his hand up and down my naked hip. "It means you're crazy about me."

"I am."

"Good." He leaned down and starting kissing my shoulder. "Because I lost all reason the night I met you, Lou."

"Hm." I pretended to ponder. "Drunk Wren might say you even love me."

I felt him still behind me, and I watched the ring turn black as my stomach filled with dread. Did I push him too far too soon? Would he retreat as he'd always done?

Before I could take it back, give him an out, he said, "He's not the only one, Lou."

"Then tell me," I urged. "Say the words."

"I can't." I started to move away when he locked his arm around my waist. "I'll tell you when I get back."

"Back?" I frowned. "Where are you going?"

I was turning to face him when he lifted my leg, and after

testing my readiness, he slowly slid inside me from behind. My breath caught. Nothing else before that mattered.

"Again?" I gasped.

He was already moving inside me, long strokes that reached deep and stole my breath until I could think of nothing else. "Again."

The sun wasn't shining through the windows when I awoke much later. The room was pitch black and silent, and after looking over my shoulder, I realized I was in bed alone. I ran my hand over the sheets on his side, and when I felt the warmth he left behind, I sighed.

Until I remembered his promise just before he took me.

Heart racing, I shot up from the bed and looked around, but the bedroom and the bathroom were both empty. I hurriedly checked the rest of the guesthouse as well, but Wren was nowhere to be found.

In a fit of desperation, I flew out into the cold night. I only had the T-shirt he'd slipped over my head just before I passed out to cover me. I ran down the paved path leading around the side of the main house to the driveway out front.

Once there, I stopped short when I spotted him dressed in dark jeans, shirt, and that brown leather jacket I loved so much. And he was headed toward a green Crown Vic.

"Wren!"

He spun around and cursed when he saw me standing there shivering in the cold. His long, angry strides had him reaching me in no time. "What are you doing out here?"

I slammed my hands against his chest and pushed him. "You were just going to leave?"

"I told you I was."

"Yeah, right before you fucked me senseless so that I wouldn't ask questions!" I shot back.

He shook his head and was already turning away. "Go back to bed, Lou."

How could I when I knew he was charging from the safety of the castle to slay my dragon alone? I ran around him. "Tell me why you're leaving."

"You know why."

"I don't!" I shouted without regard for the people sleeping inside. "Fox doesn't matter anymore, so why are you going back?"

Tired of my tantrum, his hand suddenly gripped my neck, pulling me until his mouth pressed against my cheek, and I could feel every one of his words as he spoke. "You want to live long enough to have those babies you promised me?"

Slowly, I nodded.

"Then I need to find Fox before he finds you."

My arm shot out, and I pointed to where his Impala waited. "To the Batmobile!"

He let me go and took a step back. "Very funny."

"But it's not funny," I whined. "You're not Superman, and you're not Batman. You're mine. You belong with me where it's safe."

"But it's *not* safe, Lou. He'll find us here eventually, and the longer we stay, the more we put the rest of them in danger."

"So let's just go now." I pressed myself against him and let his warmth surround me. "Somewhere out there is a beach with our name on it." I peeked up at him. "Maybe even a nude one?"

Leaning down, he kissed me slowly. He even copped a feel when his hands trailed up the shirt I was wearing and began kneading my butt. But then he ended the kiss with a groan. "As tempting as that sounds…I can't."

I narrowed my eyes at him. "I'm getting sick of hearing you say that."

He smiled and kissed me again. "I promised Ever I'd bring his mother home in exchange for keeping you safe."

I blinked in surprise. "His mother?"

He shook his head. "No time to explain."

I huffed. "So you just expect me to wait here patiently in the dark for you to return?"

"I'll be gone a day. Two days tops." He then rested his forehead against mine. "And when I get back, we are going to have a long conversation before anything else happens between us."

"How long?"

He grimaced and pulled me closer. "Very."

"It can't be that bad," I said as I wrapped my arms around his neck. I wanted him to kiss me, but he didn't. His eyes seemed gray now, reflecting the bleakness he felt as he stared down at me.

"Yeah, Lou, it is."

"You think I won't want you anymore?" I stepped back and pulled the ring he'd given me from my pointer finger.

"Lou..."

Holding his gaze, I slid it onto my ring finger. Light entered his eyes turning them blue again. "There's nothing else I could ever want."

"Lou..."

I grinned at his speechlessness.

"Say the words, Wren." He swallowed hard, and when he looked to me for help, I leaped into his arms, wrapped my legs around his waist, and stole the kiss I wanted. "Tell me you love me because I know you do."

Trembling hard enough to rock a mountain, he squeezed me tight, buried his face in my chest, and then he said the fucking words.

CHAPTER THIRTY-TWO

The Flame

I TOSSED ONE LAST TIME BEFORE RIPPING OFF THE THICK BLANKET AND fleeing from the overbearing warmth underneath. I checked the time and swore. My skin was nearly soaked in sweat, dampening the thin T-shirt I wore. I didn't allow myself to acknowledge what else had dampened in the hour since I'd fallen asleep.

The heat flowing through the air ducts wasn't even the culprit for my misery.

It was the couple locked away in the next room.

The sound was faint, but it was loud enough to keep me awake given the nature. And just when I thought maybe she was in trouble and needed my help, she'd beg for more, making it clear what she needed and it sure as shit wasn't me.

Two days had come and gone, and Wren still hadn't returned, but his parting words echoed in my mind. It was the only thing offering me comfort when so much was unknown. Was he okay? Would we be when he got back and finally told me whatever he thought would make me walk away from him? I'd offered him assurances, but lying in the dark, left alone with my mind, so many of my insecurities ran wild.

Tonight, at Four's insistence, I was sleeping alone in her room while she slept around the corner in Ever's bed. I had a feeling I was a decoy. Thankfully, his room was further away from the master suite or else their parents would be getting quite an earful.

With my hand over my ears, I made my way downstairs and to the kitchen.

If I couldn't sleep, I'd eat.

My eyes were barely open as I sleepily searched for the light switch. When my fingers finally connected with the switch, I flipped it up, causing light to flood the room. It took a few seconds for my vision to adjust, and when it did, I suddenly wished I was blind.

Standing in the middle of the kitchen, naked as the day he was born, was Jamie. He looked like a deer caught in the headlights as he held a sandwich bursting with what looked like turkey, cheese—maybe provolone or Asiago—lettuce, and tomato.

"Jesus! Jamie! Why are you naked?"

"Why are you looking?" he retorted, his tone flat.

My eyes quickly averted but not before I caught the playful crook of his lips. "I didn't see anything," I quickly defended. It wasn't entirely untrue. I hadn't seen any of the important parts but what I did see had my eyes burning for another peek.

Jamie was slender, not packing as much muscle as Wren or even Ever, but what he did possess, he'd perfected. Every. Inch. I was curious about the tattoos covering his body and why he had so many. I mean, there were only so many things important enough to permanently scar your skin.

I would have already had one or two myself if Wren had let me. Whenever I brought it up, he simply said he hadn't found an artist that he could trust enough to touch me with a needle. What he *didn't* say was that this famed artist also had to be female. One day, I'd call him out on it.

"Then maybe you should take a second look."

I'd teased Wren enough times to recognize a come-on, and knowing Jamie, he wouldn't bother asking questions if I bit the bait.

"All I'm looking for is a drink, thank you."

My gaze was still firmly fixed on the manicured lawn visible through the open windows so I could only listen as Jamie strolled on bare feet to the refrigerator. I heard a cabinet open and close, some pots bang around, and then the flicker of gas igniting on the stove.

Taking a deep breath, I took a peek.

Jamie had his back to me as he oversaw whatever he was concocting, so I took the time to admire the tanned skin marked with tattoos and fresh scratches stretching a red path down to his tight ass. I knew very well what those marks meant since I'd given Wren a few myself.

Right now, there was a girl feeling very satisfied, and because it was Jamie responsible for that feeling, I imagined she was feeling guilty, too.

"Why are you awake?" I asked to distract me from my musings.

"The same reason you are." I could hear the amusement in his tone and was thankful he couldn't see me blush.

"Should they be that loud considering their parents sleep a few doors down?"

"I don't know what Rosalyn's deal is, but my uncle has always been a heavy sleeper."

"Still…it's a huge gamble. I guess I can see why they risk it, though. They sounded like they were having fun."

"Yeah…I can't wait for it to blow up in their faces."

I paused at that. There was no malice in his tone, which only confused me more, so I went with the only explanation to pop into my head. "You want Four?"

He snorted. "That ship sailed a long time ago. She might as well be Adara."

"Who's Adara?"

"My sister."

The sheer pride and adoration in such a simple answer painted a picture—albeit murky—of the affection he held for Four.

"If she's like a sister to you, why do you want to see her unhappy?"

He snorted. "I don't. I just need the asshole she's wrapped around out of my way."

I panicked when, without warning, he reached for the cabinet next to him and produced a glass. I quickly resumed my watch of the quiet lawn. I heard the pouring of liquid, and a second later, through my peripheral, a glass of milk appeared in front of me.

"You seriously didn't bring pants down with you?" I griped.

"It's two in the morning," he argued. "I wasn't exactly expecting company."

"Right." Feeling like a skittish kitten, I lifted the glass and felt the heat. "Warm milk?" I was careful to keep my gaze on the milk and nothing else.

"It'll help you sleep."

"I'm impressed," I said with my eyebrows high.

"That I can warm milk?"

I pictured him frowning but was too chicken to confirm. "That you cared." I took a sip of the milk and let out an appreciative hum when I realized he'd added sugar.

"You think I'm a jerk?"

"Is that a serious question?" I shot back before taking another sip.

"Yes."

I started, not expecting his answer. Forcing down the milk, I looked into his eyes. "If it bothers you, why do you act this way?"

"Like what?"

"Like the world wronged you."

He shrugged and ran his hand through his already unkempt hair. I loved how the light made his hair look more red than brown.

"Maybe it has."

"That would imply that it owed you something in the first place."

"So you're not angry?" he countered.

"About what?"

"You've been here for few days, and no one has come beating down the door looking for you." I heard the hidden question in his statement.

"Maybe I just hide really well."

"Or maybe they never bothered to look."

I pushed air through my lips but said nothing. The Hendersons would be busy preparing for their new life in Austin. Of course, my social worker would be looking for me, but that was her job, and with a caseload her size, a seventeen-year-old who was mere months from aging out of the system would be the least of her priorities.

"What about your family?" he pressed.

"What about them?"

"Wren told us about your parents."

I snorted. "Yeah, well, Wren talks too much."

"If it helps, he was wasted when he told us. Why hasn't the rest of your family claimed you?"

"Because I was never theirs to claim."

He frowned at that. "What do you mean?"

"Brian and Emily," I said, speaking their names for the first time in five years, "weren't my birth parents. They adopted me when I was a baby. I guess that's why it was so easy for them to leave me behind for greener pastures." I wasn't of their flesh and blood, so when they left, it hadn't felt like a piece of them was missing. I only wished I could say the same.

"Fuck, Lou," was all Jamie said. I could feel his horror creeping under my skin and cooling my blood.

"My mother, whoever she was, gave me up so I could be left behind by strangers again and again and *again*."

"Maybe she thought she was doing what was best for you."

I chuckled at the idea of Jamie being a romantic. I bet if he were wearing clothes right now, I'd find his heart on his sleeve. Instead, he'd chosen to let something else hang free.

Keep your eyes up, Lou. Don't even think about it.

"The only thing good intentions prove is that no one knows what's best for you other than yourself," I spat.

"If that were true, instead of mating, we'd be sprouting from the ground like plants with no need for the bonds we hold close to our hearts. You like to think you're a wolf without a pack, Lou, but you're not completely alone. If you were, you'd be dead already—inside or six feet under."

I sneered at him. "And how do you know that?"

"Because we're not that different," he muttered. And then with a sigh, as if all were truly lost, he added, "That's why I can't fuck you."

I didn't even try to keep my eyes from rolling. "Right...*that's* why."

He gave me a knowing look. "Don't try to convince me that it never crossed your mind."

"It hasn't," I lied bitingly.

I suddenly felt him hovering behind me, his breath warming my nape. "Not even to make him jealous?"

"Who?" I asked, playing coy. He only sucked his teeth in response. "I don't know what you mean," I insisted.

"Like I said," he whispered while slipping his hand under my T-shirt, "I won't fuck you, but I can be of service." He let the offer hang in the air as he ran the back of his fingers across my belly, heating every inch of skin on the way. "You won't be the first girl I've helped out of the friend zone."

I forced a laugh as my mind raced. "So that would make you, what? Some kind of relationship gigolo?"

"A gigolo with a ninety-nine percent success rate," he bragged.

"What happened to the other one percent?"

"She fell for me instead." He leaned down and pressed his lips against my forehead, but that wasn't all I felt pressed against me. Resting against my hip was the hard and rather long evidence that he'd make some lucky girl *very* happy one day. I just hoped she had the patience and fortitude to put it to good use. "Sweet dreams, sweet Lou."

I lingered long enough to finish my glass of warm milk, and when I finally made my way back upstairs, I ran into Ever and Four, covered in sweat and wearing nothing but their wide smiles.

What the hell did these people have against wearing clothes around here?

"Oh, shit!" Four quickly ducked for cover behind her boyfriend's back.

Ever, however, peered into the dark, completely unbothered by his nakedness. Obviously, he and his cousin were more alike than what met the eye. It was no wonder why they were often at each other's throats, locking horns, and battling for dominance.

A quick peek was all I needed to confirm who had the *slightly* larger edge.

"Lou? What are you doing up?"

I glared at them both. The words *you kept me up* were on the tip of my tongue.

"We need to talk."

The next morning, Four kept shooting me apologetic looks. On the stairs last night, I informed them that I could hear every moan, plea, and squeak of the bed springs. Of course, I'd been exaggerating—they weren't *that* loud—but it got my point across.

I don't think the red has left Four's cheeks since.

Her oh-so-charming boyfriend, however, acted as if nothing happened, other than the glare or two I caught him throwing my way. I was sure that it had more to do with Four spending the rest of the night in her bed with me instead of his. I stuck my tongue out, taunting him with the possibility of me stealing his girl right from under him, and he sent me another scathing glance. I could barely hold in my laugh when he immediately pulled her from her chair and into his lap.

Boys.

For a heartbeat, I wondered if I was overreacting about their late-night sex marathon. After all, misery loved company, and the thought of no one getting any if I wasn't, sounded strangely bittersweet.

"It's not that big a deal," Jamie chimed from his place at the end of the island where he devoured a bowl of Lucky Charms. "We just need to get her laid. Wren basically hit and quit it. Of course, she's bitter."

Ever's tight mouth loosened into the grin. "Is that right?" he said slowly, and if anyone—most especially Four—didn't know any better, it would have seemed suggestive. "The douchebag did leave *explicit* instructions to provide for your every whim, and if I couldn't, I was to call him *immediately.*"

My stomach dipped.

"Don't you dare," I warned, but Ever was already reaching for his phone sitting next to his plate. Four tried to intercept but Ever was faster.

Retaliation for last night lit up his light brown gaze, making them look golden as he watched me. He thumbed the screen without taking his gaze away, and then he held up his phone as ringing filled the room.

Oh, he so better sleep with one eye open.

I shot up from my seat at the same time he carefully placed Four on her feet and backed away.

"And here I thought your bullying days were behind you," Four said as she stood with her feet planted and her arms crossed. I realized at the same time Ever did that she was blocking his chance of escape as I approached from behind.

He stared at her in disbelief as if she'd betrayed him. "Whatever happened to for better or worse?"

"We're not married," she retorted dryly.

"Yet."

That promise, however real, was the distraction he needed to toss the phone over her head—to Jamie.

Four whirled on him and screeched, *"What the hell?"*

"Sorry, kitten." Jamie grinned at her. "Blood is thicker than water."

The phone stopped ringing, and I said a quick prayer that it went to voicemail, but then I heard his voice for the first time in two days, clipped and to the point.

"She better be alive."

"She is," Jamie confirmed. "And all the soft hairs on her head remain intact. You're welcome." Without warning, he tossed the phone over the island to me, and I managed to catch it before it hit the ground.

Wren was remarkably quiet on the other end. Knowing he was probably seething, I disabled the speakerphone and put the phone to my ear.

"Wren."

"What the fuck is going on?" he barked. "Are you okay?"

"I'm fine. Ever and Jamie were just being pricks, is all."

Silence, which stretched so long I thought he'd hung up, but then he sighed. "Remind me to kick their asses when I get back there."

"Done." I clutched the phone tighter hearing that he was coming back to me. "I'll even help you."

He chuckled despite the tension I could feel even through the phone. "That's my girl."

"So…where are you?"

"Safe." It was all the assurance he gave me.

"How much longer?" I chewed my lip.

He took a deep breath, but his voice was gentle when he spoke. "If all goes well, I should be back tonight."

If all goes well… But what if it didn't?

"Lou?" he prompted when I was silent for too long.

I felt a tear fall and wiped it away. "Yeah?" My voice shook, and I prayed he didn't hear.

"I have to go, baby."

"Okay." I took a deep breath and let it out slowly. "Say it again?"

He made a sound that told me he was fighting the urge to do so. I held up my hand and saw that my ring turned gray as I waited, but then it changed to a blue that matched his eyes when he said it. "I love you, little Valentine."

"I thought you said you had to run errands." I stood back and watched Jamie kick over rock after rock in search of something. Probably his sanity. I knew then that I should have stayed in my lonely corner, sulking where he'd found me. It's been hours since the phone call with Wren, and I was in no better state than before. Worse, actually.

"I am," Jamie claimed before looking around with a frown.

"This is the errand? Breaking and entering?"

"We're not breaking in," he said as he lifted a plant and smiled. "We have a key." He plucked the single gold key from the ground and carelessly tossed the plant aside. The sound of the pot shattering had me cringing, and I wondered how pissed Wren would be when he had to bail me out of jail.

"Whose place is this anyway?"

"Not relevant." Jamie nonchalantly climbed the steps leading to the terrace, and I nervously followed him.

"It will be when I'm asked to testify against you."

"Funny," he said, sounding salty. He then shoved the key in the lock. "You don't look like a rat."

"You smell like one."

"Sorry." He shrugged and smiled apologetically. "I didn't have time to shower after my workout." Just as quickly, he was back in true form. Waggling his eyebrows, he said, "Besides,

I read somewhere that fresh sweat can be...stimulating...to women."

"So you're hoping to seduce me with your smelly pheromones?"

His smile changed. As if the reason was a secret. "Not you. Not this time."

I would have asked who he planned to seduce, but he quickly stepped through the French doors and disappeared inside what I hoped was an empty home. I was still standing in the same spot, debating if I should follow him, when he suddenly reappeared.

"Coming?"

I folded my arms. "Not unless you tell me why we're here."

"Mystery creates wonder, and wonder is the basis of *this* man's desire." He was gone again by the time I realized he'd quoted Neil Armstrong.

"That's not how that goes!"

I heard his chuckle, but then the sound faded along with his footsteps, and I realized he'd left me to decide alone. Cursing, I stepped inside on silent feet just as Wren taught me. One glance around and I realized I was standing in someone's kitchen. There were cozy looking nooks on each side of me, one with a small dining table and the other designed with two fancy looking armchairs perfectly positioned to enjoy the sun. I didn't see Jamie anywhere, but I did see another set of double doors. One of them was cracked, making it clear where Jamie had gone.

"Jamie!" I called in a harsh whisper after I carefully slipped through the door. I didn't want a single strand of my DNA left behind. I liked Jamie, but I didn't trust him. Not yet anyway. There was a storm brewing in him, but his friends were too wrapped up in their shit to notice. I just hoped they were the kind to stick around to pick up the pieces.

I stood in the middle of the large foyer—although not nearly as grand as the McNamara's—and wondered where he could have gone. Ahead of me was a staircase and just beyond that was the front door. I knew which option was the smarter choice, but curiosity got the best of me. Jamie had seemed determined so I could only assume whatever business he had here was important.

At least to him.

I was ready to climb the stairs when I noticed another door just feet from the front door. It was probably nothing, just a harmless coat closet. The closer my feet brought me to the door, however, the less likely it seemed.

My only hope now was that the door would be locked. Of course, when I turned the knob, it wasn't. And it wasn't a coat closet, either. It was an office.

One that made my fingers sticky with anticipation. I mean, I was practically foaming at the mouth. My original plan had been to rob the McNamaras blind before I left. Unfortunately, they were smart enough to keep their small but pricey valuables locked away.

Judging by the ostentatious décor, whoever lived here preferred to flaunt their wealth. I looked around wondering what I should pilfer first when I noticed the large portrait hanging between two windows.

Jackpot!

Where there was a portrait, there was probably a safe. And if lucky, it would be unlocked, but what were the chances of that?

I tiptoed across the room and gaped when I saw the people posing in the portrait. I recognized them instantly from the Thanksgiving dinner. The girl I'd teased Jamie about had her father's eyes and her mother's striking beauty. While the man looked stern and the woman proud, their daughter seemed resigned. I figured she felt the same way I would if I were forced to take such a stuffy photo. My gaze drifted back to the mother and the glistening string of pearls around her neck.

I'd bet my next meal they were real.

I used to dream of finer things like any little girl. A pony, a castle, and a prince charming to dote on me, but after my parents took off, my dreams changed, and the only thing I wanted was to never depend on anyone ever again. But then I met Wren, and my dreams changed once more.

Grabbing the portrait by its sides, I started to lift it when a shriek of outrage had me jumping away. Thinking I'd been caught red-handed, I spun around with my hands raised high but quickly realized I was still alone.

What the hell?

The moment I heard shouting, I took off for the stairs. I should have made for the door, but Jamie was sort of my friend. Leaving him behind wasn't something I could do. I made it upstairs and called his name, but there was no response, only more shouting that sounded too muffled to be close. That was when I noticed another staircase and took it at a jog to the third floor.

"Jamie?" I shouted, not caring anymore if whoever he pissed off knew I was here.

"Yeah?" he answered, sounding way too calm. I followed his voice and found him in a standoff with the beauty from the portrait. I raked over my memory for her name.

Was it Barbara? Betty...Babar?

She was seriously pissed off as she clutched a towel around her naked body. She was dripping water all over the pristine carpet, but she didn't seem to care as she glared daggers at Jamie.

Those daggers were suddenly aimed my way when she noticed me standing in the doorway. She turned back to Jamie but not before I caught the flash of jealousy in her eyes. "And you brought one of your sluts?"

"Jealous?" I teased her with a giggle. I didn't take offense to being called a slut. I'd have done much worse if I caught Wren even breathing around some chick and wouldn't give a fuck if she was eighty years old or eight.

"I wouldn't give you the satisfaction," she spat without sparing me another glance.

"All the same." Jamie shrugged. "She's not a slut. She's my friend."

"What's the difference?" she shouted.

"The difference is," I interjected before Jamie could make it worse, "we never have and never will."

She looked at me, studied me, and I mean really studied me. I felt like a bug under a magnifying glass right before she squished me under her heel.

"You were at the dinner," she said when she was done picking me apart with her eyes.

"Yup."

Her eyes narrowed. "But you don't go to Brynwood." It wasn't a question.

"You couldn't pay me to wear the uniform."

I wasn't sure, but I could swear I saw a small smile forming on her lips before Jamie wiped it away.

"Why aren't you at the country club with your parents?"

"I wasn't feeling well."

His eyebrows pulled together before he stepped closer and placed his hand on her forehead. His touch was familiar despite the tension between them. "You don't feel warm."

"It was just a bit of nausea," she breathlessly assured him.

He didn't respond, and I realized he was watching her closely for signs that she was being untruthful. It was shocking to see that he cared this much. I knew he wanted to bang her, but he also acted like he couldn't stand her. It wasn't until they stood nearly toe-to-toe that I realized just how tall she was. Jamie still towered over her but not as much as he did me. He had maybe four inches on her while he stood nearly a foot over me.

"How tall are you?" I blurted, interrupting the tension. They both shot me questioning gazes, but I had eyes only for her.

"I'm five ten," she answered with an arched brow. To Jamie, she said, "Why are you here?"

"I'm not prepared to answer that since you weren't supposed to be here."

"*I live here.*"

"Where are your babysitters?"

"You mean the staff?" He only stared down at her waiting for an answer. "They have Sundays off."

Rather than be placated, his frown only deepened. "Since when do they get days off? Your dad thinks he's too good to wipe his own ass."

She nervously looked away when she never had trouble meeting his glare before. Either Jamie didn't notice his questions were making her uneasy or he didn't care.

Somehow, I felt compelled to defend. "Why don't you lay off?"

I caught her grateful glance the moment Jamie looked over his shoulder with a bored expression. "You find the safe yet?"

"What are you talking about?" It was my turn shift and look away guiltily.

"The combination is 0618, and the safe is loaded. Cash, jewelry, bonds—make yourself scarce."

My jaw dropped while the Barbie, who rolled her eyes, didn't seem the least bit surprised. "How do you know the code to her father's safe?"

Jamie stared back at me long and hard. I knew I was pissing him off, but I wanted answers. Besides, no one was scarier than Wren Harlan when pissed off, and his moody glares didn't faze me, either.

"Because the code is my birth date," she said quietly.

"Oh." It was all I could think to say.

It didn't matter because they'd already forgotten me as Jamie and his plaything seemed to get lost in each other's gazes. Feeling like a third wheel, I quickly retreated, escaping the awkward feeling. Pressing my back against the wall, I closed my eyes and opened my ears.

"Why do you keep breaking into my house?" she demanded the moment I was out of sight.

"Why do you keep making the key so easy for me to find?"

"My father would get suspicious and would want to know why."

"And you'd get lonely," Jamie announced knowingly.

"It hasn't bothered me in four years."

"I guess I should thank my cousin?"

My eyes popped open at that. I hadn't missed the way Ever had stayed at her side for most of the evening three nights ago but could barely keep his eyes off Four. I wanted to ask questions at the time, but I kept hearing Wren's voice echoing in my head to mind my business.

"Give it a rest, Jamie. No one's feeling sorry for you."

His voice lowered and became huskier when he said, "You wouldn't be saying that if you knew just how long I can go."

I heard her intake of breath, and when she spoke, her voice had lost some of its venom. "So I guess the rumors are true?"

I threw caution to the wind and peeked inside just in time to see them drift closer at the same time. The crazy part was that neither one seemed to notice. It was as if they were drawn by the same invisible force, the push and pull that plagued Wren and me.

"About my stamina?" The edges of his smile became sharp as he looked her over. "Take me for a test drive. See for yourself."

Her gaze turned mocking as she regarded him with her nose in the air. "You shouldn't start something you can't finish."

Jamie smiled wider, not the least bit perturbed. "I always finish, Bette...just not with them."

It was then that I remembered her name. *Barbette.*

Believing I'd learned maybe more than I bargained for, I slowly backed away, and the moment I was safe from being detected, I bolted down the stairs. I could wait for Jamie in the car.

But first, a little pitstop.

After a couple of minutes of unsuccessfully attempting to lift the portrait, I discovered that it was attached to some kind of swinging mechanism. Keying in the code that Jamie gave me,

I did a little victory dance when it disarmed. However, my glee died a quick death when I opened the safe and looked inside. The longer I stared, the more disbelief gave way to confusion.

The safe was completely empty.

Had Jamie not known Barbette's father was broke?

I took a look around and shook off the thought. Maybe he'd decided safes were old fashioned and gone digital. Hearing Wren warning me to mind my business, I pushed the Montgomerys' finances aside and drifted from the house.

Ten minutes later, I was so lost in my head that I didn't notice Jamie coming until he was hopping inside the Wrangler.

He didn't speak, and neither did I.

I watched him pull something white and lacy from his pocket, press it to his nose, and take a deep sniff. Once done, instead of stuffing them back into his pocket, he carefully arranged them around his rearview mirror. He then glanced my way and caught me staring.

"What?" he asked as if his actions were normal. His eyes were low as if he'd gotten an actual high from sniffing his cousin's girlfriend's panties.

"You took me on a panty raid…"

"You had something better to do?" he shot back.

I pressed my lips tight. "I hope those are clean."

He smiled wickedly as he started the truck and sped down the long driveway. "I hope they aren't."

"You fucking stole them, didn't you?"

"It wouldn't be as fun if I asked her nicely."

"Do me a favor," I drawled as I eyed the panties hanging over the dash. "Count me out of the next panty raid."

"What are you complaining about? We both got what we needed."

"I'm going to ignore the obvious and *insulting* fact that you used me to rob and piss off your girlfriend's father and tell you that you were wrong about the safe."

He took his attention away from the road and turned to me with a frown. "What do you mean?"

"The safe was empty. No cash, no bond, no jewels. Not even the back to an earring."

He blinked and hit the brakes, coming to a stop in the middle of the road. "That's impossible."

I shrugged. "There's a plausible explanation."

"Like?" he prodded.

"Aaargh!" I said mimicking a pirate. "Mayhap he moved all of his booty to another treasure chest, matey."

Jamie seemed to think it over before hitting the gas, and taking off again.

Thinking of treasure, I slipped the gold coin Fox had given me on Halloween from my pocket. A token of my debt was what Fox had called it. On one side was the head of a Fox and the other the head of a Crow—Exiled's other founder. I flipped the coin in the air and caught it against the back of my hand. Heads. I did it again. Heads. No matter how many times I flipped that damn coin, the outcome was always the same.

"It's a good thing you're loaded," I said as I shoved the coin back into my pocket. The father of the bride might not be paying for your wedding after all."

"Knock it off," he growled.

"Why? You're the one stalking her."

"At least I'm not too stupid to realize when I've been friend-zoned."

I froze and let the humiliation Jamie wrought wash over me. Was he right? Had I been friend-zoned? Had all the emotion I glimpsed in Wren's eyes and the passionate way his hands and body explored mine been a figment of my imagination? My body temperature rose, and I couldn't tell if the heat was from embarrassment or anger. "You're right," I mumbled. "I'm pathetic." Grabbing the panties from the mirror, I waved it like a white flag. "Truce?"

He snatched them from me with a laugh. "Sure."

Staring out the window, I felt my claws slowly unsheathe as I hummed along to the song playing from Jamie's speakers. I'd never heard it before, but the lyrics seemed to speak to my stupid but hopeful heart.

Wren certainly did play it like a grand piano.

"So don't get mad, but I eavesdropped on you and long legs," I said after a couple of minutes.

His face twisted into a scowl. "What?"

"I said don't get mad!" I yelled as if he were the one in violation.

Blowing out air, he relaxed but kept the scowl. "How much did you hear?"

"Before it got weird? Not much. You two are pretty intense. I've only seen stuff like that on TV. Is there something—"

"Lou," he said in that same warning tone Wren used when he meant business. And like always, I ignored it.

"I heard you tell Barbie that you have your cousin to thank for keeping her company," I rushed out. It wouldn't have been a big deal if he hadn't sounded so…jealous.

Unfortunately, he didn't bother answering my unspoken question.

"I've only met one of your cousins, so I'm going to take a wild guess and say you and Ever are in some kind of weird love triangle with sex on a stick?"

He stubbornly kept his eyes fixed on the road and his mouth shut.

Unperturbed, I continued to muse aloud. "But then where does Four fit into all of this? I thought *she* was his girlfriend?"

No response.

I gasped dramatically as if he had.

"Are you saying he's dating them *both*?"

The muscle in his jaw began to tick, but he stubbornly remained silent. I was starting to think he and Wren were carved from the same stone.

Tapping my chin, I said, "No, that doesn't sound right. Four doesn't seem like the type to share her man."

This time, he snorted. It wasn't much, but I could tell I was getting closer to a real reaction.

"Then again, Ever is *so* dreamy," I cooed. "I bet he could get any girl to do *whatever* he wanted."

Finally, I'd found the right nerve, and without mercy, I hammered at it until he exploded.

"From what I heard last night, he certainly appears to have the stamina to keep them both satisfied. Maybe even all at once?" I leaned over until my lips nearly brushed his ear. "All. Night. Long."

"All right!" he shouted as I sat back in my seat. "Stop! Damn! I'm sorry. Wren wants you, and I know it. The whole goddamn world knows it." He peeked over at me. "Okay?"

"Okay!" I agreed cheerfully.

He shook his head and barked out a laugh of disbelief. "Jesus, you're a bitch."

I nodded and returned to staring out the window. "As long as we're on the same page."

"I'm telling you, Lou. Clexa is going to happen! Mark my words."

"But you have *nothing* to base that on!" I shouted. "You're just being a perv."

On the way back to the manor, I'd discovered that Jamie was another *The 100* fan. Right now, we were arguing over the possibility of Clarke and the commander getting some girl-on-girl action.

Dusk was just beginning to fall as Jamie drove through the gate, and I was trying to hide my anticipation of seeing Wren again. Soon. Hopefully. That anticipation skyrocketed when the house came into view, and I spotted the Crown Vic parked in the driveway. The Impala, in all its glory, would have been easily recognized by Exiled once he hit the city, so Wren had chosen to use the car Ever had loaned him.

Jamie hadn't been able to stop the Wrangler completely before I was hopping out.

He'd come back.

Wren had come back to me.

I ran through the front door, eager for Wren to carry me off into the sunset, but stopped short at the scene playing before me.

Four and Ever were there along with Thomas and Rosalyn and a slender woman I didn't recognize. She had dark hair that was unkempt, olive skin, and only wore a pale pink nightie. As if she'd left in a hurry.

The tension in the foyer was heavy as they all faced off with one another. Ever looked shell-shocked, Four looked worried, Rosalyn was clearly distraught, and Thomas...he looked seriously *pissed*.

I didn't hear Jamie come up behind me until his voice rang through with so much emotion.

"Aunt Evelyn?"

She whirled around, and a kind smile covered her face when she spotted Jamie. "Hi, Jameson. I've missed you."

Jamie made a sound, grasping for words, but when none came, those light brown eyes Ever inherited fell on me, and her smile disappeared. She took a hesitant step forward and reached out to me before thinking better of it and covered her lips with trembling fingers.

"Are—are you Lou?"

"Yeah..."

She took a deep breath before her tears began to fall. "Oh, honey. I'm so sorry."

CHAPTER
THIRTY-THREE

The Moth

WITH NOTHING TO DO BUT STARE AT FOUR LOG WALLS AND bleed on Fox's floor, I ran through my plan for the umpteenth time trying to figure out what I did wrong or what I could have done differently.

The answer was always nothing.

Evelyn was free, and Fox had plans for me. Maybe this was how it was supposed to be. My capture gave Evelyn the time she needed to get away, and I didn't regret it. I only regretted not getting to see Lou one last time.

I snorted in the dark. Wasn't that just a fucking cliché?

I didn't care, though. I'd give anything, including my dignity, to see her again. I closed my eyes picturing her black as midnight hair, her sweet and subtle smell, and her soft skin. I should have told her the truth, begged her forgiveness, and made it all mine a long time ago.

The door opened, and Shane walked in wearing his signature scowl. "You really screwed yourself, boy."

I licked the bloody lip he gave me at Fox's command. "And you care?"

"No, but Bethany and the kids would want me to talk some sense into you."

I stared up at him through my one good eye. "Would you give up Bethany?"

"Fuck no." He rubbed his bald head. "Which is why I'm

not going to bother trying to convince you." He looked me over probably admiring the number he did on me. "Are you sure she's worth it?"

I was surer of it than my own damn name. "Yes."

He nodded. "You're a prick to make me kill you."

I laughed and was surprised that it was genuine. "I'm pretty sure I'm the one drawing the short stick, motherfucker."

He scratched his chin as he eyed me. "Boss isn't going to make it easy for you."

I already knew Fox planned to torture me. If the threat of death wouldn't make me give up Lou, he hoped that pain would. He'd first break a few bones and cut away pieces of me before removing limbs entirely. No, I wouldn't be dying any time soon, but it would be a cold day in hell before I sold Lou to save myself. "I expected no less."

Shane grunted as the door opened and three of my former brothers entered with equally savage scowls. "You'll be singing a different tune soon."

My expression remained impassive as I met each of their gazes.

"Relax," Shane said with a chuckle. "We won't be fucking you up just yet. You have a visitor."

Two of them grabbed me and hauled me to my feet. Resigned to my fate, I didn't bother fighting when they tied my hands and taped my mouth shut. Ever had everything he needed to make sure that Lou would be okay.

I was herded from the basement of his mountain hideout and through the cabin until we reached outside. The air was crisp and cool, and the sky was bright and blue, telling me that it's been at least a day since Evelyn's escape. In the distance, I could see the gathering clouds and the storm brewing miles away. It would hit us hard and soon, though no one else seemed to notice. Fox, with his back turned to me, was too focused on something else, something I couldn't see past his wall of guards. They eventually noticed us approaching and parted, and when we stepped through, I almost fell to my knees at what held their attention.

No.

Before I could collect myself, Fox turned to me with a satisfied smile. "So good of you to join us, Wren. Now we can begin."

My gaze wandered back to Lou standing there, head held high even with all the guns pointed at it.

"As I was saying," Lou said without acknowledging me. I knew she was putting on a brave face for Fox's benefit, and if I weren't living out my worst nightmare, I would have puffed out my chest. "I've got friends now. Friends who have copies of those pictures and won't hesitate to share them if I don't walk out of here with him in the next five minutes."

"I'm sure your friends are loyal to your cause, but I also have friends dedicated to mine as well. Friends who have the power and resources to find your friends. So tell me, little lady, who do you think strikes more fear? Your friends…or mine?"

If Lou was affected, she damn well didn't show it. "I'm well aware of your goons who hide behind badges and call themselves cops, but in *this* century, Grandpa, it's the *internet* that will judge who is innocent or guilty. Your friends may have the law, but mine have YouTube." She smiled then. "And you can't pay off every cop in this country."

"No…only the ones with jurisdiction."

"Except, when you abducted those children right along with their parents and *set them on fire*, your crime became a big, fat federal one. And when those angry moms around the world start rallying for your head, those local cops in your pocket are going to need backup—and lots of it."

Fox was silent for several seconds. The only sound was the occasional sway of the trees in the wind and the shifting feet of the suddenly nervous guards surrounding us. The fox had just been outfoxed, and everyone within hearing distance knew it.

"I'm impressed with you, Louchana." The sound of Lou's

name on his tongue made me want to rip his throat out for the gall. She was too precious to even be in his presence. "Coming here to rescue him was a very brave thing—generous even—considering what he's done to you."

My heart dropped to my stomach. The air I was breathing suddenly felt too thick. The blood in my veins ran cold as the world around me began to crumble. I struggled against my bonds, wishing that I weren't muzzled so I could tell Lou the truth. The truth that Fox was ready to so carelessly dump at her feet.

Not like this.

Her gaze shifted to me for the first time, and the minute she saw the plea in my eyes, she lost some of her bravado. "What are you talking about?"

Fox feigned surprise. "Didn't our dear Wren tell you about his initiation?"

Her chest rose and fell faster now, and her voice was heavy when she answered him. "No."

Fox nodded his understanding and began pacing. "I suppose he wouldn't." He looked at me then and tsk-tsked as he shook his head in admonishment. "You were orphaned five years ago, were you not?"

"How do you know that?"

He ignored her question and asked another of his own. "It was all rather sudden, wasn't it?" Stopping in his tracks, he faced Lou again. "Would you like to know?"

Lou's eyes narrowed as she sneered at him. "Do you really think I'll believe anything you say?"

"No, my dear, I don't, but I know you'll believe him."

Fox turned and nodded to the men holding me. My gaze was fixed on Lou, but it was Fox I addressed when the tape was ripped from my mouth. "Don't do this."

There wasn't an ounce of compassion to be found in him when he said, "Tell her what you did."

"I'd rather die," I said with a snarl at my former boss.

"Oh, no, I won't kill *you*. First, I'll tell her what you did, and then she'll be reunited with her parents after I have Shane here blow her brains out right in front of you. You, my dear boy, will live the rest of your life knowing she died hating you."

Lou's head slowly turned to me, and her eyes welled at Fox's words. "Dead?" Her voice quaked.

"Yes, dear," Fox confirmed, and then his head tilted as he regarded Lou. "Where did you think they were?"

Paris.

She thought her parents had run off to live there. A missing person's report was filed, but no bodies were ever found, only two one-way tickets to Paris in Brian and Emily Valentine's names.

"Wren, what is he talking about?"

"We're all waiting, Wren, with bated breath," Fox goaded. "Tell us how you single-handedly betrayed and ruined this oh-so-sweet and innocent girl."

The remaining part of my world that hadn't crumbled away faded to dust at that moment. Lou's face was an expression of horror as she stared at me through unfocused eyes—as if she didn't see me at all. As if she were playing her parents' murder in her head. Tears flowed down her cheeks and over her trembling lips in an unending stream.

Seeing her gut-wrenching reaction to the truth, I knew it wouldn't have mattered if I'd told her sooner. I'd done the unthinkable, the unforgivable. Lou and I were irrevocably through.

"I'll make a deal with you," Fox said when I couldn't find the courage to speak, to beg. "Leave now, without Wren, and I'll give you a two-minute head start."

For a moment, hope flared when she didn't immediately leave, but then that hoped died when she took one last look at me, a look full of betrayal and hatred, before turning away.

I watched as Lou slowly walked away, and my heart tore a little more with each step she took. It didn't even come close to being the pain I deserved. When she reached the edge of the trees, she looked over her shoulder, and I drank in the sight of her one last time.

"Hey, Fox?" He turned back around at her request and frowned when she smiled. "The enemy of my enemy is my friend."

She flicked something with her thumb, and the two-headed coin I never knew she had landed in the grass at his feet.

Crow's head up.

By the time Fox and I looked back toward the trees, she'd already disappeared, and the silence she left behind was heavy… tense—the calm before the storm.

In quick succession, the two men guarding me collapsed with one bullet to the head. By the time everyone had shaken off their surprise, they were already dropping like flies.

The world seemed to spin out of control as I came to, and while the events—however long ago—were still fuzzy, I immediately sought her out. First with my hands, reaching out to feel her curled up at my side where she belonged. Coming up empty, I sniffed at the stale air void of honeysuckle, jasmine, and green apple. Finally, when I shivered, I pried my heavy lids open enough to search every corner and crevice of the cold motel room. It was similar to the one I'd found Lou in what seemed like a lifetime ago.

When my blurred gaze landed on the corner diagonal to the bed I'd been tossed in, I stilled.

Having instincts honed within an inch of paranoia's reach, I spotted the aberration taking cover in the dark.

"Who the fuck are you?"

I didn't receive an answer.

Ripping away the sheet covering my waist, I jackknifed into a sitting position and immediately grunted from the pain slicing across my stomach. *When the fuck did that happen?*

"Careful. I had to stitch you up myself, and I'm no seamstress."

My head whipped toward the sound—a voice that was familiar and impossible all at once. As the pain dulled, I peered into the seemingly empty corner, seeking out the source of the deep timbre.

The shadows shifted, taking shape until a tall, bearded figure with sharp blue eyes cloaked in black from head to toe stepped into the sliver of moonlight peeking through the curtains. Taking in his height, broad shoulders, tapered waist, and sharp jaw were like looking in a mirror thirty years later. The only difference was the dimpled chin I knew was hiding underneath his beard.

I'd somehow been granted the small mercy of not becoming my father's complete clone and inheriting an ass for a chin.

"Crow?" My voice shook, and I silently cursed the implied vulnerability.

"Hi, son."

I felt my blood cool. He had no right claiming me. "You're dead."

"Afraid not." He hesitated, mulling over his next words. "Disappointed?"

"Confused."

He seemed to deflate before my very eyes. "I'm sorry about that."

I scoffed at the notion of him regretting anything. My father was a selfish son-of-a-bitch. When he wasn't murdering innocents, he was leaving a trail of broken hearts and tears in his wake. "Are you? You sure as fuck took your time coming back."

"It wasn't that simple."

"It never is," I forced through my teeth. My mind was already shifting gears, uninterested in Crow's excuses, and wondering where the fuck was Lou. I needed to see her, to explain, to run to her so I could crawl, to fucking beg until my knees turned bloody. I only wished it would be that easy. I'd tried so hard to keep Lou from being hurt ever again, and in the end, I'd caused more pain than anyone.

"How have you been?" Crow probed.

"I'm still alive. Enough said."

"You almost died today, Wren. Say more," he barked.

"Like what?" I was surprised I didn't chip a tooth with how hard I clenched them. "I don't owe you an explanation."

"I'm still your father."

The reminder only inflamed the rage uncoiling in my stomach. "You were never even close to being that."

In fact, he'd done me a favor when he left my mom to raise me alone. After her death, my grandparents were too terrified to fight him when he stole me from their home thinking I was safer with him. If it weren't for the glaringly obvious, I would have never believed he was my father—mostly because he'd left me to figure it out for myself. Five years ago, Fox hadn't dropped quite the bomb he intended. Instead, he'd only confirmed what I'd already suspected.

"It was too dangerous to come back for you. Fox knew I was still alive. He kept you and Evelyn close to either flush me out or keep me at bay. The moment I came near you, he would have killed both of you."

I regarded him but just as quickly looked away, refusing the plea in his eyes for me to believe him. "He says you betrayed him."

The air around him seemed to darken. "You'd take the word of a man who would turn a son against his father?"

"I sure as shit wouldn't take the word of a father who abandoned his son to save his own skin."

"I was trying to protect *you*."

I scoffed, ignoring the pain as I swung my legs over the side of the bed. "The first or the second time?"

"Both."

I hid my wince as I shoved to my feet and came to stand toe-to-toe with the man who sired me. He was out of his mind if he thought I'd believe for a second that he cared about anyone other than himself. "There's a reason you were born a predator, *Pops*. You wouldn't have lasted long if you were prey."

Turning away after one last look of disgust, I patted my pockets for my phone and wallet before remembering that I'd left them both in the Crown Vic. I looked around wondering what the hell I was going to do now when I spotted them both waiting on the nightstand. My hand paused, however, when I noticed the Impala's keys lying next to them.

I'd left them behind in Blackwood Keep with Lou.

Noticing where my attention had gone, Crow said, "She's smart. She drove the Impala right into the heart of Fox's territory and used it as some sort of bat signal." I wanted to drive my elbow into his face when he chuckled. "Luckily, I got to her before Fox's men did. She's got balls."

Risking Exiled finding her had been a chance she was willing to take…for me, all without knowing why I didn't deserve it.

"She didn't try to save you alone," Crow continued. "She left with them…after making sure you were safe. Bear was there, too. Helped me take those guys out."

I ignored his nervous rambling as I considered leaving the keys to the Impala behind. Since my father wasn't as dead as I thought, the car technically still belonged to him. I snatched them up along with my wallet and phone. The car still wasn't safe, but I had nothing left to lose.

Spotting my shirt tossed over the back of a wooden chair, I pushed past my father to retrieve it. It was still torn and bloody, and suddenly, I remembered Jackal attempting to disembowel me to save himself. I shoved it over my head.

"I have a clean shirt you can wear."

"I don't need anything from you," I shot back. I knew I sounded like a brat, ignoring what was practical, but I didn't give a shit about that, either. I'd taken care of myself for five years, and I'd continue to do so.

"Then why are you so angry?" he pressed.

"Because I did need you!" I roared before I even knew what had come over me.

For a moment, his shock mirrored mine. But then my chest began to heave, my hands balled into fists, and my nostrils flared. I was a flurry of emotions. He stood so very still. Long seconds passed, each of them a wave of control until I was once again drowning in it.

"I did need you," I repeated without the turbulence from a moment ago. "But I don't anymore."

An eternity seemed to pass. The room became a bubble, bringing a solitude so silent that I swore I not only felt but heard my heart splintering right down the middle.

Relief washed over me when I saw him deflate.

"Then I won't stop you from going." His words sounded like the echo of a key turning inside a lock. The moment the catch released, I didn't hesitate to make a break for the door. "But you should know," he called out before I could step over the threshold, "I never left you, son, and I won't leave you now, so if you ever do need me again, I won't be far away."

I could feel his gaze, and even though he didn't move an inch, I could feel him reaching out for me.

I fled before I could reach back.

CHAPTER
THIRTY-FOUR

The Flame

ONE BY ONE, I PEELED AWAY THE FRAGILE PETALS OF WREN'S heart.

He loves me not. He loves me forever.

Best friends forever. Soul mates...never.

When I got down to the very last petal, I sighed.

He loves me.

A week ago, I would have run to him, shown him the evidence, and gloated over owning his heart. I would have made him confess and promise me forever.

A week ago, he hadn't been the reason my parents were dead.

I stared hopelessly at the flower petals littering the ground. Wren hadn't tried to defend himself or make excuses. All of this time, he'd been carrying the guilt on his shoulders, and when the truth had come out, he'd laid it at my feet like an offering. His dishonor was now mine. To enforce ...or forgive.

Before I could decide Wren's fate, a chorus of giggling that may as well have been nails on a chalkboard interrupted my brooding. Jamie and I were hanging out at the local park while Ever and Four were both at school. Jamie, who'd been a senior when he got kicked out of school in Ireland, had completed all the credits he needed to graduate. He only had to sit back and wait for the actual ceremony in June.

A breath of fresh air was what Jamie called it when he

pulled me out of bed this morning. I couldn't remember leaving it before then.

The shameful part of it all was knowing that it wasn't the loss of my parents that made facing the world hard. For five years, I grieved losing them. The only thing I felt now was a twisted sense of closure.

No, it was walking away from Wren that made me feel like I'd died, too.

"Sorry, ladies," Jamie said to the trio of girls twirling their hair around manicured fingers and flirting with their eyes. "I'm flattered, but I'm not interested."

My eyebrows rose as I looked over the group. They were attractive and willing, the only standards Jameson John Buchanan possessed, yet he was passing up the opportunity to sleep with them?

Maybe there was hope for him yet.

"Hmm," the sole male member of their group mused aloud. He was a short Latino with the biggest brown eyes and mile-long lashes. "I'd say you were batting for my team, but my radar isn't picking up anything." His eyes then turned to slits as he studied Jamie.

Jamie's smile was wolfish as he said, "Why don't you come closer? You might get a better reading."

One of the girls gasped, the second sighed, while the third rolled her eyes.

"It's always the hot ones," the one with the attitude whispered.

"Good for you, Matty!" another one cheered.

I pursed my lips, knowing Jamie was full of shit, but I propped my elbow on my knee and rested my chin in my palm, more than curious to see how far he'd go.

Matty shrugged and strutted over without an ounce of shame and his friends' jaw dropped when Jamie leaned back on the bench and made room for him on his lap.

"I'm Jamie," he introduced once Matty was settled. Jamie

looked perfectly relaxed, and I had to say I was surprised. Most guys treated homosexuality like it was a contagious disease. Even now, some of the men walking by scowled with distaste, but one look from Jamie had them scurrying away. "So?" he inquired after a few seconds passed.

"I'm torn between integrity and my wildest fantasies," Matty answered with a sigh.

"Well?" one of his friends badgered. "Is he or isn't he?"

Matty ignored his friend and pouted over his shoulder at Jamie. "I'm afraid you're as straight as an arrow."

"Darn," Jamie replied with a grin.

Matty asked Jamie for his phone, and after unlocking it, Jamie handed it over without hesitation. We all watched as Matty tapped at the screen before handing it back to Jamie. "Give me a call if you're ever curious enough to bend that arrow a little."

Jamie's only response was to wink, and with another sigh, Matty stood from his lap and walked away with an extra sway of his hips. His friends sent one last longing look at Jamie before rushing after him.

"You really don't give a shit, do you?" I asked him once Jamie's giggling group of admirers were out of earshot.

Jamie lit a cigarette and blew smoke in my face. "Why should I?"

I didn't answer him because I was too busy coughing, trying to clear the smoke from my lungs. "You're dead inside, aren't you?"

"Not yet," he said with a chuckle and then paused. "But if you're offering to make me feel alive again, then *totally*."

I laughed, and even though it was genuine, it felt weird and wrong. I'd just found that my parents were dead and that my best friend was responsible. I didn't think I'd ever laugh again.

"Are you ready to talk about it?" Jamie asked when my laughter died.

"You were there...what is there left to say?"

After Evelyn broke the news that they had captured Wren, I hadn't said a word. In fact, I didn't react at all—which, in hindsight, was probably what gave me away. Later that night, I'd attempted to sneak away, to go after Wren alone, but Ever and Jamie had other plans. As soon as I'd reached the Impala, they emerged from the shadows where they'd been lying in wait.

"Where you go, we go," Ever proclaimed. *"If he's already dead and something happens to you, the fucker will haunt me the rest of my days."*

"You tell me," Jamie countered with a knowing look.

"Are you asking me to *share my feelings*? Should I get the tissues?"

He barked out a laugh. "You're a dick, you know that?"

I shrugged. "I may have heard that a time or two."

"You know he's not going to stay away," Jamie warned.

"It's been a week, and he hasn't come crawling." I quickly flattened my lips when I realized I was pouting. "I think he knows better than that."

Jamie laughed as he blew smoke in the air. "I just saw you face down a monster with nothing but a wing and a prayer and *win*. I know you're not that naïve."

I looked away so that he wouldn't see my heart galloping in my eyes and stared down at my empty ring finger. I'd only worn it for a few days, but it had already left its mark. "He's not going to come."

And even if he did, it wouldn't change anything.

Wren and I could never go back to a time when he *didn't* kill my parents.

The next evening, I wandered into the kitchen with Jamie by my side and found Ever glaring down at a small notebook as if it had personally offended him. Vaughn and Tyra were also there, but they seemed more interested in each other than their friend's woes.

Jamie let out a loud groan when his gaze landed on his cousin. "Dude, why don't you just buy her diamond earrings for Christmas? Bitches love diamonds."

My eyes nearly popped out of my head as I took a subtle step away from Jamie. I still didn't know Ever all that well, but he seemed like a no-nonsense kind of guy. I couldn't chance getting an elbow to the face if they came to blows. Jamie was clearly baiting Ever and knowing the reason why only made me more curious. Anyone with eyes could see that Ever was irrevocably in love with Four. He didn't see anyone else when she was in the room.

I could tell by the way Vaughn and Tyra tensed that my assessment was spot on. However, Ever didn't react. After only a withering glare, he returned to staring at his drawing. The bleakness I glimpsed in his eyes might have been the reason.

In all my grief, I'd forgotten that Ever had just been reunited with his mother thanks to my treacherous, former best friend. The reunion couldn't have been heartwarming considering Evelyn had found that her husband and son had both moved on with another family.

Curious, I inched closer until I could see over his shoulder. Jamie, Vaughn, and Tyra had also moved forward.

"It's missing something," Ever said to no one in particular.

We all studied Ever's sketch, and after a full minute passed, I figured we'd all drawn a blank until Jamie shouted, "Pigtails!"

"When have you *ever* seen Four wear pigtails?" Tyra argued.

"Maybe she should," he shot back with a grin. "And high… like a naughty girl."

Frowning, Tyra propped a hand on her hip. "How would you—"

"Know?" Jamie finished. "Those walls upstairs are thinner than you think." He winked, causing Tyra to blush before scowling at Vaughn. It seemed Jamie knew more than Tyra was comfortable with.

While Jamie and Tyra bickered back and forth, I studied the wicked looking skull and concluded that Jamie was right although, as usual, his delivery sucked. Even for a tomboy like Four, the skull was too masculine. The pigtails would help soften it and even give it a Harley Quinn vibe. And what guy didn't want their very own Harley Q?

Still, I wasn't a part of their inner circle, so I didn't think they'd welcome me taking sides. Glancing at Vaughn, I wondered if he'd step in, but unfortunately, he looked his usual bored self as he tossed back peanut M&Ms.

"He's right," I heard myself saying. I instantly regretted it when Tyra and Jamie immediately fell silent, and Vaughn paused mid-chew.

Ever was slower to react, but when he looked over his shoulder, he didn't seem at all annoyed. Only curious. "Yeah?"

I slowly nodded when I couldn't find my voice. I wasn't usually passive, but it was safe to say that I'd lost myself in those mountains. When Ever smirked and lifted a brow, as if goading me to grow a pair, I cleared my throat and said more firmly, "Draw the pigtails."

He held my gaze for a few more seconds, and when I wouldn't fold, he turned back around with an approving nod and said, "Sounds good."

He began to sketch, and I could feel his friends watching me as we all stood around waiting for him to finish. All the while, I wondered where Four was at the moment. I shrugged figuring she was walking Jay D.

"It's still missing something," Vaughn said when Ever finished.

"It needs color," Jamie said.

"How about yellow?" Tyra suggested. "It's her favorite color."

"Yellow won't be as eye-catching as purple," I pointed out.

"It should be pink," Vaughn voiced.

With a snort, I said, "I've known Four about five minutes now, and even I know she won't be caught dead in anything pink."

"Careful," Vaughn said, and I was taken aback by his blatant contempt. "You're new here."

Ever frowned disapprovingly at his best friend while Jamie rolled his eyes, and Tyra nudged me with her elbow. "He's just grumpy. Ignore him. I usually do," she muttered.

Jamie leaned over and laughingly whispered in my ear. "Ask her why he's grumpy though."

"Something tells me you already know," I whispered back.

"Yup," he whispered a little too proudly. "She's been leaving his balls fifty shades of blue lately. I'm talking no hand jobs, blow jobs, or any jobs."

Jamie's laugh was infectious, but even then, I still felt my stomach turning as I sneaked a peek at Vaughn. Our eyes met, and I could see from the way his green eyes glowed that his anger had nothing to do with Tyra. He was wary of me. He might even hate me. Now I just needed to figure out why.

Jay D ran into the kitchen, and when Four appeared seconds later, everyone kind of moved at once. Ever hurriedly flipped his notebook closed while Jamie grabbed Four in a bear hug and twirled her around for no good reason.

"Jamie, what are you doing? I want to see what Ever was drawing."

"Have I told you lately that you're hot as hell?" Jamie cooed.

"Yeah, last night...when you tried to cop a feel."

Ever's head whipped around so fast I was surprised his neck didn't snap. "What?" He growled as he shot to his feet. The stool he was sitting on would have toppled over if I hadn't caught it.

Looks like I might catch that elbow, after all.

"Calm down, cousin," Jamie drawled. His gaze never left Four as he set her on her feet. "She's just trying to get you to punch me."

Four's eyes twinkled, confirming Jamie's claim.

"Come on," Ever said, inserting himself between them. "Let's get this over with."

"Get what over with?" Tyra inquired.

"I'm teaching him how to ride," Four announced as she led a reluctant Ever out of the kitchen by the hand. Jay D didn't hesitate to follow. The rest of us shared a look, and we all seemed to be thinking the same thing. A second later, we were pushing and shoving to get through the door first.

"Oh, this should be good," Jamie said when we made it outside. He was rubbing his hands together with a mischievous smile.

Four and Ever were standing by her bike, and she was talking as she pointed to different things. Ever listened with his arms crossed while looking like he'd rather be anywhere else. Jay D sat dutifully by his side, tongue wagging as he watched his mama.

"I'm her best friend," Tyra griped an hour later as we sat on the steps watching the spectacle playing out in the driveway. Ever did not make a good student, and Four was beginning to lose her patience. "She never even offered me lessons."

"It's not about the lessons," Vaughn told her. "Ever's mother just showed up after four years. His head is fucked up. This"—he waved to where Ever was straddling the bike and nuzzling Four's neck, making her blush and grin—"is a distraction."

"Where is Evelyn anyway?" Tyra asked, voicing my thoughts.

It was Jamie who answered her. "Unc arranged for her to stay in a rental nearby."

"Does Rosalyn know that?" Vaughn asked.

Jamie chortled. "God no."

The three of them talked and joked among themselves while I traced every crack and crevice in the ground to keep myself from thinking about Wren.

"Jamie, you're sitting awfully close to Lou," Four teased as she and Ever approached. "Give it up already. She doesn't want to be your girlfriend."

I was still staring at the ground when I heard Jamie say, "What do you say, Lou? Wanna give it a try?"

My head shot up, and I frowned at him. "What?"

"You and me. Girlfriend and boyfriend. Think of the mischief we'll cause." His eyebrows waggled, making me chuckle.

"Sure, Jamie. Why the fuck not?"

His eyes shone with delight making me second-guess if he was joking or not. "Seal it with a kiss?" Jamie's soft lips stole mine before I could tell him no, and even in my surprise, I couldn't help but notice that he was a damn good kisser. Before I could pull away, I heard the deep rumble of an engine that sounded all too familiar.

Paula.

Heart racing, I snatched away from Jamie as my entire body flushed. *Shit.* What if he saw?

I forced myself to calm down, realizing that I didn't owe Wren my loyalty or an explanation. He was the one who ruined us.

Maybe I should fuck Jamie.

Who better to exorcise Wren completely?

I peeked at Jamie and found him staring straight ahead with only a barely-there smirk to tell me what he was thinking. I sighed, knowing screwing someone else wouldn't cure my broken heart.

I heard the Impala shut off and then a car door slam shut. Taking a deep breath, I forced myself to look at Wren for the first time since learning he was a murderer.

He lied to me.

Wren was maybe three steps away before Jamie suddenly stood, blocking him from getting to me, and Ever, to my astonishment, joined him.

I gaped at them even though they couldn't see me with their backs turned.

So much for being a lone wolf.

Ever and Jamie had just made it clear that I was now part of a pack—whether I liked it or not. I looked around. Four, Tyra, and even Vaughn as he stood to join Ever and Jamie, wore equally hostile expressions. My gut told me that none of them were going to make it as easy to push away as the Hendersons had.

"We really need to learn to lock that gate," Jamie muttered.

Ever grunted, his only response as he waited for Wren to make his move.

I hugged my legs to my chest and waited, too.

"Lou, come here," Wren ordered, ignoring both Ever and Jamie. I should have known, even in the wrong, he'd never be anything else but arrogant. The ache in my belly intensified along with disgust at myself for actually wanting to go to him.

"What do you want?" I asked him quietly.

"To talk…to explain."

Feeling rage overcome my vulnerability, I shot to my feet and pushed past the wall Ever, Jamie, and Vaughn had made. I felt the heat from their bodies on my back as they closed ranks around me. "You had the chance to explain, and you just sat there. Do you want to know why, Wren? It's because there was nothing to say then, and there's nothing to say now."

"I was going to tell you, Lou."

"When?" I shouted. "After you grew tired of fucking me?"

He shoved his fingers through his hair. "I didn't want to touch you until you knew the truth but you—"

"Right," I cut him off. "It's my fault."

"No!" His chest started to heave, and after a few seconds, he forced himself to calm down. "You convinced me that it wouldn't matter what I did, and I was selfish enough to believe it."

"Killing my parents and believing that it wouldn't matter to me doesn't just make you selfish, Wren. It makes you a fool."

He flinched and looked away. Behind me, I heard a feminine gasp and was genuinely surprised that Jamie nor Ever had spilled the beans. They all seemed pretty tight, but Wren had just taught me that, close or not, we all had our secrets.

"I didn't," he said after a long and tense silence.

"You didn't what?" I snapped.

He turned his head, nostrils flaring as he met my gaze. "I didn't kill them, Lou."

I didn't react at first, but then I felt my hands ball as I turned his words over in my head. He didn't kill them? How could he say that to me? How could he *lie*?

Before I knew it, I lunged forward and slammed my fist into his nose. Satisfaction and adrenaline rushed through me, so I did it again but aimed for his eye this time. He didn't even try to protect himself when I went for a third, but a hand suddenly clamped around my wrist kept me from doling out more punishment.

"Let her go," Wren growled to whoever held me.

"So you can get your ass kicked?" Jamie mocked. "Happy to, although I'm pretty sure she's hurting herself more than she's hurting you."

I realized Jamie was right, and I grimaced. Not only was my hand throbbing from the pain but my heart twisted so cruelly seeing him bleed that I almost cried out.

It wasn't fair. I shouldn't care, not this much and not at all.

I cradled my hand against my chest, and Wren's gaze followed and darkened. I could tell he wanted to comfort me but knew I'd scratch his eyes out if he tried.

He sighed and looked wary when he met my gaze again. "Fox talks small businesses into cutting him into their profits in exchange for protecting their interests. He's the biggest threat to any of them, and they all know it, so they pay up. Usually." He took a deep breath. "After I convinced Fox to let me work for him, I still had to prove myself like everyone else. Every initiation is different. Some have to complete a task, and some have to take a beating. It's always their choice. I was the only one not given one. Fox had set his sights on your parents' bodega, but they wouldn't budge, so...he tasked me with convincing them to pay up."

"And when you couldn't, you killed them." It wasn't a question.

"I couldn't convince them, but I didn't kill them, Lou. I begged them to run, but when they told me they had a daughter, I panicked. I didn't give a fuck about who they were leaving behind. I couldn't have their blood on my hands. I pulled my gun out, and I tried to make them leave with me, but it was too late. Fox had been watching, waiting. He knew all along that I wouldn't go through with it."

"What happened?" I snapped when he became mute.

"Lou—"

"*Tell me*," I demanded without mercy. There was nothing he could say or do to hurt me any more than he already had.

"Fox had them tortured, and he made me watch. He wanted me to remember their screams and how they begged for death the next time I chose mercy."

"And you still worked for him?"

His eyes narrowed. "Do you honestly think I had a choice after that?"

No. I didn't. The moment he'd gone to Fox, I knew he was already in too deep. Still, I wasn't about to give him an inch. Compassion and understanding wouldn't bring my parents back.

"What about the one-way ticket to Paris that the cops found?" I grilled. "What about my parents' bank accounts that had been emptied? Did Fox do that too?"

He frowned, but when his expression cleared as if understanding dawned, he looked away. It was a few seconds before my heart sank.

They had been planning to leave me, after all.

I felt the wall behind me push in closer, ready to let me lean on them. I shouldn't have been ready to accept them after my parents and Wren all let me down, but I knew I couldn't go on never allowing anyone close. I had to leave my heart open to pain. It was the only way to strengthen it. Each lash was a lesson and each scar left behind a new stronghold. All the love I'd wasted on the wrong people was now returning to me tenfold.

"What do you want from me, Wren?" My voice reflected the weariness I held in my heart. I refused to cry anymore.

"You deserved to know the truth."

"And you were expecting me to forgive you."

I realized he left himself completely open as he gazed into my eyes. "Hoping," he said the moment I felt my resolve melting.

"Let's say I do forgive you…what does that mean for us?" My heart galloped in my chest as I waited for him to answer.

"Whatever you want."

I chewed on my lip as I looked away. "You didn't hurt my parents, Wren, but that doesn't change anything. Not only did you lie to me for nearly *three years*, I know you'll never let that guilt go, so…maybe you were right. Maybe we only stand a chance as friends." I took a deep breath and faced him again. "And *only* friends."

"Just friends?" He took a step that was threatening but somehow my pussy clenched and warmed, finding it promising. "Because of you, I stopped thinking of us as friends and started seeing you as mine." His heated glare shifted to the three males hovering behind me, and the warning was clear. "*Just* mine."

I heard a snort that I knew came from Jamie and was thankful when he chose not to goad him further.

I lifted my chin, and Wren paused in his tracks. "It's friends or nothing, Wren. Take it or leave it."

Later that night, there was a single, hard knock before the door to Four's room flew open, and Jamie burst in. "What's up, ladies? Four."

She didn't bother looking up from her phone as she flipped him off. I had the feeling from the heat pinking her cheeks that she was busy sexting with Ever. After I'd given Wren his ultimatum, he'd left without a word, but the promise I'd glimpsed in his eyes just before he turned away kept me from knowing what to think.

Jamie crossed the room and shoved open the window before taking up a seat on the wide sill with one foot hanging from the window and the other planted on the floor. He then dug in his pocket and pulled out a pack of cigarettes, popped one in his mouth and then dug for a lighter.

"Jamie, I don't want my room smelling like smoke."

"Hence, the open window, kitten." He ignored the rest of Four's protests and lit up. Jay D, enamored by the newcomer, rushed to his side, and Jamie greeted him with a cloud of smoke blown in his face. Jay D barked but didn't move away, so Jamie took another drag with a twinkle in his eye.

Seeing this, Four rushed over and grabbed her baby before Jamie could do it again. "I don't think there is a person in this room who won't say that you *fell* out that window and broke every bone in your body."

"You wouldn't dare and not because your balls aren't big enough but because you'd have no one to use when you need to make Ever jealous."

"And why would I need to make Ever jealous?"

"Because his attention is divided." He looked over at Tyra, who was painting her nails. "You're shit at that," he remarked.

I couldn't argue with him and neither could Tyra as she frowned at her toes.

"Well, if you're going to crash our slumber party," Tyra griped, "you should at least make yourself useful."

He didn't respond other than to lift his lithe yet powerful body from the window and stroll unhurriedly to the tall white chest in the corner of Four's room where an iPod was hooked to a pill-shaped speaker.

"Thief." He snarled at Four before plucking the last of his cigarette from his lips and putting it out on the pristine wood.

"Jamie!"

He ignored her and thumbed through the iPod. 'She Loves Me Not' by Papa Roach came through the speakers, and Four cocked her head with a teasing smile.

"Something on your mind, James?"

"Bite me," he said before taking a seat on the bed and yanking Tyra's foot into his lap.

"Careful!" she scolded. "I'm delicate."

"But your tongue is sharp," he retorted with a snicker. "If you're looking for ways to get Vaughn to stick around, I wouldn't suggest giving him a blow job."

Twenty minutes later, he was applying a final coat of red polish to Tyra's toes.

"Good boy." She patted the top of his head, so he pushed her feet off his lap, making her shriek and inspect her toes for smeared polished.

Sighing, he looked between Four and me. "Who's next?"

Four snorted, so I wiggled my toes in invitation and tossed him one of Tyra's many blue polishes.

"How are you so good at this, anyway?" I asked him as he applied the first stroke.

He frowned before he ducked his head, and I had the feeling he was hiding. "My dad sometimes painted my mom's toes. After he died, she would always cry whenever she did them herself."

"So you painted them for her."

He shrugged and dipped the brush inside the bottle for more polish. "I didn't like seeing her cry."

"Aww, Jamie!" we all cooed at the same time.

The vicious scowl he wore in response had us laughing until we cried.

"Laugh all you want, but the joke's on you," he grumbled. "I lied so one of you would sleep with me."

I shook my head while Four rolled her eyes. Jamie hadn't lied, but the way he avoided our gazes told me he was afraid of being open. So afraid that it made me wonder if he'd been hurt before and how deeply.

"You're shit at that," Tyra said, throwing his words from before back at him.

"At what?"

"Keeping people from seeing who you really are."

"Perhaps I'm a magician, and you're too busy watching the wrong hand to see all the magic happening in the other."

"Now who's the thief," Four teased. "You totally stole that from *Now You See Me!*" She bent over clutching her stomach while Jamie glared daggers. It didn't faze her one bit, and after a while, Jamie grinned, too. I realized then that their friendship was an honest one despite its flaws. Something Wren and I never truly had.

I hadn't realized I had Jamie's attention until gentle fingers lifted my chin. "Your eyes don't belong down there."

I smiled at him. It was hesitant and small but the best I could do.

"Are you okay?" Jamie asked.

"I will be if you throw in a foot massage, too."

He shook his head and laughed. "Sorry, but I have to draw the line there. No one's going to buy the cow if they can get the milk for free."

"I don't think that saying applies to foot massages and pedicures," Tyra pointed out.

He looked her up and down. "You'd know, wouldn't you, virgin?" She rolled her eyes, and he turned to me. "So yeah, even though we had a good thing going," he said as he finished up, "I hope you and Wren work things out."

"Jamie," Four said as she pinched the bridge of her nose. "You dated her for like *two seconds.*"

He stood from the bed and grinned down at me. "And they were two glorious seconds, weren't they?"

Jamie thankfully left before I could respond, and Tyra said her goodbyes shortly after. It was just Four and me, and with Jay D asleep at the foot of the bed, both of us were content with the silence.

I wasn't sure how much time passed when she produced a paper out of the top drawer of her nightstand, stared at it for a few minutes, and sighed. It was wrinkled as if this wasn't the first or even hundredth time she'd stared at it.

"What's that?"

I didn't miss her hesitation or the way she clutched the paper tighter before she replied. "A form...to change my name."

I sat up quickly and rounded on her. "What? *Why?*"

"Because Rosalyn is a schizophrenic with an addiction to falling for the wrong man."

My lips parted, but when no response came, I frowned. "Yeah, you're going to have to explain that one to me."

So she did.

By the time she was done telling me about her mother's failed relationships and the three miscarriages that led to her mental spiral downward, I realized I'd underestimated Four.

But so had she.

"Did you know my birth mother was the one who named me?" Four blinked at me, and I shrugged. "I'm sure she picked it out with so much love in her heart right before she left me in the cold with a note that said *I'm sorry, Louchana.*" Taking the form from her hand, I ripped it in half, making her eyes bulge. "It's just a fucking name." I ripped the form again into fours. "Your mother could have given you the most beautiful or exotic name in the world, and she'd still be messed up." I ripped the pieces of paper in half again. "That's not your fault. These scars you bear are what made you who you are. Bold, beautiful, and badass. Wear them, Four. They're your crown."

CHAPTER
THIRTY-FIVE

The Moth

I 'LL TAKE THESE." JAMIE SNATCHED THE BOUQUET OF ROSES FROM MY hand and tossed them over the railing of the porch. It was a long way down given the blue beach house was sitting on stilts, so I watched them land in the sand, the petals scattered and ruined, before glaring at Jamie. "You'll be showing your hand the moment she sees you," he explained. "You need to sweep her off her feet before she has the chance to put her guard up."

"And fix your face," Vaughn criticized. "You want to look sorry, not pathetic." My scowl deepened, and he grinned before saying, "Much better."

"Now put this on," Ever ordered while handing over a blue and gray sweater that read 'Snow's Out Ho Ho Ho's Out' with a snowflake pattern.

"Why?" I said, finding my voice for the first time since they bombarded me. It's been nearly two weeks since Lou's ultimatum, and I was running out of air. It was only a matter of time before I drowned, so when Ever invited me to this party, I readily agreed after he casually mentioned that Lou would be here as well.

"It's the theme."

I looked them over realizing that they were all wearing sweaters. Jamie wore a tank that looked like the top half of a Santa suit. His tattoos were in full effect, which I suspected was the reason he decided to risk the biting cold. Vaughn wore a black and white sweater that read 'Snowtorious' above a scowling snowman wearing a tilted crown. Ever's was a Christmas-patterned cardigan and tie.

"The theme is ugly-ass Christmas sweater?"

"Exactly," Jamie confirmed as we stepped inside the crowded house. "We're having a contest," he shouted over the music.

After shoving on the sweater, I looked around and saw everyone wearing one, each uglier than the last. 'Get Low' by Lil Jon, The Eastside Boyz & Yang-Yang Twins was playing, and everyone started pushing and shoving to out-hype each other. We escaped into the kitchen where the drinks were, and with one bellow, Vaughn cleared the room.

"What does the winner get?" I asked even though I didn't care. I just needed to distract myself from searching the crowd for Lou.

"Our respect," Vaughn answered.

"At least until the party's over," Jamie added.

"Wow," Lou drawled as she stepped inside the kitchen. "A bit douchey, don't you think?"

I spun around, eyes wide, but thankfully, her gaze stubbornly fixed on Jamie, which gave me time once Vaughn nudged me to compose myself. And admire her. Lou had her hair pinned up in a ponytail, curls cascading down her back while a few framed her face. The sweater she wore was white with red and green ribbons covering the front. She looked so soft and wholesome, concealing the hard edge I knew she possessed and often displayed proudly.

"There's also a five-hundred-dollar cash prize," Four wryly informed me. I hadn't even realized her and Tyra were standing there wearing sweaters just like Lou's. "Unfortunately, ninety-nine percent of Brynwood's population have rich mommies and daddies, so a high-five from these three is as good as it gets."

Ever fought a smile as he moved behind Four, who stood in front of the island and started mixing a drink. Four tensed at his closeness for some reason before looking around in a panic.

"I don't know what you're getting tight about," Jamie scoffed. "You're one of us now."

Crossing her arms, she moved away from Ever and squared off with Jamie. "How is that, exactly?"

"You made your bed," he answered, jerking his chin toward his cousin, "now lie in it."

Vaughn, Tyra and, to my surprise, Lou sighed, telling me this may have been a reoccurring argument.

"Make up your mind, Jamie. You either want me with your cousin, or you don't. Frankly, I couldn't give a shit what you think, but the bitch fits are getting old."

"Careful not to say that too loud," Jamie taunted. "Someone might hear."

"And why would I care?"

"Because you sold your soul for that dick. But look on the bright side," he continued before Four could rebut, "at least you can't tell anyone."

Four stood still for God knows how long, with Ever at her back practically blowing steam from his nose, before she blinked away the tears forming and stormed from the kitchen.

"Jamie!" Tyra scolded before punching him in the arm and running after Four.

Ever started to follow, but Jamie stopped him in his tracks.

"So how many times am I going to have to make her feel small before you do something about it?"

Ever approached him, each step silent but lethal, until his chest brushed Jamie's. "You mean other than kicking your ass?"

Jamie shook his head as if Ever were the one who was hard to believe. "You and I both know a bloody nose and busted lip won't do shit but piss me off."

"What the fuck do you want me to do, Jamie?"

"The right thing," he bit out.

"You don't have the facts to tell me what's right and what's wrong."

"But I've got twenty-twenty vision." Ever's answering silence had Jamie narrowing his eyes. "You really don't see what your little arrangement is doing to her?"

"And you do?"

"I can relate," was all Jamie said.

"She's fine," Ever said, gritting his teeth.

"Now. Maybe. But for how long?"

Ever pinched the bridge of his nose. When he met Jamie's gaze again, the same mask he wore when he was Danny Boy was in place. "Don't say shit else to her about our relationship, Jamie. I'm fucking warning you."

"Can't do that, cousin. You don't give a shit if I insult you, but your panties bunch so tightly they might split you in half whenever I say just one word to Four."

Jamie didn't stick around, bumping Ever's shoulder on his way out. I had the feeling he was going after Four to comfort her since he was a dick but not a heartless dick. As if realizing this himself, Ever rushed out of the kitchen a moment later. Vaughn sighed and after downing the last of his drink, he left, too.

That left me alone with Lou, who was eyeing the exit. She was probably afraid I'd pounce if she ran while I didn't know what I'd do. I felt like I was living in someone else's skin.

"Any idea what that was about?" I asked to break through the awkwardness between us.

She looked at me then for the first time since I walked away from her, and the longing I felt was sharp enough to gut me completely.

"No idea. They have so much drama exploding around here that it's hard to catch every grenade."

Just then, a crowd of people rushed inside the kitchen. Seeing the coast was clear they went straight for the drinks. We were herded into a corner until she was trapped between the counter and me. Lou tensed and refused to meet my gaze as her breathing became faster and uncontrolled.

Sensing she needed space, I took her hand, feeling like I'd been shocked back to life, and cleared the way out of the kitchen. I didn't stop until we stood outside of the beach house near one of the fires they'd lit.

"Better?"

She gave me a curt nod and looked away. My hands began shaking, so I shoved them in my pockets so she couldn't see my nervousness. It had never been this awkward between us.

"I'm sorry," I said when no other words would come. It was then that I realized I'd never actually told her just how fucking sorry I was. I simply told her what happened five years ago and expected her to forgive me for the truth without actually apologizing for it.

The truth was just as ugly as the lie I'd let her believe.

Her head whipped around, and the shock in her eyes told me just how much I'd fucked this whole thing up. I shouldn't have left her that day. I should have got on my knees and stayed there until she forgave me—morning, noon, and night. I never expected that losing her heart would hurt a hell of a lot more than losing her friendship. I would have walked away the moment I realized I was falling in love with her.

She didn't respond right away, and I counted each agonizing second until she decided my fate.

However, instead of putting me out of my misery, she said, "Did you know who I was the night we met?"

I swallowed. "Not right away, but...yes. After what happened to your parents, I couldn't resist seeking you out. I needed to make sure you were okay."

"I wasn't," she spat, and I hung my head.

"I know." But I'd forced myself to forget about her anyway. There was nothing I could offer her but more pain. "When I saw you during that snowstorm, I knew I couldn't walk away again."

Her lips flattened into a tight line. "So you became my friend out of guilt? You thought it would absolve you?"

"Yes," I admitted even though it burned. "I thought if I took care of you, I could fill the hole your parents left behind, but you ended up filling all of mine, instead."

All around us, music played, the ocean waves crashed in the distance, and people were reveling, but somehow, I was only aware of Lou and me and the empty void left between us.

"I suppose I should thank you," she said after a few tears had fallen and she'd wiped them away. "For trying to help my parents."

I had trouble swallowing the lump in my throat. "You don't owe me anything. I should have done more."

She shook her head and stared into the flames. "You were only fifteen."

"That's no excuse," I growled, pissed at myself rather than her.

"You're right," she conceded. "It doesn't matter if you were fifteen or fifty. If you had done something, you would have died and I—" Her eyes closed, and I could sense the war waging within her. "I wouldn't want that," she finally admitted. Her eyes opened and found mine. The vulnerability she never allowed herself before shone brightly within them now. "Not then and not now."

Feeling like the gates of heaven had just opened up, I grabbed her and pressed her against one of the wooden stilts raising the house from the ground. Before she could protest or ask a million fucking questions, I sealed my lips to hers. It might be the last time I'd ever get to kiss her. With an impending sense of doom, I deepened the kiss, drawing all I dared take from her while giving her everything I had left to give—my heart, my soul, and my life if she asked for it. I'd slit my wrists right here and now so that she could see how I bled for her. How much I wanted to carry her pain for her.

As if hearing my thoughts, she ripped her mouth away with a startled cry and gripped my sweater as she rested her head on my chest.

Leaning down, I kissed the top of her head and inhaled when I caught a whiff of her shampoo.

"Do you trust me?"

"I don't want to," she admitted in a small voice.

"But you do." She drew in a sharp breath but wisely remained silent. We both knew if she gave an inch, I'd take a mile and feel no shame for my greediness. "If nothing else, trust that I won't give up on us."

She lifted her head, her mouth opening and closing until she finally said, "I—I just want to be friends, Wren."

"No, Lou. You don't." I kissed her again, and it felt like my heart was in her fist when she greedily sank into it. This time, I was the one to pull away although it felt like chewing off my limb. "But I'll wait."

"Forever?" she challenged, her tone skeptical.

"However long you need me to," I confirmed as I backed away. "I'm yours, Lou. I'll always be yours."

Lou looked like she wanted to argue, but then, with a frustrated cry, she fled back to the safety of the house. A moment later, Jamie emerged from the shadows, clutching the lit cigarette hanging from his mouth.

"How much did you hear?" I said as my nostrils flared. I was getting sick of this fucker putting his nose in my shit.

"Enough." He propped his shoulder against the side of the house and grinned. "You should invest in kneepads," he suggested while looking like he was enjoying every minute of my fall from grace.

"Why?"

"Because you're going to need to grovel better than that."

Gritting my teeth, I turned away, knowing he was right, but then a sudden thought had me turning back to him.

"Whether she forgives me or not, I'm going to make damn sure you don't get her, either." Whatever was left of her that I hadn't ruined, Jamie would surely finish the job.

Standing up straight, he shrugged. "Then you'd be wasting your time barking up the wrong tree."

My gaze narrowed on him. "You expect me to believe that?" I saw him kiss her two weeks ago, and it had been all I could do not to rip his throat out. Since I'd come to beg and not to demand, I refrained. Somehow.

"You can keep your little Lou Who," he told me cockily. "I've got my heart set on a much bigger challenge." Shoving his free hand into his pocket, he swaggered away before I could knock his teeth down his throat.

I considered going back inside and finding Lou to plead some more, but knowing I had work to do, I made an about-face and headed for my car.

CHAPTER
THIRTY-SIX

The Flame

ONE MINUTE I WAS WATCHING THE SNOW DESCEND OVER THE city much like it had the night I met Wren, and the next, I was tearfully watching the glass surrounding the scene shatter and crumble to the floor after it crashed into the wall.

Two months.

It's been two fucking months since I'd seen or heard from Wren.

My eighteenth birthday had come and gone *two weeks ago*, and he still hadn't shown his stupid face—all the promises he made me shattered. Just like that fucking snow globe.

Seconds later, Ever appeared at my door, looking dapper in dark jeans, a white button-up with the sleeves rolled up to his elbows, an open gray vest, and a red tie.

I was now staying in the spare bedroom his father had surprisingly offered to me. Any other parent would have called social services by now or at least asked questions, but Thomas hadn't. I tried not to dwell on the reason why, but the question lingered in the back of my mind.

Ever's gaze lingered on the broken snow globe before shifting to me on the bed with my knees now to my chest. "I'd ask if you were okay but…"

A laugh-barked from my raw throat and I cried even harder. "I-I'll c-clean it up. I pro-promise."

I had no idea if he understood me or not, but in a flash, he was next to me, pulling me into his lap before my next sob was free.

"Falling is easy," he said. "Sometimes it's even painless. It's getting up and walking away that cripples us."

"I'm not broken," I angrily cried into his shoulder. I hated the thought of anyone believing me weak. "I'll be okay. I just…" I suddenly looked up and found him watching me patiently. "You didn't mean me."

His lips twitched, but he said nothing.

"But I was the one who walked away," I argued.

"Were you?"

I scoffed and released his shirt I'd balled in my fist, before climbing out of his lap. The asshole was making it hard to be selfish and think of only my feelings. Didn't I at least have the right to mourn what could have been?

He chuckled at my attitude and stood from the bed.

"Take a ride with me."

I blinked, wondering if he'd smacked his head or something. "It's Valentine's Day. Shouldn't you be with Four somewhere celebrating?"

"Later."

I looked out the window and frowned seeing nothing but darkness staring back at me. It didn't get much later than that.

Pulling me to my feet, Ever tossed me the hoodie I left at the foot of the bed.

"If it's another party, I'll pass."

One thing the elites of Blackwood Keep knew how to do was have a good time. We'd partied nonstop throughout their winter vacation, and I had a feeling they were attempting to keep me distracted.

A lot of good it did.

The moment I was alone, all bets were off, and I was right back where I started.

I hadn't heard from Wren. Had no idea if he was even still alive. Fox was still out there, after all. Weakened but not beaten.

"No one told you to take all those shots."

"Ah, but that's what made it so much fun." I followed him outside to the G-Wagon and awkwardly waited as he transferred the dozen yellow roses from the passenger seat to the back seat. "Seriously, don't you have somewhere to be? You're dressed for a date, and there's no way I'm dating you." In addition to my immense respect for Four, I knew there was no way he'd let me get away with half the shit I pulled with Wren. Hot or not, Four could have that headache.

"Jesus, you really are a pita."

"Like a loaf of *bread*?"

"Like a pain in the ass." He helped me inside the truck before rounding the front and hopping into the driver's seat.

Ten minutes later, he drove us through a large cul-de-sac. He hadn't offered much in the way of conversation mostly because he'd been texting furiously every chance he got, and I spent the entire ride trying to figure out his nervous energy. Every so often, he'd strangle the steering wheel, glance at me, and then quickly focus on the road before I could ask questions.

At least he wasn't stingy with his radio like Jamie.

Banks was just beginning to croon 'Under the Table' when Ever turned into a cul-de-sac with tall houses lining each side of the street. Three months ago, I would have been in awe, but after living in a mansion and seeing all the luxury hidden within that sleepy town, I was only mildly impressed.

Until I saw it.

The wide navy blue two-story at the end with white trim and a charcoal roof.

Just beyond the stone archway was the front door, which was painted black with a large glass window cut to resemble a snowflake. I could only imagine all the natural sunlight the huge windows allowed in during the day. It was the perfect setting for capturing beautiful moments.

The front yard, small but immaculate, had a single large tree towering high over the house and a wide paved driveway leading to a garage.

I hoped whoever called this place home shared it with a family. It was the perfect size to offer space without feeling alone. Because the memories, the laughter, and the tears would be hard to miss.

It wasn't just a dream. It was my dream.

I'd spent too much time trying to find my place in someone else's.

"Who lives here?"

My door opened before he could answer, but judging by the secretive twinkle in his eyes, he hadn't planned to anyway. Shivering at the sudden blast of cold air, I turned to confront the culprit and found Vaughn standing there with his hand out.

Waiting.

I hesitated only a moment before accepting his hand. My heart was already beating fast, and I had no idea why. I allowed Vaughn to help me from the truck, and once my feet touched the floor, Tyra appeared out of nowhere, dressed to impress in a light pink dress, and carrying a small wicker basket filled with red rose petals. She smiled at me, and I offered her a trembling one in return.

My gut, which was currently somersaulting all over the place, told me I wouldn't get answers if I asked for them, so when she started walking tossing rose petals on her way, I followed her. The moment I stepped onto the path, the lanterns lining the sides lit up one by one until I found Jamie standing at the bottom of the porch steps holding a guitar.

Our eyes met and his fingers began to move, creating a tune that was light and full at the same time. It was familiar, and I didn't realize why until Barbie appeared from behind the archway and began to sing.

"Wise men say…"

My heart started pounding so hard that it nearly drowned out the rest of the song.

I knew without a doubt what—or rather who—was waiting for me.

The front door slowly opened, but all I could see were more petals flooding a seemingly empty foyer. Instead of the lanterns, however, candles led the way up the stairs directly across from the door.

I looked back feeling unsure.

My gaze landed on Jamie, but his attention, even as he continued to play, was locked on Barbie. She didn't even notice the emotion, stripped of mistrust and anger, spilling from his gaze, her eyes closed as she sang, completely unaware. Her voice, deep and soothing, had him locked in a trance as she gave it her all.

Since I had arrived alone with Ever, it was my guess she had come here with Jamie, and judging by the way she was dressed in the freezing cold—tiny pink shorts and a thin cream camisole— she had been pulled from her bed in a rush.

Or, knowing Jamie, unwillingly.

Finally, I looked to Ever, who was leaning against the passenger door of his G-Wagon with his feet crossed. The soft smile he gave somehow gave me courage, and with my heart in my throat, I stepped inside the candlelit house.

The moment I cleared the door, I felt someone at my side. Four looked absolutely stunning in a red dress of floral lace with a high round neckline, cap sleeves, and a skirt that flared below the waist and stopped inches above her knees. On her feet were patent leather ballet flats, and around her ankle was a thin gold anklet, which I'd never seen before, with the words 'My Wild' connecting the links.

I realized she must have been the one to open the door and had hidden behind it to stay out of sight. *So much for that*, I thought when she pressed a kiss to my cheek and winked before ducking out the door. I watched through the glass as she ran to Ever. He stood up straight in time to catch her in his arms and kiss her deeply.

A bolt of longing shot through me, leaving behind a gaping hole that I knew only Wren could fill.

My legs threatened to give out as I started up the stairs and saw the framed black and white photos of varying sizes filling the wall. Each memory was more precious than the last. They told the story of Wren and me from the harrowing start to its heartbreaking finish.

I'd left them behind hoping to make new ones when I ran from the Hendersons what seemed like a lifetime ago. How were they here? Had he risked going back for them? Sadness crept in knowing the Hendersons were long gone, and I wouldn't be able to say a proper goodbye—or thank them.

Following the rose petals to the top of the stairs and through an open set of black barn doors, I paused.

Shock.

Disappointment.

Confusion.

I felt it all as I took in the furnished bedroom.

Straight ahead, floating in the middle of the room was a single heart-shaped balloon and tied to it, a small slip of paper. I approached on cautious feet and seized the note.

He'd only written two words.

Two small words that squeezed my heart until it shattered, much like the snow globe had.

Welcome home.

My next breath snagged. With my throat burning and a hot river flowing over my cheeks, I crushed the paper in my fist.

I didn't want it. Not without Wren.

Why couldn't he see that? Why wasn't he here?

Anger overtook me, and I spun around, ready to find a match and burn this house to the ground when I stopped, a gasp frozen on my lips.

Wren was standing in the open doorway, hands shoved in his pockets, looking very much afraid.

"You don't like it?"

The words "I love it" threatened to spill, but I swallowed them back down. He didn't deserve praise. "Where have you been?" I cried instead.

He winced, and I wanted to go to him, to tell him that I forgave him, now and forever. I didn't. "I didn't want to face you again empty-handed."

I stared back at him in disbelief. "So you think you can buy me?"

"Of course not." He took a step closer. "You were an orphan because of me. You lost your home because of me. This was the only way I could give at least one of those things back."

I took a deep breath as another tear fell. "Wrong again, Wren. You once told me that my home was with you, and I believed you."

"Because it's true," he growled.

"Then why did you leave? Why did you leave me homeless all over again?" My entire body started to tremble then my legs buckled.

"God, baby." He rushed to catch me before I fell and carried me to the large bed with a sheer gray canopy falling from the ceiling and tied off at each corner. It was perfect.

I immediately melted into the comfy mattress underneath me and inhaled his tantalizing scent as he hovered above me. *God, I hate him.*

"I suck at this," he admitted after a long silence.

My tears continued to leak through when I closed my eyes and fought the laugh that was bubbling up. "Yeah, no kidding," I mumbled.

When I opened my eyes, I saw him biting his bottom lip to keep from laughing. "So am I welcome?"

I shrugged, pretending that my stomach wasn't tightening with hunger for him. "It's your house."

"Not according to the deed."

I blinked once before I spoke in a shaky tone. "You really bought this for me? How?"

"I had help," he admitted cryptically. His expression darkened before he shook it off. "But none of that matters now. I just hope you like Blackwood Keep because we're here to stay."

I loved it, but I couldn't help but wonder if we had run far enough away from Fox's reach. "What about Fox?"

"We're the last of his worries now, Lou. The best he can hope for is prison."

"I don't understand..."

He shook his head and bent down to kiss me. "Later."

Sitting up, he pulled me with him then dug into his pocket.

My breath caught in my throat. Sitting in his palm was the mood ring I'd left in his car when I thought I'd walked away from him for good.

Meeting my gaze, he let me read every single page I'd written on his heart. "Three years ago today... you became my onus, my light... and I'm hoping... starting now... you'll just be mine?"

Seizing my left hand, he slipped the ring on my finger, and we both watched as it turned a startling violet. However, I didn't need a mood ring to tell me I was in love. I had my heart beating wildly for him.

Wren couldn't give me back my parents, and he couldn't turn back the clock three years and decide not to lie to me, but with this ring, this home, and his open heart, he was asking for the chance to start over again. It was the only way to make it right, the only way to piece us both back together again.

I wanted to hate him, to hurt him by denying him my

heart, but I knew neither of us would survive it. Love couldn't exist without forgiveness.

So with one word, I set us both free.

"Yes."

"Slow down."

I moaned as I shook my head and sped up. The sound of him sliding in and out of me intensified, and I could feel his heart racing under my hands. We had our eyes closed tightly, our heads thrown back, too lost in the sensations we created to care about our surroundings.

Because I couldn't be bothered to wait until we returned home for my riding lesson, we'd climbed into the back seat of Paula right there in the store parking lot. Unfortunately, the 'lesson' quickly turned into me taking control, leaving Wren to find the will to shake free of the fog he was in long enough to take it back.

The windows had long ago fogged up, keeping anyone from seeing us, although the rocking car probably gave them a good idea of what we were up to.

I'd been perfectly okay going without food, but Wren insisted we shop for groceries, so I made sure to pick up enough to last us the next month or two. Seeing Wren push that damn cart around, looking so domesticated, was what had driven me crazy in the first place.

We'd been going at it all night, barely taking a breath as we made up the time we'd spent apart. I never wanted to go that long without him again. He might as well save space for me in his suitcase if he ever had to take a trip. It felt like someone had taken a goddamn lung. I didn't breathe the same.

"You're going to hurt yourself," Wren weakly warned.

I didn't care. I wanted it to hurt. It was a fitting punishment for needing it this bad and never getting enough. It had to be wrong, right? The deaconesses at the Hendersons' house of worship would certainly think so. The first women's seminar Mrs. H had forced me to attend was the last after my brazen comments turned every single one of those ladies a deep shade of red.

I was naked from the waist down, my shirt and bra bunched above my breasts while Wren's sweatpants pooled around his thighs. Our hurried state of undress was as far from proper as it got. Smiling, I planted my hands on Wren's knees and leaned back as I moved up and down on his cock. The new position created friction on my overeager clit that would have had me coming in seconds if Wren hadn't intervened.

Sitting up, he clutched me tighter as he rapidly lifted his hips meeting me halfway and bringing tears to my eyes. "Why are you crying?" he taunted as he pounded me from below. "You wanted this, right? You wanted my cock? Huh? Answer me."

I tried to be a big girl, but I found myself wailing at the top of my lungs. I wasn't even sure what I babbled to him, but without an ounce of remorse, he viciously grabbed my messy bun and licked a trail up my neck until he reached my ear where he whispered, "And it's all yours."

I desperately tried to regain control, but he only sped up his strokes until it became clear that top or bottom, Wren would always reign. Unfortunately, by the time I finally submitted and allowed him to fully have his way, we were both too far gone to stop.

The cry I let out when I came caused the scandalized shopper passing by to gasp and shout, "Oh my goodness!" I listened to her hurried footsteps carrying her away and grinned.

Our eyes slowly drifted open at the same time, and with one look, we both knew neither of us was done. The sweat and sex clogging the air in the enclosed space made it hard to catch our breath, so neither of us bothered to speak. Shifting my weight, I realized he was still hard and frowned.

"You didn't come?"

"You ready to do what you're told?" he shot back. I whimpered my response. "Good. Now walk before you run." He grabbed onto my hips and started a slow pace that was sure to torture me. "Take your time. I'm not going anywhere."

"You promise?"

The nipple he'd only just drawn between his lips fell free. "Promise?" he echoed. His eyes were a glittering blue as he stared up at me. "That's a warning, Lou. Learn the difference."

I rose up and moaned, feeling every inch of him as I sank back down on him so slowly he groaned as his eyes nearly rolled back. *This could work.* Leaning down, I kissed him. "I love you too, bestie."

CHAPTER
THIRTY-SEVEN

The Moth

A FTER TWO WEEKS OF SECLUSION, I SNUCK OUT OF THE HOUSE, leaving Lou alone in our bed. That didn't stop me from itching to get back to her as I sat next to my father in Thomas McNamara's office.

I wasn't sure when Thomas had figured out who I was, but it saved me the trouble of convincing him when I confronted him a few months ago. Coming clean was the only way I could think to keep Lou safe in Blackwood Keep while I got my shit together. To my surprise, however, Thomas had not only figured out who I was but he also knew that my father was still alive. Even though he owed me nothing, it was hard not to feel resentment toward him for taking part in my father's lies rather than seeking me out.

The only reason I even agreed to this meeting was that both men had helped me secure the home I now shared with Lou, which was the least either of them could have done. My father had forked over the cash thinking it would buy my forgiveness while Thomas handled the legalities.

I'd been locked in this office with both men for over an hour now while my father poured all of his dirty deeds on the table, including the real reason my mother had died, which wasn't because of my father's infidelity as Fox had claimed. Finding out that my father never loved my mother or even cared enough to make her his woman stung, but like all the other hurt he'd caused me, I brushed it off.

My mother had somehow discovered the real treachery that led to the formation of Exiled and was killed when she attempted to enlighten my father. Thirty years ago, Crow unwittingly stepped on Fox's toes when it became obvious that he was favored to be the next Father of Thirteen. So Fox, in an effort to secure his own succession, killed Father and set up Crow to take the downfall. However, what Fox had done was discovered before he could take over Thirteen, and he was cast out with a hefty price on his head.

Crow, unaware of Fox's role in his downfall, agreed to form Exiled when Fox sought him out. Their partnership ended when Irma, my mother's best friend, found the courage to tell Crow why she didn't believe my mother's death was an accident. My father confronting Fox didn't end in his favor, leading him to hide in the shadows for the past five years. And Fox knew he was out there, which is why he'd kept me close. I'd been as much his prisoner as Evelyn, but I'd been too naïve to see it.

And then there was my father's other piece of news…

"You were too young to remember, but the two of you had met before. Once." My father reached inside his pocket and pulled out a photo that was folded and worn as if he'd looked at it a thousand times.

I accepted it from him when he handed it over and instantly recognized myself—even at two—as well as the baby I was holding in the photo. It was the same one my grandmother had although I never understood why. Whenever I asked about the baby, she'd always explain him as a distant relative.

"Both of your mothers have the same photo."

I was still reeling from finally learning why I'd felt connected to Ever all this time.

We shared the same sperm donor.

I shifted in my seat feeling uncomfortable. I wasn't sure having the same father was enough to make us brothers. There was too much red tape. Like the fact that Thomas was more than willing to put up a fight. He'd been the one to hear Ever's first words, watch him take his first steps, and grow into a man.

"I know," I answered coldly. "I've seen it." I handed him back the photo, refusing to give him the reaction he was hoping for.

Seeing this, he turned his wrath on Thomas as he stood. "This is your fucking fault. I asked you for one thing. Take care of my son and my woman. Instead, you fucked them both up."

"Me?" Thomas barked.

"Evelyn went looking for me and got herself kidnapped by Fox, and *my son* went looking for her when you couldn't be bothered. He could have got himself killed!"

Thomas slammed his fist on his desk and shot to his feet. "You don't know for sure that he's your son. As I recall, we were *both* there that night Evelyn got pregnant."

I blinked as my ears began ringing from all the new information that, frankly, I could have done without. Sean and Thomas, unable to win the whole heart of the woman they both loved, had foolishly shared her, and now they were all suffering the consequences.

"If you're so confident," my father shot back, "why didn't you get him tested?" Thomas didn't respond, so my father went in for the kill. "It's because you already know who he belongs to."

They both looked ready to come to blows as the former best friends glared at each other from across the expanse of the desk. I was just grateful that Ever was at school, or he'd be getting an earful. If these two fools couldn't protect him, that left me, his big brother. It felt awkward assuming the role, especially since I could never tell him, but listening to these two bickering like children fighting over a toy, I knew I didn't have a choice.

"No one is going to tell him," I dictated as I stood to my feet.

Both men's gazes flew to me—Thomas's filled with relief while my father's filled with defiance.

"Why is that, son?"

"Because I'm not going to let you do to him what you did to

me. Ever has a father, and I don't know Thomas, but I know you. He's probably a better father than you'd ever be."

I watched my father stroke his chin. He looked deep in thought, but there was also anger there. "I stayed away to protect him just like I did for you. I did what I thought was best."

"Then continue to do so." I gritted my teeth. "Or I swear to fucking God, I'll save Fox the trouble and kill you myself."

Surprise and pride shoved aside my father's anger, but I was numb to it. I meant every word. With one last warning look, I left them both standing there, gaping.

By the time I reached home, my father and all his fuckups had left me feeling empty. That bleakness he caused, however, was magically swept away the second I stepped through the front door.

As if on cue, Marvin Gaye began to croon 'Let's Get It On,' and with my heart suddenly bursting, I chuckled knowing Lou was somewhere waiting to do just that. I knew then that in the lifetime that we'd spend together, there would never be a dull moment. She was the magic filling me with light, and I was hopelessly bound to her flame.

Stripping off my clothes one by one, I went hunting.

EPILOGUE

The Flame

Three months later

"WHAT THE HELL ARE YOU DOING?" WREN BARKED. Startled, I jumped and dropped the bundle I'd been carrying as I stepped out of our room.

"Oh…" Bending down, I scooped up the clothes—his clothes. "I thought you were going to be another hour." He'd left this morning to meet with his father, who now that Wren knew was alive couldn't seem to stay away. No matter how much Wren pretended to want otherwise.

"I missed you, so I ditched him." His gaze dropped to the bundle in my arms and narrowed. "Doing laundry?"

Ducking my head to hide my blush—and shame—I moved around him. However, he was hot on my heels as we entered the guest room closer to the stairs. The moment Wren saw more of his things already waiting inside, he cursed.

"Lou, what is this?"

Sighing, I dropped his clothes on the bed and tried not to wring my hands once they were free. "We need to talk."

"So talk," he urged while trying to rein in his anger and suspicion.

I took a deep breath. "The things we've been through forced us to grow up." At Wren's reluctant nod, I added, "Faster than we should." He swallowed as his gaze shifted nervously, and it made me think twice about the blow I was about to deal. However, in my heart, I knew it was the right one. "Maybe we should think about slowing down?"

His confused frown morphed into hurt as understanding dawned. "You want to break up?" His voice broke at the end, an echo of his heart splintering down the middle.

I hurriedly closed the distance between us. "Of course not." Grabbing his hand, I placed it over my heart, showing him that it still beat for him and *only* him. "It's just that most people date a while, sometimes years, before they live together, and it still doesn't always work out."

"S-so you want me to leave?"

I immediately shook my head. I was Wren's home, and he was mine. There was no way I was letting him leave. "I thought we could use a buffer. Someone to keep us from moving faster than we already are."

He looked ready to argue when the doorbell rang. Nostrils flaring, he wordlessly left the room, and I listened as he stomped down the stairs. I couldn't keep my grin from spreading knowing that the worse was yet to come. After running my sweaty palms down my purple cotton shorts, I quickly followed and found Wren holding open the front door. I couldn't see his face, but I could tell by the tension in his shoulders that he was *not* happy about who stood on the other side.

"What are you doing here?" he asked.

"Wren Joseph Harlan, if you think I'm going to stand by while you *shack up*, you've got another think coming, young man."

Wren's hand began to strangle the doorknob, so I rushed across the foyer and pushed him aside before he could continue being rude. "Hi, I'm Louchana," I greeted the tiny woman with a head full of gray and a stormy visage. "Please, come in!"

Wren watched wide-eyed as his grandmother stormed inside.

"Don't just stand there," she snapped when he didn't move. "Pick up my bags and take them upstairs. I'll be staying in whichever guest room is nearest this precious thing." His grandmother smiled as she pinched my cheek, making me blush.

Wren snatched her suitcases up and met my gaze over his grandmother's head. If looks could kill… Without a word, he marched up the stairs, and I released the air I was holding. The ache in my chest remained.

"You did the right thing calling me," Winny said when she noticed my troubled expression.

"I'm not so sure anymore." I knew Wren's anger was only masking his hurt. If the shoe were on the other foot, I'd feel the same. Especially if he'd gone behind my back like I did to him and made this decision for us.

"He'll come around," Winny assured me with a pat on my hand.

I took her into the kitchen, and we talked over the tea and sandwiches she whipped up. She was more at home in my kitchen than I was. A homemaker, I was not. After an hour passed, and Wren still hadn't come down, I excused myself to go face the music. I knew he was waiting for me and judging by the smile Winny tried to hide, she did, too.

Peeking inside the room that would now be his, my heart started to race when I found it empty. Shaking off my fear, I moved down the hall toward the master bedroom. Wren was sitting on the edge of our bed, bent forward with his arms resting on his thighs. His head slowly lifted as I stepped inside and crossed the room.

"You called her?" he asked once I stood before him like a child awaiting punishment. It was more of an accusation than a question.

I nodded.

"Why?"

Biting my lip, I struggled over a way to make him understand. "Because the honeymoon stage has to end sometime, and I don't want either of us to end up feeling overwhelmed."

"That's not going to happen," he bit out.

"I'm only eighteen, and you're only twenty. We have forever, Wren. There's no need to rush."

His eyes widened before he shot to his feet, nearly knocking me over. "Is this about last month?"

I had trouble swallowing past the lump in my throat. "It scared you, too. Admit it."

"It was a false alarm, Lou."

"But what if it hadn't been?" Last month, my period was late, and the aftermath when I counted the days had nearly been catastrophic. Neither of us reacted to the possibility of my being pregnant well. It made me realize that maybe we weren't quite emotionally equipped to handle all the responsibility we now had—for ourselves and one another.

"Then we would have gotten through it. *Together.*"

"I know that, but that doesn't mean we shouldn't be cautious." He'd taken me to get on birth control, but it wasn't enough to ease my mind. What if we had a kid, and one day, because we weren't ready, we abandoned it too?

Rather than consider my point, his eyes narrowed. "I still think it's a little convenient that you're having this revelation now," he grumbled.

I quirked a brow as my lips twitched. "You mean after I've gotten in your pants?"

"Yes," he hissed.

I snickered, finding his insecurity adorable. But when he pulled me into him, and I saw the fear in his eyes, my amusement died.

"Are you running from me, Lou?"

I held his gaze as I shook my head. "Never again." And then I kissed him. Soft, tender kisses that reassured him of my love. "It's only for a little while," I told him when I felt the tension easing from him.

"How long is a little while?" he grilled.

I bared my teeth as I peeked at him out of one eye. "A few years?" He growled so savagely that goose bumps appeared on my arms. "I'm kidding!" I rushed out as I laughed. "Just a few months, silly. Six months tops."

"Three."

"That's not enough—"

"Three."

"Okay, three," I agreed with a sigh.

"And I'm not staying in another room," Wren announced. More like dictated.

"But, Wren—"

He gave a curt shake of his head, cutting me off. "No, Lou." I started to argue, anyway, when he gripped my waist and tossed me on the bed. "This," he said as he moved between my legs, "is *our* bed. And no one is going to kick me out of it." Kissing me, he started moving his hips, letting me feel how hard he'd gotten. "Not even you."

I was ready to agree and promise to give him anything he wanted when a throat clearing froze us both. At the same time, our heads swiveled toward the bedroom door where a glaring Winny stood.

It wasn't until now that I truly regretted inviting her to stay.

Sensing my thoughts, Wren smirked as he climbed off me and headed for the door. I watched him bend low and kiss his grandmother's forehead before disappearing altogether.

Winny and I locked eyes, and when I saw the question in hers, I shrugged.

Chuckling, she shook her head. "I suppose I'll be running for the hills long before you two send me packing." With a wink, she quickly spun on her heels, likely to terrorize her grandson some more.

Later that night, I was standing in front of the full-length mirror frowning at my phone when Wren swaggered into our bedroom.

"What's wrong?" he asked me as he wrapped his arms behind me. Even under all the tulle of my royal blue ball gown, I could feel his muscles and the heat warming me from underneath his black tux. It had been hard keeping my chin free of drool when he stepped out of our closet an hour earlier.

"It's Four," I told him as I read the text a second time. "She said she's not going to prom." It seemed the intervention we all ambushed Four, Ever, and Barbie with last month had worked but not in the way any of us expected. My stomach twisted painfully, not wanting to see Forever—as I dubbed them—end, but I knew she deserved better. Barbie, too, although I wasn't sure Jamie was any better for her than Ever. Jamie could be brash, cruel, and un-forgiving. Who knew what he'd do if he ever got his hands on Barbie. Their story was one I was very interested to hear but also one he refused to tell.

I felt Wren tense behind me as I texted Four that we were coming over.

"Then why the hell are we going?" he immediately griped. "It's not even our prom."

I turned around to face him. "Because it's too late for either of us to go to our own. And because I said so."

Wren was a high school dropout, and now, under the circum-stances, I guess I was, too. I should have cared more than I did, but I couldn't help thinking that I had everything I wanted at the moment. Wren, after all, had been right about me. What I desired most was a home I couldn't run away from, and now, because of Wren, I had it. And he wasn't just my home. He was my universe, too.

That didn't mean I wouldn't shoot for other stars eventually. I've never cared much about conquering the world, but after ev-erything we'd been through, maybe one day we could both help to make it a better place.

Until Fox was finally eradicated, laying low was our best chance for survival, and now thanks to the friends we found in

Blackwood Keep, Fox wasn't the only one with a pack watching his back.

"I guess it's not so bad," he admitted as I straightened his bow tie. "You look damn beautiful."

I blushed despite this being the third time he'd told me since I'd gotten dressed. "I know, right?"

Snickering at my response, he sat down on the edge of the bed and pulled me between his legs. "I am so goddamn grateful for snowstorms," he said then kissed the top of my breasts, which spilled from the sweetheart neckline.

My breathing became heavier and faster with each press of his lips, and it was all I could do not to hike up my dress and mount him. Knowing Winny was somewhere lurking, I refrained. *Paula, it is.*

"And barbershops," I said with a wistful sigh.

"And a certain homeless girl who wanted my cock." I punched his shoulder making him grin. "All right," he said with a sigh as he stood. "Let's get this over with."

"Quit your bellyaching," I ordered as I crossed the room to grab my camera, "or I'll make you dance with me twice."

He groaned but wisely remained silent as he waited for me by the door.

When I reached him, I held up my pinky finger. "Best friends forever?"

Ignoring my finger, he stole a kiss, and with our hearts finally and forever open, he answered.

"Nope."

Stay tuned for *The Punk and the Plaything*!
Jamie and Barbie tell their riveting story in the third installment
in the When Rivals Play series.

Subscribe for monthly updates!
www.bbreid.com/news

Add on Goodreads.

Keep reading for an announcement.

Coming May 27th-31st!

Read Me Romance is a FREE podcast hosted by *New York Times* Bestselling Authors Alexa Riley and Tessa Bailey. At **Read Me Romance**, we bring you a new, original audiobook novella *every week* from one of your favorite authors! One section of the audiobook will be released each weekday, beginning Monday and ending with a perfect happily ever after on Friday! Don't forget to subscribe to the podcast so you don't miss a single installment!

EVERMORE

Return to the world of Blackwood Keep for an exclusive, bonus novella!

Four Archer was the toughest girl around. Just ask anyone. She's the street racing daredevil who brought the King of Brynwood Academy to his knees. But watching her boyfriend fawn over his childhood playmate—even though it was just an act—would be her toughest challenge yet.

When jealousy rears its ugly head, Four questions if she can handle playing the sideline.

Ever McNamara has the world at his fingertips, but not even a private jet and a seven-figure trust fund can get him out of this rock and a hard place.

When a childhood pact puts their fairytale in peril, Ever must risk it all to keep her.

Visit the Read Me Romance website to learn more:
readmeromance.com

CHARACTER INTERVIEW

Adriana B: What was the first thing you noticed about Four when you first met?

Ever: Those big brown eyes of hers. I knew the moment I looked into them that she was going to ruin me if I didn't ruin her first.

Sabrina D.C.: Vaughn, we know you are in love with Tyra. What are you waiting for?

Vaughn: Better circumstances.

Carla D.C.: Four, let's play *Kiss, Marry, and Kill* between Jamie, Wren, and Vaughn!

Four: Hmm…I'd kiss Vaughn on the cheek because he doesn't seem to get much affection at home, I'd marry Wren if Lou doesn't claw my eyes out first, and I'd kill Jamie because I've already planned the whole thing out.

Jasmine S: Jamie, why are you still chasing Barbie when she treats you like a non-factor?

Jamie: They tell me the best things in life aren't free, and I love a challenge.

Tamara M: Tyra, will you except Vaughn if he has to take over for his father?

Tyra: It's not something I lose sleep over. There's nothing Franklin Rees can do or say to make his son ever fill his shoes.

ACKNOWLEDGMENTS

I hate writing these things because it's always at the last minute so I'm sure I end up forgetting someone who played a vital role in helping me finish this book. It took many ears for my ranting, space for my pacing, and patience to talk me off the ledge to get to the end, so I'm raising my glass to all of you right now.

Mama, I'm sure no one has listened to me whine about how doomed I am more than you have and no one has shown more patience or been more supportive. I couldn't have asked for a better mother and friend.

To all my friends and family who waited a week for me to respond to a text when you read this book, I hope you see that all the neglect was worth it. If not, lie to me. What are friends for?

Rogena and Colleen, no one has shown better resilience than the two of you. Thank you for your patience, kindness, and most importantly, your tremendous editing skills. I'm sure I'll forget everything I've learned by the time I write the next book. I hope you're ready.

Amanda, pregnant throughout the whole designing process, and I never once noticed when you were cranky…because you're always grumpy. Your amazing skills more than make up for it though. The cover and all the marketing that came with it were an absolute hit, and no one could have captured this book better.

Happy Anniversary, Stacey! Nope, I didn't forget. I'm assuming I'll drive you crazy with my million and one changes before and probably after I hit publish. This is my 'thank you in advance' and 'please don't fire me.' No one can make this as beautiful inside as it is on the out better than you can.

Tijuana, fear of being whipped to death came in handy. If it weren't for you asking me when I'll finish every other day, I'd probably still be writing. Peer pressure really works! Thank you so much for listening to my sixty-seven ten-second voice messages and letting me bounce ideas off of you. Most importantly, thank you for being honest with me when I needed it most. Beta reading isn't always an enjoyable job, but you do it with finesse.

Sarah, I'm going to call you the Grim Reaper because it's just too clever not to. Sarah Grim Sentz…get it? Also, you were the one standing over my shoulder holding a gun to my head while Tijuana screamed "Finish the fucking book!" If you haven't seen that meme, you really should. It's awesome.

Sunny, Charleigh, the rose to my prose. When I think of whom I can depend on, whom I can trust, and whom I can run to, I always think of you. Thank you for being the douche to all my baggage. Ew…wait…that didn't sound right.

Reiderville, the reason I'm willing to spill so much sweat, tears and blood, thank you for sticking around through all my ramblings, randomness, and ridiculousness. You are at the heart of my inspiration because you challenge me to be better than I was the last time. Your posts and comments make each day a little brighter.

And to anyone I didn't mention, I must have said 'thank you' a thousand times because that's how much you've helped me. Thank you.

CONTACT THE AUTHOR

Follow me on Facebook.
www.facebook.com/authorbbreid

Join Reiderville on Facebook.
www.facebook.com/groups/reiderville

Follow me on Twitter.
www.twitter.com/_BBREID

Follow me on Instagram.
www.instagram.com/_bbreid

Visit my website.
www.bbreid.com

ABOUT B.B. REID

B.B. Reid is the author of nine novels including the hit enemies-to-lovers Fear Me. She grew up the only daughter and middle child in a small town in North Carolina. After graduating with a Bachelors in Finance, she started her career at an investment research firm while continuing to serve in the National Guard. She currently resides in Charlotte with her moody cat and enjoys collecting Chuck Taylors and binge-eating chocolate.

30093514R00255

Printed in Great
Britain
by Amazon